To my mother,
and in memory of my father

DOWN CEMETERY ROAD

MICK HERRON

JOHN MURRAY

First published in Great Britain in 2003 by Constable,
an imprint of Constable & Robinson Ltd

First published in 2016 by John Murray (Publishers)
An Hachette UK company

This paperback edition published in 2020

3

A CIP catalogue record for this title is available from the British Library

Paperback ISBN 978-1-47364-697-1
eBook ISBN 978-1-47364-698-8

Typeset in Bembo Std by Palimpsest Book Production Ltd, Falkirk, Stirlingshire

Printed and bound in Great Britain by Clays Ltd, Elcograf S.p.A.

John Murray policy is to use papers that are natural, renewable and
recyclable products and made from wood grown in sustainable forests.
The logging and manufacturing processes are expected to conform
to the environmental regulations of the country of origin.

John Murray (Publishers)
Carmelite House
50 Victoria Embankment
London EC4Y 0DZ

www.johnmurraypress.co.uk

WHEN HE OPENED HIS eyes he expected to find all the light squeezed from the world, but no: he was alive still, strapped to a bed in a sterile room, angry red claws of pain scratching channels in his flesh. *They have tied me down to keep me from shredding myself,* he managed, in a moment of clarity. *To prevent me ripping the skin from my bones, and not stopping until I'm dead.* This was a good thought: it pretended they had his welfare in mind. But the pain remained, like being chewed by fire ants, and even when he slept he felt it working in his dreams. In his dreams, he was back in the desert. His companions were dead soldiers, their meat dropping off their bones.

The loudest thing in life was a helicopter. All around, the boy soldiers disintegrated; made puddles in the sand.

Here, when he was awake, there were other noises to occupy him. Outside his room, he imagined a long corridor of swept tiles and white light; an echoey tunnel that carried sounds past his door, some of which lingered to mock his boredom. A dropped fork rattled in his mind for hours. He heard voices, too, a low mumble that never separated into language, and once he thought he heard Tommy; thought he recognised a man he knew in a noise mostly animal: a rising scream, cut off by a slammed door. Footsteps clattered into distance. Something on wheels might have been a trolley. He tried to shout a response, but his voice got lost in the deep red caverns of his pain, and all he could do was weep silent tears that scorched his cheeks.

A doctor came once a day. He had to be a doctor: he wore a white coat. The nurse with him carried a tray; on it, a precise array of tools – different-sized needles, small bottles of coloured liquids. Both nurse and doctor wore gloves and surgical masks, and both had olive skin and hazel eyes. Only the doctor spoke. His sentences were short and to the point: Breathe in. Breathe out. I take blood now. Even without the mask, he'd hardly have been fluent. It was another clue to his whereabouts . . . Not all the needles were for him, so he knew he wasn't alone here; there were other rooms, other patients, though 'patients' wasn't the word he meant. 'Prisoners', his mind supplied. He was a prisoner here, though where 'here' was, he couldn't be sure.

The doctor said, 'Sleep now.' As if it were a magic instruction, and he was a rabbit being put back into a hat.

The nurse, though, was beautiful, as nurses have to be. The nurse came more often and fed him, wiped him, saw to his bowel movements. Nothing he did made her speak. Even an erection, to him little short of a miracle, left her unmoved. For the rest, all he had were a few schoolboy phrases – *Parley voo? Spreckledy Doitch?* – which it wouldn't have helped him if she'd answered. And anyway he knew, was certain, that if she spoke it would be in a sand language, whose vast syllables would leave him adrift and uncomprehending, like a traveller caught between settlements. Soon, he forgot she was human. When he didn't want to see her, he turned his face to the wall.

Days passed. There was no way of knowing how many.

His body was healing, but slowly: red weals marred all his flesh he could see, and a small detached part of his mind – his black box – told him he'd always be like this now; that his body was scarred and monstrous for ever, but at least the pain was dimming. He was no longer kept strapped down.

An ankle chain secured him to the bed. In time, he might do something about that.

Once, he stole a spoon during a careless moment; filched it from the tray when the nurse looked round at a noise from the corridor. He hid it under the mattress, but within the hour they'd come to fetch it – three of them: male, silent, dark-featured. Two held him against the wall while the third retrieved his prize, though not roughly. He didn't struggle. But the effort exhausted him anyway, and he crashed as soon as they'd left. His dream took him back to the desert and the boy soldiers. Sand crunched as he fell from the truck, and the chopper's whine was the loudest noise in the world. And the boys were melting again, their faces turning runny while his black box recorded it calmly, noting that *it's like watching a very wet painting hung in the wind* – but he was sweating when he woke, and sure he'd been screaming. There was nobody to tell him if that were true. Just as there was nobody to tell him if it were night or day.

He'd have sold his soul for a window. For natural light.

And then one day – he had an idea it might be the winter; there was a cold bite to the air – they took him out of the room. The same three men came to secure him to the bed. He was blindfolded and taken through the door, down the corridor he'd only imagined; wheeled past – he was sure of this – windows, from which light fell on to his face in a gentle strobe. He racked his body against the bed, but remained locked in place. When they removed the blindfold, he was in what looked like an operating theatre. The doctor was there, masked, suited up, and had the three interns – guards – untie him and fasten him in what resembled an open coffin. Because he thought they were going to kill him at last, he didn't struggle. But instead he was loaded into a large mechanical device, of a kind he might have seen in hospital films. Some kind of scanning machine. He was kept there for twenty minutes or so. The noise was constant but not too loud, like knowing there were bees nearby. He almost fell asleep.

Afterwards the doctor said, 'Good.' He was strapped down again, eyes covered, and wheeled back to his room. Again he felt the windows pass, and his one wish in the world was not even escape, but just to be able to stand in the light, and imagine the wind pulsing against his damaged skin.

After that, it became regular. Once every three days, as far as his body could tell . . . There were no other clocks available. That was one of the discoveries he'd made: that the body was a kind of clock. It couldn't be rewound and couldn't be replaced. When it finished telling the time, its job was done . . . Once every three days they took him to the theatre and scanned him with their device. He never asked a question. This was his plan: for them to forget he was there and turn their backs for one moment. Even without a spoon, he thought he might win an eye or a tongue.

. . . He never knew this, but it was on a Wednesday that it all changed; that he caught his glimpse of the outside world, and found it upside down.

He was asleep when the nurse came. Genuinely asleep. The pills did this, along with the blood they took: he never did anything, but often felt weak and sleepy. By the ankle chain, he was tethered to the bed. She must have thought this enough. Perhaps the others, the men, were having a day off. He never knew. It didn't matter. She wheeled him from the room like that, just the ankle chain holding him down.

It was the movement woke him. He'd been dreaming again – the dream never left him, or perhaps he never left the dream – his head full of boiling faces when he forced his eyes open, the way he always woke. For a moment he thought it hadn't started yet, that he was back in the truck, and instinct tipped him over the side where he hit the floor with a crash of spilled metal. The bed jerked to a halt. And with his gown flapping open, bare-arsed to the world, he lay with a window just two feet above him, its blinds pulled tight against the light, and both his hands untethered.

Even then, the nurse didn't speak. She pressed something on her belt instead, though he heard no alarm, and as he reached a hand for the blind, came round to arrest him. He thought she'd be soft. She punched the back of his head. It had been a while since he'd been hurt quite like that, and he collapsed back to the floor, taking the blind with him. It sounded loud as a helicopter. And then there were feet coming, and a pricking in his arm to send him back into the desert, where he really didn't want to go, not now he'd seen the light – not now he'd seen the sky, and the treetops, and the arch of the building opposite, with its grey stone scrolls and pigeon shit and everything about it screaming *England* – but then the needle opened the window in his head, and he flew back to the desert. The light was just the morning sun, building its killing heat. The boy soldiers were dying again, but nobody heard their screams.

ONE

BHS

I

ON DISCOVERING A FIRE, the instructions began, shout *Fire!* and try to put it out. It was useful, heart-of-the-matter advice, and could be extended almost indefinitely in any direction. On discovering your husband's guests are arseholes, shout *Arseholes!* and try to put them out. This was a good starting point. Sarah was one glass of wine away from putting it in motion.

But the instructions had been pinned to the wall in her office when she'd had a job, and did not apply in the kitchen. Here, Mark would expect that all emergencies be met with predetermined orderliness – crisis management was his latest big thing – and graded instantly by size, type and career-damaging potential: earthquake, conflagration, shortage of pasta. His guests would not figure on the chart, since they came under acts of God, and were to be borne as such. Of course they're arseholes, Sare, he'd say, when they were gone and he could afford to be ironic. He's rich and she's dumb: what did you expect, they'd be *nice*? But if Sarah asked when rich got important, he'd lose a little of the irony. Since rich got on my client list, he'd say. Since rich started buying lunch. Self-promotion was his other latest big thing. He had these in pairs now, so as to be sure of not missing anything.

And now he came into the kitchen, to make sure she missed nothing either. 'Coffee done?'

'Just about.'

'Anything I can do?'

'You could try asking that first in future.'

'In *future*? You think I want to go through this again?'

She banged a cupboard, just quietly enough to sound accidental next door, but loudly enough to leave Mark in no doubt.

'I mean,' he went on – hissing – 'Wigwam? *Rufus*?'

'You said,' she said, through gritted teeth, 'another couple. You wanted company.'

'I *wanted* Stephen and Rebecca.'

'Busy.'

'Or Tom and Annie. Or—'

'*Busy.*' She took a breath. From the living room came that awful dead sound you probably got on battlefields before the buzzards swooped. 'And you said, when I said it was awful short notice, you said *just get anybody*. Anybody who could make it.'

'I didn't mean—'

'Well, you should have said so at the time. Because it's a bit late now, isn't it?'

Mark gave a short laugh, which might easily have been aimed at himself. It was one of his characteristic declarations of surrender, though she had no doubt this would be temporary. And his next words, anyway, were 'You did get some of those mints, didn't you?'

'Yes. Mark.'

So he changed tack, put his arms round her: 'Come on. It's not been that bad, has it?'

He really didn't get it. Two hours he'd sat watching war being declared in slow motion, and he still thought it hadn't been *that* bad. 'Did you just arrive?'

'He has firm opinions, that's all. Gerard does.'

'Well, I didn't think you meant Rufus.'

'He's used to playing rough. Cut and thrust sort of—'

'He's a vampire.' She pulled free and checked the kettle lead, for something to do. It was plugged in okay. It just hadn't boiled yet. 'Get back in there and stop him biting my friends.'

'It won't hurt them to have their Greenpeace sensibilities challenged once in a while.'

'Challenged is fine. But he wants a pissing contest, and that's not.'

'Sarah—'

'Just go away. Go and smooth his ego. Use the bloody iron if you think it'll help.'

'He's nearly a *client*,' Mark hissed on his way out. 'I'm *that* close.'

And you were staring at her legs, she added. *The Trophy Wife's. You shit.* But Mark had gone.

She poured the water, found a tray, emptied the mints into a bowl. They were foil-wrapped, chocolate-covered mints, and she ate one while waiting for the coffee to draw and another while hunting spoons. The cups did not match. One comment from Mark and it was a separation issue. Then she counted the mints: two each and one over. She ate it, and carried the tray through.

'Guns,' Gerard was saying, with the air of a conjuror producing a toad when the kiddies had been expecting a bunny.

'You collect *guns*?' Wigwam asked. You molest *babies*? Wigwam apologised when people trod on her foot. Gun collectors were out of her range.

'What did you imagine, stamps?'

'Well, I don't . . .'

'Gerard has some *awfully* expensive guns.'

'Cheap guns,' Gerard said, 'being better avoided.'

'I thought,' said Rufus bravely, 'that sort of interest was, you know, compensating . . .'

'That's easy for you to say. I don't suffer penis envy myself.'

Sarah put the tray on the low table around which they sat: Gerard in an armchair; Wigwam on the floor; the others sharing the sofa. Gerard *needed* a whole armchair but did not act like he did, and this Sarah found irritating. The overweight should own up and be made to suffer. But Gerard moved like a man half his size. She had read of the peculiar grace to be found in heavy men and had assumed it propaganda, but his gestures were small and controlled, as if part of his overactive mind were engaged in choreography. He made dainty movements now with his unlit cigar, punctuating sentences with careful darts and jabs. He had asked permission to smoke and seemed hardly put out at all by her refusal. Now it wagged like a totem in his long but chubby fingers, as if he were warding off evil. She'd have felt happier with a crucifix herself. Gerard Inchon was a total bastard.

'What *do* you suffer, then?' she asked.

'I beg your pardon?'

Mark sprang forward and began rattling cups. 'Who's for sugar?'

'I said, what do you suffer? We've heard a lot about your perfect life, there must be something goes wrong occasionally. The Porsche's ashtrays fill up? Your tailor sleeps in?'

'Gerard gets all his suits—'

'Sarah's making a joke, dear.'

'Or is this as good as it gets? Flaunting your wealth in front of the help?'

'I'm hardly the help,' said Mark.

'I wasn't talking to you.'

Gerard Inchon smiled. 'I suppose you get a lot of this,' he said. He was talking to Sarah. 'Dinner guests at short notice. Strangers you're supposed to be polite to.'

'Not a lot, no. Mark's not that important yet.'

'Sarah—'

'Well, he will be. So you'll have to get used to it. Because a lot of them'll be worse than me.'

She found that hard to believe.

'And they'll find your perfunctory small talk and poorly

hidden contempt rather more unpleasant than I do. And then your husband's career will suffer. And then what will you do?'

'Hire a band,' she told him. 'Throw a real party.'

Wigwam said, 'Gosh, I'm *dying* for a coffee. Are those mints?'

'So it's not me you're objecting to, it's your husband's job?'

Mark said, 'Look, I'm really sorry about this—'

'Don't you *dare* apologise for me!'

'No apology is called for. But I am interested to know what Sarah proposes to adopt. As a matter of policy, I mean.' Gerard Inchon surveyed the company as if awaiting suggestions, then turned back to her. 'You don't work, do you?'

The switch threw her. 'I— No. Not at the moment.'

'Publishing, was it?'

She gave Mark a hostile look. 'If you know, why ask?'

'I didn't. I was guessing. Let's see, not one of the big ones. Something worthy. Third world? The environment?'

'Is this meant to be funny?'

'Alternative medicine? All of the above?'

'Green Dolphin Press,' said Sarah. 'If it makes you happy.'

'With print runs of three hundred, and selling less than half.'

It sounded like he'd seen the books. 'Lots of businesses fail.'

'And lots don't. So what happened then, charity work?'

'Christ, what a phrase. But then, you'd like that, wouldn't you? Soup kitchens. Workhouses.'

'Don't get me started. What was it, one of these homeless shelter places? That's the guilt trip of choice, isn't it?'

Wigwam said, 'Oh, there are so *many*—'

'Let me guess,' said Gerard. 'They couldn't use you.'

Sarah was shaking her head in disbelief. 'What is this?'

'Oh, I see a lot of it. Hubby brings home the bacon, and the little woman has nothing to do. The ones that don't have affairs, shop. The ones that don't shop get charity jobs.'

'You really are disgusting, aren't you?'

'So these jobs are oversubscribed. The interesting ones, anyway. What was it, you didn't have the experience?'

She'd failed the screening.

'Which leaves the dull end of the market. The retail bit. I can't see you sticking that, though.'

The Oxfam shop had let her go.

Gerard Inchon leaned back into the armchair. 'What I like to call it, I call it BHS.'

Nobody ask him, Sarah prayed.

'Bored Housewife Syndrome. Most women enjoy being bored, of course, but you still get some who—'

'You insufferable bastard.'

'—end up throwing wobblies at dinner parties. You're enjoying it now, though, aren't you?'

'*What*?'

'Little bit of aggro, little bit of rough.' He made his cigar pass from one hand to the other, like an amateur conjuror. 'I bet you haven't had a scrap in ages. What you need is more excitement.'

That was when the house blew up.

The evening had started badly too. The Trophy Wife arrived first, ten unfashionable minutes early: overdressed and faintly disappointed, she must have been expecting a different party altogether. Sarah was having a kitchen crisis and did not retain her name; it was Mark who poured drinks, extracted information. Gerard was parking the car; Gerard would be along in a minute. Gerard was forty-five minutes, in fact: something of a record even for south Oxford. Meanwhile Wigwam turned up without Rufus, who was doing something vague and would be along soon. Most things involving Rufus became vague, even those that were fairly concrete to start with. Wigwam was Sarah's oldest, most annoying friend; Rufus her startling new acquisition, but startling only because younger, and prepared to take on her children. In all other respects he was distinctly run of the mill, and given half the chance Sarah would have forgotten his name too.

'How lovely to see you,' lied Mark, who thought Wigwam an historical curiosity, and usually developed an interest in being elsewhere when she was about. 'Glass of wine? Red? White?'

But Wigwam refused a drink, citing an article she'd read outlining various urinary complications attendant upon alcohol consumption, while the Trophy Wife regarded her as if Wigwam were an exhibit lately wandered from the zoo.

There was a whole world between them; a gap that merely started with their clothes. The Trophy Wife wore a red dress four measured inches above the knee, and lipstick in a shade to match; this plus the kind of face that usually came with a slogan slapped above it, and a figure men would pay money to see with staples through the middle. Mark, damn him, looked like somebody had hit him on the head with a broom handle. His new man credentials kept his tongue from hanging out, but the thought police probably held a warrant for his arrest.

Standing next to her Wigwam looked like a hippie, though Wigwam would have looked like a hippie standing next to Bob Dylan. What she was wearing tonight defied description unless you were a qualified 1970s anthropologist, but was possibly what Abba rejected when they settled for the white trouser suits; it was purple, all of one piece, and had probably covered a sofa in its previous life. The rest of the image assembled various influences: jewellery by Friends of the Earth; hair by Worzel Gummidge. She had a beautiful smile, which was turned on most of the time, but in repose Sarah had seen in her face an almost heartbreaking sadness, as if her natural optimism were based on the knowledge that life couldn't treat her worse than it had done already. She had taken up with Rufus six months ago. The smile hadn't wavered since.

'Can I help in the kitchen?' she asked Sarah.

'Nothing can help in the kitchen. It's past saving.'

'Are you cooking it yourself?' asked the Trophy Wife, her tone suggesting Sarah had a live elephant through there rather than a dead salmon.

'I plan to.'

'Sarah's a wonderful cook,' said Mark, in what was probably intended to be a show of loyalty. 'Aren't you, darling?'

'Yes.'

'Except, remember those scrambled eggs,' Wigwam said, disappearing behind a fit of giggles.

'The eggs were fine. It was the pan got ruined.'

The Trophy Wife looked puzzled while Mark poured further drinks. He was nervous; it was a big night for him. This Inchon character was a prospective client of The Bank With No Name; having him for dinner was tantamount to the Queen turning up at your garden party. Mark had announced the invitation as a fait accompli two nights ago; had insisted on a second couple – he'd told Inchon they were expecting friends; that this wasn't, far from it, a schmooze-the-money do – and he'd wanted, of course, Tom and Annie, or Stephen and Rebecca. Who would *behave*, even if they might mock afterwards. So Sarah had retaliated by asking Wigwam and Rufus instead. Briefly, she wondered now how fair that had been. Fair on Mark, she meant. Later she revised that, when it became clear it wasn't fair on Wigwam and Rufus.

'Have you lived in Oxford all your life?' the Trophy Wife asked.

'Not yet,' said Sarah.

'We moved here from Birmingham,' Mark cut in. 'A good ten years ago, wasn't it, darling?'

Her role tonight was to say Yes, No, Three Bags Full.

'*I've* lived here all my life,' Wigwam offered. Then Sarah's comment penetrated, and the giggles came again.

Sarah excused herself, pleading business in the kitchen, and stretched making a salad dressing so it filled ten minutes. Meanwhile Rufus arrived without noticeably adding to the party atmosphere, though at least he had bothered to wash his hair. This was grubby-blond and crawled over his collar in untidy clumps that suggested he cut it himself. He had not shaved in several days, though, and wore the stubble like a badge of proletarian valour in a middle-class world, his one apparent attempt at making an impression. A less intentional one was signalled by the little scraps of tissue paper clinging to the front of his sweatshirt, indicating how many times he'd sneezed into toilet roll. A martyr to hay fever, he bore his cross bravely.

So it was to the Trophy Wife's undisguised relief that the doorbell rang at last, announcing her warrior hero's arrival. Alone, unarmed, he had parked the Porsche. Sarah emerged from the kitchen to catch their pantomimed kisses:

'You've been *ages*.'

'It's all residents' parking. I left it the other side of the park, and had to walk round.'

'Where's your briefcase?'

'Left it in the car.'

'But I thought—'

'In the boot, darling. It'll be safe enough.' He turned to Sarah. 'She thinks the local yobs'll be attracted by the shiny bits. You must be Sarah. A very great pleasure.'

And this was her first sighting of Gerard Inchon, a man she'd heard much about; even read about occasionally, in heavily vetted stories in the business section of the paper. He wasn't more than mid thirties, but appearances placed him at forty or higher: paunchy, heavy-featured, he was coming into middle age like a man entering his kingdom. What remained of his hair was dark brown, oily and scraped back over his head, leaving a widow's peak that added years, to which his double chin was a multiplying factor. Maybe that's what Mark had meant when he'd called Inchon a big catch. But no, because he'd gone on about it: Inchon was 'expanding into the East when everybody else was running for cover', whatever that meant. 'He's a player, he's a mover and shaker,' Mark had said. Once he'd have said wanker and meant the same thing. And for Sarah that first look was enough: here was a man with a fine veneer of civilisation, under which he was living in a cave. The civilised version played Beggar My Neighbour. The real Gerard Inchon ate his.

And made no bones, now, about establishing the fact. 'Nice place you've got here, Mark. God-awful city, though. When are you moving to London?'

'Well, we've no plans—'

'God, man, you can't stay out here in the sticks. Your fax machine'll rust in the damp. Hello, you're—?'

'I'm Wigwam and this is Rufus.'

'Bloody hell!'

'Sorry,' said Mark, 'I should have made the intro—'

'No, no, they're just damn strange names, that's all. Damn strange names. Call me Gerard. That's a *Christian* name, in case you've not heard it before. Wigwam and Rufus, eh? Sound like a pair of goldfish.'

'Can I get you a drink?' Sarah asked. Arsenic? she added. Liquid mercury?

'Vodka Mart, if you've such a thing. I'll trundle straight on to the wine otherwise. White.'

Lacking the Mart part, whatever it was, she poured a glass of Chardonnay, which at least he didn't try to identify. He was interrogating Wigwam by then. 'You have *four* children?'

Like he was from population control, sorting out a persistent offender.

'By my previous.'

'Oh. So they're not, er, Rufus's, then.'

'Oh no. But he married me anyway.'

'Damn brave of him,' said Gerard. Presumably in reference to the children.

'Rufey was an orphan,' Wigwam said. 'A ready-made family, it's just what he wanted.'

Rufey didn't deny it. He irritated Sarah. He let talk wash over him, a small rock in a large stream, never poking out no matter how shallow the conversation. How had he come to charm Wigwam? Perhaps by being available.

Which was an evil thought, but Gerard Inchon had her in an evil mood. He turned to her now. 'And what about Sarah?' She hated that: being addressed in the third person. 'Any plans for children?'

'None that aren't private,' she said sweetly.

'Oh, we want kids,' said Mark. 'Soon as possible, in fact.'

'Is that right?'

'Well, not entirely,' said Sarah. 'Mark wants kids. Soon as possible, in fact. That part's right.'

Mark glared at her. Wigwam said, 'Oh, you'll feel differently when—'

'Everybody says that. But what if they're wrong?'

'Treat it as an investment,' Gerard said. 'You can get a good price for children, some parts of the world.'

Which seemed the right moment to regroup, as it was unlikely that anything more tactless would be said in front of an orphan and an earth mother for the next little while. Because they were eating in the sitting room – a large, knocked-through area, taking up most of the ground floor – shepherding everybody from one side to the other didn't take more than about five minutes, with Wigwam and Rufus being hardest to organise. Perpetually eager to please, Wigwam tried to sit everywhere at once, while Rufus looked like he'd be happiest with a bowl in the kitchen. It was her Imp of the Perverse, Sarah decided – her own personal demon – which had made her invite these two.

The food, she'd kept simple, partly from common sense but also out of the desire to show Mark she wasn't spending thirty-six hours in the kitchen making him look good. So: stuffed peppers to kick off, then salmon with lime juice and apple. Avocado salad. Fruit salad. Some of the snobbier cheeses from the market. Nothing desperately exciting, but nothing to generate complaint either, unless Gerard was expecting raw meat, though in that case he'd probably just bite whoever he was put next to.

In the event Gerard proved easy to feed, eating everything put in front of him as if eager to watch Miss Manners starve to death. Shutting him up was trickier. Practised guests, Sarah thought – and Inchon looked like a man accustomed to eating other people's food – should be used to sounding out strangers; to defining common ground on which to meet their fellow guests. But Inchon explored new territory merely to lay mines and retire; he sized people up, then chose what would bring them down. To Mark he was perfectly affable, chatting with him in terms incomprehensible to the rest of the company, who knew little about finance and cared less; to Sarah he was slyly polite. But to Wigwam and Rufus he was positively dangerous.

The war, for instance. Or the nearly war. For the Middle East was hotting up again; Iraqi intransigence over UN inspections prompting sabre-rattling across the Western world. Politicians threw solemn press conferences while secretly creaming in delight; the tabloids squeaked, the broadsheets thundered. Foreign correspondents checked out their designer khakis. And the Wigwams of the world threw up their hands in shame and horror, while the Inchons tuned into cable TV, their remotes in one hand and a copy of the stock market listings in the other.

'Nothing boosts the economy like a good war.'

'Are you serious?'

'Of course. I'm not talking about the price of a tin of *beans*, my dear. I mean sums of money. Contracts for helicopters, jobs for whole towns. All the media hustle gets people excited.'

'What if we lost?'

'That's not an option.' He gave a condescending smile. 'We're talking about ragamuffin conscripts with second-hand weaponry. The Western armies have toys they haven't tested yet. And these people are more or less in the Stone Age anyway. They just got lucky with the oil.'

'Nobody would win a nuclear war,' said Wigwam.

'That's a naïve and foolish thing to say. Anybody who has nuclear capability when the other side doesn't can win a nuclear war. It's simply a question of public relations.'

'That's despicable,' Sarah said.

He gave a smug smile. 'That's realism. Not that it would come to that. There are quicker, cleaner ways. No point winning a war if you're landed with a huge bill for compensation afterwards. What do you reckon?' This last to Rufus.

'I – I don't . . .'

'Maybe you should ask your wife what you think. She'll probably know. Do you think I could have a refill, Mark? Thanks so much.'

Rufus had turned pink. 'There won't be a war,' he said.

'Won't there? Why not?'

'People'll see sense,' Rufus said. 'Nobody wants to go through that again. All those charred bodies, and . . .'

Gerard threw back his head and laughed. 'Priceless,' he said. 'Priceless.' Then he drained half a glass of wine. 'People will see *sense*,' he repeated, his voice thicker now. 'Thank God for a bit of serious analysis.'

Rufus turned two shades darker. 'So what do you think, then? You think they'll just do it?'

'Just do it. There could be a slogan in that. I don't know. Maybe they will and maybe they won't. I can think of half a dozen scenarios to back up either. But none involve people *seeing sense*. We're talking geopolitics here, not some playground squabble.'

'These are *human lives*,' Wigwam said. 'You can't talk about it as if it didn't involve *people*.'

Gerard looked at Mark. 'The trouble with discussions like this,' he said, 'is that the women always have to drag sentimentality into it. You can't discuss war or sport with women because they never understand how crucial the *result* is. They always feel sorry for the losers.'

Mark said, 'Yes, well, obviously . . .'

'Obviously what?' Sarah asked.

'Obviously there's a lot to be said for looking at the human element. But in the long run . . .'

'In the long run what?'

'In the long run it's not the people on the ground making the big decisions. Can I get anybody more wine?'

'So you're coming down pretty firmly on the fence, then?'

The Trophy Wife spoke for the first time in a while. 'I'd like some more wine.' Mark tried hard not to beam in gratitude, and disappeared to the kitchen to find another bottle.

Sarah turned to Gerard. 'What's your stake in it, anyway?'

'I beg your pardon?'

'I don't know what you do, other than it involves supplying commodities to a variety of customers. I mean, you don't actually *make* anything, do you?'

'I make money, my dear. A great deal, actually.'

She'd walked into that one. 'And that's what you'll be doing if there's a war, is it? Making profits out of the dead?'

'You make it sound as if I go grubbing round battlefields picking the pockets of corpses.'

'Well, you might as well, mightn't you?'

He looked at her. 'No, in fact. My "stake" in it is the same as yours, actually. In that I'll be a member of an involved nation.

Other than that, I've no direct interest. But *unlike* you, I gather, I'll actually be supporting the troops sent out in my name. Because the fewer of them die, the happier I'll be. Is that what you were getting at?'

Sarah bit her tongue. Slippery bastard.

Gerard looked at Rufus. 'So much for world events. What is it you do?' He put a slight stress on *do*, as if the notion of Rufus in action, hard as it was to swallow, had to be faced up to sometime.

'I, er, freelance.'

'Freebase? That's some kind of drugs thing, isn't it?'

Rufus coughed. 'Freelance.'

'Oh, *free*lance. At what? Quantity surveying? Window cleaning?'

Mark came back with an open bottle and began waving it vaguely, as if expecting a queue to form in front of him.

'I teach,' Rufus said. 'Adult literacy,' he added.

'How *fas*cinating,' Gerard breathed.

Sarah had had enough. Much more of this, and Gerard Inchon would be wearing her cutlery in his back.

'Wine, er, anyone?' Mark said at last.

'I'll go and make the coffee,' Sarah said.

But the explosion, when it happened, drew a line under the conversation. It seemed to come in two distinct stages, though afterwards Sarah could never recall in which order they occurred. The room shook, not violently, but more than was usual during the average dinner party; the prints on the walls rattled in their frames, and the light fitting spiralled, sending shadows swinging from their corners. And then, or possibly slightly beforehand, there was a dull thump followed by a sliding noise, as if a geological event were taking place at an unexpected venue. Wigwam dropped her empty wine glass; the Trophy Wife's eyes grew round in alarm. Mark rose to his feet, looking automatically to Gerard for enlightenment, as if having more money than anybody else made Gerard the expert on everything. To her fury Sarah found she'd done the same herself. Gerard put his glass down very carefully and turned to look at the curtained window, then nodded to himself, as if an earlier suspicion had been confirmed, and turned back to Sarah. 'That was a bomb,' he said.

'A *bomb*?'

'Unmistakable. A gas explosion would—'

Rufus brushed past him on his way to the front door.

There was a moment's confusion, as if nobody were sure whether to follow Rufus or listen to Gerard; then a general exodus in the former's wake. Probably the only time Rufus could expect to upstage Inchon, but Sarah only managed this thought later. At the time, her mind was locked in that off-kilter clarity in which all perceptions are heightened and everything happens in slow motion, but nothing is capable of articulation. She wished afterwards she'd savoured the look on Gerard's face, but had to make do with imagining it.

It had come, the explosion, from several hundred yards up the road, maybe as far as the river itself, and even against the night sky inky black smoke was visible, clouding the air the way a squid might stain the lower depths. But there was little flame, and if it weren't for the crowd already gathering under streetlights, Sarah would not have known which way to look. The noise that remained was the sound of aftermath: a kind of muted roar still echoing off the houses. Sarah bit her lip, tasted blood tinged with mint, and half of her wanted to understand what had happened, and the rest didn't want to know. They stood in a group, with only Rufus apart; a few yards closer to the destroyed house, as if that slight edge gave him a different perspective. And under the roar she could hear the muttering of the crowd ahead; the appreciative undertone you get at a bonfire. For there was a fire. If you looked closely you could see a glow from an upper window, as if a dragon breathed against the pane.

'Must be a gas main,' Rufus said.

'What can we do? We can't just stand here!'

Mark put an arm round her. 'There's nothing we can do. Just wait for the professionals, that's all.'

'But whose house is it?' asked Wigwam. 'Is it somebody we *know*?'

As if this made all the difference, thought Sarah. Or any difference at all.

'I can hear sirens,' the Trophy Wife said. Sarah wished she could remember her stupid name. 'There!'

They could all hear them: a high-pitched keening, curling over the rooftops and echoing down the street.

Gerard lit his cigar. The flame from his lighter threw a devilish cast across his round face, stressing his widow's peak. 'Bit more excitement to wind up on,' he said. 'You lay this on especially, Mark?'

'Oh, shut up,' Sarah said.

She did not know whose house it was, but it lay hard by the river. The crowd was keeping a distance; no amateur heroics this time of night. Maybe it was empty, after all. But Sarah wished somebody would do something, if only to absolve the rest of them from the crippling sin of being useless in a crisis. She took a step away from Mark, whose arm dropped from her shoulder. And now fire engines came crashing round the corner, still blaring their sirens to underline the nature of emergency. Nothing serious ever happened quietly. Not while men were driving, anyway.

'There's nothing to see,' Mark said, in unconscious parody of a policeman in move-along mode. 'No sense rubbernecking.'

'Isn't there an ambulance?' asked Wigwam.

'It's coming.'

It tailed after the fire engines, its blue light scooping in and out of the gaps between houses. Because there was an ambulance did not mean anyone was hurt, Sarah thought. But it was pointless reaching these rational little conclusions. The house could be stuffed full of infants for all she knew. The fire engines pulled up near the house, and all sorts of efficient things happened. Hoses snaked from the backs of trucks, while men in yellow helmets shouted instructions to each other. The crowd moved back in awe or obedience while two men in white pulled stretchers from the ambulance. At this remove, it all had an air of unreality, as if she were watching a not quite accurate account of a small disaster. She heard glass breaking, then a hose whooshed on, trained on what was left of the upper storey. At this angle she could not be sure, but the house had a lopsided appearance, as if part of it had been swallowed by night and shadow, or something with an altogether larger appetite. It was the house on the corner, she decided. So any part of it that had collapsed had probably fallen into the river.

'Shall we go closer?' fretted Wigwam. 'I can't see whose *house* it is.'

'We'll only be in the way,' Mark snapped.

Rufus reached out and caught Wigwam's sleeve, whether in comfort or prohibition, Sarah had no idea. There was another rupture from the emergency scene, and uniformed men danced back from sliding rubble.

'I can't bear this,' she said. 'Let's go inside.'

They straggled back in, Gerard alone reluctant. Perhaps he got a kick out of other people's tragedies; more likely he wanted to finish his cigar. Sarah found two inches of it squashed upright on the gatepost the next morning, like the offering of a particularly acrobatic poodle.

All were subdued, and at least two of them deeply upset by what had happened. So Mark approached the matter in best masculine fashion, producing the brandy he held back for private emergencies; he and Gerard made the most of this one, though everybody else declined. Rufus never touched spirits.

Gerard wasn't surprised. Other than that, an armistice had been declared, which lasted until the dinner guests called it a night. It had gone twelve, to Sarah's surprise. She thought she'd been excruciatingly aware of every minute, but the last hour had passed her by entirely.

The thank-yous rang phoney in her ears. Half her guests she never wanted to see again; the other half she wished she'd not invited. Mark, come to that, was scoring small in the good husband stakes. So pleading a headache, she retreated to the kitchen almost before they were out the front door. At the back of the house, she could pretend the noise outside was a party. That way all she had to grieve about was the fact that she hadn't been invited.

She could hear Mark heading upstairs. Once he'd have been in to clear up. Now it seemed this was her domain; he'd cancel his subscription to the *Guardian* before using the phrase 'woman's work', but he'd justify not helping nevertheless. Hard day at the office; long journey back; had to stand all the way from Paddington. Plus she'd been pissy with his guests, which was hardly the way to further his career. And underneath that, no matter what kind of day he'd had, no matter what she'd said to whoever, there'd be that nasty little jingle that she heard all the time these days, although he'd yet to say it aloud:

It's not as if you do anything else. Is it, Sarah?

She stacked dirty dishes. Fifteen minutes' work here, but she was tired. The morning, she thought. She'd do it in the morning. Then a sudden, unwanted vision attacked her of them both being blown away in their sleep, and morning never coming. But that wouldn't happen, not twice in the same street. Not two gas accidents so close, though she might just get the boiler checked while she had accidents in mind . . .

Gerard, remember, had been sure it was a bomb.

Something moved outside the back door, shocking her from her thoughts. Probably a cat, she quickly decided. Which it was.

Moving closer she could make it out, sitting on the patio, grooming itself; a familiar local black, the opposite of a stray in that about six different households fed it. No way was she joining in. But she stood and watched it for a while, until it became too difficult to focus on the world beyond her own reflection, chopped and multiplied in the dozen glass panels that made up the back door. See yourself as Picasso sees you, she thought. In her case, heavy. Lifeless, shoulder-length hair. A smidgin over-made-up this evening . . . *This woman has low self-esteem.* Which didn't make her wrong, Sarah thought bitterly. Let's get Mark's opinion on the subject, shall we?

He was not available. The cat was subjecting her to pretty close scrutiny though; its eyes reflecting the kitchen's glow, its gaze steady and unforgiving, and it seemed to Sarah that it was weighing her according to some feline scale; checking out her potential for survival on the other side of the glass, where the wild things were. She didn't rate highly. *Too old, too slow, too fat.* Only thirty-three. Never what you'd call fast. She could stand to lose some pounds, it was true. *The other Sarah Tucker would have done just fine. But I don't know about you.* It was the judgement of a superior creature, she felt; a creature that never suffered a dinner party for its mate's awful client, or squandered its emotions keeping house.

But for all that, Sarah Trafford, née Tucker, thought, it was only a cat.

2

South Oxford had its compensations. North Oxford had the parks, the houses, and one or two minor colleges; east Oxford had Tesco's and an energetic police presence. West Oxford had the railway station. South Oxford had the river.

Not all of it, true, but as much as fitted into a long stretch beween two locks: Old Lag River. Between Osney and Iffley it meandered, with the pedestrian bridge at Friars Wharf marking the midway line: a harmless if unattractive structure, its metal frame daubed with uninspired graffiti. Twice a day this saw heavy traffic as infants from the estate were ferried across it to school. Sarah used it habitually as a shortcut into town, and from it could make out the exploded house next morning, an end of terrace whose exposed side stood on the footpath that ran by the river. Or had stood, rather, since now the house had folded in on itself like a used-up cardboard carton, all that remained of the wall being a faint outline the eye drew on the air, as if bricks and mortar had been reduced to an architect's plan. The front door stood upright; a bright cheeky red which could have illustrated the spirit of the Blitz. But everything to its left had collapsed, laying the interior bare to the gaze of onlookers like Sarah and the gaggle of women still returning home two hours after dropping their kids at school: they huddled nearby, smoking, telling lies about seeing it happen, while on the riverbank groups of policemen did much the same, except kitted out in dayglo overalls. The footpath had been cordoned off, along with the top of the road giving out on the river; little strings of yellow bunting flapped in the wind. The second storey of the house was gone, and the ground floor a mess of smashed furniture and broken walls, as if a whole collection of worldly goods had been dropped from a great height. The wallpaper on the inside upright was scorched and shriven, and on it Sarah saw the shadow of a chair which no longer existed, one the blast had reduced to matchwood. What was left of the roof sagged, still shedding tiles at irregular intervals. To all intents and purposes, the house next door was now nearest the river. South Oxford had grown smaller by one address.

There was a seal splash as a wetsuited policeman dropped into the water. One of the women detached from her group and came over. 'They carried three out. I saw the stretchers.'

Sarah didn't know what to say. She had never spoken to this woman, and didn't know three was a significant number. 'Well . . .'

'And she lived alone. Just her and the kid.'

'Who was—'

'Nobody knows.'

There was a shout from below. The frogman surfaced, holding what looked like an intact teapot.

'I don't even know who *she* was.'

'Maddie. Maddie Singleton.'

The name meant nothing. 'And the child?'

'Just a bairn. Could have been one of us, couldn't it?'

'What could?'

'Something like that. The mains it was, they reckon. See our block?' She waved a hand at the flats behind them. 'It happens over there, Boom! Goodnight, Vienna.' She was much the same age as Sarah, but her smoker's features added years. 'Goodnight fuckin' Vienna.'

'Were they killed?'

'Course they were killed. It was an explosion.'

A policeman had taken the teapot and was trying to fit it into a polythene bag. The frogman dived once more, his flippers breaking the surface briefly, then disappearing with hardly a ripple. The women on the bridge murmured, as if giving points for style. It was a strange new spectator sport: catastrophe aquatics. The frogman would collect what used to be a life, and pack it all in polythene bags for the experts to put together again.

'Shocking, I call it. They should do something about it.'

'Like what?'

But the woman didn't know.

She went back to join her mates, the word spread, the message passed on. Sarah felt she'd fumbled the encounter, but couldn't think how to recover it. And felt clumsy, too, standing here; looking on someone else's accident. Then she saw the man on the other side of the river, standing on the apron of grass below the flats: he too was a voyeur. But something about him held her gaze.

He looked to be forty, though that was an outright guess. The first glance told Sarah he'd lived a life that had aged him fast, though she'd have been at a loss to supply the detail to back up that notion. His long hair flopped untidily across his forehead and was tied in a knot at the back; it also sprouted in a stringy, undernourished beard that looked fairly recent. Outfitted by Oxfam, Sarah thought: denim jacket, patched jeans, scuzzy white T-shirt; he could have been one of the dozens of homeless who mumbled round the city centre, carting bundles of newspaper and litter-filled plastic bags, but something took him out of the category; she couldn't fathom what. His air of concentration perhaps. Something, anyway. She'd work it out. And all the while Sarah gazed down at him he didn't once look up, yet she was sure he was as aware of her presence as he was of all those presences on the bridge, enough to have described any one of them a week hence . . . Perhaps she'd drunk more than she'd thought last night.

Enough, anyway, not to notice Wigwam until she was nearly on top of her. Or recognise, rather, for Wigwam was not unnoticeable. Bright yellow shorts this morning, with a pink, hugging T-shirt that walked a line between brave and downright stupid; turning a figure you might call generous into one that looked plain greedy. Though Wigwam, Sarah had long since known, cared nothing about her appearance.

'Are you all right?' were her typical opening words.

'I was miles away.'

'Poor thing.'

But Wigwam, Sarah realised, wasn't addressing her any more. 'Did you know her?' she asked.

'Maddie? Yes, of course. Didn't you?'

'Don't think so.'

'You must have done. Tall woman, blonde hair. Her daughter's just a tiny.' Wigwam's eyes filled with tears.

Sarah was remembering a flitting shape, a head of hair, an outline without a voice. 'Red overalls?'

'Maddie?'

'The child.'

'Dinah. I think so.'

She had sat on the towpath throwing crusts to the swans. Sarah remembered her now; a fair child with her hair in bunches, and grubby clothes, and bright yellow jellies. She couldn't have been much more than three. 'Swans,' she'd said to Sarah, and pointed. There'd been a mother there, but she hadn't left a mark on Sarah's memory.

It had only happened once. But now, even looking at it, she found it hard to picture a towpath without a grubby blonde child casting stale bread into the water.

'Poor love. All alone now, even if she does—'

'She's alive?'

'Oh, she wasn't killed. Not Dinah.'

'I thought she was.'

'She was shielded by a wardrobe or something. From the blast. She was in bed, and the bed just dropped through when the floor caved in. She didn't even fall out.'

'How do you know all this?'

'Rufus was talking to one of the firemen. They were still here this morning.'

'What about Maddie?'

'Oh, she died.' Wigwam's face crumpled. 'She was downstairs when it happened—'

Sarah hugged her friend. She felt weepy herself now, having latched on to an image: a fair child, a pair of yellow jellies; the kind of tear-trigger newspapers relied on, but genuine enough for that. 'Come on. Let's go.' They were surplus to requirements, rubberneckers at a tragedy, and it wasn't a role she enjoyed seeing herself in. But looking for somebody specific to share the blame, she saw that the man on the waterfront had gone, and a couple of policemen now stood in his place. This was not necessarily a significant development. But Sarah could not shake the man's picture from her head, and it stayed with her as she and Wigwam walked into town.

That morning she had cleared the dinner party debris, vacuumed the sitting room, changed the bed linen and polished the wooden handrail that ran alongside the stairs; she had cleaned the mirrors in the bathroom, swept the front path and had a long internal dialogue as to whether to defrost the fridge or wait until the weekend. She had eaten two bowls of muesli, five digestive biscuits and all four mints left over from last night. She had opened the *Guardian* jobs section, closed it, and turned to the TV listings instead; had watched the last half of a programme that taught her how to find the railway station in Italian, and the first half of one about early colonial administration in

Australia. She had been seriously thinking about the remaining digestive biscuits, trading the calories against agreeing to defrost the fridge that afternoon, when common sense had prompted her to leave the house instead.

Now she was eating a slice of strawberry cheesecake while Wigwam explained the Singleton family:

'Her husband was killed a few years ago.'

She'd never realised south Oxford had such a high body count. 'Killed how?'

'He was a soldier.' Wigwam made the statement a flat inevitability, as if being in the military were itself a terminal condition. 'He fought in the Gulf War, can you imagine that?'

Sarah could. It wasn't as outrageous as Wigwam seemed to think: somebody had to have fought there, else it would have been over too fast. 'And that's where he was killed?'

'No, of course not. Dinah's only four. Four and a bit. No, he was in some kind of accident in a helicopter or something. I think in Cyprus.'

'You only think so, Wigwam? You're slipping.'

She stuck her tongue out. Then said, 'It was four years ago. There was a few of them killed. Him and some other soldiers. Dinah wasn't even born.'

'Did you know him?'

'Course not. This was before they moved here, silly.'

Talking to Wigwam was a window to another world. If the BBC ever started a rolling gossip channel, they had their anchorwoman right here. On the other hand, she did expect you to keep up. Sarah should have known when Maddie Singleton moved into the area: more than a duty, this was her holy obligation. What happened where you lived was of paramount concern. A war might rumble into life thousands of miles away, but who the neighbours were having round next Friday, that was news.

'Exploding, though,' Wigwam said, and shook her head. 'If

you were a soldier you'd expect it, wouldn't you? Sort of. But not a soldier's *wife*.'

Sarah avoided confronting whether soldiers expected to be blown up by taking a bite of cheesecake. 'I don't suppose she knew much about it.'

'That's the best way to go,' Wigwam said with an authority that sounded born of experience, though presumably wasn't. She nibbled at her apple pie. 'But so *young*,' she added, muffled. 'You wouldn't wish it on anybody.'

'I don't know. How about Gerard?'

Wigwam winced to indicate that there were some things you couldn't joke about, but also gave a quick smile to show that Sarah was forgiven. 'Is he very important? Gerard Inchon?'

'He thinks so.'

'I didn't like him very much.'

Sarah laughed. 'Neither did I, Wigwam. Neither did I.'

'Why are rich people horrid?'

'Maybe you have to be horrid to get rich, I don't know.' She looked at the cake on her fork. 'You know what I found myself thinking, though? That he was also horrid because he was fat.' She shuddered. 'This is me speaking. A couple more mornings like today, I'll be the same size as a helicopter.'

'You're not fat.'

'I eat. It's all I do these days. I do housework and I eat. I also watch telly, but I eat while I'm doing that too. Sometimes I have the telly on while I'm doing the housework, come to think of it. If I did that *and* ate all at once, think how much time I'd save.'

'You're just depressed. Have you been looking for another job?'

'Barely. The first month I applied for everything, and got exactly no interviews. You lose heart.'

'You should take up something.'

Sarah groaned. 'I don't want a *hobby*, Wigwam. I want a life.'

'Jobs aren't everything.'

Wigwam would know. She had about seven, luckily all part-time. Sarah felt a pang of guilt: doing housework kept Wigwam's kids fed. Other people's housework. It was probably easier not to obsess on it when it wasn't your own, but even so it didn't make for a career.

'Why did he say it was a bomb, though?' Wigwam asked suddenly.

'Who?'

'That Gerard. Rufus says it was probably a gas main. That's what it was, wasn't it? When houses blow up, it's usually the gas. Or else they've been keeping something inflammable in the cellar.'

There were times when Sarah wondered what it was like inside Wigwam's brain. She was either gifted with unusual insights, or had been stranded on this planet as a small child.

'But Gerard said straight off it was a bomb. Why did he say that?'

'I don't know.'

'It was an *awful* thing to say.' Wigwam's eyes filled with tears again. 'Who would want to blow up Maddie Singleton?'

'Or whoever was with her.'

'What?'

'Maybe it was the man with her they were trying to blow up.' A thought occurred to her. 'It *was* a man, wasn't it?'

'I expect so. She was Catholic.'

There was a certain tortured logic to this, so Sarah let it pass.

Besides, she'd had another thought. 'If she was seeing somebody on the quiet . . .'

'Maddie?'

'Yes. Somebody might be missing a man.'

Wigwam let this sink in. Then her eyes grew round in horror, tinged ever so slightly with delight. 'Oh *no*!'

'Hell of a piece of news to wake up to.'

'That's *terrible*. To find your partner was unfaithful and it got him *killed*!'

'I'm not sure. If I found out Mark was having an affair, I'd be quite pleased to learn in the next breath he'd been blown to kingdom come.'

'That's horrible.'

'I know. I'm not as nice as you are.'

'You're not getting on, are you?'

'Me and Mark? No, not really. At least, we're not *not* getting on, it's just that there aren't any buffers any more. Or not for me. He's got his job, and all I've got's him. I think he likes it that way, that's what bothers me.'

'Is he doing well at work?'

'Seems to be. It takes up most of his time. But we don't talk about it much, because it just leads to rows.'

'It's bad when you can't talk about things.'

'Don't I know it. What really gets me is how much he's changed, or how much his beliefs have changed, and he just doesn't seem aware of it. Or he takes it for granted, as if it were part of growing up. Getting older.'

'Everybody changes.'

'I know. And we don't all grow up either, I know that too. So maybe I should be grateful. But the people he works for now, he used to hate all that. Working for the clampdown, he called it.'

'Mark did?'

'Sure. He was never going to save the world, you know? But he was always on the side of the people who were going to. If critical theory was radical action, he'd have been Che Guevara. These days he thinks Tony Blair'll do nicely, thanks.'

'*I* like Tony Blair,' Wigwam said loyally.

'You like everybody, Wigwam. That doesn't count. You know what he said to me the other day? Mark, not Tony Blair.' She scraped her plate with her fork for the last crumbs. 'I was handing him a cup of coffee, and he said, "Thanks, em, Sarah."' Wigwam was looking distraught. Sarah remembered, not quite soon enough, that Wigwam hated information like this; she'd rather everybody had a wonderful life. So she added, 'Anyway, I didn't know your Rufus was taking adult lit.'

'Oh, he's not. He just said that to shut Mr Important up. Well, he did try it once, but he didn't like it. So he stopped.'

'What *is* he doing now?'

'Well,' Wigwam said. 'He doesn't actually want anybody to know.'

Male prostitute? Sarah wondered. Librarian? But Wigwam wouldn't say.

Wigwam had to go to work after that, so Sarah drifted around town on her own for a while: window shopping, before succumbing to the genuine article and buying a summer dress in a closing-down sale. There it was, she scolded herself on the way home. You grouse about Mark's job, but it lets you buy whatever you want. Even things you don't much want but you're too bored not to buy. That was the problem, really. She was bored.

Bored too, a bit, by south Oxford, she decided, as she crossed the bridge again going home. Not that it was worse than anywhere else. There was more to it, of course, than just the river: some dreadful pubs; two primary schools; a lake by the railway line. There was what Wigwam referred to as a community spirit, which in effect meant that neighbours felt free to complain when you painted your house, and everybody moved to north Oxford as soon as they could afford it. The last eighteen months had seen two local murders: one domestic – a battered wife became a murdered wife – and the other opportunist: a daytime burglary that went 'tragically wrong', according to the paper, as if there were some ideal template of burglary that this had failed to live up to. The same paper had written of a neighbourhood living under the shadow of fear, and this was crap also. Most people did not expect to be murdered, all but a few justifiably. They got on with their lives regardless of the terrors of the world: the wars brewing up whether they wanted them or not; the houses that exploded in the middle of the night. When forced to consider the ugliness that lurked on the fringes of life, they did so in a way that confirmed their views of what that life should be like. It was not a world, Sarah thought now, to bring children into – the standard excuse used by those who did not want children anyway.

Which Sarah didn't. Her considered view was that from the age of about three children were incredibly dull, until they got to twelve or so, at which point they became unspeakable. Wigwam's brood, her favourite example, were particularly obnoxious: snotty, ill-coordinated, perpetually whining, though she had to admit Wigwam seemed quite fond of them. The opinion remained untarnished, however. Which made it all the stranger now that she could not get from her mind the picture of a small girl asleep when a blast ripped her house apart, and of a wardrobe falling, its doors flapping open, forming a protective coffin to shield the girl from harm. The girl, in her mind, wore red overalls and yellow jellies.

And, like Sarah, was a survivor.

It was the notion of a protective coffin which haunted her. A sort of instant resurrection. But what kind of life had Dinah Singleton been born again into? With a father dead before she was born, and her mother newly following him, orphanhood was what remained. Probably not the Dickensian nightmare it used to be, but not something you'd wish on a small child even if small children did not figure highly among your priorities. And where had she been taken? Since her own survival, still not long enough ago for comfort, Sarah had nursed a dread of hospitals and the institutionalised anonymity they imposed: for all the best efforts of the nursing staff, you could never be anything more than the next patient. Not that what happened to the child was any of her business. But the image, the overalls, the jellies, nagged at her like an unquiet conscience. This was what she got for thinking children obnoxious. Something very like guilt.

Down by the exploded house, busy teams still sorted through wreckage. One or two individuals stood to one side, heads cocked, as if trying out a new perspective which might make sense of the strewn rubble: like puzzlers newly arrived at a half-completed jigsaw, they were looking for the important pieces that made sense of the rest. And with sudden clarity it came to Sarah what had been unusual about the bearded man, the man who had stood on the grass apron watching these professionals. It was that he was the only one there who looked like he knew what he was seeing. As if such damage were as much a part of his everyday as any other element in that scene: the river, the bridge, the swans who had not been fed.

3

SHE DID NOT LIKE hospitals, and with reason. All one winter she'd spent incarcerated in one, feeling – she'd wished – like a princess in a tale; her view a dismal car park, though at least it had had an ornamental fountain as its centrepiece. And out of nowhere, now, as she parked her car, she remembered waking one morning to see that this had frozen, and a rather dour piece of statuary become a thing of beauty. Encased in ice, as if a glacier had swooped on it overnight, the statue might have been the relic of a long-gone society, preserved by chance and freak weather; its survival made possible by the forces that sought to destroy it. A bit like those mammoths people were always finding, or hoping to find. Had that ever been true, the deep-frozen mammoth discovery? She didn't know. But it made a good story.

That was then, and this was now. Three days had passed since the night of the explosion, the first of which had seen a flurry of press interest. But the story had dwindled, relegated to small paragraphs on inside pages, all of which explored different ways of saying the same thing: that no progress had been made; that nobody knew who the dead man was. Dinah's existence had been established that first day, and the child not mentioned since.

At any other time Sarah might have found it odd, this hasty burial of what was surely a major story. But the wind from the

East was blowing all other news from the headlines: Iraqi troops had been mobilised in defiance of Western dictates, and the mutterings of US hawks were growing shrill, if mutterings could do that. Last year's news was being dredged up once again: the old accusations about missing Iraqi soldiers. The *Guardian* covered this one in detail, even giving the names of the six conscripts Iraqi ministers claimed were being held – claimed had been murdered – by Western troops. But the conclusion remained that these soldiers had perished in the storm they'd been lost in, on the Syrian border, a couple of years ago; their 'disappearance' simply a useful legend to a government hostile to UN inspectors.

All of which mattered more than two deaths and one small child. But it was happening in other time zones, whereas this was a short distance away. She locked the car and went in to Reception.

Where she found a lone harassed woman dealing with three telephones and a short queue. The latter dissipated after a while; the telephones remained substantial and in full working order, and it was against their clamour that Sarah made her request: to see, talk to, Dinah Singleton. A child. No, she did not know which ward, though the children's would be a good guess. Yes, this was the little girl who had been brought in after an explosion.

'Are you a relative?'

'A neighbour,' she said. 'A friend,' she added.

'You're not press, are you?'

'Do I look like press?'

The woman didn't appear to want to comment.

'I'm not press,' Sarah said firmly.

'You'd better take a seat. I'll see if there's someone can talk to you.'

So Sarah took a seat, while no obvious effort was made to find someone, anyone, to talk to her.

There were posters on the walls: the dangers of smoking, of drinking, of taking drugs, of making love. In a student city, it was a pretty forlorn hope that anyone was paying attention. She remembered a piece of graffiti she'd once seen or read about: a picture of a newborn baby, with the legend *The first three minutes of life can be the most dangerous.* Under this had been added *The last three can be pretty dodgy too.* The girl she was here to see, Dinah Singleton, could grow old and die without ever being in so much danger again. She could smoke, drink, shoot up, screw around; she could take up lion taming. And all through her life she'd know, when she was tiny, she'd slept through an explosion, and would never be in so much danger again. There was no need to mention miracles: you could talk about wardrobes, and the random order in which things happened. And what you could take away from such an event, if you happened to be the one who lived through it, was a belief that your life had been weatherproofed, stress-tested, and the ordinary dangers, the ones the posters warned you about, no longer applied. At the very least, you might think yourself bombproof. Nobody outside a war zone was surely called upon to survive explosions twice.

This, then, was the link. This was why she was here. It was not just the vision of the blonde child in yellow jellies, but the secret sharing of the gift of survival: Dinah, like Sarah, had come through the fire, and while the circumstances could not have been more different, the simple fact of it shone like a talisman. And because this was so, she needed to track the story to its conclusion. She needed to know that Dinah had not just survived, but would continue to do so. She wanted to know her condition.

So, anyway, Sarah told herself while she waited; wondered, too, why she had not told Mark she was doing this. Probably because to have done so would have been giving him ammunition. Any weakening on the question of children, he'd jump on in an instant. Which was maybe why she'd given her maiden name at Reception. This was not her usual habit.

After a while somebody came: a small, fiftyish woman who evidently wore the rule book like a whalebone corset. Possibly she was a robot in a white smock. 'Ms Tucker?'

'I'm looking for—'

'You can't see her.'

There was such a high-definition quality to this, Sarah hardly knew how to respond. 'Why not?'

'It's completely irregular.' She spoke impatiently, as if she'd exhausted this subject more than once. 'This is a hospital. You simply cannot wander in and be given free rein.'

Deep breath. 'When would it be possible to see her?'

'I can't answer that.'

'It's a simple enough question. When are visiting hours?'

'I cannot allow—'

Sarah turned and walked away, while behind her the robot choked to a halt. At Reception, Sarah asked the young woman when visiting hours were.

'Mondays to Fri—'

'I'll deal with this, Dawn,' the robot said. 'Ms Tucker, I'll have to ask you to leave.'

'This is ridiculous.'

'You are interfering with the smooth—'

'I'm interfering with nothing. I'm concerned about a child. That is all.'

'Are you a relative?'

'No, but—'

'Then there is nothing more to be said.'

'I don't agree.'

The robot's mouth twitched once. Twice. Somewhere deep behind her eyes lurked an unassuaged affront.

'Just tell me this. Is she all right?'

'I have no information on the patient.'

'What do you mean you've no—'

'I have no information on the patient.'

Sarah's anger tipped into fear. All around, walls pulsed with the consequences of emergency. How could one small child survive the damage by the river? Wardrobe or no wardrobe. 'She's dead, isn't she?'

'I have no—' said the robot. Then she stopped.

'You know which child this is, don't you? There was an explosion.'

The mouth twitched again.

'It's a police matter. Shall we call the police? Do you want the police here instead of me?'

'You'll have to leave now. Or I shall call security.'

'If I go without seeing her,' Sarah said, '*I'm* calling the police.'

'That won't help you.'

'Why not?'

A wrestling match took place in the robot's head: Sarah watched the coverage broadcast live on the robot's face. The disinclination to give out information versus dealing the clinching blow to Sarah's wants. The blow won.

'The patient,' she said, 'is no longer in the hospital.'

The patient was no longer in the hospital. What did that mean: she'd been transferred, discharged, what? Abducted by aliens? 'Are you actually in charge?' Sarah asked. 'I mean, who else can I speak to about this?'

The robot's eyes narrowed to slits, the kind you find on coastal defence bunkers. The ones they fire cannons through. '*I am in charge*,' she hissed. 'Any enquiries you have will be dealt with by *me*.'

Sarah did not wait to hear it but turned and walked smartly out the front door, the best she could manage on the way being a wink at Dawn on Reception, pressganging the poor woman into an alliance against her horrible boss. Who was probably herself a harassed, overworked woman, but there'd be time for rational sympathy later. At that moment, Sarah hoped the robot would soon step into a malfunctioning lift.

Out in the fresh air, she took a deep breath. It had been years since she'd smoked, but at times like this, of which there were thankfully few, she tended to monitor her stress receptors, putting that old chestnut about there being no such thing as an ex-smoker to the test. Everything seemed normal. No outraged nicotine centre screaming its shredded lungs out. She expelled air carefully, relieved that tobacco slavery was a thing of the past, and headed for the car.

Where a man leant against her driver's door: long-haired, bearded; wearing shades today, but she recognised him. Anywhere but here and now – broad daylight, people, a *hospital* – she'd have screamed. You read about this: women finding strangers by their cars, wielding sob stories, looking for lifts. Afterwards, you'd know they had tools in their bags: saws and pliers, cutting knives. Never trust anybody you meet on the street. If Sarah had children, that would be lesson one. Never trust anybody you meet. But this man carried no bag, and his hands hung loosely by his sides, palms out, as if he were aware of the dangers flashing through her mind, and wanted them out of the way. He spoke first.

'Who are you?'

Bloody cheek.

'You were on the bridge, with the other women. Now you're here. What do you want?'

'I want my car,' Sarah said. She had her keys in hand, prepared to throw them in his face. Or slash out; leave railway tracks down his bloody cheek.

'I don't mean to scare you. But you're here for Dinah, aren't you? Where is she?'

'I want my car,' she said through gritted teeth. 'Would you get out of the way?'

He didn't move. 'Are you a social worker?'

'Fuck off!' She moved round and opened the passenger door. He didn't try to stop her. But he watched through the windscreen as she squeezed into the driving seat, and she wished she'd worn a longer skirt. She wound the window down. 'And who are *you*?'

'They're friends of mine,' he said.

'The Singletons?'

'All of them.'

'There were only two,' she said stupidly. Then he turned and walked off, his ponytail bouncing against his neck as he went. He didn't look back. Whatever he'd wanted, she didn't have.

Sarah's hands were shaking, even once she'd taken a grip on the steering wheel. She felt, now it was over, that she'd spent the past five minutes being beaten up. *The patient is no longer in the hospital.* Where the patient was, was no business of Sarah's. But it could not be right, this humourless rejection of a simple enquiry; nor did she enjoy being lurked for in car parks, when all she wanted was to ascertain the fate of one orphaned child. A spurt of anger fuelled her into action, and she twisted the ignition key harshly. There were other uniforms, she thought, than the white one the robot wore. Not a natural-born police enthusiast, she at least recognised when matters fell within their jurisdiction. And as she reversed from her parking space the statue in the fountain stirred in the back of her mind, as if it could tell her a thing or two about survival, about resurrection; about how they did not always end in the happy ever after.

4

THE AGENCY WAS SANDWICHED between a pub and a newsagent's, and while the advert in Yellow Pages specified hi-tech, the reality did not run to a working doorbell. After pressing twice Sarah tried the door, which opened on a staircase leading up to a small landing, where a framed print of dreaming spires hung next to another door. The legend read OXFORD INVESTIGATIONS, and below that, in upper case, JOSEPH SILVERMANN *BA*. She tapped on the glass. Maybe Joseph Silvermann BA was hard of hearing. When she pushed it, this door opened too – hard of hearing and short on locks – and Sarah found herself in what looked like a secretary's room: a desk with a phone and intercom and electric console, and a couple of plastic chairs lined against the wall. A coat stand stood next to a closed connecting door, and more dreaming spires, taken from a different angle, brightened the wall. Through the door came voices, mostly a woman's. It did not sound pleased. A male kept attempting a counterpoint, but she couldn't hear what he was saying: it was just a bass stutter, poking through the gaps in the harangue.

'—just try growing up, even. I mean Jesus Christ, you're old enough. Or is that too much to ask?'

'———'

'Oh fuck off, Joe.'

Leaving suggested itself as a bright next move. The last thing she needed was a home-grown version of *Moonlighting*, especially after her brush-off from the regular cops. The police station was opposite the Crown and County Courts, a proximity helping to foster the illusion that the law was efficient, travelled in short, straight lines, and knew exactly where it was headed. There was a busy road to cross between the two, though, and maybe this accounted for the casualties along the way. Certainly Sarah's experience suggested that justice was not so much abstract as unobtainable, given the materials at hand, chief among these being the bored, or possibly stupid, desk sergeant who had taken the details she offered him and proceeded to put them together in a bewildering variety of ways, their common thread being his inability to come anywhere near the truth.

'So it was your house that exploded, then.'

'No. I live in the same street, that's all.'

'But your daughter was in the house.'

'She's not my daughter.'

Three-quarters of an hour of this, and she'd been transferred to a detective, or at any rate somebody without a uniform. Maybe one of the cleaning staff. But he had at least seemed aware of the existence of the Singletons, the fact that an explosion had occurred, and that the police were nominally looking into it. What he didn't seem too keen on was complicating this knowledge with further details. He listened to Sarah's story with barely suppressed boredom before the brush-off proper commenced.

'If the child is no longer in the hospital, we have to assume that she was discharged.'

Brilliant. 'Into whose care?'

'You'd have to speak to Social Services about that.'

'I've tried. Nobody seems to know.'

He sighed. 'Ms Tucker, they're hardly likely to have let her wander off on her own. If she's not there any more, it's because she's been taken somewhere else. And if they won't tell you where, it's because they don't regard it as any of your business.'

Which was as close as he came to saying he didn't either, but near enough for there to be no mistake. Sarah could just see him opening a mental file on her, labelling it 'Nosy Neighbour', and shutting it again. So she kept pestering him long enough to be an actual nuisance, rather than merely irritating, then left abruptly when his phone started ringing.

And now she was in north Oxford, in the lobby of a private detective agency picked from the phone book, and the impulse that had carried her this far was waning now she'd arrived. What, she asked herself again, was Dinah Singleton to her? The ghost of a child, a walking shadow; not even an actual absence in Sarah's life, just the possibility of one. An invisible girl with whom she shared a knack for survival. What mattered was that she hadn't slept last night for wondering about the girl; not all of her sleeplessness arising from a disinterested concern for the child's welfare. A good part of it was consuming curiosity.

'—last time, Joe, I mean it.'

'———'

'Yeah. I've heard it all before.'

The door opened and Sarah jumped. The woman that came through was taller than her, and older, with the kind of naturally curly hair that must have been a wow at eighteen but could get to be a nuisance in later life, when people thought you wore it like that to look younger. It was dark, very nearly black, and cropped so it fitted the woman's head like a cap one size too small. Her face was laughter-lined around the eyes and mouth, but she wasn't laughing now. Nor was she expecting company. She started when she registered Sarah, though recovered quickly. Her eyes, like her hair, were almost black, and looked properly sardonic when she spoke. 'Well well well. A customer.'

'The door was open.'

'You looking for Joe?'

'Is there any of him left?'

The woman laughed without a trace of humour. 'It bites. Let me guess. You've got a husband, he's got a secretary. Am I getting warm?'

'Actually, I want him to kill someone for me.'

'Joe doesn't do that. What he does is, he pines away in front of you. Bleeding hearts haemorrhage to death at the sight.'

'You're a big fan of his, then,' Sarah said.

'I've known him twenty years, man and boy. In that order. And the fact is, dear, Joe's a bit of a case.' She plucked a handbag from behind the desk and pulled a packet of cigarettes from it. 'Zoë Boehm,' she said. 'By the way.'

'Sarah Tucker.'

'Delighted. Joe's what you might call a hopeless romantic. He's hopeless at everything, in fact. But I don't mean to put you off. He's a sucker for the right client, and you look his type.'

'Which is?'

'God, you know. Sort of doe-eyed and a bit helpless.' She lit her cigarette with a disposable lighter. 'You want one of these?'

'No. And I'm not helpless.'

'Good for you. Won't help telling Joe, though. He tends to believe what he wants to believe.'

'Some detective.'

'He has his moments. Same as a puppy does. You keep throwing sticks long enough, he's bound to bring one back eventually. Probably have hold of the wrong end, though.' She opened the connecting door. 'Incoming, Joe!' Then she turned back to Sarah. 'He's all yours. But don't be too hard on the silly sod. When he acts hurt, he's usually not acting.'

'Are you his secretary or his nanny?'

But Zoë Boehm had left.

For a moment, maybe two, Sarah was on the point of following. The signs indicated that Joe Silvermann was more in need of help than in any position to dispense it, and a new lame duck in her life she could do without. But backing out now would mean learning to live with unanswered questions, so of the available doors, she took the one leading into the office.

Most fictional private eyes Sarah had encountered were politically correct women who specialised in investigating crimes their friends and family members were wrongly accused of. The pages Joseph Silvermann had sprung from were the Yellow ones, and she assumed he'd be a little less witty, a little less fit, a lot less ethical and wholly unarmed. That said, she hadn't known what to expect, so Joe in the flesh was neither a disappointment nor a relief. He was sitting behind a desk, and had greying, curly hair doing its best to surround a bald spot covering about half his head, and large features arranged in the usual way but producing a face maybe kinder than you usually get. All told, that first sight of him awoke a nagging memory she couldn't pin down for weeks: Joe Silvermann looked like the actor Judd Hirsch, who'd been in that old American show *Taxi*; not a dead ringer, but near enough. Part of it was the kindness.

After about maybe four seconds he looked up. He hadn't been reading, just studying his desktop. 'Has she gone?'

'She's, um, left. Yes.'

'Think she'll be back?'

'It was hard to tell.'

'She'll be back.' He looked down at his desk again, or at his hand, rather, which lay palm down on top of it. Maybe it was his fingernails he was studying. 'Once every eight months she's got it down to. It is July, isn't it?'

'Yes.'

'Right. Eight months, give or take. That's how often she flips her wig. Reads me the riot act then buggers off to London for a fortnight. She thinks I don't know that's where she goes. She wants me to think she's got a lover stashed somewhere.'

'Maybe there's a lover stashed in London,' Sarah said. 'It's a big place.'

'She goes to shows,' he said mournfully. '*Les Mis. Buddy.* She's seen those five times each.'

'You'd rather she had a lover?'

'I'd rather she had taste. Pinter. Early Stoppard. Though I suppose she'd not have to pretend in that case.' He stood suddenly and extended the hand he'd been perusing, as if deciding it had passed some kind of test. 'Joseph Silvermann,' he said. 'You'd probably guessed that.'

She shook his hand. 'Sarah Tucker.'

He was tall, it turned out, and bordering on heavy; possibly he still got away with people thinking it was muscle, but it was only a matter of time before they knew it was flab. 'There's a seat,' he said, waving his hand at it. She took this as an invitation, and they both sat.

He relapsed into silence, this time studying Sarah instead of part of himself. It felt pretty phoney; the Sherlock Holmes approach. Soon he'd tell her she'd been brought up in the north, bit her nails as a child, and had never been fond of dogs. Her expectations weren't altogether dashed when he spoke.

'You're a graduate, aren't you?'

'Yes.'

He looked pleased. 'Which college?'

'Birmingham University.'

'Oh, Birmingham. Yes, I've heard that's very . . . Eng lit, was it?'

In Glit.

'Yes.'

He looked pleased again. 'I can usually tell.' He got up to

close the window. On the street below, work was starting up: two men with a pneumatic drill ripping up a stretch of pavement, presumably for a very good reason. 'I was at Oriel,' he announced. 'English, yes. Taught by Morris. You know him at all?'

'I don't think so.'

'Retired now, of course. Well, dead actually. He wrote the book on the Romantics. *Furious Lethargy*. Wonderful man.'

'Mr Silvermann, I—'

'You probably don't need the small talk. A lot of people need putting at ease, they come into my office. They're gearing up to tell me things they can't tell their closest friends, and it makes them nervous, so there I go with the small talk. But you don't need it.'

'Are you good at your job?'

'Am I good at it?' He turned to look at her. In the light from the window he looked younger. 'I won't lie. Philip Marlowe, I'm not. But who is? Most of what I'm hired to do, I manage. I suppose that makes me good enough.'

'And what's that exactly?'

'Wandering husbands, missing kids. I do some process serving. But I'll be honest, a lot of it's running credit checks, you do most of it over the phone. I might as well be selling insurance half the time. There's days when it's like watching wood warp. You haven't made your mind up yet, have you?'

'I'm thinking about it.'

'You'll find better if you look around. But that might mean Reading or Bicester. I'm handy.'

'And you've an Oxford degree.'

'It helps the networking.' He produced from his pocket something which for an absurd moment she took to be a rape alarm, and triggered it into his mouth. 'Pollution,' he apologised. 'The air here, I find it hard to breathe. Would you like to tell me your problem, Ms Tucker?'

'I want to find somebody.'

'I can do that. It's difficult to go missing, you know. Really completely missing. There's so many records these days, you're under surveillance wherever you go. Credit cards, traffic control. You'd need to be an expert.'

'This is a four-year-old girl.'

'Probably not ex-SAS then.' He came back from the window and sat behind his desk again. 'I'm sorry, that was in poor taste. The girl's name?'

'Dinah Singleton.'

'She's not your daughter.'

'You sound sure of that.'

'Daughters do go missing, even very small ones. But mothers don't usually look to private investigators to find them.'

'She's a friend. A neighbour.'

He said, 'Singleton.'

'Not an immediate neighbour, actually. She lives up the road.'

'I've read that name recently.'

'Their house exploded.'

'Of course. The house in south Oxford, yes? The adults present were killed. They must have been friends of yours. I'm sorry.'

'I didn't know them. That is, I didn't know her. Nobody knows who he was.'

'But you know the little girl.'

'Yes,' Sarah said. 'Sort of,' she amended.

Silvermann nodded. 'A friend of your own children, perhaps?'

'I don't have children.'

'And wish you did?'

'What on earth—'

'I apologise. I'm simply trying to get a grasp on the situation, Ms Tucker. A little girl is involved in a tragic incident. She has since, I take it, vanished from view. You wish to find her. I'm curious about your motives, that's all. You say you *sort of* know her. You don't really know her at all, do you?'

'No.'

'But it's important to you that she be found.'

'Of course it is.'

'That hardly follows. Children vanish every day. Sometimes their own parents don't care.'

'Her parents are dead.'

'And you? Are you the Good Samaritan, Ms Tucker?'

'I don't think you get good samaritans any more.'

'This is true. We're too afraid of malpractice suits. How did the little girl come to vanish?'

This, too, she found phoney; the way he jumped from one subject to another, placing his questions where they were least expected. Perhaps, in addition to his wonderful degree, he'd spent a few years watching *Columbo*. But she told him anyway about the hospital and the long-haired stranger in the car park. When she finished he nodded as if it were all too familiar a tale. 'You realise,' he said, 'there's no reason to think anything untoward has happened?'

'The woman in the hospital,' Sarah said. 'She didn't know where the child had gone. She was furious.'

'She works in the NHS,' Silvermann said. 'She could have been furious for any number of reasons.'

'What about the man in the car park?'

'A family friend. A concerned family friend. My first guess would be grandparents. The grandparents have taken the child.'

'There are no grandparents,' Sarah said, with a certainty belying her complete ignorance on the matter.

He shrugged. 'Then I'd be forced to move on to my second guess.'

'Which is?'

He shrugged again. 'Strange things happen. The little girl is no longer an ordinary little girl, you know? She is part of a story. A miracle girl, a child who survived an explosion. So, possibly a newspaper has taken her up. This happens, you know.

Sort of a corporate takeover. They remove her to a private facility, where they'll pay for her treatment and photograph her at leisure.'

'That can't be legal. She's four years old!'

'Many things become legal when you can afford them, Ms Tucker. We live in a culture of expediency.'

'I wasn't expecting a lecture in civics.'

'I talk too much. People . . . have said so. All I'm trying to point out is, if you hire me to find Dinah for you, I will in all likelihood discover her safe and well. But this will cost you quite a lot of money.'

'How much?'

'One hundred and fifty pounds a day.'

She nodded, as if she'd been expecting that, but felt the sum like a slap in the face.

'Or any part thereof,' he added.

'And what do I get for that?' Sarah asked.

'My undivided attention.'

'The advert said hi-tech.'

'We've got a computer.'

'We?'

'Zoë – Ms Boehm is a partner.'

'She doesn't get her name on the door.'

He looked away. 'There was a mistake. The painter misheard his instructions.'

Sarah nodded again, for something to do. Her mind was ticking off sums of money: current account, savings. The joint account was obviously out. 'How long a job do you think it would be?'

'You know the adage? If you have to ask, you can't afford it.'

'I can afford it.'

'Believe me, Ms Tucker, I'm not in the business of turning work away. But nor do I wish to take advantage.' He hesitated.

'Sometimes people bring me problems they know can be solved. It's a way of dealing with the ones they can't do anything about.'

Sort of doe-eyed and helpless. 'Have you a couch I can lie on?'

'I don't mean to be intrusive. But all I can do, if I find the girl, is tell you where she is. I can't deliver her to you. I can't bring her mother back, either.'

'If I thought you could raise the dead, Mr Silvermann, I'd have found your rates very reasonable.'

'Perhaps there are cheaper ways of solving your problem, Ms Tucker. Perhaps there are cheaper problems you could find to solve.'

'I don't want analysis, Mr Silvermann. I want to find Dinah Singleton.'

'Of course you do.' He opened a drawer in his desk and pulled out a form. 'This is a standard contract. I'll need one day's pay as a retainer. If I don't find the child within two days, we can discuss the matter further.'

Sarah filled in dotted lines: name, address. Her current unemployment. 'For a partner in the firm,' she said, 'Ms Boehm didn't sound too keen on your line of business.'

'She thinks we should alter course,' he said. 'Headhunting. She likes the sound of headhunting.'

'But you don't?'

'I am a confirmed vegetarian, Ms Tucker. Also, I like being a detective.'

She couldn't resist it. 'Sometimes solving other people's problems is a way of avoiding dealing with your own.'

'Touché, Ms Tucker. I take all major credit cards,' he said. She was still smiling about that at the bottom of the stairs. The two men churning up the pavement had stopped again: exhausted by their fifteen-minute stint, they were leaning against a wall, smoking. As she stepped from the doorway into the sunshine, she felt vulnerable under their scrutiny. Private detective translated to extramarital sex. They were wondering whether she was sinned against or sinning, she thought; scarlet woman or vindictive wife. Maybe their philosophies were wider than this, but the way they stared didn't hold much hope of that.

Her immediate problem, though, was what to do next. Overheating in a woollen jacket, she couldn't face the trip home yet, so stopped in the pub next door and sat in the courtyard with a half of bitter, worrying about what she'd done. One hundred and fifty pounds was a lot to spend on a whim; especially with another hundred and fifty following it. Mark had never complained about her expenditure, but she'd never hired a private detective before either. Nor had she told him she was going to. She wasn't wholly sure why.

It was not that she didn't love him. Odd that this had to be stated, even to herself. But he had changed during their marriage, and if he'd hardly been happy-go-lucky at the outset, she sometimes had difficulty recognising the man he'd become. Targeted, he called it: jargon he'd have choked on five years back was his major mode of expression these days. He worked for a City firm, a merchant bank so professionally discreet nobody had ever heard of it. And being targeted, she'd recently decided, translated to job-obsessed; not wholly fair perhaps, but all the self-help books in the world couldn't convince her that making lists of career goals was an endearing character trait. On the other hand, he'd always had a tendency to catalogue his record collection. This should have been a clue.

She drank some beer and tried to balance the equation. What about her own goals? A career came into it, certainly; that was part of her problem. BHS, Gerard Inchon had called it: patronising sod. But it didn't help to know her talents, whatever they amounted to, were lying dormant; it disturbed the equilibrium of their marriage, allowing Mark to think that he'd found his role and that hers was obvious: she should have a child. She'd long suspected, anyway, that he'd thought her job a hobby. When you worked for The Bank With No Name, earning less than your age in thousands was a joke. And he who dies with the most toys wins. Out there in the marketplace it was a man's world, and they never let you forget it.

Meanwhile, there was Dinah Singleton: a child who shouldn't have meant anything to her but was rapidly becoming a symbol. The number of people who'd told her to stop looking for Dinah was mounting up. If she wanted to believe she set her own agenda, keeping searching was the only way to go.

Draining her glass, carrying it back in, Sarah knew she'd reached her decisions. She'd pay Joe Silvermann's bill herself; she'd do bar work if she had to.

And maybe she would have a child, but not yet. In her own damn time.

After she'd found the one she was looking for now.

5

ROUGHLY SIXTY MILES EAST of where Sarah was finishing her drink, on the fourth (and top) floor of a 1920s office block, the rest of which housed an overflow from the Ministry for Urban Development, a man stood looking down through an office window at the traffic snarled below: a belching snake of hot metal, strangely silent at this remove. He was a tall man with patrician features, and a full head of steel grey hair he wore swept back, to emphasise its weight. His suit was grey too, though more discreetly so, and the frame it covered lean and healthy-looking. His hands were long and his fingers thin; his nails clipped neatly just that morning. He appeared to be in his late fifties, though in fact had recently entered his eighth decade. Of this, too, he was proud, and while publicly ascribing his physical fortune to good genes, remained secretly convinced that strength of character held the key.

It was just a shame this was so rare.

The office he occupied was sparsely furnished. A metal desk, lower-orders issue; an ungainly shredder he referred to as the Dalek. A calendar on the wall seemed to think it was 1994. There were two chairs, which matched neither each other nor the desk, and a few oddments – desk lamp, hat stand, mirror – which looked as if they'd found their way here from different collections. Indeed, the office as a whole felt made up of left-over spaces, like a priest's hole or a butler's mezzanine. As if its existence were being tactfully passed over, and the business conducted between its walls allowed to remain a secret.

There was a knock at the door, and after a moment or two, a new man entered. His name was Howard. A lot younger than the room's original occupant, he hid it well: sparse hair, stressed features – he looked as if he'd unexpectedly been made leader of the Conservative Party, and hadn't yet found a way of passing the buck. And now was made to stand and wait while the man who'd summoned him – the man for whom Howard worked, or to whom he reported, though Howard had never discovered his name – stood looking out of the window; working up, no doubt, some piece of crap Howard would have to pretend he enjoyed. Or deserved. One or the other.

Howard often thought of his boss as C. Not because it was traditional in their field, but because it stood for a very short word that seemed to fit.

When C spoke at last, it was to say, 'Made a right bollocks of this one, haven't you, Howard?'

Howard didn't answer.

'I don't remember you receiving permission to start a war.'

'The Department was given carte blanche, sir.'

'That's very pretty, Howard. French, isn't it? And it implies pretty wide parameters, I'll grant you, but not wide enough to cover barely controlled explosions in densely populated suburban areas. Who did you have running this one? Wile E. Coyote?'

'Crane, sir.'

'Oh God. That's almost as bad.'

Though he hadn't asked which Crane, and everybody knew there were two.

C sighed. It was a theatrical sigh: sounded rehearsed. He waved a hand at a chair, so Howard sat, though C remained standing. But he turned from the window at last. Looked down at Howard like a disappointed headmaster. 'And Crane thought a bomb would do the trick? I suppose we should be grateful he didn't go after him in a tank.'

'It came out looking like an accident, sir. And there was the problem of the body, too. Crane thought taking him out solo would have caused more problems than it solved. I mean, the target was already dead, sir. Technically.'

'But his wife wasn't. Crane happy with that on his conscience, is he?'

Crane hasn't got a conscience, thought Howard.

'What about the locals? They've been pacified?'

'It was a gas leak. We're all square on that one.'

'No hungry journos looking for their name in bright lights?'

'It was a gas leak, sir,' Howard repeated. 'The story will hold.'

'I'm delighted you're confident. What about the child? Crane hasn't had her shot or anything, has he?'

'She's fine.'

'She had fucking better be fine, Howard. Dead babies sell newspapers. Dead babies blown up in cack-handed covert operations run by psychopathic idiots get entire documentaries dedicated to their short, wasted lives. Now which of the blasted Crane brothers masterminded this bollocks, and what's he planning on doing for an encore?'

'Axel, sir.'

'Axel shouldn't be let out on his own. He's a danger to the public. As I'm sure the public will all too readily agree after this fiasco. What's his next move? A small nuclear device in a crowded shopping centre?'

'Downey's still running loose.'

'And what are the bets on his suspicions having been aroused, Howard? You think he'll write it off to a faulty gas main? Luck of the draw? Or might he be a little bit jumpy?'

'Crane says—'

'Axel?'

'Amos. He's holding the reins on this.'

'So the bomb was *his* idea?'

'Axel's. It was a field decision, sir. He was given carte blanche—'

C waved his hand so Howard shut up. Axel Crane, Amos Crane: they were each as bad as the other. This time round, Amos Crane was home in the bunker, calling the shots; Axel – who was generally agreed to be a mad bugger – was out in the open, ignoring them. And civilians were being smeared across the landscape.

The older man said, 'Jesus wept. The lunatics are running the asylum. What does he say then, Amos Crane?'

'That it doesn't matter what Downey thinks or knows. Or thinks he knows. If we've got the child, he'll come looking for her.'

'This is what passes for a strategy?'

'He's gamed it every which way. There's a lot of things Downey might do, but not if we've got the child. He'll put her first. Until he's found her, he won't even think about going—'

Oh, *fuck*.

'Going what?' C asked politely.

'Public.'

'Public. Fine.' C pulled his chair out and sat down. 'Read the papers this morning, Howard?'

'Glanced at them, sir. Been a bit busy.'

'Anything grab your attention especially? Any minor events worth musing over? Like an impending fucking war, for instance?'

'Sir.'

'Fasten your mind on this, Howard. The country is prepared to take up *arms* to prevent Downey from going public. That isn't an option. If you're expecting your career to last longer than your hair did, don't even think about mentioning the possibility. Got that?'

'Yes, sir.'

'Right. What are you doing with the child?'

'We're working on it.'

'Well, work faster. Is Axel staying out in the open?'

'For the time being.'

'Good. Maybe we'll all get lucky and he'll be hit by a truck. *After* he's sorted out Downey.' C stood up again. 'Are you still here?'

Howard crawled to the door.

'And, Howard? Remind Crane he's not running a private war out there. If he can't keep his brother on a leash, maybe it's time you found him a job he can manage. Like checking ID at the car pool. Tell him that, will you?'

Howard closed the door behind him without a sound, then ran a finger round his shirt collar. The finger came away wet.

Waiting for the lift he swore fluently, obscenely and without repeating himself for just over a minute, not a single emotion showing on his face. There was a price to be paid for this, though at that moment Howard couldn't recall if it were cancer or heart disease. One of those. You couldn't bottle such fluency up and not have it go rotten. On the ground floor he smiled politely at the woman on Reception, who thought him something in forensic accounting, and walked out into groggy sunshine still harbouring violence in his heart. *Made a right bollocks of this one, haven't you?* Yes, sure, fine. From an office high above the mess, it all looked pretty easy. Down at street level, you worked with what you had. And if that included the Crane brothers, you thanked Christ they were on your side, and let them get on with it.

He would walk back across the park, he decided. If he could just cross the road in one piece, he'd walk across the park.

Howard hated being in this position, of having to defend the indefensible. The first he'd known of Crane's explosion, it was already over. And putting the fix in after the event was like making jelly in a sieve, so maybe that bastard with the view should come down here and see what real life looked like. A lot of traffic, all trying to go different places at once. All of it meeting in the middle, so what you got was smoke and noise.

At the corner, the green man told Howard it was safe to cross. Howard trusted green men about as much as he did any other kind, but crossed anyway. In the park it was a little cooler, a little calmer: there was a whisper of wind tasting less like exhaust fumes and more like something born of nature. Howard walked between flower beds Londoners had used as litter bins, past litter bins in which Londoners had been sick, and wondered again what to do about the girl.

It shouldn't have happened this way. Even Amos Crane – wolfishly protective of his younger sibling – admitted that, in a field situation, he'd not have chosen Axel's method. It hadn't allowed for total control. It demanded too much of a fix. But Amos believed in fate, too, and in the girl's survival saw something that went beyond tabloid whimsy: he saw the makings of a game plan. The girl, as he put it, was still on the board. It was up to them to use her with care.

But Howard, without being sentimental about it, wasn't sure this was a good idea. The trouble with infants was, you couldn't be sure people would forget about them. Everyone could lose an adult or two, and assume their life just took a different direction: they'd moved or got in with a new crowd – people were always prepared to write their own backstory to explain away a casual friend's disappearance. But with an infant, you didn't assume they'd made their own choices, changed their own lifestyle. With infants, the most unlikely types might get it in their heads to come looking.

The fix seemed solid: the police, the local press. The inquest should ring down the curtain. Nobody liked it much, but in the name of national security, a lot of shit got swallowed. Still, things needed checking. That was the trouble with cowboys like Axel, thought Howard: they pulled off whatever wacky stunt felt good at the time, and muggins here was left to make sure nobody got curious after the event. It could be a problem if anyone other than Michael Downey took the bait. Especially with Axel Crane running wild, morally certain the fastest solution to most problems was a shallow grave.

So Howard made a mental list (Howard made a lot of mental lists). 1. Check on the child. 2. Hang up some alarm bells – it would be nice to have warning if things went wonky. 3. Remind Crane he wasn't running a private war out there. If he couldn't keep his brother on a leash, maybe he'd like checking ID at the car pool.

He almost smiled at the thought of passing that last item on.

Amos Crane, though, was a truly creepy motherfucker, and Howard didn't think he'd be telling him anything of the sort very soon.

TWO

DEAD SOLDIERS

6

IT WAS OVER A week before Sarah heard from Silvermann again, a week in which the debris was sifted and cleared at the broken house, and scaffolding erected to prevent what was left of it sliding into the river. The police presence became nominal and eventually disappeared, and the absence of obvious developments led to the falling off of newspaper coverage in proportion to increased speculation in the neighbourhood. No husbands were reported missing. Dinah's disappearance received no coverage. Either it wasn't newsworthy, it wasn't known about, or it wasn't a real disappearance. Maybe Silvermann would let her know which, if he ever got in touch. One night Sarah awoke sure she could hear a child crying in the street, but saw nothing human through the window. Mark slept through it, even when the streetlight's glow fell on his face as she drew aside the curtain. He looked much younger sleeping, Sarah thought. Probably everyone did. But it kept alive in her a tenderness harder to maintain in the daylight hours.

Harder to maintain, too, was a sense of exactly why she'd hired Joe in the first place. The image of Dinah that had latched on to her mind had grown paler with the passage of time, as if, mission completed, it could fade away into the light. The overalls, the yellow jellies, remained, but they too seemed less substantial, as if their memory had grown confused with that of the dolls' accessories Sarah played with as a child. She was starting to wonder if her own subconscious weren't playing treacherous games, luring her into a state of maternal concern that would leave her prey to Mark's powers of persuasion. And Silvermann's silence also gave her unease; nor could she recall the details of their contract. He'd said two days and taken eight so far: would he charge for those? Several times she'd dialled his number but hung up before making the connection, unready, yet, to call him off before knowing what had happened. At this point, of course, she believed it was possible to halt events.

When he called at last, he called mid-morning. Sarah, inevitably, was involved with housework. At least once a week she found a corner – the cupboard in the spare bedroom today – she'd somehow overlooked until that moment; cleaning it thereafter became a weekly fixture, another item tagged on to a list of chores that threatened to last forever. What had been a weekly routine was becoming an eight-day cycle; she was torn between needing it and wanting to walk away. So Silvermann's call sounded like chimes of freedom, though it contained less information than you'd find on a postcard, or even a postage stamp. 'Have you found her?' she asked him.

'Are you free?'

'Right now?'

'Right now, yes.'

Because he never gave out important stuff over the phone. That was what he told her later, along with what he'd found out.

So she was free, yes, or at least released on licence. He suggested Modern Art Oxford: not the gallery, but the café, which met with Sarah's approval. While she couldn't always admire what the gallery chose to exhibit as art, she'd endorse its cakes any day of the week. But Silvermann was there first, and his offer to pay for coffee left her unable to ask for cake. Imposed virtue is not the sweetest, but she supposed she'd live. Joe Silvermann, meanwhile, steered them to a table by the wall where he could sit with one eye on the exit. It was hard to gauge whether this was professional paranoia or juvenile posing. For the moment, Sarah wasn't ruling out a bit of both.

'I spend half my life in places like this,' he said.

'Galleries?'

'Cafés. But also galleries, yes, and pubs and clubs. Anywhere people meet people, you know? Museums. Railway stations.'

'You must have a lot of friends.'

A hint of a smile swept across his mournful face: it was like watching somebody remembering a joke at a funeral. 'Strictly business. This is where a lot of cases start. Strangers meeting. Then wanting to know more before taking it further.' He picked up his coffee cup, sniffed suspiciously, then put it down. 'Maybe ten, twelve times a year I get jobs like this. It's always an older woman, she's met a younger man. And what she wants to know is, is he all right. You know?'

'Is he safe.'

'Is he safe. Times used to be, you met someone, you liked them, you got married. Now you need a credit check and deep background before the second date. Nobody wants to get married to Frederick West.'

'Or his wife.'

'But men mostly trust their judgement. I don't know why. A woman can fool a man. The other way round, it's not so easy. So I've always believed.'

'But maybe your judgement is suspect.'

'You're laughing at me. I don't mind.' He picked up his coffee again. 'I had a case once, a woman, she has this new boyfriend. And she wants to know, can I take a blood test from him without him knowing? I ask her, what am I, a vampire? But that's what she's hiring me for. She wants to know if he's got Aids, if he's HIV, without him knowing she's finding out.'

'How did you manage that?'

'Something you should understand: when a woman wants

a man checked out, ninety-nine times in a hundred she's got good cause. Her instincts have already told her what she needs to know, she's just looking for confirmation. So that's what I supplied in this particular case.'

'You told her he had Aids?'

'I told her he was already married. It was just as effective, and a lot less messy.' He drank from his coffee cup at last. 'So. Dinah Singleton.'

'You've been to the hospital.'

'I've been to the pub,' he corrected her. 'Just down the road, the White Horse? Very popular with medical staff.'

'Is that your usual procedure?'

'It's the human touch. So I'm at the White Horse, and I see some familiar faces. I've done work there before. One time I bribed a nurse to add bandages to a car-crash vic. It upped the settlement twenty, maybe thirty per cent.'

'Joe, could you stick to the point?'

'I am making a point here. Everything I've said, it's to the point. The point is, I do people work. Conspiracies, I leave to the police.'

'This is people work, Joe. I'm looking for a child.'

'A child who was blown up. You can't separate the two, Ms Tucker. These are very muddy waters.'

'Did you find her?'

'No, I didn't find her. What I found was, she was checked in at 2:37 a.m. on the fourth. They're very precise with their records. It is, after all, a hospital. It's not a cocktail party.'

'And what else?'

'Nothing else, Ms Tucker. That's what I mean by muddy waters. This is a place, you ask for a drink of water, it goes on your chart. They make a record, excuse me, when you fart. But a litle girl disappears in the middle of the night, nobody knows where she went.'

Sarah didn't say anything.

'That's not people work, Ms Tucker. This, it took organisation. I work with carrots, you know what I mean? And the nurse who took my money that time, she needed the little extra. I'm not ashamed. But this time, I'm all out of carrots. People don't want to know about carrots. It makes me wonder if somebody's been round there with a stick.'

'You're jumping to conclusions.'

'Jumping, it's allowed. You had to walk to conclusions, how far would you get?' He was pleased with this. He stopped talking to drink his coffee while Sarah received the full effect.

On the next table along a man and a woman sat, also with coffee, but too involved in argument to bother drinking. Snatches of their dialogue, intense if not yet disruptive, kept drifting into hearing. Already they were drawing glances; becoming the centre of that embarrassed fascination you get when a scene threatens to erupt in a middle-class setting. Right at the moment, Sarah had too much on her mind to eavesdrop. 'I don't understand,' she said at last. 'She can't have just gone. There has to be a record.'

'I agree.'

'But you said—'

'What I said was nobody *knows* where she's gone. Nobody I spoke to. You could call it restricted information. But there must be a record, yes. It's a hospital, it's—'

'Not a cocktail party, right. Could you get into restricted records?'

'It wouldn't be easy.'

'But you could do it.'

'Probably not.'

Sarah took a deep breath. 'That's it, then.'

'Not entirely.'

'How so?'

Joe scanned the café. It was filling up nicely; the lunch crowd drifting in to form a queue at the salad bar. Also, the rowing couple had adjusted their volume upwards. Leaving little chance, Sarah reckoned, of anybody overhearing what he was about to say; which didn't stop him approaching it from somewhere over the horizon. 'You get a feeling for this kind of work. You learn to trust your instincts.'

'What are they telling you, Joe?'

'When you came in the other day I thought, this isn't as simple as it sounds. Finding a missing child.'

'Not what you said at the time.'

'I didn't want to alarm you. But look at the facts, her mother's killed in an explosion, then she disappears. What does that tell you?'

'It doesn't tell me anything, Joe. Nor have you.'

'Somebody's got an enemy.'

'She's too young to have enemies. She's only a kid.'

'Nobody's too young to have enemies. This is news to you? Some of us, we've got enemies because of the race we were born into.'

'We should discuss this some day. But not right now.'

'That's a good idea. We should meet, talk about this and that. No reason we can't be friends just because we met professionally.'

'Joe—'

'It happens. Sometimes,' he said hopefully, 'the client develops romantic yearnings towards the detective.'

'Have you heard from Zoë?'

He sighed. 'I withdraw the comment.'

'Joe, what did you find out?'

'I talked to the cops.'

Sarah picked up her coffee. It was pretty cold. The couple at the next table were still bickering steadily, though the parameters of their discontent had widened. Something about him caring more for his damn *golf* clubs than about her talent; something else about her only talent being for shopping. The word 'bitch' was tagged invisibly on to this last complaint, or possibly Sarah imagined that.

'And?'

'And they've identified the other body. The man.'

'That's not been reported.'

'No. They're keeping it quiet for the time being.'

'So who was he?'

'They got him through his prints, and double-checked them against his dental records. Normally they'd be lucky to get one or the other, but in his case they had both.'

'Joe—'

'He'd been in the services, you see. The army.'

At the next table, the woman stood and reached into her handbag.

'Who—'

'It was her husband, Sarah.'

'Her *husband*?'

'Lawful,' Joe said. 'Wedded.'

'But he's dead!'

Two feet from where Sarah sat, the standing woman pulled a gun and fired it six times at her companion.

As the noise died away Joe said, 'Well, if he wasn't then, he certainly is now.'

7

FOR DAYS SHE COULD not get it from her head: the way the man had bled at the mouth before falling backwards, spilling his chair as he fell. All chatter died the way the man died: not suddenly, but with a great deal of painful surprise. Even once he'd hit the ground he continued to twitch convulsively, as if life leaked away in little spurts, while the woman glared down at him with a contempt suggesting she didn't think he was handling even this automatic process with much finesse. In the silence following, somebody dropped a saucer. Everybody waited until its ringing died too before shocked outrage found a voice.

'Guerrilla theatre,' Mark said. 'So-called. A bit passé, I'd have thought.'

'I know what they call it. It was still upsetting.'

'It's easy to shock. It doesn't take talent.'

Neither did being critical.

When the man sprang up, blood dripping from his jaw, to take a bow, Sarah hadn't joined the applause. Nor, to tell the truth, had anybody much. Even in Modern Art Oxford, disturbing people unnecessarily was on a par with rifling through their handbags. It might be Theatre, but it wasn't *nice*. But Sarah's reluctance was less a disinclination to bestow undue praise than shock at the uncanny conjunction of this man dying and coming back to life just as Joe was telling her that Maddy

Singleton's husband had also risen from the grave. Though returned there, in short order.

'I suppose they took up a collection after.'

'No. Just smirked a little, then left.'

'I didn't realise,' Mark went on, 'that was where you spent your mornings. In the gallery.'

Sarah looked away. 'I just stopped in for a cup of coffee.' He didn't reply, but bent, instead, to his newspaper and continued slogging his way through the Middle East coverage. Telling him about the shooting again – she'd already told him once – had been an attempt at re-establishing friendly relations, but Mark was obviously determined to continue being pissy, a determination Sarah knew from experience could see him through the day. Mighty oaks from little acorns: a lot of marital disharmony starts with the ludicrous before working up to true crime. This had begun with dental floss, or the lack of it in the kitchen.

'There's some upstairs,' Sarah had told him.

'Yes, but I'm downstairs. I don't want—'

'I'll get it.'

'That's not the *point*. There should be a tub on the fridge. I hate my teeth being gunged up after eating, you know that.'

'I'll get some tomorrow.'

'You said that on *Friday*, Sarah, but you forgot then too.'

'Well, for God's sake, it's hardly a matter of life and death. Having to walk up a flight of stairs to floss your blasted teeth.'

'I'm not talking about having to walk upstairs. I'm talking about things not being in their proper place, about running out of stuff we need. I'm at work all day, Sarah. I can't do all the shopping too.'

'I spend *half* my *life*—'

'And there's no bin liners either. How am I supposed to get the rubbish out when there's nothing to put it in?'

She'd called a halt there, though rejoinders sprang to mind. Days like this, it would be best if she could just disappear for a while: meld with the background until he'd forgotten he was pissed off, or at least what he was pissed off about. Not that she didn't give as good as she got. But soon, she knew, Mark would be on about children again, his sense of timing on the matter being flawlessly inept, and she could live without the recriminations, spoken and otherwise. *Unnatural woman*, that's what he was building up to. *Unnatural woman*, for having her own agenda. She thought of the bonsai trees gardeners slaved over. She didn't know much about it, but what she thought was this: that there were trees, left to themselves, that might grow sixty feet tall, but instead had their roots punished to produce something small, cosseted, and ornamental. Something making up in charm what it had lost in dignity. Marriage was a psychological bonsai; maybe society was. Still encouraging women, after all these years, to be small, cosseted, and ornamental. Still hacking away at their roots to keep them from growing taller than anybody else. You couldn't even call it deliberate. It had grown instinctive, a natural form of pruning. To a man like Gerard Inchon, it was a duty: barefoot and pregnant kept them quiet. You didn't talk about the Enemy, but that was what you meant. With Mark, it was a creeping form of moral paralysis. He wanted a baby; he wanted one now. What did she mean, couldn't they discuss this? They *were* discussing this: he wanted a baby. Of course her career was important. But she didn't actually have one, did she? So what better time to have a baby?

For the moment, she let him simmer. Out in the back garden, she found ivy attacking the shed, and spent thirty minutes ripping it to shreds. Mentally reliving while she did so what Joe had told her, back in Modern Art Oxford.

Once the emotional terrorists had gone, Sarah settled into a state of mild shock. Joe hadn't batted an eyelid. 'An obviously fake gun,' he had reckoned.

'You're an expert?'

'Was I wrong?'

'If he'd been bleeding to death,' she asked him, 'how long would you have sat watching before admitting you'd made a mistake?'

He didn't think it worth considering.

The chatter around them had swollen to the level of a medium-tempo uproar; a free-for-all post-mortem on the cunning, smug artistes. 'So tell me,' she said. 'Singleton. What was his name?'

'Thomas. Tom.'

'How did he die? The first time, I mean?'

'At the risk of seeming pedantic,' he said, 'the evidence suggests that reports of his first death were grossly exaggerated.'

'Thank you, Mr Twain.'

'Apart from anything else, they never recovered his body.'

'It would have been a bit embarrassing for them if they had,' Sarah said. 'In retrospect.'

'True. He was a soldier, did you know that?'

'I heard he fought in the Gulf.'

'That's right. But he died off Cyprus, in a helicopter crash. This was about four years ago. There were other soldiers in the copter. I think six died altogether. And the crew.'

Sarah nodded, as if this made sense, or indeed had anything to do with her. 'And the police told you this?'

'*A* policeman told me. In return, you understand, for a donation to the charity of his choice, which in his case begins very close to home. Sarah, you should understand this. What he told me, what I've told you, this is for your ears only. Two hours after I spoke to him, he's on the phone suggesting I forget we ever met. Even offering me a refund. This is unprecedented. It's practically supernatural.'

'Did he say why?'

'He didn't know why. Just, there's been this "information clamp-down". His very words. Leaks, he said, would be plugged.

He was worried for his pension.' Joe's shoulders rose and fell. 'Don't expect to read this in the papers.'

A thought struck her. 'How much do I owe you, Joe?'

'I gave you two days,' he said. 'I spread it over a week, that's all.'

'Are you sure?'

'None of it matters. I went looking for a child, I found a father. You couldn't call it a result.'

'It's odd, though.'

'Life is odd. You should know this, you don't grow old and disappointed. You owe me one hundred and fifty pounds, since you ask. I would offer a discount for failure, but union rules forbid it.'

She wrote him a cheque. 'What will you do next?'

'I thought I'd have a look at the exhibition. This French photographer, are you interested? It's free before one.'

'I meant about Dinah.'

He took the cheque, folded it, slipped it inside his wallet. 'Sarah. You don't mind? Of course not, you're calling me Joe. Sarah, like I said, these are muddy waters. A soldier comes back from the dead, even if his visit proves brief. We are not talking about police matters here. We are talking national security. Military Intelligence. Private investigators, they don't like. Sometimes they throw the book at them.'

'Joe—'

'Have you seen the book, Sarah? It's very big and it's very heavy. I promise you, if I wasn't a coward, I'd help.'

'You're giving up.'

'If you want to put it that way, yes. You won't shame me into this, Sarah. You want to know what else my policeman friend told me? Ex-friend. The word is, that house did not blow up by accident.'

'The papers said—'

'The papers lied.'

'You know that for a fact?'

He raised his eyes to heaven. 'Facts. A policeman wanted to give me my money back, Sarah. We are beyond facts here. We are in an age of miracles and wonders.'

'But what about the child?'

'Trust me. She'll turn up. It was a hospital she was in, they won't have sold her into slavery.'

He wasn't about to budge, Sarah could see that. Still, it wouldn't hurt to insert a wedge. 'Supposing I found out—'

'How would you do that?'

'I don't know. I'm supposing. Supposing I thought I knew where she was, would you help me look? If I asked?'

He picked up his coffee spoon and held it lengthwise between index fingers. He seemed to be measuring something with it. 'You understand what I said? That explosion was no accident. In English, a bomb was involved. It's a dangerous business.'

'I don't care about that. I want to find Dinah.'

'Why?'

Why? Because the child was a survivor: now, more than ever. Before, Sarah had imagined Dinah to have come through an act of God unscathed. Now, it seemed she had lived through an act of man. For that, if for no other reason, she deserved to have someone care about what happened next.

'Sarah?'

'Joe. It matters, that's all.'

He considered. 'You need help, it doesn't involve policemen or spies or soldiers, okay, I'll be there. But this is only because I like you, Sarah.'

'And because you don't think it'll happen.'

'That too.' He put the spoon down and reached into his jacket pocket. 'This doesn't interest you. But it's what he looked like, Thomas Singleton. I took it from a newspaper, an old one. The story about the helicopter crash.'

She unfolded a picture: two men, uniformed, but relaxed

and smiling; both about her age, maybe a little older. The one on the left was squinting in the sun. The other, Thomas Singleton, held a cupped cigarette at chest level.

Joe said. 'His friend there was in the chopper with him.'

'What's his name?'

'Michael something. Michael Downey, I think.' He scratched his chin. 'You know, come to think of it, maybe he's still alive too.'

'Oh, I'd put money on it.'

'Why's that?'

'Because he's the man who was waiting for me in the car park,' Sarah said.

She finished stripping the ivy from the shed, and piled it in a garden refuse sack. For all her musing she was no nearer finding Dinah Singleton, apart from having established that she wasn't in the garden. Back inside, Mark was absorbed in cricket, and didn't look up as she walked past. Sundays were their one guaranteed day together. Looked like they'd blown this one.

The fight proper, though, didn't start until the evening. Usually Mark was ready for bed by ten, never failing to make some comment about having to be up early. Meaning lucky old her, who didn't. Tonight he was in no hurry, pouring another glass of wine as the clock struck. 'We've been invited away next weekend,' he said.

'Really? Who by?'

'The Inchons.'

He'd deliberately turned away before dropping this bombshell.

'You have to be kidding.'

'Uh-uh.'

'Well, forget it. We're not going.'

'Yes we are.'

'*You* might be. He's not my client.'

'But I'm your husband. Be reasonable, Sarah. It goes with the job.'

'That's my point.'

'Christ, why do you have to be so *sanctimonious* all the time? You never bleat about my job while you're spending money.'

'I don't notice you being particularly supportive about *my* career.'

'What career?'

'Yeah, thanks a bunch. Congratulations, Mark. You really have turned into one of the shits we used to hate so much in college.'

'I work bloody hard—'

'You spend all day arse-licking on the phone. I tell my friends you sell crack to schoolkids. I don't want to alienate them.'

'You've been a real bitch these past months, did you know that?'

'And you turned into a yuppie prick about three years ago.'

She couldn't believe what she was hearing herself say; it was like watching somebody have an accident there was nothing you could do to prevent. The damage they did now would be with them long after they'd both pretended to forget it. Later they'd call it clearing the air, but it had more in common with biological warfare.

'. . . Turned into a *what*?'

'I didn't mean that. But Christ, Mark, what am I supposed to think? This wasn't what you'd planned.'

'This is news to me?'

'All I meant was—'

'You think I wanted it to be like this? You think I woke up one morning and thought, I never *really* wanted to fulfil my life's ambition, maybe I'll go and work for a bank instead? You think that's what happened?'

'So what *did* happen, Mark? You tell me, since I can't work it out for myself.'

'Things change, that's all. Is that so hard to take in? You

think life's all straight lines and easy choices? How many people get to live their student daydreams? Hell, people we know'd be running the world if that happened.'

'And that's your answer, is it? *Things change*. Brilliant.'

'What do you want? An apology?'

'I just want to know what happened to us, Mark! One day you were full of ambition. You were going to write *books*, for God's sake. What turned you into a shark instead?'

'I'm not a shark!'

'Your job is making bastards like Inchon richer. What would you call it, radical philanthropy?'

'My job pays for everything we have.'

'I'm not interested in what it pays for, Mark. I'm worried about what it costs.'

'Oh, pardon me while I write that down!'

'I'm being serious here.'

'So am I. You wish I'd made it in academia? Me too. But I didn't. Shit happens, Sarah. What am I supposed to do, curl up into a ball and spend the rest of my life crying about it? Would that make you happy?'

'Maybe I just didn't want you to give up.'

'Well, that's fucking easy for you to say. What did you ever work at?'

'I work at *this*. I work at *us*. But you're never here, and when you are you aren't interested!'

'Oh, *grow up*.'

She didn't realise until then how loud they'd been shouting. There followed one dull, excruciating moment when she knew the neighbours must have heard them, and another of pure pain as she realised they'd never fought like this, not even back in the early days when everybody fought. How did you get out of a corner you'd just painted yourself into? She fell back on the old; the tried and trusted: 'I'm sorry.'

He pretended not to hear that.

'Mark? I said I'm sorry. I shouldn't have said any of that. I didn't mean it. I love you.'

He mumbled something she wasn't meant to catch, and went and locked himself in the bathroom.

So Monday was hell, even more than usual. She found a space above the airing cupboard she'd never attacked, had always assumed was spider heaven, and spent the whole morning with it, though you'd need a ladder and torch to appreciate it afterwards. Then she cried for a while, skipped lunch, and walked into town to buy something expensive from the butcher's. *This is what good little wifey is supposed to do*, a voice in her head informed her, but she was too miserable to pay attention. When you were in hell, you *always* did what you were supposed to do.

And in the evening Mark played the good hubby anyway, getting home early with flowers and chocolates, which made them even. They went to bed first, then ate chocolates, and had fillet steak sandwiches for a midnight snack. It was a little like life five years ago; four at a pinch.

'I'll call him,' he said, far too casually. 'Tell him we can't make it.'

'No, let's go.'

'You don't want to.'

'No, but we have to. It'll be all right.'

'Are you sure?'

'No. But let's go anyway.'

He was pleased, but tried not to show it. 'I'll make it up to you. I promise.'

'I've been meaning to mention it,' she said. 'I spent three hundred pounds last week.'

The next few days, Sarah mostly spent gearing up for what she was calling, in her mind, 'The Inchon Weekend': a name which made it sound like a particularly dire novel. But with a dire novel you could give up halfway, and 'The Inchon Weekend' would have to be lived through minute by minute. It occurred to her, had occurred as soon as Mark had confessed they'd been invited, that this had been the point of having the Inchons to supper; the *quid pro quo* he'd been angling for from the start. Not much chance of doing business with Wigwam and Rufus about. But with a whole weekend to play with you were away, though what banking business involved, the kind you could do just talking about it, Sarah didn't know. Presumably, though, The Bank With No Name would be happy that its brightest and best was rubbing elbows with a fat potential client. At the fat potential client's country seat.

'Which is where, anyway?'

'Out in the Cotswolds.'

'Does London continue to function without him, then?'

'Just try and behave yourself, Sarah. No one's asking you to enjoy it. But try and behave yourself.'

He said that in the mock-angry tone they teased each other with, but she wasn't fooled.

They drove there, or Mark did, mid Saturday morning. It was dreamtime weather: a great big blue sky with faint tufts of cloud, like a child's drawing of summer. To Sarah, it felt like passing through a funfair on the way to the dentist. She kept telling herself that these things are rarely as bad as you expect, but couldn't help suspecting she invalidated that premise by relying on it. If she wasn't expecting it to be quite so bad any more, it would probably turn out worse.

The village was one of the modern kind whose original inhabitants have grown old and died, leaving their houses in the hands of BBC executives. And the Inchons' weekend cottage, one in a row of similar detached dwellings, had 'weekend cottage' written all over it; there was just no way you were looking at anything else. Not that it had an air of neglect: quite the opposite. The whitewash on the walls seemed fresh; the bedspread-sized garden was Britain in Bloom standard. But when Sarah tried to conjure an image of Gerard in overalls with a bucket, or Gerard on his knees with a trowel, it faded almost immediately, to be replaced by one of Gerard handing a wodge of money to a man with overalls, a bucket, etc. It was too perfect, and Gerard too much the townie to have made it so. That was what Sarah decided.

Inside, the story was the same: an interior designer had looked up 'rustic,' then thrown a lot of money at it. The stone floor presumably matched that of every other cottage in the row, but Sarah doubted there were many more Bokharas thrown casually on top of them, even round here. Eveything gleamed, and a faint smell of polish tainted the air. A wooden staircase looked both old and new at once; a triumphant marriage of conservation and conspicuous consumption, with what appeared to be a mouse carved into the handrail, in imitation, Sarah was pretty sure, of someone famous. In the nook below, on a purpose-built stand, sat a compact disc deck with associated gadgetry; next to this was a row of bookshelves holding neatly labelled videos. Through a diamond-shaped window on the far wall, an untidy countryside mocked these civilised arrangements: the crystal decanter perched smugly in an alcove; the scatter of pristine lifestyle magazines on the glass-topped coffee table. For no reason she could positively pin down, Sarah found herself recalling Britt Ekland on *Desert Island Discs*; how, when asked for her favourite book, the former celebrity explained that she never got much time for reading, and would just like a few magazines please. It was the nearest Sarah had come to throwing a radio through a window. Meanwhile Inchon, in brown cords and white sweater despite the weather, played Mein Host: a triumph of method acting. She'd not have been surprised if he'd said 'Welcome to our humble abode', or practised a sweeping bow as he'd ushered them in.

What he was in fact saying was, 'You're here, you're here. How about a drink?'

It wasn't the words or the manner; they had nothing to do with it. But afterwards she pinpointed that as the moment she decided it had been Gerard Inchon who planted the bomb that blew the Singleton house away.

8

ASKING MARK TO REMIND her what the Trophy Wife was called would have been asking for it: divine inspiration descended in time. The name was Paula and, unlike her husband, she was making no concessions to her environment; her lilac number, matching skirt and jacket, could have graced a West End opening without alteration. So could her air of boredom. But this, like the suit, didn't seem to have been put on for their benefit: a weekend in the country, Sarah reflected, was one of those relative terms. Under different circumstances, she'd have been looking forward to it. For Paula, it looked like a phrase followed by WITH NO HOPE OF PAROLE, in block capitals.

Still, she didn't labour the point; positively unwound, in fact, once Sarah and Mark had accepted Gerard's offer of drinks. Or spoke, anyway. 'Did you have a good journey?'

'Fine, thanks,' Mark said. 'Absolutely no . . . problem.'

It was like listening to people remembering a phrase book they'd glanced at. A suspicious mind would have assumed they were having an affair.

But Sarah's suspicious mind was otherwise occupied at that moment; was trying desperately to send the right signals to her body, her limbs. *Act natural. Smile. Talk about the weather.* Don't, for instance, mention Gerard turning up late the night of the explosion, leaving his briefcase in the car. (His *briefcase*? At a *dinner party*?) Don't ask why he'd been so sure it was a bomb.

Don't ask where he keeps his gun collection. Just take, which she now did, the proffered cocktail and smile, act natural, talk about the weather.

'Brilliant piece of sunshine.'

'Splendid.'

'Great summer in fact.'

'Greenhouse effect.'

'More power to it.'

'*Too* hot, really.'

'Well, yes, I'd say so.'

'They say it'll break soon.'

'But they always say that,' concluded Gerard, 'don't they?'

Mark fetched their bags, and Gerard showed them the guest-room. It was more of the same: an illustration from a catalogue; a backdrop to a tweed collection. The double bed had a bolster, and through the window sheep posed placidly beneath a spreading chestnut tree, probably. Gerard showed them how the wardrobe worked: it had a sliding door. Left to themselves, she and Mark would have cracked this fairly soonish. You could take the host business too far, she thought, but you couldn't fault his geniality.

Except you had to see it as an act. If you had decided he was responsible for the deaths of a young widow and her curiously extant husband, and, by logical extension, the kidnapping – or at any rate disappearing – of their surviving daughter, you had to take this newly jovial front with a quarry-load of salt. Sarah had, of course, no evidence. For the moment, though, she wouldn't let that get in the way; with a weekend on the premises to go, she could have him bang to rights by Monday.

'Not too shabby,' Mark said, once Gerard had left them.

'Mmm?'

'All this.' He waved a hand: the room, the cottage, the country. He was desperate for her to be pleased, she realised; for the stage to be suitable for a convincing performance of enjoyment.

So they could both pretend, even in front of each other, that it was brilliant they were here. Maybe she should tell him, she thought as she stood on tiptoe to kiss his cheek, that the entertainment potential in this weekend had increased by a factor of ten. On the other hand, though, she definitely shouldn't.

'All right?' he asked anxiously.

'Fine. Everything's fine.' And they went downstairs.

It was hard getting a handle on Gerard in his home environment. It was as if the slate had been wiped clean, and he was determined not to acknowledge in any way that their first encounter had been anything but immensely cordial. He did mention the explosion once, but addressed his question to Mark while Sarah was asking Paula something interesting about neighbours and couldn't butt in to prolong the dialogue.

'Anything ever come of that incident? Developments?'

'Not that I know of.'

'Hmph. Trouble with the police, they're so busy bending over backwards to prove they're not racist thugs, they never get anything *done*. It's like everything else, you want results, go private.' He glanced at Sarah as he said this, but she was too busy being fascinated by Paula to respond. Something about a TV star three doors away. His last party started on Friday and went on till *Monday morning*!

One of the non-bomb-related puzzles that had been exercising Sarah, why there was no activity in the kitchen, was solved when Gerard explained he'd booked a table at the local pub for lunch. *Booked*, mind. Not one of those pub lunches where you just turn up. Within a few minutes of that, they were in The Feathers, a pub that was everything the rest of the village promised, having uniformed staff, a wide choice of real ale and expensive food. Sarah, though, was on her best behaviour. So, it seemed, was Gerard. When he spoke, she listened and laughed; when she spoke he attended as if expecting questions later. Mostly Mark did the talking, though, while Paula picked at her food and didn't offer much beyond adding the odd name to her list of the village alumni. Sarah thought she'd be happier in Planet Hollywood. Even Gerard threw her odd glances, as if wishing she'd try harder.

After the garlic bread, the lasagne, the summer pudding, Gerard suggested a walk. 'Lovely walks round here, aren't there, darling?'

Paula shrugged.

'Woods?' asked Mark, to show he knew a thing or two about the countryside.

'I wouldn't be at all surprised.'

They had a brief altercation about the bill which Gerard won, depending on how you looked at it, then set off to check out the surrounding countryside. A footpath took them beyond the village limits in a very short while. Here, Sarah expected segregation to set in: Gerard would stride on with Mark and discuss manly things, while she was left to dredge up enough small talk to keep Paula from slipping into a coma. In the event she was quite wrong, soon finding herself with Gerard, some fifty yards behind their spouses. Detective finds herself alone with suspect. What do they talk about? The weather.

'Wonderful, isn't it?'

'What is?'

'Good clean air,' he said.

'You're not really a country boy, are you, Gerard?'

'I wouldn't say that. I'm from yeoman stock. Generations back, my family were farmers.'

'Generations back everybody's family were farmers.'

'Funny, isn't it? Everybody rat-racing in the City, struggling to make their pile, so they can get back where their ancestors sweated. Maybe we should all have stayed where we were in the first place.'

'Would you have liked that?'

'Of course not. This is the weekend talking. It's not real life.'

'Which is?'

'Competition. Struggle. The survival of the smartest.'

'And the devil take the rest.'

'You think I'm a capitalist monster, don't you?'

'It crossed my mind.'

Gerard stopped to examine the view. She imagined the checklist in his head: sheep, yes; fields, yes; trees, yes. This was the country, no question. He nodded in quiet satisfaction and said, 'When I meet people like those friends of yours, the ones with rather bizarre names, I must admit I play up to their expectations. They think wealth goes hand in hand with obnoxious attitudes.'

'So that was a game.'

'No. But it's not the whole story, either.'

'Underneath it all,' Sarah said, 'you're just another raging lefty.'

'That's the trouble with you middle-class socialist types.' He seemed to have had enough of the view now, and together they walked on. 'You think you've the monopoly on compassion.'

'Whereas you regard it as a free market.'

'Oh very neat, yes. A market in which there's no room for random acts of senseless generosity, shall we say.'

'Why not?' Sarah said. 'It sounds like we've said it before.'

He chuckled at that. Annoying Gerard Inchon was an uphill task. No doubt he was aware just how irritating this was.

For all that, the weekend Gerard wasn't what she'd expected. There was something to his manner – and the country clothes, the appreciative once-overs he gave the scenery – that told her he was playing a part, for his own benefit as much as hers. He wanted to be at home here but wasn't quite making the grade, and what surprised her wasn't so much this chink in his armour – she'd never met a man who didn't come with one of those – as her own response to it: a mild disappointment at his obvious vulnerability.

. . . And there she went again, treating it all like a giant game. Though the players in this case were people, and some of them were dead.

'It doesn't bother you, though,' she said after a bit, 'just to write some people off?'

See if he appreciates the subtlety of *that.*

'How do you mean?'

'Well, my friend Rufus.' *My friend* was a stretch, but he wasn't to know that. 'You decided he was a dead loss in no time flat. What gives you the right to do that?'

'The same thing that lets me get away with it. He's spineless, Sarah. Fond as you so obviously are of his retro missus, you have to admit *friend* Rufey is a bit lacking in what, in other company, I'd have to call balls.'

'And that's what makes a man?'

'I'd call it a defining characteristic.'

'Not everybody gets the same chances in life.'

'It would be foolish to deny it. But not everybody makes use of the ones they get.'

'He was an orphan.'

'He wasn't the only one.' Gerard stopped abruptly, as if he'd said more than he'd meant to, and used a stick he'd acquired to point at a speck in the sky. 'What's that, do you think?'

'A bird?' Sarah ventured. 'Mark's the expert.'

'Kestrel, probably. Or a hawk. Or a buzzard.'

Sarah surveyed once more the green sweep of landscape, receiving from it this time a sense of something large and impressive to which she could not readily put a name: possibly nature exerting its pressure; something, anyway, she didn't feel in the city. 'It's very beautiful,' she said, and because it sounded to her own ear as if the words had come out grudgingly, said it again. 'Beautiful. What's it like in the winter?'

'God knows.'

The others were waiting at a stile, and they swapped partners as if the move had been choreographed in advance. Sarah spent the rest of the walk communing, largely in silence, with Paula, reflecting the while on her conversation with Gerard. From which she had learned precisely nothing. So the man was an orphan, or that's what he'd implied: so what? As a clue, this ranked poorly against the tortured confession she might have extracted. The most interesting thing he'd said, he'd said to Mark: his comment about going private when investigating crime. Which could mean he knew about Joe, which in turn meant he was having her watched. You might come down with a bad dose of paranoia in this business. Hadn't Joe said he never spoke freely over the phone?

And Paula never spoke freely anywhere, or so Sarah was finding. 'How long have you owned the cottage?'

'About a year.'

'And do you come here . . . often?' Her voice trailing away.

'Whenever Gerard feels like it.'

From up ahead, the odd word came wafting back: parts of that complicated vocabulary people never use, but money thrives on. Interim pre-tax profits. Commercial reserves. They spoke of entire nations as if other races marched ahead with a single thought in mind: the Germans always this; the Japanese never that. As if every other country in the world had a fixed agenda, while jolly old Blighty bumbled along, full of people who didn't give a toss. That last part, in fact, felt pretty true to Sarah's experience, but there were probably Wigwams and Rufuses in every country in the world.

'And do you like it?'

But Paula just looked at her.

When they got back to the cottage it quickly became apparent that the fresh air and exercise element of the country weekend was officially at a close, and the drinking far too much aspect just breaking open. Gerard uncorked several bottles of wine at once, some to breathe, some not to get the chance, and for the next few hours time seemed to stand still for long stretches, then gallop to catch up at unexpected moments. Sarah kept a stern eye on her glass at first, until the effort of remembering her suspicions while pretending to enjoy herself started to weigh too heavily to allow for other considerations. Perhaps she was only pretending to suspect, and genuinely enjoying herself. Gerard kept up a flow of jokes which grew progressively raunchier as the afternoon wore off; Mark laughed a lot and it struck her as an unfamiliar sound. And Paula drank steadily and spoke about life in London, and where the best places to be seen were, and what made them the best places. She was starting to sound like a Muppet. When Sarah giggled at the wrong moment she found she couldn't stop. 'Sorry.' Gerard said something she didn't catch, and next moment Mark was bending over her, closer to her than he'd been since they'd last had sex. 'I think you're quite drunk, Sarah.' *I think we all are*, she wanted to tell him, but the effort was beyond her so she meekly allowed him to lead her upstairs instead, where she woke several hours later in a very dark room, with her head screwed on too tight and a mouth so dry she must have been force-fed crackers in her sleep.

She found the loo then cleaned herself up a bit. The face in the mirror was red-eyed, very pale-skinned: not a brilliant advert for your husband's career, she thought, before remembering she didn't give a sod about Mark's career, and it wasn't her fault she'd got drunk anyway. When she came out it was to the sound of a minor earthquake in the adjoining room, and since its light was on and the door open she stuck her head round to find a fully clothed Paula on the bed, snoring to wake the dead. The survivor of a thousand city nights wasn't looking too hot. Probably the country air. Feeling less a casualty for having witnessed another crash, she went downstairs in search of moving bodies.

Mark's was not among them. Draped over the sofa, head

back, mouth open, he had a washing-up bowl balanced on his knees, which Sarah's long-term experience indicated was both prudent and not his own idea. The main light was off, and for one moment his face seemed to flicker in the dark, as if she were catching a glimpse of him from a passing train. But the movement was illusory; the darting shadows the TV. Gerard Inchon was watching a movie.

'Cary Grant,' she said, more to announce her presence than to let him know who he was watching. Buried in an armchair, he hadn't looked round as she came down, and for a moment she thought he was asleep. But at last he turned his big head lazily round and nodded as if he'd been expecting her.

'Archie Leach,' he replied.

'Archie Leach was a nobody,' she said. 'Cary Grant was a star.' Why did she feel the need to duel with this man?

Whyever, he didn't join in. 'Sit,' he said. 'Have a drink.' He waved at an array of wine bottles, most of them empty. 'I can open another,' he added, reaching the same conclusion.

'Water'll do, thanks.'

'We've got some of that. I think we keep it in the tap.'

'I'll find it.'

There were more empty bottles on the kitchen table, forcing Sarah to suppress a shudder as she found a glass, poured some water, drank it, poured some more. She couldn't remember an afternoon when she'd drunk this much. Nor wished to. The afternoon anyway was long over: the kitchen clock said 11:20, and through the back window dark trees waved at her. She could make out her own reflection too. It wasn't doing her any favours.

Back in the sitting room Cary Grant was climbing a flight of stairs, carrying a glass of milk with a light bulb in it. Gerard seemed engrossed but beckoned her to sit, pointing at a tray of sandwiches somebody had fixed up at some point. Suddenly ravenous, Sarah ate four, while on the screen in front of them an improbably happy ending imposed itself on what had been, up to that point, a good film. When the urge came to tell the audience everything is going to be all right, it was definitely time to pack it in.

Gerard got up and turned the TV off.

She said, 'Do all your weekends end like this?'

'With me the last man standing?'

She nodded at Mark. 'With your guests comatose, yes.'

'Everybody arranges these things differently. I mean, how would I go about capping that evening at yours? Blow the neighbours up?'

'I wouldn't put it past you.'

'They'd have to really annoy me. Wear brown shoes, or whistle in the mornings.'

'Heinous crimes like that.'

'We've all got standards. That husband of yours, drink a lot, does he?'

'Depends on the company.'

'I would, in his posish.' Gerard had, even in his own. But except for a bloodening round the eyes and the occasional verbal stumble, you wouldn't know it. Not bad going, with a dozen empties about the place.

'Meaning?'

'Meaning his job. Keep your hair on.' He clumsily poured another glass of red. 'So how's it going, anyway? Your little problem?'

'My what?'

He waggled his fingers. 'BHS.'

'*Vino veritas*,' she said. 'You couldn't keep up the pretence, could you?'

'Which pretence is that?'

'That you're not a shit.'

'Ah, Sarah. Now, the thing is. What you have to do.' He belched, softly. 'You really have to learn who your friends are.'

Mark stirred and mumbled something in an alien tongue.

'This is really good advice you're giving me.'

'You want good advice? I can give you that. Batten down the hatches, girl. You've got big trouble coming.'

'So have you.'

He ignored her. 'You'll be wishing you were bored again. Soon. Trust me on this.'

'I don't trust you on anything.'

'Time zhit?' said Mark.

Gerard looked at him, then back at her. 'If I was you, I'd get out while you can.'

'Thank you, Gerard. You're a prince among men.'

Mark sat up straight very suddenly. 'God. Must have dropped off.'

'Must have.'

'Did I miss anything?'

'Only Cary Grant.'

Mark rubbed his eyes. 'Cary was here?'

'Come on, old son,' Gerard said. 'Better be getting you upstairs.'

Ten minutes later they were all in bed, and what felt like ten minutes after *that*, Sarah was awake again. Downstairs, a shockingly healthy-looking Gerard was making tea for a gratifyingly woebegone Paula: they looked like a normal couple, damn them, Gerard having reverted to his brilliant host role, pouring tea from a caddy straight into the pot.

'That's a lot easier to gauge if you use a spoon.'

'There's not a spoon to be had. They're all in the dishwasher.'

The downside of technology. Michael Crichton was probably writing a book about it. Gerard made a tray for her to take upstairs, and told her he and Paula were just off to Mass, they'd be back in an hour or so. Sarah was mildly surprised, but hoped it didn't show.

She went back to bed. Mark was well out of the running,

only coming round long enough to make it clear he didn't want breakfast and hadn't appreciated the offer. So Sarah drank tea alone and unattended, reflecting as she did that there were two whole rooms in the cottage she'd not been in yet. Probably she'd have been able to sleep if that thought hadn't arrived.

She showered, giving temptation time to wither and die, which it didn't, and took their bedroom first. There wasn't much to it; it looked, in fact, like a second guest-room, with even the clothes in the wardrobes having the air of being extras, spares. She imagined matching counterparts in other wardrobes in their London house; could almost picture Gerard and Paula buying two of everything, to save carting back and forth.

But poking around in other people's bedrooms was a grubby business. She shut the door quietly behind her and thought seriously about forgoing the other room, which might only be a cupboard after all. So really there was no harm in looking, she decided; a piece of deductive justification which might have been more impressive had she reached the end of it before opening the door.

This room was tiny, little more than a box room, but it looked like Gerard got a dual purpose out of it anyway: part office, part gallery to his ego. On a table which was surely too big to have got through the door squeezed a PC, a telephone, a fax machine next to what might have been a baby photocopier plus a stack of papers and a palmtop. And around the walls hung framed photographs of Gerard at different stages of his important life: young and chubby, adolescent and chubby; prosperous and fat. In one of the older shots he stood in front of a low wall, flanked by, presumably, his parents. In the way old photographs have, this one looked as if black-and-white weren't just the medium but the subject: the adults appearing straitened, uncomfortable; their very postures suggesting that their post-war years had kept oozing on into the sixties, the way they had in the north. In contrast, young Gerard looked simply impatient, as though even at eight or nine he'd been waiting for the coloured times to arrive. He was holding a model aeroplane in a proprietorial way that left no doubt he had built it himself, but Sarah couldn't discern much pride from his demeanour; more dissatisfaction that toys were all he had to occupy himself. His mother was pretty and slight. His father, much taller, stood with one hand on Gerard's head, as if attempting to keep him where he belonged.

Other photos, of more recent vintage, showed Gerard fully emerged from the cocoon of childhood, not that the result resembled a butterfly. A happy slug came to mind. Here was Gerard breaking ground on what an accompanying picture proved an office block (Inchon Enterprises); Gerard spraying champagne over somebody getting out of an expensive car; Gerard becoming married in (of course) top hat and tails, while Paula posed winsomely beside him in a dress even Sarah could see cost well into four figures. She did, it had to be said, look lovely. Even Gerard came out of this one well. Something solemn had crept into his face, forming a solid foundation for what was obviously happiness. The result was to firm up his otherwise slack features; hardly putting him in heart-throb territory, but at least bestowing a visible sense of purpose you could mistake for integrity. Sarah found the same effect in another recent picture which showed him handing a cheque to a tall, priestly man; the pair of them standing in front of a small crowd of children. The background, mostly obscured, seemed to be an institution of some sort; a noiceboard behind them had part of what was probably a name, *rimat*, visible between young heads. Some religious set-up, she hypothesised. Catholic or very high: he'd said 'Mass'.

She turned her attention to the clutter on the desk, hoping to find a bomb maker's manual among it. Nothing doing, but she picked up the palmtop to look at. She'd seen such toys but never operated one; was not really what you'd call a card-carrying member of the technological society, though had enough experience to know the average computer could take you from How Hard Can It Be? to What The Hell Happened There? in two seconds flat. That was the downside. The upside was it was very small with an obvious on-button and where was the harm in trying? This button proved remarkably simple to operate and the little screen came to life immediately, flashing a prompt she guessed was its demand for a password. What kind of password would a man like Gerard use? She went for blindingly predictable, and keyed *Paula. Invalid Password* it countered. Not a single other word came to mind. It was as if her brain had been rinsed of all vocabulary.

'What are you looking for?'

She nearly jumped out of her skin.

'Sarah?'

'I wasn't looking *for* anything. I was just looking.' She put the machine down before turning round, hoping he wouldn't notice, then switched topics in what she prayed was an undetectable, natural manner. 'My God, you look awful.'

'I feel awful.' Mark ran a hand across his forehead. 'That wine must have been a bit dodgy.'

'That fifth bottle was corked, probably. Come on, I'll make you some coffee.'

Mark took a detour via the bathroom and by the time he joined her in the kitchen, dressed, the others were pulling up outside. 'They may be godly, but at least I'm clean,' he said.

'I suppose I should be grateful you didn't go with them. Keep the client sweet.'

He gave her a hard look.

'It was a joke, Mark.'

'It needs work.'

'And you need this.' She gave him a cup of coffee.

'No, what he needs is a hair of the dog,' said Gerard, entering. Then, at the look Mark gave him, laughed and said, 'But it'll keep. Actually, I wanted a word, Mark, since you're up. Don't mind, do you?' He addressed the question to Sarah.

Be a good girl, now. Run along and play. But residual guilt from snooping, or from being caught snooping, left her unable to object.

Gerard handed her a bunch of newspapers and took Mark up to his study, while a still interestingly pale Paula mumbled something about a lie-down, and disappeared. Sarah took her bundle into the garden, and spent the next hour reading what appeared to be the same set of articles in three different papers, before drifting softly to sleep in the sunshine. She was woken by a hand stroking her cheek, though Mark's words weren't as affectionate as his gesture.

'When you were in Gerard's study,' he said suspiciously, 'did you mess with his palmtop at all?'

'Did I what?'

'His electric notebook. Only it wasn't closed down properly.'

'Maybe he forgot to last time he used it,' Sarah said, fully awake this time.

'That's what I said. He said, "Hmmm."'

'I only turned it on. I'd never seen one before.'

'Jesus, Sarah! That's like looking at somebody's diary. It *is* looking at somebody's diary.'

'Well, if it had been a diary, I'd not have been interested,' she lied. 'I was thinking of getting you one for Christmas. I wanted to see how they work.'

He became thoughtful. 'It'd come in very useful.'

'I can't get you one now, can I? It wouldn't be a surprise.'

She left him to mull that over and went inside, where Gerard was in the kitchen, preparing lunch: a joint of beef, the usual veg. Traditional, as she'd have expected, though he wasn't the one she'd have thought would be preparing it. 'Anything I can do to help?'

'I think it's under control, thanks.'

She looked out of the window at Mark, who'd settled down with the papers now; was reading the Middle East news with a worried frown which might have related to world events or just to his hangover, she couldn't tell. When she turned back Gerard was studying her with an evil look on his face.

'Is there a problem?'

'One thing would be useful.'

'Yes?'

He pointed at the bottles on the table. 'You could clear up the dead soldiers,' he said.

9

Amos Crane – tall, grey, crewcut, a bit of a problem; his face that of a man in the last stage of something wasting – sat in the glow of a VDU, whose green wash made unearthly the crags and hollows of his head. Beneath the surface wreckage, though, everything pumped in order. The body was a tool. An early riser, Amos Crane jogged three miles before breakfast; ran past Chinese supermarkets as they opened, blowsy strip clubs as they closed, and considered the lives grouped round these exits and entrances as being connected to his own by an invisible network of alliances. Crane was not a Londoner, and never imagined himself one. But on the city's early streets he felt part of a larger community, and regarded the tired dancers and busy grocers as his equals, at least inasmuch as they led lives outside the jobsworth's timetable. He was their secret sharer. He understood their passions. Now, though, he was at his desk.

He preferred to work without overhead lighting; with just an Anglepoise bent so low it scorched rings on the desk's surface, and the light of the computer screen, whose lettering reflected on his spectacles. A computer, too, was a tool only. He had no patience with those who substituted this magic box for the real world, looking to it for answers: it held only clues. All the information in the world didn't give you the answers. For these, you had to close with flesh and bone.

His brother used to accuse him of attempting philosophy.

'It doesn't hurt to think,' Amos would say. And then amend it, adding, 'It doesn't hurt *me* to think. I can see where you'd have problems.'

'Always the kidder.'

'You rush into things.' Serious now; it was Axel's big fault. Always doing, and working out the total later. Or letting somebody else do that part, which bored him.

Axel would blow him a smoke ring. Change the subject. But it was true: over the years, Amos had tried to steer his brother right over and over. Telling him a hundred different ways, he had to get a grip on the politics of the situation. Probably there was nowhere left in the world you could do the wet work and not worry about the consequences. Well, America. The Far East. Africa too, come to think of it. And most of Eastern Europe. But Oxford, no, you had to be more circumspect. Blowing up a house, even Axel had to assume there'd be raised eyebrows afterwards.

'It got the job done.'

'*Half* the job done.'

Axel had blown another smoke ring.

And it had been up to Amos to work out the details: get the kid out of hospital, fashion a lid to pop on the story; plus the tricky bit, which was letting Howard believe he'd been the one doing all the work. Credit had a way of calming him down. Thinking about Howard now, he tapped out a little riff on his keyboard, squirting a meaningless jumble of letters on to the screen.

'Your brother,' Howard had said, 'is certifiably wacko.'

'Please.'

'You're supposed to be his control on this operation. Did you have any idea what he was planning?'

'The agent in the field has the last word. Or didn't you know?'

Howard was strictly a desk-man, and didn't enjoy being reminded of the fact. He'd flushed, said, 'An innocent woman was killed. Are you aware of that?'

So Amos had told him about the early forties, in Mongolia. The experiments with the rats and the prisoners.

'You can't compare us with *them*,' Howard had said. And then shut up, perplexed, while Amos laughed at him.

He'd just come into the room, now. Howard. Without turning, Amos knew it was him: something about the clumsy way desk-men moved, even (especially?) when they thought they were sliding like grease. On the nights he worked late – which, to be fair, were frequent – Howard always let you know. 'I was in the office till almost twelve last night': not complaining, just filling you in. Wanting everybody to appreciate, Amos Crane thought now, that he had it tough too. Till almost twelve.

'Howard,' he said, before the other announced his presence.

'Any . . . developments?'

'Not exactly.'

'Are you aware of the pressure I'm under?'

Howard was always asking if you were *aware* of whatever.

'It's like chess, Howard,' Amos said kindly. 'You can watch it for hours and think nothing's going on. But that's because you're only seeing what's happening on the surface.'

'Thank you. Where's the child?'

Crane looked at his watch. 'Tucked up in bed.'

'She's not to be harmed. You know that.'

'Safe as houses,' Crane assured him.

There was a pause while both men thought about houses recently brought to their attention.

'And your brother?'

'I doubt he's in bed yet.'

Howard sat on the edge of Crane's desk, then stood up again when the other man looked at him. He sat on a chair instead. 'I've had a lot of complaints about his action.'

'You said.'

'I can't protect him forever.'

Amos smiled.

'Any word on Downey?'

'He's keeping his head down. As I mentioned he would.'

'But he'll come looking for the child.'

Made as a statement, but he was after reassurance. There was a kind of boss Amos Crane had read about: the seagull manager. Who flaps in, makes a lot of noise, shits over everything and leaves. Howard aspired to that, but he was hampered by his personality. Unless he got a lot more secure quite quickly, he was never going to be able to fuck things up in anything but a minor way. So Crane said, 'He'll be looking for the child, Howard. I promise you that. And if he finds her – and we'll make it easy for him – he'll be sticking his head right into our box.' He chopped the edge of his hand down on to his desk. 'And we'll cut his head clean off, Howard. No mess. No waste. No more Downey.'

'Whereabouts?'

Crane told him.

Howard thought about it, then nodded. 'Makes sense. Has a kind of symmetry about it.'

'Thanks.'

'And the child won't be hurt.'

Crane held up his palms: who, me?

'I'll hold your fucking brother responsible.'

'I'll make a note of that.' He wrote something on a Post-it. Howard stood, turned to go, then turned back reluctantly. 'Something else?'

'It's probably minor.'

'But I ought to know. Oughtn't I?' asked Amos Crane.

Howard reached into his inside pocket, and drew a letter out. 'This came the other day. To the Ministry. It was intercepted, of course.'

'Of course.'

'I knew there'd be a fuss. Your bloody brother . . .'

Amos was already tucking the letter away in his own pocket. He knew what kind of thing it would be. 'I'll see to it,' he said soothingly. 'It'll be like it never came at all.'

'No bombs.'

'Don't worry.' Be happy. Howard was really going this time. Amos said, 'Oh, and Howard?'

'Yes?'

'You couldn't protect my brother if he used you as a condom.'

For a while, it looked as if Howard had something to say about that, but at the last he just turned and walked away. Crane settled back into his comfortable darkness. Howard was harmless – his major failing – but he offered occasional amusements, such as *Mongolia* – where, in the course of germ-warfare experiments in the early forties, the Soviets kept prisoners chained in tents with plague-infested rats. Crane couldn't remember offhand the point at issue. Anyway: a prisoner escaped, and a minor epidemic was halted by an air strike, with the usual collateral damage. Round about four thousand Mongols died. Nobody was actually counting. The bodies were burned with 'large quantities of petrol'; a description Crane had read in a book. *Large quantities* of petrol. And Howard had said *You can't compare us to them*, and Crane had laughed and laughed. He hadn't been scoring moral points. He'd just found Howard's assertion unbelievably funny.

'Course not, Howard,' he muttered now, as he leaned forward and killed the monitor. For a brief moment, a trinity of dots shone in his eyes – red, blue, green – then they too died. In that moment, Amos Crane was thinking about Axel, and about how Downey wouldn't just be looking for a child, but looking for revenge, too; and this was a man trained to kill. Perhaps he should be worried about his brother. And then he smiled again, at the notion of worrying about *Axel*, and patted his breast pocket where Howard's letter now nestled. Whoever sent *that* should be worrying about Axel. And he turned the Anglepoise off also, and sat for a while in the dark.

THREE

THE FIRST STATION OF THE CROSS

10

MONDAY MORNING SHE HAD the panic, and was assaulted by the dead.

It happened shopping. During the summer months Oxford fell prey to hordes of foreign students hungry for the cultural experiences the city had to offer, chief among these being found in McDonald's on Cornmarket Street. As Dennis Potter once remarked, pardon me while I spatter you with vomit. Though on the other hand, Sarah conceded, these were kids far from home, and you couldn't blame them for congregating in the one corner of this foreign field that might have been mainland Europe. But back on the first hand, they got in the way and left litter everywhere. She crossed the road and entered the covered market.

Everywhere else, a covered market was for cheap food, end-of-line clothing, plastic shoes and party junk. Oxford being Oxford, it was where you bought stuffed olives, Greek bread and T-shirts costing thirty pounds. But there were still ordinary shops, mostly butchers', and through one of their windows now she watched a boy in a white coat arrange a tray of offal: heart, tongue and liver neatly displayed according to a set pattern, as if butchery were an ancient religion, and this its sacrament . . . For some reason she was thinking about Gerard Inchon; about her new-found conviction he was responsible for the explosion up her road. Over the phone she had shared this with Joe, who wasn't impressed.

'He was late for your dinner party.'

'And arrived without his briefcase.'

'Sarah. How can I say this to you? They lock people up for less.'

'I'd think we need more evidence,' she said doubtfully.

'I meant you. Paranoid fantasies; you're a danger to yourself.'

'Do you never get moments of inspiration, when you just know you're right about something?'

'And then I wake up. Sarah, this man, he's got money, right? Lots of it.'

'That's the story.'

'Enough so he wouldn't have to do his own dirty work.'

'Maybe that other guy, the one with the hair—'

'Stop right there. You establish an accomplice, your *evidence* goes out the window. He's got an accomplice, why was he late? If he was late, why think there's an accomplice?'

She changed subject. 'Does the word "rimat" mean anything to you?'

'Rimat?'

'Or "rinat", possibly. Part of a longer word.'

'Like a clue?'

'Something like that.'

'Peregrination,' he said. 'Farinated.'

'But probably "rimat."'

'Where is it from, this clue? Written on a cigarette packet? A scrap of burnt paper, perhaps?'

She told him about the photograph.

'Ah. With plenty of children standing about.'

'Maybe it was a school of some sort,' she said.

'Would you listen to yourself? Would you care for some advice, Sarah? From my heart to yours?'

'I'm not going to like it.'

'Have a kiddy. One of your own. Stop worrying about this Dinah child you think someone has spirited away. If she was missing, people would be looking for her. They're not. She isn't.'

'I want to know where she is,' she said stubbornly.

'You're not meant to know where she is. It isn't your business. Now you're having fantasies about this friend of your husband's you don't like. Heaven forbid you should not like me, you'll think I did it.'

'Joe—'

'Dinah isn't there. Zoë isn't here. That doesn't mean either of them are missing.'

'Have you heard from her?'

'There was a postcard,' he admitted. 'From London. With the last of the Mohicans on it.'

'Dinah isn't sending postcards.'

'This child, she's too young to write. Besides, how do you know? Would you be the one she sent postcards to?'

She didn't answer.

'You hardly know this girl. Let me guess, you're mid thirties, right?'

Early thirties. 'Careful, Joe.'

'Have a baby. It will change your life, I mean it. All your problems, all these mysteries, *pouf*, they're gone. Your life will be happiness and nappies. They're not incompatible.'

'How many kids have you got, Joe?'

'As many as I have paranoid fantasies.'

'You're supposed to be a detective, not an agony column.'

'Hey, I solve problems. I don't choose them.'

But talking to Joe, for all that, had helped, if only in demonstrating that it would take more than undiluted scorn to blow away her suspicions. Though maybe he'd come close to the truth, picking up on that *rimat* business: she'd only retained the fragment because of the picture: all those children, crowded in front of a big old house. *Where was Dinah Singleton?* A hundred times a day she wondered that. And all her other notions faded as she did, even the chilling memory she had told nobody about: that Gerard Inchon had threatened her in the dark, with only a sleeping husband for a witness.

In a notice on a board near the centre of the market, the council congratulated itself on the standard of busking it demanded. Today's entertainment, though, was provided by a strange drunk woman with sharp ferrety features, playing the same four notes over and over on a recorder. She wore a woollen cap of bright, Latin American design, and her puppy – they all had puppies – was a brown, shivering wreck. These four notes trailed after Sarah as she wandered buying meat, vegetables, olives; not buying sweatshirts embossed with gargoyles. It only slowly dawned on her that the music was not the only thing following. That was the beginning of the panic.

First, she saw the man with the placard: a tall man in a dull grey suit, his trouser legs bunched around his ankles, a bowler hat perched on his head like an egg on a tray. Where his face should have been was a rubber mask. Looking tearfully at the world from between bow tie and bowler, Stan Laurel bowed low for her and walked on by, the large wooden sign he carried swaying ominously as he passed. PARTY FAVOURS, it read. FANCY DRESS, BALLOONS, NOVELTIES. There was a whole industry based on such ephemera. Today, though, Sarah felt a slight shiver – a goose on her grave – as the living image of the dead comedian passed, large as life and twice as monochrome: it felt more than an advert; it felt a warning.

On the street outside the crowds were desperate as ever. On any given day, you could easily believe rationing had been introduced that morning. Manoeuvring through shoppers, the feeling grew upon her, as intangible yet certain as hearing her name whispered in a crowded room, that she was being followed. When she stopped and looked round, she couldn't pick anyone out. But the feeling remained, went hand in hand with the music in her mind, the four erratic notes the small battered woman had played on her recorder. As if the tune had drifted from the market in her wake and dogged her now like one of those sick puppies.

The feeling grew gradually, but when the panic arrived it arrived full fledged, forcing her to stop dead, drop her shopping, take her left hand in her right and squeeze. It was years since she'd had one of these: a doom attack; a paranoia fit; after her accident they'd arrived regularly, once every few weeks, but had faded with time. She'd never learned to control them. But knew, nevertheless, what to do now: find somewhere quiet to sit until the world ceased to be a hostile mass, became the usual whirl of busy people who had nothing to do with her. All she had to do was move. She released her hand, saw the purple indentation marks her nails had left, and could think of nowhere to go. Muttering people bumped into her. At the top of the street was a church, a grubby square, a couple of benches. Winos hung out there, like everywhere else, but it was close. Her bruised hands collected her shopping while she faked normality: breathe in, count down, breathe out. One step became another. There was a booth where you could buy coffee, but she gave it a miss and sat in the shade, where, in the space of ten minutes she noticed, repeatedly: a female jogger in a purple tracksuit, her hair tied back so it bounced off her collar; a dirty man in need of a shave, with an indestructible dog-end cupped in a scarred right hand; a man in a used-car salesman's coat, and a face that belonged on Gollum; a teenage girl hugging a filthy child, waving a polystyrene cup in the face of everyone who passed; and, this one only in her mind, a woman – herself – skydiving from the roof of a high terraced house, the lights of the city cartwheeling in her head as she turned over and over, and never hit the ground.

She was breathing hard now. It was a vision that recurred at moments of crisis; her own private ghost no rite of exorcism ever managed to lay. It happened, she said – not aloud – to the other Sarah Tucker. But the only answer her mind gave was the same frightening picture from the same impossible angle: a woman – herself – skydiving from the roof of a high terraced house, the lights of the city cartwheeling in her head as she turned over and over, and never hit the ground.

'Spare s'm change, miss? F'food like?'

It was just a voice from the never-ending street parade but it startled her anyway; she must have made some noise or other because he backed off, startled himself.

'Wz only askin'.'

He had black teeth and a bruised head; his features were puffy with drink or assault.

'Fuck off,' she snarled.

'Wz only askin',' he muttered again. But he backed off further, fucked off in fact, leaving her alone again and the skydiving picture shattered. In its place hard knowledge.

Which was this. In all the films, all the books, it was the little things gave you away: the typewriter with the raised T; the spare key still on its ledge above the door. With her, it was that damn palmtop. One switch flicked at no gain to herself, and Gerard knew she was digging, knew she knew what he had done. So now she sat on a crowded street, people milling every which way, and she was alone and frightened because Gerard *knew*, and had already killed two people and disappeared a third. Maybe more, because nothing about planting a bomb suggested you were an amateur: amateurs used kitchen knives. Gerard had blown people away for motives she hadn't even thought about yet, and now she'd provided him with a reason for doing it to her. And this was a man who collected guns. *Batten down the hatches, girl. You've got big trouble coming.*

Just two days ago she'd been thinking there was entertainment value in this.

Her blouse clung to her now: she wore jeans, a blouse, a summer jacket; all light enough until fear had set in. Her shoes were no help: flat but narrow, running to a point at the tip, which ruled out breaking into a jog. And where would she run? Who was she running from? *He's got lots of money, this Gerard?* Joe had asked. *Enough so he doesn't have to do his own dirty work?* He could have hired anyone. They could all be in his pay.

Tall, mournful Stan Laurel bobbed past once more, and it seemed to Sarah that he picked her out for special scrutiny; that the living eyes behind the rubber mask found her out in her junkies' corner, and recorded a secret amusement at the sight. She clutched her own hand again. A silly exercise, but it used to help, and could do no harm now. And nor could Stan Laurel. If anyone was watching her, it was somebody from the colourful now, not out of the black-and-white past.

There was an odd sort of comfort in this, though; knowing there was a real enemy, a specific danger. Whatever had happened in the past, whatever scars left on her imagination, it was not her own mind she had to fear now: this was happening, and was therefore not without solution. There were rules for these situations, and number one was that you didn't panic. She released her hand again, and studied the nail marks in the flesh: once, when she was younger, they'd have disappeared as she watched. But the self-inflicted pain had done the trick, and she felt ready to leave now. Gathering her shopping, she stood. With the dimming of the panic, knowledge of her essential safety gathered about her like an overcoat. Nothing could happen. This was important to remember. Here among the Monday morning shoppers, nothing would happen.

Home, then. She crossed the road and headed down St Michael's Street. Not much more than a lane, this carried little in the way of traffic, and few pedestrians compared to the main shopping grid. Her bags were growing heavier by the step, and she stopped twice before the corner, rearranging them to achieve the perfect balance. Which would be the day, she thought ruefully. Already her panic was strange to her, like a familiar object viewed from an unusual angle: a worm's-eye view of a cheese grater. What had got into her? How likely could it be that Gerard was having her watched? On the one hand you could add up all that had happened: the bomb, the missing child, Gerard's threat, all the rest. And on the other you took an ordinary day in the centre of Oxford, and a young (thank you) woman fetching the first of the week's groceries. Nothing ever happened. There was a kind of middle-class privilege about lives like hers: for all the drama she hovered on the edge of, there would always be the home to go to, the food on the table, the bath before bedtime. Sinister strangers had their place, but only in guest appearances. Life was *slow* dying. Her bubble would burst like all bubbles, but not without the usual drawn-out ending: the doctor's charts, the nurse's warnings, the soft words spoken around a bed with fresh linen. Death didn't happen on a side lane in the city. Cemetery Road was very long.

A car pulled up behind her and she jumped.

A man leaped out and disappeared into a printers' shop. Sarah's heart changed gear again; climbed right back down into first. *Idiot*, she thought. Meaning herself, mostly, but also whoever that had been, who had no right to exist while she felt so fragile. All that equilibrium shot to pieces. She reached the corner, turned it, and bumped into Stan Laurel.

'Sarah,' he said.

She screamed, or tried to, or thought she did, but no sound came out: not much more than a hiccup. He'd already put one white-gloved hand out and taken her by the arm, while with the other he carefully leaned his placard against the wall.

Then he pulled his face off.

11

SHE WORE A NECKLACE of cubic wooden beads, like little dice but with letters, spelling WIGWAM. Which was probably fashion, but might just have been utilitarian: of all the people Sarah knew, the one most likely to need reminding of her own name was Wigwam.

'I should have told you.'

'You said he didn't want people to know.'

'He was embarrassed at first. A grown man dressing up. Then he was disappointed nobody recognised him.'

'He wanted an Oscar?'

'My performance, he calls it.' Wigwam laughed. '*My performance went very well today*. I think he's hoping a talent scout will clock him.'

'If it's being clocked he's after, he almost had his wish. When he started pulling his mask off, he nearly got six kilos of assorted vegetables in his face.'

'He was really sorry.'

'So he kept saying.' But Sarah had her doubts. There'd been a hint of malice in Rufus's eyes when he'd seen how frightened she'd been; the kind of private glee a worm must feel when it turns. Though afterwards he'd hidden it, and complicated her attempts to pick her shopping up in his familiar ineffectual way. And then presumably reported in, because Wigwam had turned up before she'd been home ten minutes. 'No harm done anyway.'

'Are you sure?'

'Just a little on edge, that's all.'

'You're not . . .' Wigwam's query trailed away, hardly worth the question mark.

'Pregnant? No.'

'Oh.' With a carefully judged amount of sympathy in the tone: Wigwam was sorry, but aware that Sarah wasn't. 'Rufus and I are trying,' she went on.

Several short remarks occurred to Sarah, any one of which could have destroyed their friendship. 'Gosh,' was what she said at last.

'You think five's too many, don't you?' said Wigwam, a little sadly.

'I think one's too many, sweetie. But that's just me.'

'At the moment.'

'If you like.' The kettle boiled, and she got up to pour. 'I can see that Rufus might want one of his own,' she said. 'But won't it make things awkward?'

'Oh, he's lovely with the kids. He really is.'

'And that won't change when he's an actual father?'

'Oh, no. It'll strengthen the bond.' Wigwam sounded like she'd memorised the manual. But still, she'd had the experience. What did Sarah know about children?

The phone rang in the other room, and she excused herself to answer it. Left to herself she could ignore a ringing phone, but Wigwam grew nervous in the face of such disrespect. What if it's *important*? she'd say. A doctor, a policeman, the Queen. It was none of those, but it did turn out to be important.

'Arimathea.'

'What?'

'Arimathea. As in Joseph of, no relation. It's me, Joe.'

'Hey Joe,' she said automatically. 'Rimat. Arimathea. Right.'

'He was a merchant, a trader. Friend of the Christ family.

You know, Jesus Christ, Mary Christ. Legend has it he supplied the tomb Jesus was laid in.'

'That was kind of him.'

'He got it back. Plus, the story goes, he brought Jesus to England as a lad.' Not a minute of research was being wasted here. 'And did those feet in ancient times, and so forth. The Holy Grail passed into his keeping after the crucifixion. Basically, he was the gospels' Mr Fixit.'

'Did you get his phone number?'

'All it took was a certain skill at crosswords and an encyclopedic knowledge of everything. There's no need to thank me.'

'You're a genius. So now all we want—'

'It's in Surrey. Little place called, well, Littleton.'

'A hospital?'

'An orphanage.'

Behind her, Wigwam had come into the room. She was carrying Sarah's tea and her expression said, I am not listening to this conversation. She hovered uncertainly, a strange reversal: a waitress trying to catch the customer's eye. And was definitely capable of interrogation afterwards, so Sarah wrapped Joe up quickly. 'When do we go?'

'Let's not get excited, Sarah.' She could picture him adopting his Wise Man expression. 'What are we looking at here, really? He makes donations to an orphanage. You're saying he supplies orphans too? That's quite a leap.'

'Maybe it's some complicated tax dodge.'

'You could save more money not bothering. I owe you, Sarah, but this, it was just a puzzle. A word game. It's not something to get hyperactive over. Maybe I should have kept the answer to myself.'

'I'm a big girl now.'

'This is what troubles me.'

'I'll talk to you later, Joe. Thanks.'

'Friend?' asked Wigwam. On the off chance, presumably, that it had been a wrong number.

Sarah took her tea. 'Thanks. Somebody who did some work for me.' Trying to make Joe sound like a jobbing plumber. 'Do you want a biscuit to go with this?'

'That'd be nice. He doesn't do gardens, does he? This Joe of yours?'

'I'd have to ask.'

'Only I've a branch needs sawing down. It's a bit high for Rufus.'

'We've a ladder you can borrow.'

'It's safer going professional, isn't it?'

Thus it was that, without actually having to lie or make false promises, Sarah arranged to ask the private detective if he did gardens at four pounds an hour. Not long after Wigwam left, she was back on the phone. There was little else for her to do. She'd not yet had replies to last week's letters.

'Oxford Investigations.'

'Joe, I want to take a look.'

'So take a look. I'm stopping you?'

'Will you come with me?'

'I'm a tour guide? Sarah, I want wild goose, I hang around Port Meadow in the autumn. I want a drive in the country, I head for the Catskills.'

'Cotswolds.'

'Whatever. Surrey, I don't touch. It holds bad memories. I had a dreadful case there once.'

'Murder?'

'Flu. And I'm busy at the moment, or I expect to be. Any day now.'

'Okay.'

'So I'm not going.'

'Okay.'

The silence down the line was very loud. The humming of unsaid words snarled up in the wires.

'This happens in films,' he said at last. 'One scene you get the man saying no way is he doing it. The very next he's doing it. Whatever it happens to be.'

'I've seen that,' Sarah said.

'But that's not going to happen here.'

'No, Joe.'

Whatever she had been expecting, the building was a brilliant cacophony of wings and crenellations, with small round towers jutting up at available corners, suggesting that it had been built to the specifications of a six-year-old. But all of it was tired, too; rain-streaked, mossed over in patches, and even in the bright sunshine looking like it suffered a chill. Or an ague, Sarah amended. Sometimes only the old words fit.

'Miss Havisham's wedding cake,' Joe said.

'Gormenghast,' she countered.

'Bit obvious,' he muttered as they got out of the car.

Oxford to Littleton had been no drive in the country, involving enough plastic bollards to throw a ring around the moon, and barricades of metal signs conveying cryptic instructions, small sandbags slung over their crossbars like dead piglets. Joe proved both neat and nervous behind the wheel; choosing his lane and sticking to it, and assuming every other road user was a homicidal incompetent. This didn't stop him talking. 'I need my head examined,' he'd said.

'You're a very good man.'

'I'm a schmuck. You know the expression?'

'It doesn't apply.'

'I'm a sucker for a pretty face.' He glanced at her sideways, but she didn't register the compliment. 'I need a tougher contract. No refunds, no guarantees. That way, I wouldn't be taken advantage of.'

'Is that what I'm doing?'

'If the cap fits . . .'

'You've probably got it on upside down,' she finished, and immediately regretted it. 'Joe, you're kind to do this. But I'll pay for your time.'

'I promised,' he sighed. 'Remember?'

She did. And thought she was pretty good, actually, not to have reminded him herself. 'At least let me pay for the petrol.'

'Okay.'

They had set off early, no more than ten minutes after Mark left for work: as long as she was home before him, he'd never know she'd been gone. Except he might wonder why there was no supper. That was a problem she'd shelved; meanwhile she savoured the fact of setting out on what might be an adventure. With a real live private detective, authentically grumpy to boot. Though he thawed once they were under way; showed an alarming tendency, in fact, to wax nostalgic.

'I remember when I first came to Oxford—'

'Where were you born, Joe?'

He thought about it. 'Croydon.'

'Nice part of the world?'

'You don't want to hear about Oxford?'

'I live there.'

They were jammed up already: lots of cars going God knew where on a midweek morning. Reps, Sarah supposed. Spare shirts on hangers hooked above back-seat windows. A sense of purpose to journeys like that: hers didn't bear too much thought. If she pondered it too long, she began to see just how much weight she was hanging from a thin thin thread.

'He said he was an orphan.'

'Said it or suggested it?'

'Well, suggested it. But there were pictures of him with this couple, they had to be his parents.'

'Doesn't mean he didn't *get* to be an orphan. Everyone's an orphan eventually.'

Which was not entirely accurate, but Sarah let it pass. 'What's his business anyway?'

'Inchon Enterprises.'

'Sounds suitably vague,' Joe allowed.

'I'm not sure what they do, exactly. Something financial.'

'There was an Inchon at Oriel,' he began.

'Is that a kestrel? Over there?'

Joe's mouth set in a hard straight line, but Sarah suspected there was a smile in it somewhere.

They listened to the news: Oxford made the headlines. A local girl, *thirteen*, had died at what was still, apparently, called a rave; had died of dehydration, after taking Ecstasy. There followed one of those short interviews with an angry, grief-stricken parent which, as much as anything, were a hallmark of the decade.

'Tragic,' was Joe's only comment. He turned the radio off. They stopped for coffee and a strategy session at a service station: the coffee was okay but the strategy didn't pan out. They could pretend to be prospective foster-parents, but weren't sure how the system worked; they could pretend to have money to donate, but didn't think they could do a convincing rich. Or they could tell the truth, but this had all sorts of drawbacks.

'Not least being,' Joe said sourly, 'that it's a fools' errand.' But once they were back on the road he cheered up again, as if simply working towards a destination were enough for him, and the problems of what to do once he arrived could wait. Probably a good attitude for a detective, Sarah thought: concentrate on the mystery, not the solution. Though Joe, as he said himself, had never solved a mystery; just ironed out the odd problem.

'So why this line of work?'

'Lots of holiday. I only work one day in ten.'

'No wonder you charge so much.'

'Also, I'm a romantic.'

'How nice for you.'

'It's a cross I bear. Women, they don't want romantic men. Have you noticed this?'

'No. But thanks for the tip.'

'They want practical, they want plumbers and chefs. Not dreamers.'

'Are you a dreamer. Joe?'

'When I was at Oriel—'

'What was your tutor's name again?'

'Morris. Abel Morris.'

'And what years were you there?'

'Ah, '70 to '73.'

'Which staircase did you live on?'

'What?'

'What was your scout's name?'

'Sarah—'

'That's what they're called, isn't it? Scouts.'

'Yes,' he said glumly. 'That's what they're called. Scouts.' But when she started laughing he joined in, and after a while seemed to enjoy the joke more than she did.

And now they'd arrived, still with little idea of what they were doing. 'It's your party,' he said, locking the car.

'I want to explore. They'll have records, files.'

'They'll say, Sure, go ahead. Look all you like.'

'I wasn't planning on asking.'

'You're a dangerous woman, Sarah Trafford.'

'Can you distract their attention?'

'Only because it can't hurt. It's an orphanage, Sarah. Stolen children, you're not going to find. Likewise explosives and plans for world domination.'

'You're no fun.'

'But you'd best take this,' he said, handing her what, for one absurd moment, she thought was his asthma inhaler.

'A rape alarm?'

'Not that I imagine the fathers, they're Catholic priests here, will be overcome with lust at the sight of you.'

'*Thanks*, Joe.'

'But if you meet any trouble, whistle and I'll come.'

Already coming was a man who could only be a priest: not just for the black trousers, black shirt, white collar, but for that certain air of bland superiority Sarah remembered from her youth, much of which had been spent listening to withered virgins explaining how awful sex was. From the corner of an eye she registered the sign from Gerard's photograph. Before she could take it in, the priest was upon them. 'Can I help?'

A young man, twenty-two or -three, he had shiny cheeks and square black glasses as unflattering as anything Sarah had seen on a face, including acne and brush moustaches. Unfortunately, that was all she could think of, and saying it didn't seem a fine idea. But before she could pretend to be sick, Joe spoke: 'You see, honey? I told you there'd be priests.'

Everything but the accent was American.

The priest was understandably hesitant. Joe was smiling in such an open, friendly way, he looked deranged. 'This is an orphanage,' he said.

'Of course it is, of course it is. And you are—?'

'My name's Sullivan, Father Peter Sullivan.' He pushed his glasses up his nose. 'I'm an administrator.'

'Ah, the man in charge.'

'Well, not exactly—'

'You hear that, honey? I told her, I said, you want something done, go straight to the man at the top. And here you are.'

'I'm not in charge here, Mr—?'

'That's a good idea, let's leave it plain Mister.' He winked loudly. 'Let's not stand on ceremony. *Mr* Gold, Joe Gold. You can call me Joe.' He put out a hand. 'This is my assistant, Missy. We were just passing.'

Sarah had been reading the sign when she heard her new

name: it read THE ARIMATHEA HOME, and under that, in smaller lettering, FOR CATHOLIC BOYS AND GIRLS. Gerard had stood there, on that patch of grass, bestowing his largesse on a tall, elderly priest – not this one – whose expression suggested it was he who was doing Gerard Inchon the favour. And now she was here, the pointlessness of it hit her: so this was where Gerard had had his photograph taken. So what? She might as well have gone to that office block he'd had built, gone through it room by room. Looking for Dinah. Who would never be found.

'Missy?'

'It sure is a nice place,' she said, letting some remembered Brummie creep into her voice.

It sure was. Spooky, true; deafeningly Gothic, but charming the way illustrations in old books of fairy tales were charming: the kind of houses that never existed, but ought to. This one had obviously found a loophole in the laws governing the fabric of reality, and had materialised in the Surrey countryside, presumably wreathed in fog, never to find its way back to Goblin Land. Which was what Joe was basing his pitch on, in fact. 'You must get lots of offers.'

'The property isn't for sale, Mr Gold.' With just that degree of irritation the Pope allowed when speaking to a Jew. 'Now if you don't mind, this area—'

'Lord, man, I didn't mean to *buy* it. You hear that, Missy?'

'Certainly did, Goldie.' Damned if he'd get to stay Joe.

'I'm talking about an afternoon's use, two days max. Just the frontage. Couple of good exteriors in the bag, we're away down the road, you're fifteen hundred richer. Never know we were there, otherwise.'

Sarah picked it up. 'Interiors would be on the elevated scale, of course. That'd be two thousand and up. But only if we could use it. Depends on the ceilings, what do you say, Goldie?'

'We need a boom rig in there, you're talking twenty foot.

Eighteen minimum. How big are the rooms, Padre? Excuse me, Father.'

Father Sullivan was groping towards the daylight Joe let in with the mention of money. 'You're in television?'

Joe laughed. 'Television, movies, video. All in the best possible taste, of course. Our properties win awards.' He made like he was reaching for a cigar, but remembered in time he didn't use them. 'It's like Missy says. We shoot interiors, the rate rockets. I shouldn't be telling you this.'

'Our ceilings are, um, spacious.'

'We're a ways from town, Goldie. You add catering costs, you're looking at megabucks.'

'Point.' He grimaced. 'Shame. *Excellent* frontage. *Classic.*'

'Those turrets. They'd die for them, Stateside.' Having lost all shame, Sarah was starting to enjoy herself.

'Yeah, but they're not as high as the overheads. Out of town is out of pocket, that's what Quentin always says.'

The priest could see fifteen hundred, maybe two thousand, taking wing. 'Would you like to see inside? The ceilings really are rather special.'

'Missy?'

Sarah shrugged. 'Come this far.'

'Thanks, Padre. That'd be real.'

'Quentin?' she whispered, as they followed the priest through the main door.

'Quentin Taylor. Runs the deli next to the office.'

Inside, the building lost a lot of charm, felt like a school: plenty of corridors, peeling paint. A smell of overcooked carrots and powdered custard. But strangely quiet, as if the children were kept sensibly gagged, or had been Pied Pipered away; she asked the obvious as Father Sullivan led them into what must be the main hall and he explained, as you would to a primitive, about school hours in England. 'There's a good school two miles down the road. We bus them in.'

Joe was looking at corners through a little square he'd made by joining fingers and thumbs together. Perhaps, somewhere in the world, real people did this when sizing locations for filming. Even if they didn't, Father Sullivan thought they did.

'Are the ceilings high enough?' he asked, a little anxious.

Sarah wasn't much of a judge, but thought you could safely have juggled elephants.

'We could squeeze in,' Joe allowed doubtfully.

'What's your film about?'

'Is there a little girls' room?' she asked.

'Um, through that door, second on the right. No, third.'

'Spare no details, Goldie,' she urged as she left, intending to get lost.

Which she did. The first door she chose, neither second, third, nor on the right, took her into a chapel: a cold, tidy, chapel, with the peculiarly religious air of being older than the house which contained it. Two rows of benches flanked an aisle; eleven deep on one side, seven on the other to accommodate the pulpit, a thoroughly traditional little chamber from which its doubtless thoroughly traditional incumbent could harangue his flock without needing a microphone. On its panels was embossed a strange device, which Sarah could not make out clearly. The only light, barring the small red altar lamp, came from two stained-glass windows, each too high to help much, though she could see, around the walls, the Stations of the Cross glaring down: a particularly stern accounting of what was, she supposed, a particularly stern journey. No attempt here to gloss over the barbarism of judicial murder . . . For a moment childhood felt so close she could taste it, then shimmered away into the cold, faintly incensed air; a ghost of something that had not yet died, or at least not been laid to rest.

Funny that the air was so cold, though. On a day so warm outside.

. . . She had not told Joe what had happened in the market;

nor would she tell him about this. But the chapel's atmosphere reached into her, feeding its ache to her bones, and while she did not feel it as a *presence*, something in it spoke to her nevertheless, and nothing it had to say was welcome. It spoke of raw Catholicism; of threat not faith, death not resurrection, and all the accoutrements on view, from the First Station of the Cross to the last blade of glass in a painted window, seemed tricks for the propagation of a fundamental error. For as long as she'd had thoughts on the matter, she'd known religion meant nothing if it did not preach compassion. What she discovered now was that she'd always been wrong about this; a lesson learned at last in a chapel made of stone, built on rock, and hard as nails.

None of which was much use. What she had been hoping for was an empty office, an administrative nerve centre, a helpful register open on its desk with a brand new name inked in. Even if it hadn't actually read Dinah Singleton, she'd have been prepared to accept the clue. The next door she knocked on, and when an elderly female voice responded hurried along the corridor, ducking into the first unoccupied room. Not a nerve centre. More like the staffroom of a second-rate public school – there was no rule that said such judgements had to be based on experience. What she saw: a worn three-piece suite; a little table with bottles of scotch and gin and a soda siphon. Bookcases around the walls, their contents all bound in drab leather; to the side of the one window was a little glass display case with more of the same. The view from the window showed the grounds to the rear: a well-mannered garden, a playing field, then just fields. The carpet beneath her was threadbare, the curtains dusty; the floorboards squeaked. The door creaked too, and opened now: she felt her heart thump as somebody entered. *Caught*.

'Lost?'

'Joe!' You nearly killed me she was about to add, but Father thingy, Sullivan, was just behind him. 'Third on the right going meant third on the left coming back. Right?'

'Doubtless.'

'Ah, miss, um, Missy.'

'Did Goldie give you the rundown?'

'He seems to think we might, ah, come to an arrangement. E. M. Forster, he tells me.'

'*A Passage to India*,' said Joe. Sarah raised an eyebrow. 'Just for the flashbacks.'

'You know, I'm sure I've already seen a film of that.'

'This is a miniseries,' Joe said firmly.

She turned to look out of the window, worried she'd start giggling, just as a phone rang which Father Sullivan answered. Joe sidled to a bookcase and began fingering spines; the phone call was about dinners; not the faintest hint of a clue. Which did not surprise her. The heart-stopping seconds when the door opened had given way to something deeper than anti-climax. There were no clues here; there was nothing to be found. If she'd wanted wild geese, she should have listened to Joe.

The phone call droned on. Sarah too plucked a book from the shelf; opened it at random. *So the first angel went and poured his bowl on the earth, and foul and evil sores came upon the men who bore the mark of the beast and worshipped its image.* She nearly dropped it when Sullivan spoke behind her: 'Find something interesting?'

Joe strolled over. 'Your books, they're very nice. A worthwhile library.'

'Thank you.'

'I'm speaking as an educated man. Oxford. Perhaps you—'

'Oriel,' Father Sullivan said shortly.

'Jolly good. Jolly good.' Oddly, Joe didn't pursue this co-incidence. 'So, Missy, time we were off? Scout some more locations?'

Admit defeat, in fact. She ignored him. 'I believe Gerard Inchon's a benefactor of yours.'

'Mr Inchon. You know him?'

'Just through friends,' Sarah said. 'The Singletons?'

The priest went through a phoney memory search. 'I can't say I do.'

'They're dead now,' Sarah said. 'They were blown up.'

He looked pained. Joe said, 'Missy?'

'Just Dinah left now,' she said. 'Dinah. Singleton.'

'What is this about?' Father Sullivan asked.

'Just one of those things,' Joe said. 'You're in a new place, you suddenly remember being told about it—'

'I'd heard she was here, you see. I'd heard this was where they'd taken her.'

'I'm afraid you're mistaken.'

'I don't think I am.'

'Sarah—'

Father Sullivan said, 'You're not making a film at all, are you?'

'Sorry about this, Padre, but we're—'

'I think you're lying. I think she's here.'

'Jesus, Sarah – sorry, Father – you can't accuse him of—'

'I think you should leave,' the priest said. 'Both of you. Right now.'

'We're going,' Sarah said. 'But we'll be back. And you can tell Gerard bloody Inchon I said so.'

Outside the weather was calm and unruffled; what few clouds there were hovered motionless above them.

Inside, Sarah was storms and hurricanes. Twisters. Summer madness.

They drove in silence until they reached a school a mile or two down the road, whereupon Joe pulled up and advised Sarah to wait. He was angry with her, as she was with herself.

Once, as a teenager, she'd thrown up at her parents' wedding anniversary bash. This felt worse.

'What did you think you were *doing*?' Joe had asked, once they'd got back to the car.

'I don't know,' she said miserably. 'I wanted to see how he'd react.'

'You as good as accused him of child molesting. Under the circumstances, I think he reacted very well.'

'I did *not*!'

'He's a priest, Sarah. You accused him of having spirited a child away. Read the papers.'

But she hadn't meant that. She wasn't sure what she'd meant. Just that once she'd started, she couldn't stop herself. Like being on top of a tall building, and falling all the way to the ground.

He was back within minutes. 'Sometimes it's quicker,' he said, 'to tell the truth.' He pulled his safety belt on before starting up.

'And?'

'Mostly the truth. That we're looking for an abducted child. Who possibly hasn't been abducted. And may or may not be blonde. And might answer to the name of Dinah.'

Rubbing it in, yes. 'Would you just tell me, Joe?'

'I'll just tell you, then. I've just driven all the way from Oxford and I'm just about to drive all the way back, so before I do that, I'll just tell you what we've found. Nothing. No new child at this school, female, male or monkey. No Dinah Singleton. She isn't here. She never was.'

'I'm sorry.'

'Paid in full, Sarah. No more favours.'

'I really am sorry.'

'Yeah, right.' He sighed. 'Me too. I'm sorry. But this vast trek across the country, Sarah, that's it. All done. That was just an orphanage, Sarah. One you happened to see in a picture on the wall of somebody who happened to be at your house the night your neighbours died. That's all. Not even a string of coincidences. Because coincidences mean something, and this doesn't.'

'I know.'

'This girl, your Dinah, I don't know what she's mixed up in. Something to do with having a father who wasn't really dead. But you're not going to find her by throwing darts at a map. Are you with me, Mrs Trafford?'

'Have you been checking up on me, Joe?'

'Never trust the client. That's lesson one in Private Eye School.'

'Because that's twice you've called me Mrs Trafford. And I gave you my maiden name.'

His voice turned clipped: very Basil Rathbone. 'You thought you were being so clever, didn't you? But you made one tiny error. And for that you must pay.' She wasn't amused. He sighed. 'You wrote me a cheque.'

He started the car. For quite a long time, she thought she was going to cry.

12

FOR THE REST OF the lousy journey back, they hardly spoke: Sarah didn't like to think about it afterwards. To her, it felt less a rupture in a friendship than the sudden descent of a wall between two worlds: the one she had inhabited until now, and the one she was about to fall into. The fact that when Joe did speak – comments on the traffic, the roads – he was perfectly friendly didn't help. A blanket of misery fell over her anyhow, an all-enveloping lack of self-confidence undermining all she knew. Nothing she did could be trusted. When she gave a false name, she followed it up by writing a cheque.

And Mark, when he got home, matched her mood: his own day had been sodding awful. A deal had gone up in smoke, gone down the tubes; 'Gerard' had become 'that *bloody* Inchon'. Without being Mark's fault, it was his responsibility; a distinction existing solely in the workplace, as Sarah remembered from occasions when troubles had flared closer to home. She could barely piece together the details. The last two months, though, had just come crashing round Mark's ears; the cultivation of Inchon, of Inchon's *money*, had failed to produce the expected crop. This came out over the course of two bottles of wine, of which Sarah drank almost a glass . . . There was a letter too, a letter sent by *bloody* Inchon to bloody *Mayberry*, who was Mark's bloody boss. The letter contained aspersions, downright *accusations* . . . It was libellous, obviously. Mark had said as much to a tight-lipped Mayberry.

'And what did he say?'

'That it remained to be seen.'

Mark was white with anger throughout, or mostly anger. But there was fear too. You didn't fuck about with your career, he'd explained to her once; not halfway up the ladder, with everybody above you kicking out. It was so different from Sarah's experience that she'd taken issue, arguing that if that was how the game was played he'd be better off leaving the board altogether. He'd told her she didn't understand; it became a familiar row. But she didn't have the heart now to get involved in a post-mortem: just kept filling his glass and nodding, agreeing that he had indeed mentioned that he'd always seen the danger signs, had never trusted Inchon, had known it would come to this. After a while the words slipped over and into each other, and what had never been fully comprehensible to her became totally incoherent. Mark went to lie in the bath and reconstruct the case for the defence. Sarah went through to the kitchen to examine the possibilities of comfort food.

Every kitchen, she was reminded on entering, needs a place you can put things that don't live anywhere else. The top of the fridge was where buttons, screws, pill bottles and biros went when they died, all haphazardly interred in a recycled ice cream tub; it was where Mark's *downstairs* dental floss lived. It was where she put the rape alarm Joe had given her, because he'd forgotten to ask for it back. She had one of her own somewhere, very likely down the back of the fridge by now. Even in her most aggressive bouts of spring-cleaning, she'd avoided that kind of heavy lifting. It was a problem she felt immediately nostalgic for, now that larger ones had loomed into view.

It was unthinkable that Mark should lose his job, unthinkable to *her*, because there was no doubt in her mind what had happened. If Inchon had pulled out, leaving Mark twisting in the wind, it was Sarah's fault; it was the kind of indirect revenge a sneaky bastard like Gerard thought clever. Too late now to complain that revenge was undeserved, or that her 'investigating' had got her nowhere. She had had the temerity to stick her neck out; if Mark's head got chopped off in her place, that was what Gerard would call fair. All she could do now was play the traditional dormouse role and settle back into everyday life. Maybe things would work out, by which she meant return to the way they'd been this morning. There was nothing she could do for Dinah. It was time she admitted that. And whatever Gerard was up to, he had too many weapons at his disposal for her to assail: this was a man, she reminded herself, who collected guns.

Time to give up, then. Time to be a *good girl*. She began unpacking the fridge to make sandwiches for Mark, and found a packet of biscuits to eat while she did so. Come the weekend, come next week, she'd start over. First thing needed, a damn good cleaning job.

By the weekend, her life was to have altered course. Two things happened first, though.

In the days that followed, immediacy seemed to drain from the situation. Nothing serious developed. Mark became reticent, unwilling to discuss work in detail, though he gave her to understand things weren't as bad as he'd feared. Bloody Mayberry, the boss from hell, might still be breathing smoke, but the word 'fire' had yet to be uttered. Jobs like Mark's, they didn't give you notice; the least competent moneyman could bring a bank to its knees in a week. He still had a desk, then, which was as good as an anchor; he was keeping his head down, his nose clean, his tie straight, and every other cliché he could think of ironed and buttoned. Gerard Inchon, maybe, didn't have the clout he thought he had. One word from him, and nothing much occurred . . .

But the first thing that happened was, Sarah found Dinah Singleton. Or rather, discovered that she'd never actually missed her.

For the child was not Dinah, this was the sad and awful truth of it. The child was somebody else entirely: the overalls, the jellies, the fondness for feeding the swans. Sarah chanced upon her one afternoon coming back across the bridge; her eyes drawn to the devastated house, she did not see the child at first. By the time she did, it was too late to undo anything.

The blown house was a familiar landmark by now: one local children were proud of and adults tutted over as something which should have been *seen to* already. What had been done was not enough. Though boarding had been erected, indicating to the civic-minded that this was a no-go area, it was not so effectively constructed that it actually prevented ingress to anyone with even a mild curiosity as to what lay behind. From the bridge, what this was was clear enough: a slew of rubble, of bricks and mortar, of broken pipes and shards of porcelain, all of it liberally studded with jewels of broken glass, adding a touch of glitter to the sad remains of a suburban life. And there were rags and ends of household bric-a-brac poking like weeds through the rubbish; stuff that might have emerged of its own accord, seeking the light, for most things portable of even minimal value had been carted off long since. It was strange what refused to remain buried, Sarah thought. Even a battered fish slice, a frayed lampshade, could be exceedingly tenacious of whatever life it thought it possessed. Unwilling to surrender what had never knowingly been bestowed.

Lost in this ontological speculation, she nearly fell over Dinah. Not-Dinah. The child was standing beneath the bridge, fishing lumps of bread from a Marks and Sparks carrier bag and tossing them into the water, while her superintending adult, a woman, stood smoking a cigarette. Ducks quacked and, oddly, barked in the water. The adult studied Sarah suspiciously. It was not ordinary, it was not *normal*, for a woman to respond this way to another woman's child . . .

For Sarah had come to a dead halt, all the motion knocked out of her body.

'. . . Dinah?'

The child laughed; bread flew. In the water, the word had spread. A pair of swans arrived late for the feast, running across the water; their large feet rattling the surface as if it were a snare drum. The woman dropped her cigarette and ground it underfoot. 'Come on, Kylie.'

'I haven't *finished*.'

'Dinah?'

'What do you want, then?'

The woman's overt hostility masked fear. There was nothing in modern urban mythology to suggest that lone women acting strangely were not as dangerous as men, and nothing in Sarah's behaviour to suggest she wasn't hovering on the edge of some calamity. Women squawking *Dinah* without reason were best avoided. She held her Kylie's hand and began to pull her from the riverside.

As for Sarah, in that first moment of mistaken recognition, several things seemed to come together at once to make an awesome truth: here was Dinah, back from the unknown, just as her father had come back from the dead. But, as in his case, this was but a temporary reawakening: he had emerged from an apparent state of death only to be catapulted into a real one, just as Dinah now had reappeared only to reveal that she was not Dinah, had never been Dinah, and all of Sarah's confused actions of the past few weeks had been based on a misunderstanding. The picture she'd formed of Dinah when first told about the child had been true enough. It was simply that it hadn't been Dinah she'd been remembering, but this stranger, this Kylie, who was regarding her now with part pity, part amusement, while whatever tiny amount of confidence Sarah retained disappeared like the bread on the waters. She began to weep. While Kylie's mother watched, revising her opinions and drawing her own incorrect conclusions: that here was a woman who had lost something; that here was a mother who had ceased to be.

By the following morning this, too, Sarah had accommodated. It was beginning to look like there was no end to her incompetence; that the whole world was involved in some complicated conspiracy aimed at destroying her self-respect. But when you started thinking that way, you ended up gibbering on the streets. She vacuumed most of the house in the two hours following Mark's departure for work; then took a break which rapidly degenerated into a biscuit festival. Something had to give. She had not yet paid Joe for the petrol he had wasted; that seemed a fitting way of starting the bothersome business of forgetting. Mid morning, she took the bus up to the north end of town.

The last time she'd been to Joe's office, the *only* time, there'd been roadworks to navigate: today the street, never what you'd call a thoroughfare, was empty. Though even as she realised this, its condition changed. A man in a white jacket appeared in the doorway of the Italian restaurant opposite; he looked one way then the other, cast a hopeful glance at Sarah, and finally admitted defeat and lit a cigarette. Meanwhile, a tour bus trundled past the end of the road: what on earth did they find to look at up here? She tried the outer door and, finding it unlocked, climbed the stairs to Reception, the door to which was swinging ajar. She called Joe's name, but he didn't answer. For a moment she wondered if Zoë were back, and hoped for Joe's sake that she was, but there was only silence from Joe's office. If Zoë had come back, Sarah was pretty sure silence would not be on her agenda.

She knocked, waited, and knocked again. The first had been

pretty feeble; a very English am-I-supposed-to-be-here? knock. Something about empty premises made her feel in the wrong. The second was a firm businesslike rap, but she already knew Joe was out; had probably nipped to the paper shop or pub; somewhere, anyway, near, to account for the doors being left unlocked. If she went to check these places, she knew she'd end up back at the office anyway, in case he'd returned in her absence. Simplest to wait. Simplest of all just to leave a cheque. He'd find it on his desk and know she'd been; as soon as she wrote the damn thing, she'd feel forgiven. It was the quickest way over the hurdle. She tried the inner door, the one leading into his office, and it was open too.

Afterwards, she tried to reduce it to the barest essential. *Sarah thought he was wearing a tie.* That was how this fiction began; she entered Joe's office and Joe was wearing a tie, a bright red tie. It didn't last more than a second or so, that impression, but it was a lot more comforting than the truth. Nor was she fooled by the fact that it was Joe's own hand that held the razor.

13

THE BOAT LOOKED ABOUT the size of a matchbox if you squinted; it bobbed on the waves like a damn matchbox. Eight miles from the nearest town, and every last inch under water. There were maybe worse ways to die than drowning, but Amos Crane hadn't tried them yet. Just the thought set his teeth on edge. Probably some evolutionary memory. This was where we came from: well, he wasn't ready to go back just yet.

He had drowned somebody once, in a hotel bathroom. It had been enough to get the basic picture: the subject had thrashed about as much as he'd been allowed, eyes wide open, and must have spent every second (the process had taken a good few minutes) knowing it was all over; that he wasn't going to breathe again, and was wasting what was left of life trying. Or not wasting, exactly, because there wasn't much else he could have been doing. Saying a prayer, perhaps. With his eyes wide open and his mouth tight shut.

One way or the other, Amos Crane was glad to be back on dry land.

The harbour, what there was of it, was barely big enough for one boat: just an inlet above which twenty foot or so of rock face sheered steeply. A flight of steps had been carved in the rock, and he stopped halfway up to look back at the grey blanket of sea. Forget about the boat: the island itself was the size of a handkerchief. One decent wave, and everything local was going to get wet.

He looked down at the boat, and at Jed, who'd driven the boat here. Did you drive boats? Sailed, perhaps, though it had involved an engine. Jed was maybe twenty, had grown up by the edge of this sea, and probably thought he had a lot in common with the local rocks. He nodded at Crane curtly, now. Crane offered his sunniest smile in return. It was like watching a grave open, though Crane was unaware of this. He climbed the rest of the steps, clutching all the luggage he'd brought: a sealed polythene bag holding a teddy bear.

'An hour,' Jed called.

Crane nodded.

With his teddy bear under one arm, he turned and set off down the path to the Farm. From this point, there was a fairly good view of the east side of the island, which was not a handkerchief, not really; maybe a mile and a half in length, and shaped amusingly like a banana when seen on an aerial photograph. It was hard-scrabble land, where you still found the odd sheep skull, picked clean by the salt wind and noisy birds, though it had been years since the last shepherd packed his bags. Crane wondered why they'd bothered in the first place. Was there that much money in wool you'd spend your days on a rock that God forgot, watching a pack of dumb animals tear their lunch from the gorse and tough shrubbery? There still stood the remains of a bothy in the dip on the south side: not much more than a pile of stones arranged with a little forethought. No electric, no plumbing. Jesus Christ.

But it could have been worse. Not so far away was another island. In 1942 a small bomb was detonated there. In 1981 a bunch of scientists went back. They took a seven-and-a-half-month course of injections first, and any birds picking at the sheep skulls *there* were found dead by the bodies of their dinner.

To the west, the opposite side of the island, was a stretch of pebbly beach which rattled constantly. He'd jogged it, his last time here. There'd been no street girls or Asian porters to watch him, and stones had crept into his Reeboks.

Previous visits, Crane had arrived by helicopter, which would put down on a relatively flat, turfed expanse just behind the Farm. He had enjoyed those trips, for all they felt like being carried in a bucket. Felt himself a prince, with all the powers of the air. By the second or third trip, the pilot was showing Crane which controls did what. Now, though, there were 'budgetary restrictions', which loosely translated as 'no more helicopters'. Howard's business. Crane wondered sometimes precisely how much fun it would be to bring Howard out here: boat or helicopter, it didn't matter which. And drop him halfway like a penny in the ocean, where he would never be found, nor ever washed up. It wouldn't actually be a just return for him having spouted on about budgetary restrictions, but it would certainly make Crane feel better about having had to listen.

Thinking about Howard had him checking his watch. Round about now Howard would be getting into the office, sorting through his in tray, finding Crane's memo; which would tell him – if he didn't already know: Crane wasn't too sure about Howard sometimes; he suspected him of having hidden resources – what had happened in Oxford. What had *transpired*. Little joke on 'spire' there. In his memo, Crane had quite deliberately used the word 'neutralised'. Howard had a shit fit when words like 'neutralised' were used on paper: there wasn't a journo born of woman who couldn't translate 'neutralised' as 'killed', he said. Crane's other little joke being, it was the woman who'd been neutralised. As far as the detective was concerned, Crane mentioned that Axel had killed him.

He could see the Farm now. See its roof, anyway. Another rough-stone dwelling, though much bigger than the tumble-down bothy: this one, anyway, largely underground. Like a James

Bond hideaway, though severely low-tech; more like, now Crane came to think of it, an ancient church – one of those secret caves where the early ones gathered to celebrate Mass, always with one ear open for the coming of soldiers. Now *that* was a long time ago. Here, the Farm, was a different kind of throwback. When it was built, the people responsible had had one eye on the skies and the other on the rock. The skies were where the bombs would fall from. The rock was the best chance of surviving them.

Crane had never known, and did not particularly care, exactly what the original purpose of the Farm had been. That something nasty had been explored here was a given. Images of men in protective clothing nursing volatile liquids came to mind. But the old order, when it faded, had carried many such institutions with it: budgetary restrictions weren't entirely Howard's invention. Came the day, the Farm was shut down: he wondered now what had happened to the equipment that must have been used here. Most of it dismantled, trashed; compacted into cubes that might have been anything. But the product wouldn't have been so disposable. They could have dumped it in the sea, of course, but that would have had something of an impact on the local marine life, no doubt.

But he didn't know, exactly. That was speculation. Nowadays, the Farm was a largely empty building with a number of underground rooms carved into the rock, and as far as he was concerned, it was a great place for putting people you didn't know where else to put. Scream their lungs out, there wasn't going to be anybody passing. Start a signal fire, no one would ever see. And in the end – because it would always come to this, that was one thing Crane had learned in the business; there was always a bottom line, and everybody reached it – when you didn't know what else to do with them, you just packed your bags and left. Wave at them from the back of the boat, or the helicopter, whatever. And a year or so later you could come back and clean away their bones, because Christ knows that's all there'd be left when the salt wind and noisy birds were done.

Of course, there'd always be fuckers like Singleton and Downey.

He had reached the inner compound of the Farm now. Like its original purpose, the name was something of a mystery. No guessing games, though, about the figure waiting to meet him: he was six two, face like a brick, and wore a gun in an underarm holster. Muscle. Crane had specified muscle when he'd arranged for a team to be put together, because trainees had been used back when Downey and Singleton were here. And that was a mistake that was never going to be put right, because all the trainees were dead.

'That's far enough.'

'I'm Crane,' he said.

'Put the bear down.'

He put down the bear.

This time it was just a little girl, and her chances of causing maximum havoc had to be rated at nil. Which was exactly the same rating a number of others had given the chances of Downey turning up here, looking for her. *He'd have to be a complete fucking madman*, Crane had been told, and he'd laughed. *He'd have to be a twisted thinker*, somebody else had said. And he'd laughed again. In the end, though, he'd told nobody his true reasoning: that this was where he'd have come looking, if he'd been Downey.

Simple as that.

'Jacket off.'

He removed his jacket.

'On the ground.'

Hence muscle, he thought, as he lay on the ground.

This particular muscle kicked his legs apart so he'd have a clear shot if Crane tried anything. Then he picked the bear up.

'It's for the girl,' Crane said.

Muscle didn't say anything. He tore open the transparent bag, and dropped it at his feet.

'Before we go any further,' Crane said pleasantly, 'anything you do to that bear, I'm going to do to you.'

Muscle stopped.

'Just so we know.'

'You're Crane, huh?'

'I'm Crane.'

'You're older than I thought you'd be.'

Crane didn't say anything.

After a while, Muscle said, 'You got any ID?'

'Is that supposed to be funny?'

'Only we weren't told you were coming.'

'If you were any good, you wouldn't need to be told. You'd have seen me three miles off.'

'There's only two of us.'

'The reason I look uncomfortable,' he said, 'is because you're breaking my heart. Can I get up now?'

'I need to check you for weapons.'

So he lay there while Muscle patted him down; or patted him along, rather, Crane being horizontal. He wasn't carrying a weapon, so Muscle didn't find one. Then he was allowed to stand up.

'You haven't said why you're here,' said Muscle.

'I'm trying not to say anything too complicated,' Crane said. 'I hate to watch a grown man's head explode.'

'Fuck you.'

Crane smiled. 'Now we've done the small talk, can we go inside?'

'You've not convinced me you're Crane yet.'

'Who else would turn up holding a teddy bear?'

Muscle laughed, a surprisingly high-pitched bark. 'You really are him, aren't you? Everyone says you're a mad piece of shit.'

'I hear good things about you, too.'

Muscle spat. 'Well, you've been here before, then. Christ knows why you'd want to come back. Place is a fucking hole.'

'I'll just get my bear.'

He picked up the toy and its wrapping, then preceded Muscle to the door. As they passed through Crane paused, waved a hand: the big man went ahead. And Crane, behind him, dropped the bear; stretched lightly on his toes and pulled the polythene bag over Muscle's head, wrapping it round him with one deft twist even as Muscle reached up to claw himself free. Crane kicked his knees from under him, and he dropped to the ground still clawing. And Crane leaned forward, his right hand twisting a tightening knot in the bag, to bend over Muscle's shoulder, to watch his dying face.

'Are you listening?' he asked. 'Can you hear me?'

Muscle thrashed back and struck him in the face. Crane didn't even blink.

'You listening?'

– He thought he was speaking aloud, but couldn't be sure. Such moments always squeezed him full of joy; he could feel his own vitals, his testicles, tightening with each twist of the knot. And anyway, they never heard, the dying: that man in the bath in the hotel room; he'd been deaf at the finish too. Crane might as well be talking to himself –

'I don't care how much iron you pump,' he said. 'You show disrespect to me, and I'll cut you in half. We clear on this?'

Muscle's face was turning blue. And they were on the same side, Crane reminded himself: that was undoubtedly what Howard would say. But he'd never done one like this before. Like watching someone drowning on dry land.

From the stairs leading down to the cellar a young blond man appeared, chewing an apple. Crane dropped Muscle, who hit the floor with a thump, then flapped for a bit, reaching for great ragged breaths. Blond dropped his apple too, which hit Muscle on the head. He didn't appear to notice.

Blond looked down at Muscle, up at Crane. 'You must be Crane,' he said.

Crane nodded.

'I heard you were a mad piece of shit.'

'People exaggerate,' said Crane.

Blond was Brian. Muscle was Paul. Or that might have been the other way around. Neither was especially delighted to be here, on a lump of rock in the middle of nowhere; a place that only existed, Brian said, in case God needed somewhere to take a dump. The Farm offered nothing in the way of comfort. The walls were bare, as were the floors; light bulbs swung uncovered from the ceilings. Count themselves lucky there were light bulbs, in fact. There was no Cable, and you couldn't pick up ITV worth shit; and they only had three videos, one of which was *Dumbo*. The real *Dumbo*. The food was all tinned and the microwave was bust so they had to use the frigging *stove* to cook on. There was a cat they all hated. And, Brian summed up, nobody told them fuck all. Who was the kid supposed to be? And who could they expect to come looking?

Did they think he'd come all this way to find out if they had any complaints?

Instead he asked about the nurse, and from the looks that passed between them he knew that yes, the nurse was female, and yes they were doing her. Probably both of them. Probably not at once. So much for the lack of creature comforts, then; he just hoped they weren't doing it in front of the kid. Crane had a theory about kids: he thought they remembered everything that happened to them even before they could talk about it, and bad stuff came back and fucked them up in later life. He knew this wasn't an original theory, but that made it more likely to be true.

He didn't remember anything particularly bad happening to

him and Axel in early life. On the other hand, they were both pretty balanced: not bad, considering the jobs they were in . . .

They were looking at him as if he'd just flaked out in front of them. 'So where is she?' he said.

'Downstairs. With the kid.'

He left them discussing just how weird he was, which bothered him not at all, and on the way downstairs passed the cat on its way up. It shot past, as if it recognised him. He found the nurse in one of the former cells. The kid was with her. Dinah. For a moment, Crane was left without anything to say: how was he supposed to make conversation with a four-year-old kid? Then he remembered the bear. 'Here,' he said. 'I brought you this.'

Dinah looked at him with big Disney eyes.

The nurse was about forty, a battle-scarred blonde. Crane wondered briefly how hard she'd had to angle for the job: just her and two men, with no channels worth watching. But the way she was holding the kid, who clutched tight to her knee, maybe she had other qualifications. Her name was Deedee. Deedee and Dinah. It sounded like a sitcom.

'You're frightening her,' Deedee said.

'Me?'

'She's scared.'

'I'm trying to give her a toy. I'm not going to hurt her.'

'Have you any idea what she's been through?'

Amos Crane thought about it and decided the honest answer was yes, he had a bloody good idea. But he also decided, with a rare flash of insight, there wasn't much point in saying so. Instead he put the bear on the floor, a foot or so in front of the girl, and stepped back, looking around the room. Still very much a cell. There'd been attempts – all around the wall, at Dinah height, splashes of paint added a four-year-old's version of decoration; the duvet was cartoon lions – but nothing much could be done about the absence of windows, or the way the walls rippled here and there, where the drills hadn't sheared them smooth. Not what you'd call a nursery feel. Deedee was talking to him. 'Have you come to take her away?'

'No.'

'Because wherever she goes, I'm going with her.'

He nodded vaguely, as if answering a question. You'll do what you're fucking told. 'I haven't come to take her anywhere. I've just brought her a bear, that's all.'

'Why is she here?'

'Circumstances.'

'None of us have been told anything.'

'None of you need to know anything. Have you been with us long?'

'Seven years.'

'And how often do you get the background on an op?'

She bit her lip. On the bridge of her nose, Crane could see the pinchmarks left by spectacles: perhaps she'd just been reading to the child – a scatter of soft books lay all around: pictures of talking crocodiles and huge round babies. He realised the child was staring at him, though she'd not yet relinquished her grip on Deedee's knee. With his foot, he edged the bear a little closer. For Christ's sake, anyone would think he was going to eat her.

Deedee said, 'And what happens after?'

'After?'

'After whatever it is we're here for happens. What happens after that?'

Crane didn't have the faintest idea, nor did he care to speculate. Once or twice – not in a long time, but you could never rule it out – things went so spectacularly wrong on an op, you didn't so much mop up afterwards as hose everything down. If that happened here, the chances of Dinah being among those left standing weren't so high they'd make you dizzy. This was a shame, and would leave Crane in seriously poor odour, but there was little point in getting sentimental.

'Well?'

'Arrangements are in place. She'll be cared for.'

'Why did you come here?'

'I had to see her.' Startled into honesty, he let the answer roll around his mind another time or two: *I had to see her. I had to see her.* Back at his desk, he'd gamed the situation just about every which way there was, and there wasn't really call for anything else. There was a blip on the screen called Nurse; two other blips called Men. It didn't matter that the Nurse was also called Deedee, or that her colouring came out of a bottle. He didn't have to wrap a bag round Muscle's head to mark him out of ten. And nor did he have to see for himself that the blip called Child had Disney eyes, untidy hair like a feathery cap, and limbs like sticks wrapped in pudgy lagging. It was just . . . It was just that he'd felt so out of it, that was all. Axel playing King of the Castle in Oxford; Howard nagging him, *Amos*, whenever Axel got overexcited. Everybody on the screen, all the players, they were all more involved than he was, even the kid. He'd just wanted to take a look, that was all. So when drastic changes occurred, at least he'd know what the ex-blips had looked like.

Especially the kid. She was at the heart. It was like when a pawn reached the far side of the board, and got to be queen: one moment she didn't matter, the next she was at the centre of events.

Deedee was watching him too now, a look of quiet horror on her face, as if his thoughts had just unravelled in front of her. He wiped a hand across his mouth; tried to fit a smile there instead. She shook her head, though whether in denial at what he had said or what she'd thought he meant, he'd never know. And the child blinked. Was that the first time she'd blinked in all the while he'd been standing there? And how come she was so quiet? Weren't kids her age talking yet? The vague impression he'd had was they never shut up.

'She's very quiet,' he said.

'I know.'

'Does she talk at all?'

'I expect she could if she wanted. But she's four years old and her mother's disappeared. That's all she knows about it. Wouldn't you be traumatised?'

Crane didn't answer. And none of it signified anyhow, he thought suddenly: talking, dumb – the kid could be dead, as far as that went, so long as Downey didn't think she was. An aspect of his gaming he'd be foolish to forget: blips were, in fact, more important than the people.

He said, 'The bear's for her. Do your job. And remember – whatever happens, she'll be taken away from you. She looks just like a little girl. But it's no different from guarding a parcel.'

'You bastard!'

Maybe so. But it was said now, anyway. He turned and walked out on them, aware that if the woman had had a weapon, she'd have been a whisker away from using it. But that whisker would always be there. It was the weakness in women, he thought; that they always waited until the last possible moment instead of taking the first possible chance.

Upstairs he walked straight past Muscle and Blond, who were waiting for a chance to pump more information. The cat, which had got behind him somehow, darted out in front again: Muscle aimed a kick at it, missing by inches. 'I hate that bastard cat,' he said. Amos Crane shrugged his shoulders as he stepped into the light. He'd done what he'd intended to do; he'd given the child a bear.

Amos Crane started to jog.

FOUR

THE OTHER SARAH TUCKER

14

A LONG TIME AGO, THINGS *were simpler. The other Sarah Tucker ate what was put on her plate, never answered back, worked hard at school and passed exams. The real Sarah –* this *Sarah – grew to hate her. But she was always there, out on the fast track; making friends easily, cooking like a saint. She could sing, dance, roller skate. It was like sharing headroom with Supergirl.*

Once, she told somebody about the other Sarah: one of those mistaken moments of confidence that mark the road to adulthood like accidents mark a motorway. It reverberated round the school like a disco beat. Sarah Tucker had an imaginary friend. No: Sarah Tucker had an imaginary enemy. *Sarah Tucker was deeply weird. She'd end up in a bin.*

Meanwhile, the other Sarah Tucker had a boy for each day of the week. She did not get spots; her hair did not hang limp. Her friendships were as painless and uncomplicated as her periods, and the way she modelled school uniform made her a walking definition of Style. This was a girl to make the whole school proud. She didn't need a weatherman to know which way the wind blew.

Sarah struggled, scraped, passed by. With a handful of O-levels, ascended into the sixth form.

'And Mr Silvermann's body was behind the desk.'

'Yes.'

'Did you touch anything, Mrs Trafford?'

'You asked me this yesterday.'

'And now I'm asking you today. Did you touch anything? Did you touch the body?'

'No,' she said. 'I didn't touch the body.'

She hadn't even touched the telephone. Had left Joe's office and called the police from the pub on the corner.

'And what were you doing there, Mrs Trafford? In a private detective's office?'

There was a careful absence of sneer when he said 'private detective'. In fact, Sarah thought, you only noticed the sneer at all because of the thoroughness with which it wasn't there. She said, 'I had . . . there was a job I wanted him to do.'

'And what was the nature of this job?'

Which was policeman talk, she decided, for 'And what was this job?'

'Mrs Trafford?'

'That's private.'

He sighed. 'We're investigating a suspicious death. Nothing about it is private.'

'Was he murdered?'

'It's a suspicious death,' he repeated. 'I'll ask you again, Mrs Trafford, what was the nature of your business with Mr Silvermann?'

'I wanted him to . . . follow somebody,' she said.

'And who might that be?'

'My husband.'

'Your husband,' he said. 'I see.'

The first time she blew the other Sarah away was at a sixth-form party in a huge terrace house on the north side of her hometown. Somebody's parents were away, and Sarah went because everybody went: it was that kind of party. There was a schizophrenic soundtrack – Led Zeppelin v. The Clash; Born to Run *alternating with* Rattus Norvegicus *– and the punch was spiked with everything: by nine* *o'clock the back garden was full of vomit and thrashing bodies. Sarah was handed a roll-up – she'd smoked cigarettes before – and had already breathed it in before she realised it wasn't tobacco. The music got softer after that, though a great deal more important, and she was filled with the wonderful sensation of having done something the other Sarah wouldn't, but which was much more fun than anything the Other Sarah did.*

A boy she'd never met told her she had beautiful eyes, and she told him she wasn't born yesterday, though it felt like a lie at the time. After a while they were in the bathroom together, looking for something he kept hidden in his trousers. Eventually they found it, though it wasn't worth the bother.

Next day she was sick as a pig, and endured a fortnight's torment before turning out unpregnant. She never saw the boy again. But still remembered those first few minutes of it: not the sex, the dope. It had felt like putting down something very heavy, something she'd been carrying round in her mind. It had felt like something she'd do again.

It was easier this way. It was almost certainly safer. What she should have done, she knew, was leave Joe's office quietly, pretending it never happened; or, at least, that she'd never been there to see it. But there were other factors. The man outside the Italian restaurant, for a start; he'd seen her. And, more important, Joe himself, whom she had not been able to leave like an unmade bed, an unwrapped parcel, a dusty shelf.

She did not for a moment believe he had killed himself. Forget about the razor in his hand.

'You suspected your husband of having an affair, and set about hiring a private detective to confirm this.'

'It can't be that unusual.'

Or original, he seemed to want to say. 'But you never got to speak to Mr Silvermann yesterday, did you?'

'No,' she said honestly, offering silent thanks for that *yesterday*.

'Or actually meet him.'

'No.'

This was not denying Joe exactly. It was simply, she preferred to think, what he would have advised: Take care of yourself. Don't get involved. Look what happened to me. *My fault, Joe. I'm sorry, so very very—*

'In which case,' the detective said, 'you wouldn't expect to appear in a case file of his, would you?'

Birmingham was a large, disappointing city, neither different enough from the one she'd left for her to feel she'd travelled any distance, nor similar enough to allow her to feel at home. The streets had the same grey rained-on air, though, and you never had to go far in any direction before reaching a betting shop or a row of boarded-up windows. Clusters of warehouses dotted the landscape like enemy settlements. This was where she had come to make sense of literature, or at least convince enough people that she had that they gave her a degree. Back then, this was still thought an advantage in the job market.

They put her in a hall of residence which contravened seventeen health and safety regulations, and armed her with timetables and reading lists, and no guidance whatsoever on how to be a grown-up. But she made this discovery: that every second person she met was scared witless, and desperately trying not to show it. It was the sort of perception that bestowed confidence. She began going out; crashed parties like everyone else. The other Sarah Tucker, she left in her room.

Their first encounter was tediously banal. He was tall, blond, amused; with chinos, a white collarless shirt, a blue sweater draped over his shoulders, and the lazy good looks of a Test cricketer who never quite achieved his potential.

'Some party,' he said.

'As in good or bad?'

'Which would you prefer?'

Another poseur. She left him decorating the doorway and found another cup of sweet warm wine abandoned on a mantelpiece. The first rule of parties was, Never bring anything you'd drink yourself.

The second was, Drink anything you find without cigarette ends floating in it.

'My God, he spoke to you!' This was Mandy, a round, spotty second year.

'Who did?'

'Mark Trafford!'

'Who's he?'

'Who is *he? Only the hunkiest piece of talent in the whole of Brum, that's all. We are talking* fit.*'*

'Never heard of him,' she lied.

'But he's gorgeous*! Who did you think he was?'*

'I don't know who I *thought he was,' Sarah said. 'But he thinks he's Jesus Christ.'*

Sarah thought: *Oh shit.*

This was how it started: you told the first lie to minimise your involvement; the second followed from that. Then you found they'd known everything from the start, and basically were just keeping you talking while someone fetched the handcuffs. Joe would have kept records, that's *exactly* what Joe would have done. This policeman already knew why she'd hired Joe; knew she'd seen him more than once.

Then she realised it hadn't been a question.

They were in Sarah's house. Yesterday, they'd talked to her at Joe's, out in the waiting room, while inside the office a police pathologist had conducted the grisly routines expected of him. Then she'd been given a lift home. When this policeman – Ruskin was his name – had rung this morning, he'd said he had more questions. They'd turned out the same ones, though, until now.

'I beg your pardon?'

'I said, that would explain why there's no file on you. Though you'd have thought there'd be a note of the appointment.'

Relief washed over her, but soundlessly. She didn't respond.

Ruskin had a sandy moustache which curled round the corners of his mouth, making him look deeply unhappy about something, and similar coloured hair arranged about an irrevocable parting. Maybe this was what he was unhappy about. He had two uniformed officers with him, which Sarah thought surplus; one of each gender, they sat on the sofa, not talking. Ruskin took his own notes. Presumably, with his name, in his job, in this city, he felt it incumbent to behave in a vaguely unorthodox fashion.

He sighed now, as if reminded about hair loss. 'The thing is, Mrs Trafford, there are one or two oddities about this business.'

'You think he was murdered?'

'No, I think he killed himself. I have no problem with that.' His voice was harsh. 'He had good reason.'

'What on earth—'

'We looked for a note, of course.'

She shook her head. 'I didn't see one.'

'There wasn't one. This is interesting, though.' He produced a folded slip of paper from nowhere; he magicked it out of the blue. 'You never actually met him,' he stated.

She tried to look blank.

'In which case, Mrs Trafford,' Ruskin went on, 'how did he come to have a cheque of yours in his wallet?'

The next time she saw Mark Trafford he was in the Union bar, presiding over a discussion on Walter Benjamin: the critic as martyr. He wore the same amused expression, which she suspected only root canal treatment would shift, and the air of a man who not only has the answers but knows in advance what the questions will be. He was drinking Perrier while all around had pints of bitter. Next shout, she guessed, the groupies would be on Perrier too. She took a seat nearby so she could eavesdrop, nursing a rum and Coke, and found to her surprise that Trafford remained silent unless called on to arbitrate, when he did so with gnomically vague utterance. He was marked down by all as a sure-fire first, but she classed him now as a bullshit artist. Though knew not a whit about Benjamin herself.

Her third rum and Coke arrived apparently of its own accord. By this time she was reading a film society handout listing all the black-and-white foreign movies she'd never wanted to see and would now have an excellent opportunity to avoid as they were all showing in the same grubby little fleapit on the other side of town. She looked up to see that the alcohol was attached to Mark Trafford; setting it in front of her, he asked, 'Are you an admirer of Benjamin?'

'Oh sure,' she said. 'I'm in favour of dead critics. There should be more of them.'

'Would you like to join us?'

'No.'

It was one of those nights – any day with a Y in it – which ended in a gathering in some unfortunate's room: heading on for closing time, the bar had that tense atmosphere you probably get on the veldt when the lions draw straws to see which gazelle to have for dinner. Playing host meant no sleep till morning, and all your best records going walkabout. So it was a definite event when Trafford announced it was back to his place: the entire bar wound up at the house he shared with some other golden boys. In front of them all, when he asked her to dance she refused: she didn't dance. Ever. She said. Then dragged a scrofulous chemist in an Oxfam leather vest on to the floor for an energetic bop to 'It Takes Two'. Trafford's studied indifference made it worthwhile, though she had to dead-leg the chemist to get rid of him.

Afterwards, Trafford started sending notes: pseudily phrased suggestions that they meet for an espresso, or a cappuccino, though never just a coffee. She ignored them. When word got round that he was dating a third year well hyped as an easy lay, she ignored that too. And there were parties to dance at, pubs to discover; there was a girl who knew a guy who knew this bloke he could always score dope from. Her work coasted along on a very average average because there was so much to do that wasn't paperwork it would be criminal to *ignore it. So every third night she got stoned; every second night she made it to the bar, where Mark's coterie had a new game: trying to guess the title of his inevitable PhD. He had his eye on Oxford somebody told her, but she ignored that too. When they passed in the corridors they never spoke, but always another little note turned up the next day. A girl told her Mark Trafford was in love, though nobody knew who with. She ignored her. And then came the night of the Big Crash, when she almost ignored the rest of her life, and the holding pattern she'd fallen into crumpled while the other Sarah Tucker laughed.*

'It was a deposit.'

'It's dated almost two weeks ago.'

So why hadn't he cashed it, the stupid *stupid* fool? Dead fool.

'There's also a credit card slip for a similar sum, one hundred and fifty pounds, dated the previous week. Also a deposit, Mrs Trafford?'

'All right,' she said quietly.

'I beg your pardon?'

'I said all *right*. You've made your point.'

Ruskin glanced at his colleagues, then back at Sarah. 'You know why we're here.' It wasn't a question.

She was confused, worse than confused. She wanted them all away; she wanted to pick up the phone and reach Joe, who would assure her she'd been asleep for hours. That good old standby, *it had all been a dream*. Failing that, she still wanted them away.

Ruskin wasn't going anywhere. 'We searched his office, of course.'

'But you didn't find a note,' she said wearily.

'I think you know what we found.'

'I haven't,' she said, 'the faintest idea.'

'We found certain controlled substances, Mrs Trafford. In

quantities that would suggest your Mr Silvermann's business didn't stop at private snooping.'

She didn't believe him. She believed him, but she didn't *believe* him.

'Heroin. Marijuana. MDMA. You know what they call that, Mrs Trafford?'

She nodded, numbly.

'Yes, I thought you might. They call it Ecstasy. It's the drug that killed young Lizbeth Moss at the weekend. And I rather think we're going to find that your Mr Silvermann supplied young Lizbeth with the Ecstasy that killed her. You understand now what I mean by good reason?'

'You're wrong,' she whispered.

'Time will tell. Is that what the money was for, Mrs Trafford? Were you one of Mr Silvermann's customers?'

She shook her head. *You're crazy* was what she wanted to say, but she couldn't wrap her tongue around the words. And was afraid, too, that it was she who was crazy.

'Because I've been doing a little digging since yesterday, Mrs Trafford. And it wouldn't be the first time you've had trouble with drugs. Would it?'

Sarah felt her past open up and swallow her alive.

It was another basement party. They were always popular. 'Everybody has to go down, man. Now that's what I call a party,' some relict told her on the stairs: a relict in a T-shirt advocating the legalisation and widespread use of soft drugs. A packet of Rothmans poked from his jeans pocket like an admission of defeat.

She passed him again hours later, on her way up.

It was her first time on LSD. Dope had long been her drug of choice. Speed was okay. Sometimes she'd do a line before a party or a dance; it injected a little craziness into an ordinary dull event. But it had its downside; it wasn't mood altering so much as mood magnifying, and once when she'd taken it feeling low, she'd wound up suicidal.

Dope was safer. It made you hazy and stupid and friendly, none of which she was the rest of the time. It was a nice place to visit, though she wouldn't want to live there.

But until this evening, she'd never tried LSD.

Like most events of its kind, the party segregated early: dancers, drinkers, snoggers. The previous week, she'd spent so long with the second group she'd ended up in the third, so avoided catching anybody's eye as she collected an unattended bottle of wine and joined Jane in a corner of the drinkers' room. Jane was the only woman on her corridor she could stand. Malcolm, her boyfriend, supplied them both with dope.

'Guys.'

'Cool,' said Malcolm. He passed his polystyrene cup. She filled it.

Jane, leaning against the wall, giggled. 'Hello, Sarah. Sarahsarahsarah.'

'God, what's she on?'

He mouthed something she didn't catch.

(There'd been warnings, of course, from various authorities; even a policeman once, who had held a seminar on drug abuse. Attendance, being voluntary, had been minimal. More useful were the snippets of etiquette you picked up at parties; for instance, that somebody always stayed straight, to look after the others. In case of a bad trip . . . *What could put you off drugs faster than anything, Sarah thought, was the bloody hippie-speak you had to use.)*

'You what?'

'Acid.'

The negotiations took forever. Throughout them, Jane planet-hopped without moving a step; transfixed on the dancers – or on whatever it was she thought the dancers were – she looked like she was approaching a state of transcendental calm from a particularly interesting direction. Malcolm, though, wasn't selling Sarah any.

'It's not the money, baby.'

(Some people still thought you could still say baby *then.)*

'I'll be okay. She's *okay.'*

'Everyone takes it different.'

'I can look after myself.'

He shrugged.

'I'll stick with you guys.'

He shrugged again.

In the end, it was sheer persistence wore him down. Or so he'd have said. Sarah's own take on Malcolm was, he didn't have scruples as such, but he liked women begging him for favours. By rights, she should just kick him in the balls; this evening, though, she was grateful for the acid. Which looked just like a sugar cube.

'It looks just like a—'

'Christ, tell everybody. Just take it.'

She took it.

Nothing happened.

He told her it could take half an hour or so; that for guaranteed instant results, she should drop a laxative. For the next thirty-six minutes she counted down time, watching utterly ordinary people dancing to the most banal music ever. Her pulse remained normal. Her senses worked to rule. She'd had more of a rush from neat orange juice.

'It was just a sugar cube.'

He shrugged. 'What can I say? Some people, it's a trip to Lake Placid. Just be thankful you're not in the Palace of the Zombies.'

'What makes you so sure?'

'And you still owe me eight quid.'

'You'll get your money.'

'God is in the details,' Jane announced firmly.

They looked at her.

'God is in the sideboard.'

'What colour is he?' Malcolm asked, with genuine curiosity.

'I'll just piss off, then,' Sarah said. Neither of them paid attention. She wandered off and found another drink. In the background, the music changed from a thud to a smooch; as reliable an indication of time's passage as the dropping of autumn leaves. She checked her watch anyway: it showed a quarter to eleven. The hands waved at her, then clenched into fists.

When your watch starts misbehaving, she realised, it is definitely *time to go. More worrying was the floor. For some time it had been melting, and only a few chunks remained solid enough to stand on; it took great care to reach the staircase without mishap. The last crumb of floor hissed and sank behind her as she jumped. Everybody else was doomed. The stairs, however, were wonderful, and she determined to climb them to the top.*

It was on the first landing she encountered the sad hippie again. 'Hey, you shouldn't be going up there, man. The party's downstairs.'

'Fuck off.'

'That's cool. Hey, you, er, going to the roof or what? They got a roof up there. They keep it at the top.' He tagged behind her while she fought her way up Emerald Mountain. On each landing a small sun burned overhead, circled by tiny pterodactyls, who ate each other then shat each other out again. Ice had formed on the walls. A girl could lose herself in a landscape like this. She could just keep going up and up, where no search party would ever find her.

'You ever make it on acid? It's like fucking with angels, you know? King pleasure. You gotta do it once just so you don't die never knowing about it.'

Sarah put recent practice to good use, and ignored him.

There was, it turned out, a roof at the top. You reached it through a door marked FIRE ESCAPE *in letters formed by serpents: before her eyes they rearranged themselves into* IFOR OSTRAPE, *which was a secret message meant only for her. She pushed on the bar and the door opened with a thud. Behind her, the hippie started re-evaluating his position vis-à-vis property rights.*

'Er, should you be doing that?'

The door led on to a fire escape; an actual ifor ostrape, which ran down the side of the house all the way to the ground and far beyond. Leaning over, Sarah could make out the dim lights of hell winking miles below . . . It seemed sensible to continue onwards and upwards. The ostrape rattled and shook beneath her feet. As she climbed, the city lights grew brighter. It became apparent that this was the nub of the world; an undiscovered pole. The tragic hippie had sloped off, rattled too by her courage and daring. There was a mission awaiting her at the very top. Already it transmitted a sense of urgency, which in the dark glowed like powerful green beams.

At the very top, she found a playpen.

It was shaped like a playpen. In fact, it contained the whole world, each corner stretching far into space: in one of them lurked Jesus. In another, the holy devil. Both called to her, and for a long moment of pure luxury, she knew that she alone had the choice on which the fate of the world depended, but the moment couldn't last. It ended with her finding that she was not, in fact, alone, for beside her, the other Sarah Tucker was baring teeth in a smile of pure benevolence. There was no doubt which choice she would make. The world was snatched from Sarah's hands.

From below came a growing uproar, as assorted humans bewailed her amazing escape.

It was futile to attempt to stop her. This was the thought that embraced Sarah now. Everything has to balance. This was a truth as deep as gravity. As the other Sarah Tucker ran to her corner, the real Sarah, the only *Sarah, took the sole choice available, and rushed for the crooning deity. Because she could float, she had to cling to the railing with both hands, to keep from blowing away.*

The people from the party arrived at the top just in time not to save her. She had already remembered that here was a dream the other Sarah Tucker had never had: the dream of wingless flight, and when she let go it was with a sense of being released; of submitting to a truth that was deep, inescapable and kind. The lights of the city cartwheeled for her, as if it were the landscape and not herself that was being sucked out of the picture. One by one they winked out, and as the last died she learned about pain, and the secret of staying alive.

Later, in her nightmares, she would never hit the ground.

They searched the house.

'You have a record of involvement with drugs,' Ruskin said flatly. 'And a connection with a dead man who turns out to be a dealer. Obviously we were given a warrant.'

The female officer, who remained with Sarah throughout, kept asking if she was all right. But of course she wasn't all right: what kind of idiot question was that? From the kitchen and the rooms upstairs, she heard thumps and scuffles as her home, her *life*, was ransacked by these ridiculous men, who had already gone rummaging through her history, as if that had anything to do with poor dead Joe. It was the absurdity of their reckoning as much as anything else which had produced this numb reaction; this inability to reach for the phone and call Mark, their lawyer, anyone.

'You're very pale. Would you like a glass of water?'

But something in the voice persuaded Sarah not to respond. Something technical and efficient, reminding her that this was a cop doing a cop job, which would get a lot more awkward if Sarah were to faint.

Cop two appeared in the doorway. Ruskin came through from the kitchen.

'Well?'

Sarah saw a gloved hand; an arm sleeved in blue; and a policeman who wore a grim smile, as if his satisfaction were tinged with dirty thoughts. From his fingers dangled a polythene bag, packed with a powder so white Sarah knew it was anything but innocent.

Already, in her head, she felt the lights cartwheeling once more.

15

THAT DAY, TOO, SHE fell off the edge of the world. They took her to the police station where they questioned her ceaselessly about drugs and Joe and drugs and Joe and drugs, until she was as convinced as they were that whatever she was hiding would come to light eventually, so she might as well make a clean breast of it now. Their words: a clean breast. So she told them about Dinah and the man in the car park and they gave her a cup of tea and asked about Joe again. So she mentioned the bomb in the house up the road, and they wondered what this had to do with the drugs. The name Lizbeth Moss was remembered. Did she know about Lizbeth Moss?

No.

They supposed Ecstasy meant nothing, either.

Foie gras to the sound of trumpets.

But Lizbeth Moss was a girl who had died; a thirteen-year-old girl who had died after taking E. And they were reasonably sure that what she'd taken would match what they'd found in Joe's office. So would Sarah like to tell them again about Joe and drugs and Joe? She told them instead about the tie she thought he'd been wearing. She'd entered Joe's office and Joe had been wearing a tie, a bright red tie. She hadn't been fooled by the fact that his hand still held the razor. But when they asked why, she just stared at the ceiling.

They sighed, and wanted to talk about the money. Why

had she given a man she said she'd never met so much money? If she hadn't been buying drugs?

A few details slipped her way too. The razor, she learned, had been Joe's own. As for the bag, the bag with the *drugs*, the bag had been behind a loose tile in the bathroom; Sarah had never noticed a loose tile there. It had, in turn, been inside a small purse, which she did remember: the purse she used for small change destined for the charity envelopes that dropped weekly through the letterbox. How it had ended up full of white powder, she didn't know. She didn't even know what the powder was. (Nor did they.)

But if it's talcum powder, Ruskin said, why hide it away like that?

Eventually the questioning came to a close; a man in a uniform took her downstairs and spoke at her in a rather formal though meaningless manner, and this either meant she'd been charged or not charged: she wasn't too sure about the details. Then they let her use the phone, and unable to remember Mark's work number, she called home just to hear his voice on the answering machine. He cut in almost immediately.

'Where the *hell* are you?'

She started to cry.

It was eight in the evening, this was what frightened her. They had kept her for hours, and she no longer knew where she was, or how to respond. It seemed like days since she'd slept. Everything that had happened before finding Joe had happened in another life. She dimly remembered a girl on a towpath, a girl who had not been Dinah: had there ever been a real Dinah? And remembered, too, the man in the car park, Michael Downey, the one with the hair. What was it he'd said? That he was a friend of the Singletons. *All of them.* Sarah wondered if he'd killed Joe.

This she brooded on through her tears: her tears were a mask so they'd leave her alone. Up to a point, that is. And up to a point, they worked. She was given a glass of cold water and tepid sympathy by an Asian policewoman who kept calling her Sally; kept asking, too, if it was coke she needed; if she was starting to get the shakes. Sarah cried some more to shut her up. And before these tears dried Mark arrived, together with a man she recognised, Simon Smith, who carried a black briefcase and spoke very loudly about lawsuits. He seemed to be enjoying himself. Mark, though, was livid.

'Who the *fuck* is in charge here?'

The Asian woman gave Sarah a look of shared citizenship. As if they had this in common: loud male voices which knew they were right.

What she remembered afterwards were harsh details: the lighting, the shabby paintwork; a voice in the corridor complaining about a database being down. But of the human contact, of Mark's intercession, almost nothing remained. At one point he hugged her, it was true, but it was the smell of trains and smoky rooms on his jacket that stayed with her. It was the irritation in his voice as he spoke of how worried he'd been, as if everything that had happened to her had been just another way of something happening to him.

Later, he'd say, 'It's all that Jewish detective's fault, isn't it?'

'Why say that?'

'Well, if it hadn't been for him—'

'Why say Jewish?'

'Oh, Christ, don't start playing PC games. I just meant he was Jewish, that's all. He was, wasn't he?'

He had been. That much was true.

But that was later, when they were home. Though in fact not much later, for Simon Smith's talk of lawsuits, along with his lethally efficient briefcase, had them out on the pavement by nine. He could, he said, have got them a lift home in a cop car, but it didn't always pay to be too pushy. He was of an age with Mark, but a savagely receding hairline gave him an authority Mark was still aiming at. He also had the smallest teeth Sarah had ever seen.

'But you should have called me yesterday,' he said. 'We could have nipped this in the bud.'

'I didn't *know* about it yesterday,' Mark said, exasperated. He ran a hand through his own thick hair. He often did this in Simon's company. 'I mean, nobody tells me *anything*.'

They both looked at Sarah. But she was transfixed by the passing traffic; the bright headlights slicing up the evening.

Simon hailed a taxi. The way he climbed into it left no doubt that getting into taxis was a way of life with him; something he had aspired to, earned, and enjoyed demonstrating in public. 'Call me later,' he said to Mark. It was about halfway between advice and instruction.

They walked the rest of the way in silence, though the electricity generated by what Mark wasn't saying buzzed in Sarah's ears. She felt disoriented, out of it; the time she had spent in the police station already receding to the status of a bad dream, but one she had yet to wake from. She wanted Joe, that was the worst of it. She wanted Joe to tell her what was happening; more importantly, to tell her it would stop. But Joe was dead, and when alive his advice had never been top-notch. Already she was mythologising. Pretty soon, Joe would be everything her father had never been. He'd be the husband her mother had wished for her.

Her own real husband had been that once, though he was falling down on the job badly now. 'I have my keys,' he said redundantly as they walked up the garden path, as if affirming a disputed claim to home-ownership; he opened the door and allowed her in first, the kind of gesture he insisted on when pissed off. So she was waiting for the lecture; prolonged silence always led to the lecture. It was the last thing Sarah needed, and a list of the first things would have filled a book: a hug, a bath, an ear, some sympathy. But once inside Mark went straight to the phone: not the one in the living room, but the extension in what he claimed was his study, though had never been more than a den. It was where he read Q magazine and listened to Oasis on headphones. He had never really lost his youth; he just kept it in a small room off the landing.

In the kitchen, Sarah spent a short while picking things up and putting them down again. This was the room Ruskin had searched, and the effect now was of having endured an untidy guest. Small objects – a sugar bowl, a mug holding pencils – had been shifted from their accustomed positions, reminding Sarah of one of those magazine puzzles: *What is wrong with this picture?* But you had to have lived in it first. Upstairs, Mark hung up the phone, then dialled again. The phones, at his insistence, were the old-fashioned, alarm bell kind. It had been a fad at the time; part of a trend that had done its best to suggest that adherence to tradition was a form of integrity.

She adjusted the calendar, which was hanging out of true. The rest of the month was a chequerboard of appointments and deadlines: visits to the dentist, bills to be paid; black scrawls noted weeks in advance, when there had still been a chance that they might be important. For Joe, there'd be no more of this. For Joe, the weeks and months ahead would remain blank; the calendars unbought. This was what death was. It was the point at which calendars were wiped clean, and all the pre-Raph ladies and Warhol etchings decorating them blurred into nonsense.

On the stairs, the thump of Mark's feet. He entered the kitchen guns blazing. 'You realise this couldn't have happened at a worse time for me?'

'I didn't have a great day either. Thanks.'

'Oh, that's right. Turn it into my fault. What got into you, Sarah? Coke in the bathroom? For Christ's sake!'

She did not need this argument now. On the other hand, it was all that was on offer. 'I didn't put it there.'

'Are you saying I did?'

'No, of course not!'

'So what happened, the police planted it? Is this one of those seventies things? The pigs framed me, man. It was a bum deal. That it?'

'You're being ridiculous.'

'*I'm* being ridiculous? Well, thank God for that. I knew one of us was off the wall. Sarah, when I went out this morning, you were a housewife. I come home, you're public enemy number one. What the fuck is going on?'

'I don't *know*.'

'Well, who does, then? Yesterday, you find this man dead in his office. You told me you'd never met him before, that you wanted to hire him to find this girl you'd never mentioned either. Am I on the right track so far?'

'I didn't tell you because I knew you wouldn't understand. And I was right.'

'Today it turns out he's running a Colombian franchise in north Oxford, and half my income's in his bank account. Not to mention his product under my bathroom sink. Which part haven't I understood yet, Sarah?'

'None of this is true. This isn't what's happening.'

'What *planet* are you on, woman? Of course it's fucking happening! It's half past nine, I haven't eaten, I've just dragged you out of a police cell. How real do you want it to get?'

'I. Don't. Take. Drugs. Joe. Doesn't. Sell them.'

'Not any more he doesn't. And whose word do we take for your being clean? Have you forgotten what—'

'*Of course I haven't!*'

There was a ring at the doorbell and Sarah burst into tears; events so perfectly synchronised, they might have been a Pavlovian illustration. Mark looked at her for a long while. He started to say something, changed his mind, then went to get the door.

The sugar bowl was still out of place; the time still out of joint.

When next she was aware of company, it took the form of a man she had never met. He was gently guiding her to sit, as if this were his kitchen and Sarah some waif wandered through the back door; he was speaking, but the words rushed past in a warm, musical flow. This was a trick everybody used when speaking to a strange dog or a grizzling baby, and a sudden flash of anger riled her entire body. But it left as quickly, leaving only tremendous tiredness, and the relief of having somebody not barking at her. So Sarah cried herself out; it did not make her feel noticeably better, but at least released tears that had been building since she found Joe's body.

The man – Sarah already suspected he was a doctor – made her a cup of tea.

She could never remember what he looked like. Small and shiny was the best she could manage in retrospect, and even that was a mental quirk: he could have been a hairy giant, and still seemed small and shiny afterwards. The same general size and shape as a little blue tablet. But at the time, what mattered was his voice. Though when she could make it out, what he actually said was: 'Why don't you drink that, and tell me all about it?' So she drank the tea and told him all about it, or as much as she could recall. About her day being ripped from her, replaced with a nightmare of custody and harsh questioning; about a drab room with overhead lighting, and nothing to mark the passage of the hours but the constant ringing of phones. And when she ran out of words, a new need sprang to the top of her list: it was to wallow in silence; to have everything about her wind down and come to a halt. Instead, there was the drumming of fresh rain on the kitchen window, and the raggy breathing of this small shiny man as he waited to be sure she was finished. Even the sound of her tears, drying on her cheeks.

'You'll be all right,' he said at last. 'Here. Take this.'

He handed Sarah a small blue tablet, then poured her a glass of water, which he placed in front of her, removing her teacup first like a fussy monitor.

'What is it?'

'Does it matter?'

'I don't like to take pills,' she said softly.

The lights cartwheeling in her head. Stan Laurel removing his face.

'It'll relax you, that's all. It's ninety-eight per cent herbal.' He carried the teacup to the sink and rinsed it under the tap.

Ninety-eight per cent, leaving two. The precise figure, the transparent honesty of it, left the very small part of her untouched by the day's tensions howling in scorn and hurling daggers at his back. Was she supposed to break down and cry again? Thank him for his *maths*? While her right hand curled and its nails bit her palm, her left took the pill and steered it to her mouth. She swallowed it without the water, her mouth still awash with her tears.

He left her then, and went to talk to Mark. She sat waiting for the pill to take effect; to feel its little blue wonder spread through her body. This didn't seem to happen. But some degree of calm arrived, she thought from the sound of the rain, and little by little she felt the panic leave, and her stress level out to a straight, flat line. The front door opened, then shut. She was alone once more with her husband.

Who ushered her upstairs with a minimum of conversation. 'You're to have a bath,' he said, as if he'd been the recipient of complicated medical advice. 'Then get some rest.'

She wondered how much the doctor charged for his instructions. A million zillion pounds, her lazy brain decided. A million zillion trillion pounds.

Later, in bed, she found the energy to ask who the small shiny man had been.

'Someone Simon knows,' Mark said shortly. 'He'll be back in the morning. Simon, I mean.'

'Why?'

'For God's sake, let's just try and get some sleep.'

It came, in the end, easily enough, and was deep and entirely without dreams. She woke to a hand shaking her shoulder; the hand was Mark's, and his other held a cup of coffee. 'Take this now,' he said, putting the cup on the bedside table, and placing beside it a small red capsule; identical in all other respects to the previous evening's blue.

'What's it?' she said, or tried to say. Her voice lost in the thick canyon of her throat.

'Never mind what it is. You're supposed to take it now.'

I'm not ill, she wanted to tell him.

'You've been under a lot of stress. Look, I know it's hard, darling. I wish I could stay with you, but it's all so bloody hairy at work . . . I'll call later. Simon's coming at eleven. I've reset the alarm. Just take this before I go.' He bent and kissed her.

It was only for the kindness in his voice that she took the pill.

She slept again, but woke before the alarm. She did feel better. The situation remained, but seemed a lot less urgent somehow; certainly yesterday's anxiety had been siphoned off in the night. Nor had appetite replaced it; the muesli she'd been looking forward to was gravel in a bowl. She couldn't remember her last meal. But it wouldn't hurt to skip a few.

The kitchen was a mess; bits and pieces all topsy-turvy. It didn't seem to matter, though. She had another bath.

Simon turned up, indeed, at eleven. It took immense effort to get him in, sit him down, ask about coffee, do the kettle, and she had to force herself to focus while he made a phone call in response to his beeper. This was important, what was happening now. Something about drugs in her bathroom. Simon's call was short, sharp, effective; when he hung up, the receiver made a noise like a cash register. This wasn't a social occasion. She had to get a grip.

'What happens now?' Her voice sounded tinny in her ears, like a mono recording.

'Your case is referred to the CPS. They decide whether or not to bring a prosecution.'

'And will they?'

He sighed. 'Does the name Lizbeth mean anything to you? Lizbeth Moss? A thirteen-year-old—'

Who had died last weekend after taking Ecstasy. Yes.

'They're not going to wag their fingers at you and leave it at that, Sarah. This Silvermann character, he was what, forty-something? Pushing pills to schoolkids? If he wasn't dead, they'd crucify him.'

'He didn't do that,' she whispered.

'And there you go. You told the police you didn't know him, and you know what? They don't believe you. Now you're defending him. What's the story, Sarah?'

She didn't reply.

'They've got a waiter from the restaurant opposite Silvermann's says he saw you going in exactly when you say you did. But when they showed your photo to a couple of blokes working on the pavements down the road, they say they didn't see you. They were on their tea break.'

He paused while this nonsense sunk in. Still, she didn't respond.

'But they recognised you anyway. They said you'd been there a couple of weeks back. Let's add this up. You're denying you ever met this man but they've got *proof* you passed him money and witnesses that you visited his premises. They've got coke they found here and more coke they picked up at Silvermann's office, in a quantity large enough to suggest he was dealing. You don't have to be Sherlock Holmes, Sarah. They think they've got this wrapped.'

He let that sink in while he drank his coffee. And in truth, it sank in easily enough: she felt amorphous, a human sponge. Everything he said, all it meant, she absorbed in an instant. It didn't matter much, that was all. Joe was still dead.

She took a sip of her own coffee, but it was tasteless, watery. Simon didn't seem to notice. The way his lips pulled back over his tiny teeth, you'd think he was enjoying the taste. Enjoying something.

'Now, what we have to work out is exactly what happened.' A response seemed required.

'I didn't do anything wrong,' she said.

'You don't have to tell me that.'

She didn't have to tell him that. But not because it went without saying. Simon Smith was Mark's friend, old buddy, and the Pals' Act was operating here. She didn't have to tell him she wasn't guilty, because he didn't much care either way.

'But what you are going to have trouble denying is that you were found in possession of four grams of cocaine. Unless you're going to suggest the police planted it.' He waited, to see if the idea took root. 'The SODDIT defence,' he added helpfully. 'Some other dude did it.'

This is my life, she wanted to scream at him. *This is not a joke.* But that voice was very far off; in another county, perhaps.

'Not that that'd go down very well. Let's face it, you don't exactly fall into the right demographic group for a police fit-up.' He made a circular motion with his hand by his face; semaphoric shorthand for a wealth of race relations. 'Which leaves us with your basic unanswered question. Unless you're saying Mark put it there.' A little light shone in his eyes here, as if the Pals' Act had just been revoked, and replaced with something much more fun.

No. She wasn't saying that.

The light went out. 'Okay. You want my best advice? What

Mark's paying for. Tell 'em the coke was yours, quote Silvermann as your source. Personal use only. Book yourself some therapy.'

'What?'

'You've been out of work, depressed, these things happen. It's the noughties, nobody'll bat an eyelid. Any other week of the year, I'd have them writing apologies while I slapped them with a writ for trespass. But less than a week after this kid gets iced taking a happy pill is *not* the time to ask the courts to take a progressive view of recreational drug use. So what we do is, we bend with the wind. It can't have escaped you, bright woman, what the police are really after. They want someone they can hold up to the press, say, "This is the one did for Lizbeth Moss." Then it's pats on the back all round, and everybody goes home early. Get it?'

She got it. She just didn't quite believe it, that was all. 'Trust me. If they can nail Silvermann as a source, it'll take a lot of the heat off. This way you become his victim, same as Lizbeth but luckier. You're a nice, middle-class woman, they'll go easy. Sort out a trick cyclist, they like that. Shows good faith.'

'But he didn't do it,' she whispered.

'Silvermann killed himself, Sarah. The police can make that look like a signed confession. They've got a result here and they don't want the waters muddied. Look, that stuff about possession, forget it. None of this'll reach the courts. They try pressing the charge, I'll ride a battering ram through that search they made, though I have to tell you it'd be a lot easier if you'd called me first. Still, under the bridge. What matters now is, you've got to give a little to get a lot. If they think you've got away with something, you'll just put their backs up, and that kind of trouble you don't want. Not if you'd like the rest of your life to consist of something other than parking tickets and nuisance phone calls. So give them the chance to be heroes, then you can melt into the background. Simple as that.'

Through the window, out in the street, Sarah watched a

blackbird come down to land. It strutted up and down the garden wall, then came to a full stop, its gaze seemingly fixed on her. But you couldn't really tell with birds, on account of their eyes being on the sides of their heads. It was an effort to concentrate on what Simon said. She had no trouble comprehending the enormity of it; it was just an effort, that was all. 'I can't do that to him.'

'Joe is dead, Sarah. Sad but true. Look, if you mattered to him as much as he obviously did to you, he'd understand. You can't help him now. But he can help you.'

Simon thought they'd been lovers. He was trying to keep the knowledge from his tone, but failing dismally. He thought they'd been lovers: did Mark think so too? Lovers and fellow druggies when, Jesus, she hadn't used drugs for . . . hours.

He stood suddenly and clipped up his briefcase. She hadn't even realised he'd unclipped it. It probably came as naturally to him as a cabbie turning the meter on. 'It's up to you, of course. Entirely up to you.' There was a *But* coming. 'But think about what I've said. I'll call Mark later.'

Of course he would. That was what old pals were for.

Once he'd gone she tried to think about it, but much of what came to mind was outside the scope of Simon Smith's understanding. If she closed her eyes she could still see Joe, his hands neatly arranged on the desk in front of him; the right clasping a wooden-handled razor blade. His shirt front stained by the passage of his blood. But while she could see it she had trouble believing; not just that he had taken his life, but that he was in fact dead and would remain so. What she half expected was the leap back from the grave, the ironic bow; the horrible silence of the onlookers breaking up as they realised that this death had been staged for their benefit, and rather than the final curtain was the prelude to an encore, to consist of the artist's smug satisfaction at having hoodwinked the crowd. If she closed her eyes she could still see Joe; when she opened them, she hoped to be in Modern Art Oxford, watching guerrilla theatre. Instead what she got was the shock of the now: she was here, at home, today. *Bam bam bam!* If he wasn't dead then, he certainly was now.

And just as he'd been wiped out of this life, so, it seemed, had she been wiped from his.

For there was no trace of Sarah Trafford, née Tucker, in Silvermann's files. Was Joe the man to be slapdash about paperwork? She didn't think so. It was true that he had not banked her cheque, but that came under a different heading: he might not get a thing done, but he'd have written down somewhere that he was supposed to do it. She could count the hours she'd spent with Joe on her fingers, but she knew him enough to know this; that there'd been a file with her name on it somewhere in his office. So somebody must have removed it, and this after killing Joe; it was the reason she knew he'd been murdered; why she'd never been fooled by the set-up. Joe had been killed; she had been warned. That was all they wanted to do at the moment: warn her. Whoever they were. And this was what passed for a warning; fixing her up as a loop in a drugs ring.

Gerard Inchon.

She yawned enormously. It was puzzling, this; one part of her mind was working step by step through the process that had killed Joe and left her in the trouble of her life, but most of her just wanted to lie down. She forced it further, though. Yes, Gerard Inchon had done this to her. Probably. The logic that put him into the frame escaped her for the moment, and it was true that she could not imagine him sneaking into her house, finding the purse, doping it up and concealing it in the bathroom. Or even, really, slitting Joe's throat with Joe's razor. Which only went to show, she yawned again, that he had an accomplice. More than one. Somewhere, he'd hidden Dinah Singleton. There must be people looking after the girl, unless she was dead too. This was as far as she could think at the moment. She really was wiped out.

But there was one more thing; something she had to pin down. The bottom line. The bottom line was, *they* had killed Joe. They'd kill her too, if she caused more trouble. There: a simple conclusion. The whole idea was, not to rock the boat. *You'll be wishing you were bored again. Soon. Trust me on this.* Gerard again. They had hidden all trace of the search she'd made with Joe, just to show they could alter the truth. Now all she had to do was alter it too, and she could settle back into normality.

It wasn't such a big thing. Joe was already dead.

An image came back to her then, of the man who'd shown up in the car park. The one everybody thought was dead. Michael Downey.

Now *him*, she could picture slitting Joe's throat.

All she had to do was tarnish Joe's name.

She wanted to weep but felt dried of tears, unequal to the effort demanded by grief. It was too much of a decision to take right now; besides, so much of it seemed to have been taken for her. She would rest now, and later think things through. Nothing in this world was so bad that a nap and a pill couldn't ease its sting.

She slept; later, she set about making a stew. There was comfort in a routine performed times without number, and what would normally have taken twenty minutes took two hours. Then she watched the second part of a film on TV, and though characters jumbled in her mind, the soundtrack provided clues to the story. By the time Mark arrived, a shade earlier than normal, she was in pretty splendid fettle. Couldn't remember, in fact, why she'd been so troubled before her rest.

'Simon show all right?'

'Yes, dear.'

He gave her an odd look. 'Everything okay? You're feeling all right?'

'Yes. Great. Fine.'

Once they'd eaten, Mark spent a good while on the phone. He seemed distracted afterwards. Sarah cleared the dishes, though it didn't feel like an urgent task. Habit, mostly. Much of her portion of stew she wrapped in paper and stuffed in the bin. Her appetite hadn't returned. It wasn't anything to worry about.

Later, in bed, Mark talked to her. 'Did you take the pill?'

Another blue one: sitting on her bedside table when she returned from the bathroom. 'Yes.' She had.

He put his arms round her, pulled her close. 'I've been worried about you.'

'Sorry,' she said, muffled by his grasp.

'But it'll blow over. Simon's got it in hand, he says. I'm glad you're going with his advice. He's good at what he does. Good man.'

So there it was. She'd taken the decision already. No need to worry.

'This man – Silver?'

'Silvermann.'

'Silvermann. You and he, you weren't . . .'

'No.'

'I thought . . .' He expelled air slowly, though didn't relax his grip. 'Doesn't matter. Doesn't matter what I thought. We'll get through this. Promise me that?'

She promised.

'You know what I don't want? I don't want you turning back into the girl you were when I first met you. Remember how you used to be?'

She remembered.

'This drugs business, I thought maybe you were turning back into her. The other Sarah Tucker. That's the way I think of the girl you were then. The other Sarah Tucker.'

That wasn't the other Sarah Tucker. This is the other one. That one was me!

'Better now, though. Everything's all right now.'

She could feel him growing against her. He rarely spoke about how they'd met, the times she'd cooled him off, but when he did, it invariably turned him on. It was as if, after all these years of making love, he still wanted to fuck the one who got away.

My diaphragm, she said. She could have sworn she said it aloud. I won't be a minute.

Mark, it seemed, didn't have a minute to spare.

16

BLUE PILLS AT NIGHT to ease Sarah's fright. Red pills on waking to quiet her shaking. They worked, though soon this became less important than their function as reminders, little nudges, of the world that waited for her when she ceased to take them. The world she'd fallen off once already. As the days went that world grew fuzzy at the edges, but this might have been the after-effects of shock rather than tranquillised stupor. So she told herself, and the calm the pills brought made it easier to believe. A spark of surviving cynicism flared into occasional life, to point out that anything the pills helped her believe was not to be trusted, but the voice itself hardly inspired faith; squeaking in the early hours, or while she was coming round from her afternoon nap. Mostly, she ignored it. Mostly, she got by.

Simon solved her problems. Police contact was minimal. She signed a statement saying that the cocaine in her possession had come from Joe Silvermann; that she had twice bought drugs from him; had met him in a pub. This cooperation, Simon assured her, effectively ended official interest in her. He smoothed a hand back over his pate as he spoke. He was the only man she had ever heard use the expression 'totty', and this was what she was thinking of when she failed utterly to thank him, leaving Mark to do so with that look of exasperated patience rapidly becoming his trademark. Little fragments of memory kept doing that; jolting loose at inappropriate times. Mostly, they were of no relevance. Sometimes they concerned Joe, but even these were usually painless.

Painless, too, were her nights; dream free and long-lasting. Mostly they began with Mark making love to her; she could not remember him so ardent since their early days, and even then, he'd often needed encouragement . . . More and more, in place of dreaming, she was wading back into her past: not the muddy, confused arena of the recent past, but her student days; the aftermath of her accident. The first few hours were a closed book, but the time in hospital seemed oddly fresh now, as if the current regime had opened doors in her mind she could step through like Alice through the glass. She replayed these times on waking. Sometimes they felt like the first days of her life.

She had been a very lucky girl. This is what she was told over and over, and where she once would have insisted on 'woman', she now accepted the demotion as another element in her humiliation; the insult they added to the injury she'd brought on herself. She had broken three important bones and four minor ones, when by rights she should have been dead; she had missed the iron railings when the combined laws of gravity and physics suggested she should have impaled herself at least twice. She looked like a human mnemonic, a living reminder of the colours of the rainbow. But the bruises would fade, and the only permanent scar lay on her upper left arm, usually hidden from view. For a while the doctors worried about other, hidden, scars, but she seemed to have suffered no brain damage. A counsellor was assigned, though, to remonstrate about drug abuse, and this Sarah suffered as meekly as she did all other treatment, though it was the least necessary. Her psychedelic period was on its way out; would be gone forever once the bruises vanished. She had discovered for herself that the immortality drugs bestowed was purely temporary. More importantly, she had convinced herself she would never be able to fly.

There were visitors. Because she had succeeded in making few friends that term – it had felt like a success at the time – she was swamped with callers during her first week: all the guilt-ridden types, mostly religious, who knew a cry for help when they saw one, and blamed themselves for not having been *supportive*. They included a tall, acne-scarred youth who had asked Sarah out back in October, and whom she had told to piss off; he arrived with a Welsh second year who was rather short but otherwise a perfect match. They brought grapes, and sat holding hands while they ate them, and Sarah suspected she was being shown what she'd missed. Seven broken bones seemed a small price to pay.

But in the absence of a hospital bed conversion, or at least an admission of romantic regret, the visits tailed off before a fortnight was out. Term had ended, and those who might be expected to have an at least theoretical interest in her well-being now had other calls on their time: exams to mark, parties to attend, important stuff like that. Her parents came, though, and wept by her bedside; whether for her injuries or her behaviour she could not tell. Her convalescence at home would no doubt clear that up once she was discharged, which would not, the doctors warned her, be for at least another fortnight. They thought it was a warning. It sounded to her like a reprieve. For two weeks she could lie in this administrative limbo, suspended in a pause between acts. All she had to do was whatever she was told, which would be nothing more taxing than drinking *this*, swallowing *that*; trying to get some sleep now, dear. Limbo was for those denied heaven. It was also a loophole for those otherwise destined for hell.

But on the first afternoon of the second week, Mark Trafford turned up; from a dream in which the words 'ifor ostrape' echoed like an ambulance siren, she woke to him by her bed, balancing about thirty books on his knee while making notes in a loose-leaf binder. He looked like a parody of a bookworm, down to the scarf wrapped twice round his neck but still long enough for the ends to trail on the floor.

'Why are you here?' Even to herself, Sarah sounded under water. *I R OO EE?* She cleared her throat and tried again.

'Be quiet. I'm working.'

Charming. Whose bed was it anyway? She thought of a very smart remark in reply, but not until she'd fallen asleep again. Next time she woke he was gone, though he'd left the collected works of William Blake on her bedside table. At first she thought it was a gift, but when she saw the paper slips marking his places, she'd known he'd be back.

One way or the other, he never went away.

Red pills on waking to keep Sarah faking; blue pills at night, to see her all right . . . It was the twelfth morning after the crash – the fourteenth since Joe's death – that she found where Mark kept the pills, and it only took this long because it had not occurred to her before to look for them. His warning that he'd be late home sparked it off. A little nudge of worry (you couldn't call it panic) that he'd be very late, *seriously* late, which would leave her lacking her bluey. This was Mark's word: bluey. He didn't call the red ones reddies, presumably because that sounded ridiculous.

They were in his bedside cabinet. Two plastic tubs, each labelled with Mark's name – not hers – above an indecipherable doctor's signature and a wealth of ominously medical syllables, spelling out to the initiated exactly what they were. She took them downstairs, thinking she'd check them against the medical dictionary. For some reason it hadn't occurred to her before that these things might not actually be doing her any good. Well, obviously they were doing her *good*, but they might not be doing her any good just the same. But the dictionary was not where it ought to be.

It didn't matter. The urgency had passed; the point was, she wasn't going to run out in a hurry. Sarah left the tubs on the sitting room floor, and went to make coffee: not because she wanted a cup, but because it was eleven o'clock, which was when people had coffee. It comforted her to keep routine in place.

Her neglected cup beside her, Sarah was back in the sitting room five minutes later, staring at the tubs. Light as babies' rattles, the pair of them; it was how light they were encouraged her to open them up and count their contents. The little plastic arrow on the lid lined up with its counterpart on the tub. Still, she had to prise quite hard to release it, and when it came free it did so with a jerk that scattered pills across the floor; a wave of little red marbles, maybe similar to what you'd find in a baby's rattle. Who knew?

The second opened easily, and she poured the blueys into a neat pile. When she'd gathered the reds, their pile was smaller, which probably meant there were a few escapees out there; under the sofa, smuggled into corners. A while now since she'd seen such places, pushing the Hoover round. Maybe later. For now, tidying up meant getting these pills in their tubs. She counted them first, though, and because she kept losing her place, lined them up in rows to do so. They looked like little soldiers, or possibly small bombs. It had been a while since she'd had thoughts about soldiers or bombs, but she was having one now.

The doorbell rang.

It felt like the very next thing: she was bent over the kitchen sink, vomiting, somebody holding her from behind, pressing bunched hands into her stomach, the taste in her mouth, underneath the acid vomit, of salt water, very salty water. She did not remember opening the door, though obviously she had done. Which had surely been a mistake, though this was the oddest form of attack she could—

'And again.'

She was hauled upright, a glass pressed to her lips. Two fingers pinched her nose, and there was the salt water taste again, and another trip down to the sink, where, for all her retching, all that came up was the salty bloody water.

As a form of punishment, it was as effective as it was undignified. Sarah was already sorry, and promising that she would never do whatever it was she'd done again.

'Okay, drink this.'

Plain water this time. Though her stomach trembled on the edge of another heave. Just in case.

'You about to throw up?'

She shook her head.

'It's your floor.' She was led to a chair where hands pressed on her shoulders, forcing her to sit. 'Speak when you can.'

Words strangled in her mouth. She wanted to spit, but swallowed instead. It was her floor. 'I wasn't . . .'

'You weren't what?'

Another swallow. 'I wasn't going to take them.'

'If you say so.'

'Just . . .' Just what? She couldn't remember.

'No harm in being on the safe side, though.'

'Not to you,' Sarah managed, sharing a little of the bile.

'My, we *are* feeling better. Remember me?'

Sarah looked up, and the movement made her squint. Tears flashed into her eyes. She shook her head.

'I'll give you a clue. We only met the once. I was on my way out already.'

Dark curly hair, dark eyes, laughter lines. She wasn't laughing now.

'I think you got my husband killed, lady. Remember me yet?' said Zoë Boehm.

*

'So how was London?'

'Not as nice as Paris.'

'Joe thought—'

'Joe thought he was a detective. There wasn't a day went by he didn't know where my credit card was. His mistake was assuming I was with it.' Zoë lit a cigarette, and dumped her burnt match in the sink. 'Joe wasn't as good as he thought he was. Oh, he had a good telephone manner, and that Oxbridge kick impressed the middle classes, if not as much as it impressed him. Once in a while he'd find somebody who didn't want to stay lost, and if one of the cleaning staff dipped into the petty cash, hell, Joe was your man. But he was operating with a serious handicap, Ms Tucker. He had the emotional age of a twelve-year-old. He was a bit of a fool, a bit of a liar, and he was the world's softest touch, as I'm sure you found out for yourself.'

'Some obituary.'

'It's not over. Because some things he didn't do, Mrs Trafford, or whatever you're called this week, and one of them was drugs. He didn't use them. He didn't sell them. Somebody killed Joe, and whoever it was planted that stuff on him. When I find him I'll have him chopped up and fed to pigs. Him or her.'

'You think it was *me*?'

'What I think is, two weeks ago he was alive. He gets mixed up with you, and now he's not. What I think is, when Joe boiled a kettle, he opened a file on it first. And there's no paperwork on you in the office. Not a scrap.'

'Maybe he forgot.'

'Joe kept a list of the lists he kept. He was more likely to forget to put his trousers on. No, whoever killed him removed your file. Why do you think he did that, Mrs Trafford?'

'I don't know.'

'How fascinating. You told the police the day you found him was the first time you set foot in his office. Why'd you lie?'

'I was scared.'

'Of the police?'

'Of everything.'

'That's your first clever thought. Because let's face it, Ms Tucker, you're short of friends. The cops think you're a junkie, and nothing about the scene through there suggests you're not. And that's as good as it gets. Because if you *didn't* kill Joe, you've got his killer to worry about.' She dropped her cigarette into the glass of water where it died with a fizz. 'And if you did kill him, you've got me.'

'I didn't.'

'You told the cops you bought coke from him. Why?'

'I . . . don't know.'

'Somebody put pressure on?'

She tried to think that through. 'It's what . . . they wanted me to say.'

'They?'

'Everybody.'

Zoë nodded; was already lighting another cigarette. 'That the same everybody got you eating tranks like Smarties?'

Her stomach felt raw; her head, oddly, was clearing. 'Was he really your husband? He never said that.'

'Surprise surprise,' said Zoë drily. 'We were growing apart. Separate prescriptions and everything, you know?'

She shook her head.

'I can read, Tucker. Those pills through there, it's your husband's name on the tub. You open the door like it's the night of the living dead, and have you looked in a mirror lately? Always assuming you still reflect. Now, either you're doing this to yourself, which makes it a guilt trip, which makes you guilty, or somebody's doing it to you. And like I said, it's your husband's name on the tubs. So where does he stand in this?'

'Nowhere. He doesn't stand anywhere.'

'Sure. I never met a husband yet who wasn't the innocent party.'

'Speaking as a detective,' Sarah managed.

'Speaking as a woman.'

'How long had you known him?' It was true she was curious. But a change of topic wouldn't hurt either. 'Since college?'

'Hah! Nearest Joe got to a college was parking on a double yellow line.' But for the first time, Zoë Boehm looked fraught. Coming into strange houses, employing DIY suicide prevention measures, none of that had fazed her. Talking about how she'd met her husband, that called on other reserves. 'We married young,' she said at last. 'We were *in love*. Hell, we were kids.'

'It didn't last.'

'It did for Joe. He was a kid till the day he died. Shit.' Amazingly, she started to cry. 'The stupid stupid *bugger*.'

'I'm so sorry.'

'He never had the slightest fucking notion. That there were people who might do him *harm*, that this stupid daydream of his might get him killed.'

Her own feelings were coming back to life now. Largely, they were physical: a raw acidity inside, and a tingling of the skin down her arms and legs as if from a rash. She was still in her dressing gown. It was only now that she realised this, along with the equally depressing fact that she'd been sick on it. Other than that, there was a large emotional numbness, though not of the anaesthetised type she'd grown used to. This was more like being trapped inside a balloon, which pretty soon would burst.

She strained at the edges. 'It wasn't daydreaming, Zoë. He was good at what he did.'

'Oh, tell me about it.' She sat on one of Sarah's chairs and lit another cigarette, making no attempt to wipe her tears. Possibly she thought smoking would dry them. 'Joe once got arrested looking for a lost dog, but even he couldn't get killed checking out some errant husband's office help.'

'He was looking for a child.'

'A specific one, I suppose. Yours?'

She shook her head.

'Do I have to pull your toenails out?'

'What did you do in the firm?'

'Worked the phones, mostly. And no, I wasn't his secretary. Ninety per cent of the job's the phone. This kid could be in Alaska, I could find her without leaving the office. Happy?'

'I want to be sure, that's all. He's dead, okay? You want me to point you in the same direction?'

'It is a guilt trip.'

'That *doesn't* make me guilty.' Her flash of anger expired, leaving her weary and next to tears. That was the trouble with emotions: once they started coming back, they chose their own order. 'There was a bomb,' she began at last. 'Up the road. It pushed a house into the river.'

The high-pitched sirens, keening over the rooftops . . .

Zoë fanned cigarettes out on the table. She'd smoked two and a half of them before Sarah reached the end.

They were silent for a while; Zoë finishing her smoke; Sarah drinking tap water, her throat raw from speaking, retching and passive vice. She had told Zoë little about the events since Joe's death, but her own state said all that.

'You're saying you've been warned off,' the woman said at last.

'Uh-huh.'

'Joe gets killed, you get warned off.' She seemed to consider this sexist as much as anything else. 'This guy, what was his name, Downey?'

'Michael Downey.'

'Six footer, late thirties, well built, stringy dark beard and a ponytail tied with a red rubber band. Carries a blue canvas bag over his shoulder. Wears a denim jacket. Warm?'

'He wasn't carrying a bag,' Sarah said numbly.

'Well, he was yesterday.'

Sarah opened her mouth, shut it again. Waited for Zoë to explain.

'I came by. You weren't alone, you had a couple of visitors.' Wigwam and Rufus, Sarah remembered. Wigwam doing a lot of creative enthusing about Sarah's achievements, Sarah's interior decorating skills, Sarah's cookery; her attitude a warm amalgam of supportiveness and solicitude, with just the faintest hint of sympathy, as if Sarah had recently won only a small amount on the lottery, say, instead of having been arrested and so on. Rufus, true to form, had chosen an armchair and ceased to exist. It wasn't so much that they were an odd couple; they were very nearly an impossible one. Faced with them yesterday, Sarah's calm stupor had come close to shaking to bits. *What happened happened*, part of her wanted to scream. *Let's stop pretending it didn't.* But at least Wigwam cared. 'In the afternoon?'

'Friends, yes.'

'He was watching the house.'

She could feel the balloon straining apart. 'My house,' she said flatly.

'He's not there now.'

She didn't know whether to laugh or cry. So if he's not there now, where is he? Should she call the police? And tell them what?

'You think he's the one killed Joe,' Zoë said.

She nodded, numb once more.

'But you've no real reason to think so.'

'Why else would he be watching? He gave the warning, he planted those drugs. Now he's just keeping an eye to make sure . . .'

'Make sure what? You don't make a mad dash for freedom and justice? Round up the bad guys? Pardon me, Tucker, but you look like the only dashing you're doing any time soon is to the bathroom.'

'Thanks a lot.'

'There's just one thing you have to do.'

'Oh, isn't that *wonderful*. At last, somebody who can tell me what to do. Have you got a ticket with a number, or did you push in?'

Zoë Boehm said, 'I'd forgotten, you bite. Sometime when you're firing on all cylinders, we can exchange recipes. Meanwhile, what you do is, you do this. You call the police and tell them it was garbage, that statement about Joe selling drugs. It's a simple thing. It's called telling the truth.'

'Are you crazy? That's *exactly* what this hairy lunatic *doesn't* want me doing.'

'Hell, Tucker, what's he going to do? He kills you, they'll actually start looking for him. Which he's gone to some trouble to avoid, up to now.'

'That's a big comfort.'

'This might come as a shock, but right now I'm more worried about the damage you did Joe's reputation than I am about anything that *might* happen to you. You know damn well he wasn't dealing, and it's only the fact that you look about two steps from a boneyard that stops me holding you over a phone and choking it out of you. So why don't you have a shower, get dressed, remember where you left your principles, and do the decent thing? Who knows, it might get to be a habit.'

The force of which took her breath away. Another new emotion, shame, came tumbling after the others. 'I never . . . Yes . . . I didn't think.'

'Doesn't look like you were given half a chance,' Zoë muttered. She picked up her bag, hooked it over her shoulder. 'I'll call you tomorrow.'

'To check up,' Sarah said numbly.

'Oh, I'll have done that long before then. But I'll call you anyway.' She cocked her head to one side. 'Look, don't feel too bad. It's not that I blame you. Your position, I'd have done the same.'

Somehow, Sarah doubted it. One thing bothered her though.

'If you loved him so much, why did you keep disappearing on him?'

'Who said I loved him? That was over years ago.'

'So why all this?'

'Because when a woman's partner gets killed, she has to do something about it. It doesn't matter what she thought of him. She has to do something about it.'

'I don't get you.'

'The Maltese Falcon,' Zoë said. 'Believe me, Joe'd have understood.'

17

SHE LEFT. SARAH SAT once more, feeling sick, weak and hungry all at once. The hunger didn't last. Most appetites seemed distant now, as if she could only focus on one point at a time, her current target being the retraction of her statement to the police – a necessary truth whose one saving grace was, it need not involve Simon Smith.

But though inevitable, it didn't have to be immediate. She showered and dressed, and made herself eat a boiled egg; and while it was a strain not to be plucking at the curtains, checking for strangers in the street, she succeeded at this too. Then she sat with the newspaper cutting Joe had given her, retrieved from a jacket pocket. She had put Downey in his early forties when she'd first seen him, from the bridge. The more generous Zoë had him late thirties. And Zoë was right; he had been thirty-four at the time of his supposed death, making him thirty-eight now. The hair added years. But what did he want from her? He had been looking for Dinah too, but why did Joe have to die? A lot more questions hovered. None with obvious answers attached. While she had the nerve, she made her call. Ruskin was unavailable. When would he be otherwise? About five, maybe six. She said she'd call back. Afterwards, she slipped into a waking doze. One of those almost states, where the clock still ticks and traffic goes by, but inside everything comes to a halt. When the phone rang, she almost hit the ceiling.

'You sound breathless.'

'I'm okay.'

'Did I wake you?'

She glanced at the clock; it had just gone five. *What am I, a baby?* But she bit it back. 'I'm okay, Mark. Really.'

'Fine. Good. Just calling to remind you, I'll be late back. A meeting with one of my accounts. Could be ten, even later. Don't wait up.'

'Mark?'

'Yes?'

Down the wires the silence pulsed. All of it carried from one place to another at the speed of electricity.

'You sure you're all right?'

'Uh-huh.'

'Okay. Call Wigwam or somebody. Have company.'

Always the assumption that Wigwam was at her beck. It irritated her that he was probably right.

It would be forever before they'd speak again. She hung up not knowing this; dialled the police while she was at it. Ruskin was in.

'You want to *what*?'

'It wasn't true.'

'What makes you think I give a—' There was a strangled arrest; the crash of a receiver being dropped, or maybe slammed. Then: 'Are you still there?'

'Yes.'

'Are you aware what a retraction will mean, Mrs Trafford? Have you taken legal advice on this?'

'Why is it I need advice now when before you were quite happy to—'

'Apart from the other implications. Wasting police time, that's still an offence.' They should lock up the whole bloody world, his tone implied. 'Making false statements.'

'It's because I don't want to—'

'Not to mention the matter of the other charges that might still, might *still*, be levied against you. You're into serious waters here, Mrs Trafford. You want to think very carefully before going any deeper.'

It had been on the news, she dimly recalled. The man who sold E to Lizbeth *Moss. Pusher cheats justice.* No wonder Ruskin was coming on like a shark.

'Are you listening, Mrs Trafford? Can I make myself plainer?'

'No, you listen to me. The statement I made, I made under duress. *Duress.* I'll be at the station to make a fresh one tomorrow. Failing that, I'll be calling a press conference. Your call, Inspector.'

Two could crash a phone.

For minutes afterwards she trembled on her feet; unable to move, unable to do anything. Except wonder, naturally, what precisely she had just done; and how, *precisely*, she would suffer the consequence.

She did not call Wigwam. Mark did that for her: she arrived a little after six thirty with a half-hearted attempt at just dropping in, which did not survive Sarah's opening sally.

'He said you sounded fraught. I think that was the word.'

'He's turning into my keeper!'

'We've all been worried, Sarah,' Wigwam said, without a hint of reproach.

It was the nearest she had come to making reference to Sarah's troubles.

'I have been,' Sarah admitted now. 'Fraught,' she said.

'I'll put the kettle on,' Wigwam said. 'And you can tell me all about it.'

But Sarah couldn't. It was not that she didn't want to; more that she wouldn't know where to start. And felt, too, something of what it would be like to listen to a friend, however close, tell you they were at the centre of a giant conspiracy in which men with beards lurked, wishing them harm. You would have to love them very much not to feel enormous pity.

She countered a yawn. This terrible lethargy; it needed fighting. Needed shock.

Wigwam sensed Sarah backing away, but did not press her. Instead, she returned to Mark. 'He called me from his office,' she said, investing the location with an awesome significance: she really was impressed, the love. The nearest Wigwam had been to working in an office was dusting somebody else's desk. 'You could hear all sorts in the background.'

'They were probably playing cricket,' Sarah said.

'It was his *office*.'

'They do that,' Sarah said. 'Bins as wickets. Paper for balls. You hit the fax machine, it's six and out.'

'He sounded ever so busy.'

'Maybe it was his turn to bowl.' She was tired of this already. 'Wigwam. He spends all day sitting in front of a green screen, making phone calls about money to other people in other banks. All of them sitting in front of the same green screen. Every day, you make more human contact than he does in a month.'

'Oh, I *like* my jobs. But they're not important.'

'Neither's his. It doesn't add or subtract a single sou to the sum of human happiness.'

'Would you rather he'd been a teacher?' Wigwam asked, a little wistfully. Wigwam had wanted to be a teacher.

'I'd rather he was happy,' Sarah said. And filled in all the blanks in her head: if he'd finished his doctorate, got the right fellowship, got stuck into his book . . .

Not married me, she thought with sudden clarity. To remind him of his promise.

And there was a thump on the doormat, as something dropped through the letterbox.

'Bit late for the postman,' Wigwam said. 'Do you want me to get it?'

'It'll be one of the free newspapers,' Sarah said. Though it wasn't, in fact, it was a letter; addressed to her in a hand she didn't recognise, and amended by several others, since the original writer had transposed the house number. *Try 217* had been added, along with *Try 271*. Postmarked two weeks earlier. Looking at it, holding it in her hand, Sarah felt her heart unaccountably sinking; as if she too had spent the last two weeks misaddressed, and was now back where she ought to be, which was not a good place at all.

'Are you all right?'

'I'm fine,' she lied absently.

'Aren't you going to open it?'

'Later. It'll keep.' But her mind was focused on it now, and for all Wigwam kept rattling on, Sarah heard barely a word.

'Because of her t'ai chi lessons,' Wigwam finished.

'. . . I'm sorry, Wigwam. I was drifting.'

'Caro's looking after the babies,' she began again. Wigwam always called her children babies. 'But she has to leave at eight fifteen because of—'

'Yes. I got that bit.'

'So I'll have to be back by then. But I'll send Rufus round to keep you company.'

'That's okay.'

Wigwam's face twisted into an awkward expression. 'We—ell . . .' she said.

'What's the matter?'

'Mark made me promise,' she confessed, 'I'd not leave you on your own.'

So what does he think I'll get up to? her inner voice snarled. *Mainline baking powder?* And then thought: no, what he's worried about is, I'll not take my pill, I'll start to be a nuisance, I'll get into trouble.

I'm already in trouble.

She thought the letter meant trouble: that's why she couldn't keep her mind off it. So to calm Wigwam down, she agreed that Rufus could come round if he must, though she had work of her own to get on with – letters to write – and would absent herself while he settled in front of the telly. A scenario which made her want to gag, actually, but better by far than actually watching it with him, or talking to him; or anything, in fact, involving being in his presence. Not that she could express any of this to Wigwam. So instead she kept herself nodding and smiling, feeling long-slack muscles in her cheeks stretch to aching point, while Wigwam ran through the local gossip one more time. All Sarah wanted was for Wigwam to go, so she could open the damn letter and find the worst. Her best friend, whom she felt she hadn't talked to for months, and all she wanted was for her to go.

Which she did, eventually.

'You're sure you'll be all right?'

'I'll be fine.'

'I'm sure Mark won't be *too* late.'

'Wigwam. I'll be fine.'

She closed the door gently but put the chain on, too, once Wigwam's steps had echoed out of hearing.

In the sitting room she sat for a while with the letter in her lap. It was from Joe. She knew that already: didn't know the handwriting, but knew it was from Joe. Too like him to get her address wrong. With anyone else, that would have been a nuisance; from the private detective, it was a kind of quiet joke. Joe once got arrested looking for somebody's dog: hadn't Zoë told her that? Couldn't detect his way out of a paper bag; but she helped him out of the envelope, anyway; unfolded the first sheet and read it through twice:

Dear Sarah

I suppose what I should have remembered is, we all have to exorcise our own demons. Who am I to tell you to stop looking?

No matter what it is you're looking for. So this little girl, since she's so important to you, I hope you find her, though I still think we went barking up a wrong tree yesterday. I shouldn't have got angry, though. I told you I'd help: I should just help. Even if that means driving to Surrey on a fool's errand. Better, I think, to start with the obvious. I enclose a copy of a letter I've sent to the Ministry of Defence. According to their press release, Thomas Singleton died four years ago, so how come he died again so recently? Perhaps they know nothing about it. If not, better they join in asking the questions, don't you think? They're much more likely to find the answers. And wherever the answer to Singleton's death lies, I think you'll find his daughter there also.

And if they do know all about it, they'll understand that a few discreet answers now might save them a lot of press coverage later. They are great pragmatists these days, Sarah, the men in suits. All they need do is give a little, right? Save you causing more trouble.

I get the feeling you could cause a lot of trouble if you tried. I'll be in touch. Joe

The enclosed letter was as he said it was: a formal *Dear Sir* laying out the bare facts of Thomas Singleton's death and his daughter's disappearance; all neatly typed; every spelling in place. He'd even put his own reference number down. This, too, Sarah reflected, had been removed from his office files. Or Zoë would have found it; Sarah had the feeling *that* woman would find pretty much everything she put her mind to.

On a sudden impulse, the kind best acted upon immediately, she picked up the phone and called Directory Enquiries, or whatever they were called these days, and after a very short wait was given the phone number to go with the address Joe had sent the letter to. She wrote it on the letter itself in big red marker pen, the only kind near to hand. Maybe she would call. Not now, obviously. Other impulses were best slept upon; they had to be given time to go away. That was as far as she'd thought things through when she heard the rapping on the door – on the back door.

Which led nowhere. Which led to the back garden, and it was true you could squeeze past the hedgerow at the far end and reach the street behind through the side passage of the house they backed on to, but nobody did this, not even burglars. Sarah didn't know the neighbours in that direction; wasn't even sure the word 'neighbours' applied. All of which suggested an unwelcome presence, but unwelcome presences didn't knock, and there was no getting round the fact that what she had to do now was stir herself, walk through to the kitchen, see who it was. It was Rufus.

Her reluctance mingled with relief, she let him in. The time it took her to reach the door, a number of horrors had ripped through her mind; none specific, but each shaded red, the colour of Joe's shirt afterwards. Even Rufus was an improvement. She let him in, closing the glass-paned door behind him and turning its key once more.

'Hello, Rufus.'

'Sarah.'

'Why the back way?'

He shrugged.

Even arriving alone, Rufus had the air of somebody tagging along. It bordered on spooky.

'Wigwam said you needed company.'

'I'm all right. Really.'

''Sno bother.'

He wandered through the kitchen, into the sitting room. It should not have been surprising that at a time like this Sarah should feel she didn't know Rufus, because she didn't. Times she'd made the effort to draw him out had been for Wigwam's sake, and wholly unsuccessful. Mostly because Rufus wasn't interested in anything. For all the impact he made, he might have remained in that limbo where all the people you've never met live.

'Would you like a cup of tea?' she asked.

'Cheers.'

So now she had to make him a cup of tea.

She put the kettle on, rinsed a cup, thought about it, rinsed another. The idea of food still made her gag, but she had to get something inside her. Meanwhile Rufus called from the sitting room, 'It's started. I heard earlier.'

'Started?'

'The War.'

'Thee' not 'thuh'. And 'War' not 'war'. There'd have been a glint in Rufus's eye, too: war did that to boys. Last time, they'd played in sandpits on the TV news.

But she had nothing to say. Nothing to offer. They'd be striking each other dead in the East right now – more charred corpses soldered to their tanks – and she wanted to know nothing of it, an ignorance as easy to achieve as turning off a radio. They'd yet to pass a law demanding you were well informed. During wartime, that was the last law they'd pass.

The kettle boiled. She made the tea. She passed a cup to Rufus, who had come through from the sitting room, and who took it by the base, apparently not noticing how hot it was. He cleared a small space for it on top of the crowded fridge, then dragged his warm fingers through his hair, a gesture that recalled him pulling his mask off. But that had been when he was Stan Laurel, and now he was only Rufus.

'She talks about you, you know. All the time.'

'Wigwam?'

'Before, it was how *nice* you are. Sarah says this. Sarah lent me that. These days, it's poor Sarah. All the time. Poor Sarah.'

'She's a good friend.'

'She's a soft touch. I can't really imagine you two being pally.'

'You don't have to imagine it,' she snapped. 'It already happens.'

He grinned, pleased about scraping a nerve. And there was the malice she'd glimpsed when he'd frightened her in town: if he hated her so bloody much, why was he here anyway? Because Wigwam asked him? All he'd had to say was no.

He plucked a magnet from the door of the fridge, examined it and put it back. 'Been resting up then, have you? After your bother with the cops.'

'I don't really want to talk about it.'

'Suit yourself. What's to talk about anyway? You're scoring dope, you got caught. End of story.'

Sods' Law, this, that now she *really* wanted him to blend into the wallpaper, he'd discovered he'd got a tongue.

'Rufus—'

'It's okay. We've all been there.'

'Look, Rufus, it's kind of you to come round. But it's really no problem. Mark'll be back soon and I don't want—'

'No worries. All I'm saying is, that should have been it. You know? You've got the cops leaning in one direction, you've got your nice cosy life in the other. It doesn't take a genius to figure out when it's time to quit.'

She rubbed her temple. There was a sharp pain buried there, and if it ever got out it would make a noise like a banshee. It was about now she'd be taking a blue pill, if she was ever going to take one again. The thought came to her unbidden that a whole stretch of her life had just come to a close, and it wasn't the absence of the pill that rang down the curtain.

'So what you doing still writing letters, Sarah? Your Jew boy's dead. Can you not take a hint?'

*

Nothing changed. The ground beneath her feet crumbled and gave, but that was all. And the only things she could think of to say were the hackneyed, the clichéd, the grim:

– *What did you say?*

– *You can't be serious!*

– *You don't mean you—*

So she said nothing.

But Rufus said, 'He to protect you, was he? Big strong man like him? Case you ran into any *bad guys*?'

'It was you. You were late turning up that night the bomb went off.'

'Mmm hmm.'

'Only nobody took any notice. Because even when you're there, you're hardly there.'

He grinned and hid his face behind his hands. 'Peep-oh!'

'Who are you?'

'Call me Rufus.'

'Who are you?'

'But my real name's Axel. Hey, what do you think that fat bastard would make of *that*?' He twisted his face into a pompous mask: not at all a bad Gerard, actually. 'That's not a *name*. That's an *abomination*.' Then untwisted, and was Rufus/Axel once more. 'Course, under fresh circumstances, I'd wipe the fucking floor with him.'

'*Who are you?*'

'I'm your bad dream, Sarah,' he said. 'I'm the stair that creaks when there's nobody home. I'm the light that goes off without warning.' He produced, from behind his back, her copy of Joe's letter; the red marker pen bawling out her intentions for the world to see. 'I mean, what the fuck *is* this? Your friend is dead, Sarah. Not to mention well stitched up. And you've got coppers wondering when you'll start shopping for a new freelance chemist. You were *supposed* to give it up.'

'I did give up. I have.'

'So why the letter? Why the phone number? Why couldn't you just let it *be*?'

She looked behind her, at the back door. The key had gone. When she looked round, Rufus held it. He smiled, and dropped it in his cup of tea. 'Won't be needing *that*.'

'You killed Joe. You planted the coke.'

'And you just had to get back on the bus, didn't you? What is it with you, is it the kid? Is it still the kid? She's a *little girl*, Sarah. There are fucking *hundreds* of them.'

'Where is she?'

'That doesn't matter any more.'

'Is she alive?'

'Do I care?'

'What are you going to do?' she whispered. Her voice barely staining the quiet air.

'I'm going to kill you,' he said patiently. 'What did you think I was going to do?'

'But they'll know, Wigwam'll *know*, she'll tell—'

'Christ. Sarah, do I care? I'd have been out of here weeks ago already, if it weren't for you. Six months I spent married to that poor cow.' He reached something down from the fridge: she couldn't see what it was. 'And just between you and me, I'd have had more fun sticking my dick down a rabbit hole. Ill of the dead and all that, but—'

'*No*!'

'Oh yes.'

'No. You can't have. You mustn't—'

'Sarah. Listen to me. You stuck your nose in something bigger than you know. And me, well, my job's to go round cleaning up other people's mess. It's a filthy business, but guess what? I love it. I mean, I *really* get off on it. Which was bad news for the missus, but hey, them's the breaks. And as for you—'

But he couldn't have killed Wigwam he couldn't have killed Wigwam he couldn't have killed—

He put his hands together, then pulled them apart. A thin cord appeared between them; he did it again. Now it was a double strand.

'As for you, I get the feeling you'd be a wet one.'

And again. It was dental floss, Sarah realised with a curious absence of shock. He was unreeling yards of dental floss, and folding it into a loose rope.

'Sadly, I'll have to make do with the foreplay.'

He snapped the cord and let its plastic box drop to the floor; then, with a quick twist of his hands, took a firm grip on the ends of his rope. It looked laughable, somehow. It was also quite enough to kill her.

'Shocking area. Do you know, they had two murders round here last year? Some mastermind put away his wife. The other one, they never caught him. Robbery gone wrong, they said.'

'Was that you?' she whispered.

'Course not. You've got it upside down. Nobody's gunna think *I* did *that*. They're gunna think whoever did that did you.' He experimented with his noose, giving it slack, then pulling it taut. Something in the process satisfied him.

The only way out was the front way, through him, and to get through him she'd need a weapon. This was the kitchen, the most dangerous room, but the knives hung in a rack by the fridge, well out of reach. She threw her tea instead, and he hardly noticed. Still hot, it splashed into his face, and he laughed. The cup glanced off a shoulder and bounced to the floor. Sarah rushed him. She didn't make it.

Somehow he was behind her; he had her in his arms and the dental rope looped round her neck was already strangling. She kicked, stamped, and thought she connected, but his grip did not weaken and he gave no hint of pain. When she tried again, he had moved. And he was right, he was her bad dream; one in which all her struggling left her more securely knotted in its grasp. Her throat was on fire now, and her tongue too big for her mouth. Strange pictures rushed to and fro in her mind as her frantic brain searched for a solution; meanwhile her body thrashed in panic, her hands grabbing at anything in reach. She pulled on the fridge door, which opened with a jolt. A carton of milk leaped out and burst on the floor. The white puddle spread out before her eyes just as a black pool opened behind them. She could feel herself falling into one or other: black, white, it didn't matter. No use crying over . . . Her hand closed round something. It felt absurdly like an asthma inhaler.

And this was Joe, come back from the dead to save her. The rape alarm he'd given her fitted like a grenade in her palm.

She raised her hand above her head, to *Rufus's* head, and depressed the trigger. And there was her banshee, wailing into the world just as the pain in her head exploded: an explosion that came like a gush of air as he released his grip while the noise bust his ears; came with light too, as the black pool vanished and familiar objects swam back into view. There was no time to cherish them now. She struggled free of his grasp, dropped the alarm; its scream whipped once round the room and died. Sarah had sunk to her knees.

She tried to stand, but slipped in the milk and fell headlong to the floor. Behind her Rufus cursed, something insane and biblical, before reaching down; intending to beat her to death with his fists. Which was not how she wanted to die. But the slick floor defeated her attempts to flee, and her throat hurt, and there was not enough air in the room to feed her lungs . . .

The back door splintered open. It was like watching a glass firework. And Sarah saw hair and teeth and a man in a crouch, his arms outstretched to make a point that was ugly, black and useful. It coughed twice. Above her Rufus bloomed red, his throat a holy mess of blood. And then, leaving a fine pink spray behind him, he was down, forever out of view, while she lay in a mess on the floor, wondering if she'd faint.

In the event, she didn't.

18

Some hours later, Amos Crane stood where she'd been standing, looking down on the vacant space where his brother had died. A faint misting of blood on the floor described the shape of Axel's head, as if death had reduced him to little more than a stencil, though it took a brother, probably, to read *Axel* into it rather than any other damaged head. Howard was there, and a number of local cops, and a man in a suit in the corner, his own head safe in his hands, who'd turn out to be the householder, Amos expected. The owner of the house where his brother had died. Looked at dispassionately, it had long been on the cards that Axel was going to die a violent death: no point blaming the bastard in whose house it actually happened. Looked at less dispassionately: fuck that. Amos would blame who he liked.

Howard came over. 'I thought this was a loose end Axel had dealt with.'

'It must have frayed.'

'It's the same woman, right? I mean, please tell me this is just a continuation of the same fuck-up, not a whole new one?'

'To you it's a fuck-up, Howard. My brother's dead.'

'Oh, Christ.' Howard pulled a tired hand down his tired face. 'I'm sorry, Amos. I didn't mean any of that. Axel – he was one of ours. Not just yours.'

'Sure he was, Howard.'

'But this – you're aware there are civilians here, Amos? I thought we'd been through this.'

'Maybe you can dock his pay.'

And Amos turned away abruptly, to the back door, to a litter of broken glass and shards of door frame. That was where the soldier Michael Downey came in. Not a difficult assumption to make. If it had been just Axel and the woman, it would have been the woman's blood on the floor, and he – Amos – would have been home in bed. And Oxford would have had another burglary gone wrong . . .

The fix, this time, would be tricky as sin. More than just the old school tie and the whisper of a gong; it would take serious handshakes and money in envelopes. No wonder Howard was wetting himself.

Oh, Axel, he thought, almost aloud. You stupid fucking—

But there was no time for that. This was damage limitation. He felt glass crunch as he stepped into the dark to look at the night sky: the heaventree of stars in all its evening glory. *Think!* He thought. Axel had been here, and for reasons best known to himself had decided to terminate the woman. Up until this evening, that hadn't been necessary – maybe *wasn't* necessary; maybe Axel had just been slipping the leash – but it was a field decision, and had to be given the benefit of the doubt. And he'd tried, and he'd used dental floss (which was possibly a first), a loop of which was still wrapped round his fist when they'd bagged the body, and he hadn't managed it because somebody had kicked the back door in and taken him down with two bullets.

Had to be Downey.

Which left them where? Which left the woman who'd been looking for Singleton's daughter on the lam with Downey, who was also looking for Singleton's daughter. Put that way, the situation hadn't changed. Downey had company. That was all.

But there was an alternative scenario: the woman screams

blue murder, and takes it to the press. But that, too, could be dealt with. Amos Crane went over in his mind what he knew about Sarah Trafford: unemployed, restless, history with drugs. There wasn't a great deal you had to add before you were dealing with a paranoid hysteric finding conspiracies round every corner, and on a day when war had broken out, the press would have better things to think about. As for Downey, he had his own reasons for staying dead. He'd not be bothering the media in this lifetime.

Not going to be a very long lifetime, either.

There was a crunch, and Howard appeared behind him. 'We found this,' he said. Wordlessly, Amos took it: a crumpled sheet of paper, with a London number scrawled across. 'The Ministry,' Howard said.

Amos looked again. It was a copy of the letter Howard had shown him two weeks back. It had been sent by the detective hired by Sarah Trafford, an unwelcome display of persistence forcing Amos to allow Axel to deal with him. Which Axel had done *very commendably*, to the benefit of all around; following it up with an excellent piece of freelancing which, if there'd been any justice, would have shut Sarah Trafford up without further pain. It was a good rule of thumb not to damage civilians, a rule Axel hadn't always followed but had produced a textbook example of in this case. And look where it had got him.

Still, it was good to know he'd had reason. In his shoes, Amos would have done exactly the same: killed the silly bitch. Nobody got two warnings.

Howard shifted uneasily. 'We need a game plan, Amos.'

'I'm thinking.'

'Think faster.'

'Thank you, Howard. That's the husband back there, is it?'

'He's a banker. Works for—'

'I know what he *does*, Howard. I'm asking if that's him.'

'It's him.'

He was problem number one, even Howard had worked that out. But Amos knew something Howard didn't: the husband was dirty. The dirty ones were easiest to deal with.

It was one of Amos's rules: when you had an agent in cover, you researched *everyone*. Even if the agent wasn't your brother . . .

'The body went out clean. Nobody knows there was a death here.'

'Except the husband.'

'Well, he found him . . .'

'And the locals.'

'It was the locals he called, Amos. Obviously.'

So nobody knew there'd been a death here, apart from absolutely fucking everyone.

'Where have they taken my brother, Howard?'

'They've taken him to the local place, Amos.' Morgue, he meant. Not place. Morgue. 'But we'll have him moved. Back to London.' Where he'd be more comfortable, Howard's tone implied. Where Amos would be able to visit; maybe take him flowers. Grapes.

'What time was he found?'

'A little after ten.'

'And was he still warm?'

Howard said nothing. He was thinking: Jesus Christ Almighty.

'Howard?'

'I don't think Mr Trafford checked.'

'Good point.' Amos looked up at the stars again. Civilian finds a body, he doesn't automatically start processing the data. Especially when the body's in his kitchen, and his wife's nowhere to be seen. 'But he can't have been dead long. Not that it counts. An hour, hour and a half, any kind of head start, someone with Downey's experience could be underground by now.'

'It's coming apart, Amos.'

'Things have come apart before. We're all still here.' He looked back through the kitchen, at the husband sitting in forlorn isolation. 'Anyone been round to Axel's place?'

'Hmm?'

'He lived with a woman. *Married* her, for God's sake.' Taking professionalism *way* too far, but that was Axel: it was often hard to tell when he was taking the piss. 'She had kids. Well, still has.'

'What do we tell her? That he's dead?'

'I don't think so.' What he did think took a moment or two to emerge. Axel had been on the point of bailing out: if that had happened, he'd have been just another husband coming to his senses. But circumstances no longer allowed for that. 'No, I think we'd better make him a terrorist.' That was the thing these days: most people could believe anything without hardly trying. Your husband? Your husband of *six months*? Well, you didn't really know him at all, did you, madam? Fact is, he's on the Most Wanted, and he only married *you* for the cover. And now he's gone. And you'll never see him again.

'Do we use the locals?'

'I think you'd better do it, Howard. It'll come better from a suit.'

'And what about the husband?'

'Oh, I'll deal with the husband.'

He turned away. After a while, Howard took the hint, and left him to the stars and his deep thoughts.

Which only looked deep. From long habit Amos Crane was able, at times of stress, to empty his mind. He did that now: for twenty minutes, more or less, he was just an upright body in the garden; at one with the dark and the waving trees. He didn't think about his brother, or the mess in the house behind him. He didn't think at all. He just allowed events to catch up with him; when he was ready, he'd be beyond the primary stages of grief: there'd be no struggling past denial, or reaching for acceptance. What was done was done. Something had happened here, and Axel was dead. This didn't mean the game was over. It just meant there was greater reason to win.

He remembered the moments on the island: wrapping the bag round that idiot Muscle's head. And he thought how fine it would be to have Downey here now: just the two of them, unarmed in the dark. We'd see how well he fared without a gun in his hand. We'd know what his flesh felt like when we ripped it open, and delved beneath.

Amos Crane shuddered at the memory, a memory from the future.

Then he went back into the house, to sort out the husband.

FIVE

BUDDY HOLLY'S LAST WORDS

19

THROUGH THE WINDOW DARK scenery rolled past, but all Sarah could make out was the gaunt reflection of her face superimposed on the landscape, as if she were one constant against a restless background, and all the things she had no control over, starting with events and ending with her own thoughts, were unfolding beneath her serious, fractured surface. Outside were empty fields and damp trees, but she was thinking about a cat; about watching a cat through a door darkly while it mocked her unfitness for life on the other side of the glass. Which lay now, she remembered, in splinters across the length of her kitchen floor.

Michael Downey had dropped the gun in three different drains between the house and railway station: the gun itself, its silencer, ammunition; all done with perfect fluidity, a dip and a drop with no hint of a stumble, so that even a close watcher would have had difficulty being sure that he had seen the actual disposal of a murder weapon rather than a clever mime. Throughout, Sarah succumbed to circumstance. *Your best friend's husband tries to kill you; your bogeyman blows him away.* Her options seemed limited, somehow. All she had taken from the house was her wallet. All it contained was twenty-odd pounds.

They had followed the dark route by the river; across the old railway bridge and over the meadow by the ice rink, through whose windows she could make out the sweeping presences of a few after-hours skaters, still at work on their figure eights. Then into the bright lights: this main road skirted the city centre. Cars whistled by. A garage dribbled neon in oily puddles. Groups of teenagers strutted past, on their way to a desperate-looking nightclub.

The station was up a gradient that seemed steeper after dark; its fluorescent lighting spilled through automatic doors like a promise of safety. Reality began seeping back into Sarah, together with an ache in her calves that served notice of how fast they'd come. She looked at Downey, and for the first time his hand fell from her elbow, as if he were offering her a choice of destination. His eyes were very dark.

'Where are we going?'

'Up there.'

'But I can't just—'

'Trust me.'

Trust him? The man was a killer.

A platoon of taxis streamed past, their beams picking the couple out like searchlights in old prison movies. A London-bound train was pulling out of the station. It moved slowly over the bridge across the road, its innocent passengers gazing down on the traffic below.

'He wasn't the only one,' Downey said suddenly.

'What?'

'That guy who tried to kill you? There'll be others.'

Something very like a wave came close to breaking inside her. 'What's going *on*?' she whispered. 'I don't even know what's happening here, there's madmen all around me . . .'

Now a police car flashed past, its American lightbar leaving a fresh blur hanging in the air like a ghostly straggler. She blinked and the spectre disappeared. I need help, she thought; apparently aloud.

'I am helping you. This is helping you.'

Another police car, this one with siren raging, split the traffic on its way west. Downey brushed hair from his eyes. 'I'm out of here,' he said. 'You want to take your chances, that's up to you.'

There was, she thought with sudden clarity, nowhere else to go.

She followed him into the station, where the promise of safety dissolved into a bleak, tiled expanse of shuttered windows and cold lighting. A booth selling coffee and sandwiches was open but held the distant appeal of life filtered through a TV commercial; she was sure that her stomach would never accept food or drink again. First thing Downey did was stop by the departure schedules, arranged on free-standing boards, while he hunted through the canvas bag over his shoulder for what turned out to be a wallet, his quick eyes scanning the lists while he did so. 'Wait out there,' he told her. 'On the platform.'

Yes boss. Sure boss. But that was a tiny voice far away in her head, and her feet were already taking her to the dark, littered world outside, which existed in a different century than the one she left. At night railway platforms are draughty, no matter how still and airless the weather. There are always takeaway wrappers scrunched into balls and left on benches. For one mad comforting moment, she considered tidying them away; gathering the whole greasy mess in a lump to her chest, as if she were starting a collection. It seemed an action appropriate to both her location and condition. She had reached a point in her life where this platform was as good a place as any. She could spend the rest of forever caught between destinations, in this ill-lit dimension where muttering, half-mad vagrants pursued their furious agendas. She could join the other transients who no longer had a home to go to.

A train pulled up opposite and began disgorging passengers from the capital; mostly men, mostly with suits, executive cases and phones; everything, in fact, bar badges reading *I work late.* A subtle race for the taxi rank began, bringing them over the bridge, towards Sarah. Almost immediately came a whistle, the buzz of electric doors locking, and with a promptness suggesting the driver was late for an appointment the train shunted off, giving a strobed view through its lit carriages of the nearly empty platform behind: one or two shadows leaning close, their movements interrupted and comical. The gang of commuters flowed down the steps, brushing past Sarah. *I don't know what they do to the economy*, Mark said once. *But by God, they terrify me.* It felt like the first thought in hours she'd spared Mark; it was as if he'd been erased from the equation. But something had brought him to mind just then, and as the end of the train trundled out of her line of vision she saw that it was because she'd been looking at him. He was one of the shadows on the platform opposite, one of two stragglers reluctant to head for home.

She should have turned away, but couldn't. The reason she could not turn was that she was watching her husband kiss another woman, a sight so unusual that it would have been a crime to miss it. The kiss bordered on the perfunctory, it was true; a quick bow and a peck on the cheek, but the fact that the woman held Mark's arm as he kissed her, that Sarah had never laid eyes on her before, that an aura of intimacy hung on them like a purple cloud: these things could not be dismissed. Mark had a lover. After what she'd been through in the last hour she'd lost much of her capacity for shock, but as she felt the knowledge settle upon her, become as much a part of her consciousness as a childhood memory, it surprised her distantly to learn that she had not yet exhausted her potential for weariness.

Mark was straightening up now; the woman relinquishing her grasp. As Sarah watched, they exchanged a few last words (endearments), then the woman left through the exit their side of the station. Mark picked up his briefcase, and headed for the staircase that would bring him over to Sarah.

Who would probably have remained there to meet him, had Michael Downey not appeared at her side. He thrust what looked like a twenty-pound note on her. 'Two returns,' he said. 'Worcester.'

She stared, uncomprehending.

'Quick. It leaves in two minutes.'

Movement reclaimed her; she took the note and hurried inside, where there was no queue for tickets, and the man selling them grasped immediately what two returns to Worcester meant. Nobody had ever spent so little time at a railway ticket booth. Which was why she walked past Mark on her way back out; though he kept walking as if she were not there, or were somebody else. He was so close as to be touched, and for a moment she wanted to do that, as if by reaching out she could erase everything and put the clock back to the days when they'd meet each other off trains and stand on station platforms making exhibitions of themselves. Before there were arguments and bodies in the kitchen; before there were lovers. She stopped, turned, and would have called out, but he was through the station doors and off down the steps, heading for the taxi rank.

'Hey!'

Downey took her arm and steered her out.

The slow train was wheezing at the blocks on Platform 3, and was a not very long string of grubby, unscrubbed carriages, as befitted a service not going anywhere important. Its individual compartments were mostly unoccupied. They took one near the rear, and almost immediately the slow grind and crawl from the station began: as a means of escape it lacked dash, perhaps, but there were no last minute attempts to flag them down. The platform slipped behind them. The racket picked up speed. And Sarah stared at her pale sister in the window and thought about bodies: bodies warm and kissed by unfaithful husbands or stone cold dead in the kitchen. She wiped a hand against the glass. Through the window, ragged stumps of hedgerow choked to death. While evening died black clouds swallowed the land and the fields and ditches of one county after another dissolved into a single bleak horizon. Everything she cared for was behind her. None of it mattered any more. She raised a hand to her throat and imagined the thin red necklace painted there, her souvenir of that frightening cord that had nearly taken her out of this world, and spoke to Michael Downey. 'I told him it wasn't a matter of life and death.'

He looked at her, not understanding.

'Mark. I told him it wasn't a matter of life and death, whether we had dental floss on the fridge or not.'

Outside the window bright settlements flashed into view, then lost themselves in the dark nowhere that swallowed up the past. This was a well-known effect of travelling at night: you felt nostalgic for snug, safe places you'd never visited, and never would.

Afterwards, she wondered if it had been the drugs. There was the numbing effect of Rufus's attack to take into account, and the shock of seeing his body hurled from one room to the next like an illustration of what was happening to his soul; but afterwards, she preferred to think it had been the drugs that produced this docility, her inability to reach a decision on her own. It remained true that the available options had been limited and unappealing, but to a rational mind the extravagance of the course she had taken, running off into the dark with an armed stranger, was almost supernatural. The irony did not escape her. Mark's purpose had been to keep her tame, domesticated, and the very tools he had used for the task had secured her liberation, as if she had shinned down the wall of her tower using the chains he had wrapped her in for a rope. Her senses dulled by medication, the first plan presented, she had acquiesced to without murmur. The first exit offered, she was off.

Which plan, it had to be said, lacked most defining characteristics of a strategy – forethought, preparation, a definite objective in mind – and boiled down, in the end, to running away. But the soldier Michael Downey had at least covered their tracks as they ran, having bought two singles to Birmingham, behaving memorably as he did so. His appearance alone might have been enough. He had pulled the band from his ponytail, allowing dark hair to tumble over his face and on to his shoulders, and looked like somebody hiding behind a curtain. His voice was strained, hoarse. Perhaps he did not use it often, though he used it now, studying her intently:

'You were on the bridge,' he said. 'After they killed Tom.'

'Yes.'

'Then up at the hospital, looking for Dinah.'

'You frightened me.'

He shrugged.

'Do you know where she is?'

'I don't even know your name.'

'Tucker,' she said. 'Sarah Tucker. Do you know where she is?'

'No.'

'Then what *do* you—'

'Not here. Malvern.'

'Malvern?'

'That's where we get off. I'll see you outside.' At her puzzled look, he went on: 'They'll be collecting tickets. We shouldn't be seen together.'

'We were seen getting on.'

'So they'll be looking for a couple. So we stop being one.' He left, taking his canvas bag. With his departure, the carriage grew colder.

Outside, the landscape unrolled both behind and in front of her reflection, or so it seemed: the dark world looked right through her just as Mark had at the station, and the thought that she could be so easily erased gave a horrifying insight into her future. It was another, gentler kind of death.

She knew you could walk past friends encountered in unlikely places; it was the brain refusing to acknowledge the unexpected. But Mark was her husband . . . An affair she might forgive, though she wouldn't put money on it. But something about the way she hadn't existed for him at that moment was an irrefutable proof that the frayed bond between them had snapped. He had failed to keep her safe when she was falling off the world. And even as she fell, he'd been playing brief fucking encounter with some pick-up on the commuter express.

It was enough to make her wonder if she had ever known anybody. Mark was not a husband; Rufus was not an airhead. But then, *nobody* had known Rufus. She thought of Wigwam's months of happiness with him, and tried to remember how he had first appeared on the scene, and couldn't: he had simply arrived, and for all Sarah knew about his past, he'd dropped out of a Christmas cracker. Another harmless hippie. It was a marriage made in outer space. Except it had been a lie, all of it; all the time he'd been waiting for Tom Singleton to return from the grave, so he could send him back there. It was a lot of cover for a simple act of murder: this impersonation of a family man, in order to trap a real one. Singleton had died because he could not stay away from his wife and daughter, and now Wigwam had died too, or so Rufus had said . . . Sarah did not know if she could believe that. Why had Rufus tried to kill her, if not for the copy of the letter he'd found? . . . She couldn't think of a reason for him to have murdered Wigwam beforehand. It was evil, then. Pure evil. He'd wanted her to die thinking her friend already dead.

But here, anyway, was one thing, one person, she could be sure of. If Wigwam were alive, she would grieve for Rufus; this Sarah knew. Whatever he had done. Whoever he proved to be. Because for six months he had pretended to be Wigwam's lover, and no man had cared for Wigwam enough in the past to keep up that pretence for so long. And with this single certainty came Sarah's own reason to cry: as the train rolled on, she grieved too. Not for the dead but the living. Whoever they were.

She left the train at Malvern. There were no whistles, no alarms; and neither sight nor sound of Michael Downey, though she waited until the train pulled away before leaving the platform. Seeing it depart was watching an escape route close before her eyes. She had barely a fistful of money; she wore jeans, a T-shirt, a thin cotton top. And she had never been to Malvern, though first impressions coloured it neat, well kept and dark. The platform lighting fell in tight pools lapped by shifting shadows. It was the wind nudging hanging baskets, from which trailed fuschias and ferns.

It came as no great surprise to find herself abandoned. Compared to recent events, it was a small betrayal: Downey was a stranger; he had saved her life and owed her nothing. That he had left her stranded hours from home was a detail. She could easily picture him, miles from here: hurrying across a field, the lights of labourers' cottages winking in the distance. A little bit of pastoral, there. But probably he had just changed trains, and was now heading into the city. Any city.

From somewhere the other side of the shadows came thumping, heaving and laughter; sounds Sarah took for porters, larking with the mails. A dim sense of self-preservation reasserted itself. Whatever happened next had best happen elsewhere: somewhere better lit, more crowded; also warmer. A sudden shiver shook her head to toe. It was the thought of that noose tightening on her throat. It was the cold and the dark and the fear, and the being alone.

Her shoes clattered on the station concourse. Everything sounds louder in the dark. Outside there was a car park and a hill to climb, and a bigger hill in the distance, and Sarah couldn't have felt further from home if she'd been E.T. Her cheeks stung where her tears for Wigwam had dried. Soon, she knew, she'd be crying again, but before that happened she needed shelter. Because once she started crying, she'd likely never stop.

A lout stepped from an alcove. 'Tucker.'

'*Jesus!*'

'Where were you?'

He had cut his hair on the train, and this oddness distracted her from fright for a second. And then it poured through her again, riding her blood like a surfer on a wave, and it didn't at first occur to her that it was relief as much as anger that made her coarse. 'You shit you frightened me half to *death*.'

'Who else round here knows your name?'

'That's hardly the—'

'We can't stay here. Come on.'

Like I'm a bloody dog, she thought. But followed anyway, like a bloody dog, up the road towards the town centre.

Downey moved naturally among the shadows, as if they were his element after years spent pretending to be dead. Sarah was forced to trot to match his pace; to stretch her legs after weeks without exercise. The blood pounded through her and her skin began to tingle. Sensations indicating that she too was coming back to life.

Coming back to it and giving it some thought. That she was here, now, was a given. That she was blindly following a man she'd seen kill without hesitation would perhaps bear examination. What it suggested was not attractive, not to the Sarah emerging from tranquillised stupor; the same inner core of selfhood that had responded to Zoë Boehm rebelled against relying on a man for instruction. Mark's betrayal was only just sinking in. Not the kiss on the railway platform, but the whole of the last few weeks: the tame doctor wheeled out to pop pills; the sex visited on her as if it were a form of therapy. Even

Simon Smith had acknowledged she had some degree of autonomy, though he'd tempered it with the unstated view that she'd be better off not exercising it. Mark thought rape and drugs would see her through. Yet here she was, having run from them all, tagging after a proven killer like a confirmed victim, lost without a source of punishment.

But that wasn't it. She knew that wasn't it. The reason she was following Michael Downey was that he'd faked death four years ago, and that lay at the heart of recent events. Joe would not be coming back to life. Her own would never be the same. And somewhere underneath all this was the shadow of Dinah Singleton, surely as unknowing a player in the game as Sarah herself . . . She could admit now that the child had been little more than an excuse. She would have traced a treasure map with as much concern. It was what Gerard Inchon had called BHS; the urge to do something – anything – to relieve the terrible boredom.

The boredom had been relieved.

And now that the damage was done, the long days when the worst she had to worry about was what to fix for supper had a prelapsarian glow; it was like those first few seconds after breaking a tooth, when you're immediately cross with yourself for not having taken advantage of all the lovely moments without a broken tooth. But there was no cosmic dentist available, and no advantage in looking back. The best she could do was arrange her own agenda. Soon they would come looking for her: the police for sure; whoever sent Rufus, possibly. The choice was to go to earth or to start back at the beginning, and not give up. To find Dinah. It had nothing to do with revenge, or even reconciliation. It was simply a matter of finishing what she had started. And that meant knowing what Downey knew.

Their location, for a start. 'What are we looking for?'

'Hotel,' he said, without breaking stride.

'We've passed three.'

'Too near the station.'

Because of the noise was her first, ridiculous thought. Though what he meant was, hotels by the station were the first places they'd come looking.

Whoever they were.

He came to a stop at a corner, just out of the reach of a streetlight, and looked both ways, like a man checking out enemy terrain. Sarah caught up, and stood in the light. 'Who are you? Really?'

'Not here.'

'Where then? I'm not coming without answers.'

'I'm the guy who shot the guy who tried to kill you. Happy?'

'I'm sorry.'

'I'd have killed him anyway.'

'Your name's Downey. You're supposed to be dead.'

He didn't answer.

'You were Singleton's friend.'

'I told *you* that.'

'And you were both killed in a helicopter crash.'

Before he could react to this, he reacted to something else: footsteps over the road, chopping little pieces off the quiet. Downey pulled Sarah into the dark and she tensed at this unexpected contact. The smell of sweat and loose clippings of hair. He hadn't shaved, just hacked at the beard with a pair of scissors. From a distance, he could have been riding the fashion. Up close he looked like an accident in a garden shed.

The footsteps stopped. 'Who's there?' It was a querulous tremor, an old woman's voice, attached in this instance to an old man. 'I heard you over there. I'm not afraid.'

They stood in their doorway, a chemist's shop doorway, huddled like startled lovers. But he couldn't see them, and they made no further noise.

'Winston? Come on, Winston.'

And the dog wheezed after its ancient owner: a boxer with a clumsy punch-drunk waddle, as if four legs were too many, or not enough. The tapping of the footsteps resumed, only to falter a few yards later while their maker hawked noisily into the gutter; possibly a gesture of contempt, or maybe just a symptom of the condition that had him wandering the streets at this godforsaken hour.

'See?'

'What?' she snapped.

'We can't hang about. There's a place up ahead.'

Which was the last one Sarah would have chosen. She'd have thought he'd go for a backstreet boarding house; the kind of refuge where the arrival of a bedraggled couple in the early hours simply meant another marriage had hit the deck. But the hotel ahead bore the same relation to a travelling reps' dive that a cruiser does a tug; an imposing stone building which looked like it had graced the town since time out of mind, and only begrudgingly hosted untitled members of the public. 'You've made reservations?'

'Think they'll turn away cash? Not on your life.'

He fumbled in his canvas bag again, and this time pulled out a folded stack of currency held by a rubber band.

'Not on your life,' he repeated.

This time, Sarah believed him.

20

SEVEN IN THE MORNING – three hours' sleep – and Amos Crane was back at his desk, back at his screen, hacking his way through railway timetables: an obvious place to start. Maybe Michael Downey used a car. Well, if so, Crane would just have to wait until he broke surface, but in the meantime here he was, chasing trains a pair of fugitives might have hopped in the small hours.

They might have split up, too, but he doubted that.

So he made a list of all possible departures, allowing a generous window of ninety minutes, then cut the London trains, because that's what he'd have done: only amateurs think you can get lost in the big city. And then cut the north train too, because the only point in heading north was putting down distance, and Downey wouldn't spend three–four hours on a train if he was expecting pursuit. Not if it meant making it as far as Durham to find a squad car waiting . . .

. . . and it occurred to him he was playing the game by trying to think like Downey; maybe he should be zeroing in on the woman instead . . .

. . . but no, it was too early for that: the state she'd be in, the best you could hope was she'd follow instructions without too much fuss. But Downey would keep her for the moment, at least until he'd found out what she knew. Which wasn't anything, which was *fuck all*, but that was the beauty of the information game: you never knew how ignorant you were without going over everything twice. Downey needed to hear her story. Which meant he'd want to hole up as soon as possible, get the debriefing under way . . .

Crane sat back, and drank coffee from a takeaway cup. He was thinking: if it had been him, he'd have bought two sets of tickets; putting down a false trail was standard. And the second pair, the *real* pair, wouldn't have been identical: he'd have bought two tickets on the same line, but for different stations. But Downey was hampered. That time of night, relatively few people about, he couldn't have risked going to the window twice: the ticket clerk might have recognised him. So he'd have sent the woman. And one person buying tickets for two different stations, that was memorable too. So Crane had to assume Downey was missing a trick. Two sets of tickets, right, but each an identical pair.

In the old days this was the point at which flatfeet wandered from booth to ticket booth, photograph in hand, hoping to get lucky. For Crane, it was a finger-hop and skip – technically illegal, he reminded himself, but that was what the word 'technically' was for. He didn't come up with many pairs. Late evening, it was mostly businessmen singles. With luck, he'd pinpoint them.

He took another gulp of coffee. Miles away, Sarah woke up.

She had slept fitfully, wakened at three by aeroplanes exploding overhead, a noise which resolved into thunder once consciousness set in. But the rain that followed soothed her, its rhythmic drumming against the wide windows washing her mind clean, for a while, of the horrors, and when she woke next the sun pouring through the gaps in the curtains evidenced a morning so perfect there was probably a patent pending on it.

Michael sat on the end of the bed.

He had spent the night in the armchair, and sometime early

had finished the job he'd started on the train, and shaved. Revealed was a thin, dark face; not much older than her own, but more travelled. A harsh crease on his chin suggested a healed scar. His brown eyes, neither friendly nor threatening, were distinctly matter-of-fact. 'You've lost weight,' he said. He didn't look well himself.

She cleared her throat. 'Thanks.'

'Are you a junkie?'

Oh, God. She closed her eyes. 'What makes you ask?'

'Because it'll save a lot of pain if you say so now.'

'No. I'm not a junkie.'

She opened them again, and looked round the room. A large room, big windows, a king-size double bed. En-suite bathroom. Trouser press. A TV she knew would get cable. Everything you looked for in a hotel room, really, down to the emergency instructions on the back of the door and the aura of mild depression hanging over it all: the inescapable conclusion that you were here on a temporary basis. As if she needed reminding of that.

Her clothes clung to her uncomfortably. She had slept fully dressed.

She sat up, rubbed her face in her hands. She was in a strange room with a strange man: it scared her. On the other hand, he had saved her life last night, and subsequently slept in the armchair.

Afterwards, Sarah looked back on this day as a series of snapshots, small moments that became shuffled in her mind. But this was always the first of them: waking and finding him sitting on the end of the bed. The hand that pulled the trigger rubbing an unfamiliar chin.

When Howard came in, saw Crane sitting at his desk, he said, 'God, Amos, should you be here? Shouldn't you be . . .'

'I be what?'

'Well, mourning.'

'I am mourning, Howard. I'm also looking for the fucker *put* me in mourning. Which is why I'm at my desk, yes.'

Howard wisely didn't pursue this. 'And last night? Um, did you sort out the, er, husband?'

'Mark Trafford. Did you know he was dirty?'

'Dirty how?'

Crane rubbed his fingers together.

'So we can expect little fuss from him, then?'

'Unless he's keen on seeing how the other half live. What about you?'

'The woman?' Howard shrugged. 'About what you'd expect.'

Crane didn't let relief show on his face, but that's what he felt. Three hours' sleep, and he'd woken thinking about the woman – Axel's 'wife', or, he supposed, 'Rufus's' wife. Depending on how you looked at it. Either way, he'd woken wondering if he'd been wrong the previous evening, and Axel really had gone into meltdown. In which case Howard wouldn't have found a wife, he'd have found another body. There were kids too. It might have been messy.

'But did she buy it?'

Distaste flitted over Howard's face. He really didn't like this part. It made Amos wonder how he'd got here in the first place, let alone being nominally in charge. 'She's not the type,' Howard said at last, 'to disbelieve anything. Not when it's backed up with a police presence.'

'The woodentops have their uses.'

'What are you doing? Exactly.'

'*Exactly*, I'm running through timetables. I think they went for a train. I'm trying to find which.'

'You said it didn't make a difference. That they'll still come after the child.'

'They will.'

'So it doesn't matter where they are now. So long as they—'

'Look, Howard, I'm fucking tracking them. All right?'

Howard didn't say anything.

'We'll find them. Sooner or later. But sooner's better. Don't you think?'

'Are you making this personal, Amos?'

Jesus Christ. Amos smiled kindly. 'Howard. Of *course* I'm making it personal. Now, fuck off, do you mind? I'm busy.'

Howard stood there for the best part of a minute before he turned and walked away. Probably, if he'd thought of something good to say, he'd have said it.

Amos returned to his screen. And if he'd been buying the tickets, he continued, the ones he'd have bought for actual use would have been for a train leaving thirty seconds later.

Bingo.

Downey had hung a DO NOT DISTURB on their door, and when food arrived, made them leave the trolley outside. He told her to keep away from the windows. And every time she wanted to think this ridiculous, she got flashes of yesterday evening like the remnants of a bad trip: Rufus with the damn dental floss – Rufus! – wrapping her throat with a cord so tight it left a mark like a thin ruby necklace. She studied it in the mirror: a *memento mori*, secular stigmata. A wound that did not bleed.

'You think they'll find us here?'

'Depends.'

'On what?'

He shrugged.

And Sarah didn't even know who *they* were yet.

He tuned to CNN, and they watched a war unfold in colour; men and women in desert fatigues, auditioning for Armageddon. Commentary was live: this was virtual reality combat. You could hold the remote and imagine pressing the buttons; lasers accurate to an inch over fifty miles; smart bombs that punched their targets while transmitting images to a watching world. You could look into the whites of enemy eyes a continent away. Study their customs, learn their language and kill them, all at once.

Michael wolfed sandwiches. Sarah couldn't eat. For information, she was hungry, but hardly knew where to start. Nor did Michael . . . There were car alarms that activated when you got too close: you didn't have to be touching. It was one of those eighties things where you not only *owned* something, you owned the space around it too. Michael was like that, though instead of an alarm going off everything shut down.

She asked him, 'Are you married?'

'Used to be.'

She waited, but he wasn't enlarging on that. 'Tell me about Singleton.'

'We did training together.'

Always, she was left to fill in the gaps, for which she leaned on films dimly remembered, and school stories devoured as a child. Parade ground brutality; men fainting in the heat. Vows of undying loyalty. Smuggled feasts after lights out. She knew the truth lay a million miles wide; truth, anyway, was a private luxury.

'You fought together?'

'Over there.' He nodded at the screen. 'Last time.'

'Was it . . .' She didn't know what to ask.

'It was war. We were kids.'

'Like this.' She gestured at the screen.

'This isn't war. It's a shooting gallery.'

She looked back at the screen. Graphs showing probable enemy dead were superimposed on a smoking background. A voice recited figures with barely suppressed excitement, as if this were a lottery rollover week, and its owner had invested heavily in the big numbers.

*

He was riding pure intuition here, but he thought they'd boarded the Worcester train. *Somebody* had, certainly: a pair of returns had been bought with just about two minutes to spare – was Worcester somewhere people went in a hurry? It was the kind of thing Howard would probably know.

He made his choice anyway; pulled up a list of stations the Worcester train stopped at, and waited to see if any jumped out. But they were ordinary places – small towns; nowhere that rang bells – and he sat back in his chair again, feeling his mind slip out of focus. Three hours' sleep was not enough.

Perhaps, too, he should have been with his brother. Axel had been taken to the small, discreet firm of undertakers the Department used: accustomed to physical trauma, to disguising cause of death. There would be no post-mortem. But perhaps there was need for Amos to sit with his brother's body a while, so he could get used to the idea that Axel wasn't coming home this time; that Amos was well and truly alone at last.

. . . Moreton-in-Marsh. Honeybourne. These were towns children's writers lived; the kind of place Winnie the Pooh would go on his day off. Just listening to the names, Crane knew nobody could hide there for long. Ten minutes after you'd found the B & B, the vicar would be popping round, inviting you for evensong.

Not that he had wanted Axel dead. But for too long he'd been forced to play the older brother role: trying to calm everybody else down when Axel went over the top. Axel enjoyed the wet work too much, that had always been his problem. Bureaucrats like Howard didn't go for that. They needed it done, sure, but they didn't want anyone enjoying it.

Pershore, Worcester itself. Worcester was biggish, wasn't it?

He made a note on a pad by his keyboard: *Hotels in Worcester?* Later, he'd find a list, find a map; use the station as its centre, and plot the hotels accordingly. It was a big job and, as Howard had suggested, not entirely necessary: sooner or later, Downey would come to him. But if it brought that moment closer, it was worth doing. Axel wasn't supposed to be one of the blips. He shouldn't have been wiped from the screen like that. Maybe Amos should be sitting vigil over his body, but he knew Axel would prefer it this way: Amos preparing to hunt down Axel's killer. In the end, you mourned by doing what you were best at, and this time Amos was doing it for love. He'd be sure to tell Downey that, when the moment came.

For a while he sat there, contemplating that moment. Then he licked his lips, and bent back to his screen.

There was a Ted Hughes poem Sarah remembered about a confined panther or other large cat; behind bars, it felt horizons rolling beneath its feet. There was something of this in Michael. The hotel room, to her, had become a prison; hourly, the walls closed in, an inch at a time, as if it were some upscale version of a medieval torture device which would squeeze the life from all their bones. But to Michael, the room was just where he happened to be at the moment. It was just another way station, away from the war.

'Where did it start?' she asked him.

She'd already told him everything she knew, which was nothing really; less than nothing, because telling it left her confused and lost.

'I don't know.'

'But please try.'

He shrugged. Talking was an effort with him. 'In the desert? I think that's where it really started.'

'During the war?'

'No. Long after that. A year ago. Eighteen months?'

'You've been dead four years,' she said. 'The helicopter crash? Off Cyprus?'

'I've never been to Cyprus.' Then what she'd said registered. 'Four years? Jesus, it is, isn't it?'

'What happened in the desert?'

'There were six of us. And the . . . others.'

'What others?'

'We called them the boy soldiers.'

He seemed to be fading before her eyes, and she was unsure whether he was waking from a nightmare or falling back into one. 'Boy soldiers?'

'They were just kids. Scared to fucking death.' He ran a hand across his eyes, then looked straight at her. 'It had to be a desert. The conditions wouldn't be fair otherwise. That's what they told us. Fair.'

It was like grasping at smoke. '*Who* told you?'

He looked back to the screen.

'Michael? You have to tell me these things!'

'Why?'

'Because I'm *involved*, dammit. Because I'm *here*.'

He looked at her again, this time with a fresh curiosity, as if he'd registered for the first time that she'd had an existence prior to his awareness of her. He had saved her life, but she knew that he'd done so simply because he'd thought she might have information; because she'd been looking for Dinah, and he'd thought she might know more than him. Returning his gaze now, she wondered if, under different circumstances, he'd be just as prepared to kill her for the same end. It was a thought she pushed away quickly.

He said, 'What's that scar on your arm?'

And she knew it was a question to draw her into his world, the one where even the innocent carry wounds. Especially the innocent. But she could not tell him about the fall from the roof; the way the lights spun cartwheels in her head as she hit the ground.

'I had a crash,' she told him.

He seemed to relate to that.

'Why did the army say you were dead, if you'd never even been to Cyprus?'

And he said, 'That's when we knew we were really in trouble.'

By mid morning Crane had settled on two towns, the time mostly spent staring through the wall, thinking himself into Downey's shoes. Like all such exercises, the longer he'd tried it, the less sense it made. But in the end he'd chosen Malvern and, yes, Worcester; the latter to allow for two possibilities: the double bluff and the stupid error. Given an hour and a half, he'd told Howard, Downey would be underground, but how true was that? Maybe, all these months, it had been Singleton doing Downey's thinking for him. Singleton was off the screen now. Downey might just be chasing his own tail, hoping to be caught.

. . . Crane held a pencil by its tip between right thumb and index finger, and as he sat, tapped the end of it against the arm of his spectacles, in time to the rhythm of his heart.

He didn't believe it. But the idea wouldn't go away, so there it was on his list.

He was waiting now for a printout of hotels, B & Bs, pubs that offered rooms, and while he did he was thinking about the woman. He didn't know much about the woman yet. If she proved as weak as her husband, who'd crumpled at his touch, she'd not be around long enough to be a problem. But Axel's ruse to take her out of the picture – drawing on her background; fitting her up with a bag of cocaine – hadn't worked, so she was either really dumb or something of a fighter, and Crane didn't think she was dumb. And by now she'd have more of an idea of what she'd fallen into.

But she wouldn't know everything. For instance, Downey wouldn't tell her the truth about himself.

Not if he wanted her on his side.

*

'Why you?'

He looked away. There were things he wouldn't tell her: not now, not ever. She knew that as precisely as if he'd actually said it, instead of what he did say, which was, 'You wouldn't understand. We were soldiers.'

'Great.'

They'd trained in a desert: somewhere in North Africa, he said; he didn't know where. They weren't told. There were no uniforms, just a vast expanse of sand and sky; a canvas-and-tin construction they slept in, ate in, returned exhausted to every evening.

'Training?'

'Up and down the sandhills. With weights. Serious weights.'

She got the picture. She even imagined the pain: the sand dragging at their limbs, trying to pull them back into the earth.

'But that wasn't the point. They were painting us. Twice a day.'

'Painting?'

She was starting to sound like an echo.

'Like they sprayed us in the war. This was different, though. They told us about it. Had to. We had to strip naked, and let the stuff dry.'

'What was it?'

'God knows.' He was far away, maybe back in North Africa. 'Could have been water. That's what we thought for a while, in fact. There were stories, you know, about the guys coming back from the war with problems. Dying. We thought it might be some kind of psych-ops thing. See if we could take it. Already knowing the stories.'

'But it wasn't.'

'No,' he said. 'It wasn't.'

'How long? How long did they do that for?'

He shrugged. 'You lose track of time, you know? A few

weeks. It stretched into months, I guess. That was when they said we were dead.'

'In a helicopter crash off Cyprus.'

'Tommy hated that. When we found out about it. That's when he knew we were really in the shit.' He looked directly at Sarah. 'Helicopter crashes, that's the kind of thing the army likes to pretend never happens. If they were using one of those as *cover*, well, Tommy said we were never coming back to life. We were on the island by then.'

'Which island?'

'That comes later.'

'Tell me what happened in the desert.'

He looked back to the TV screen, where a reporter leaned against an all-terrain vehicle, talking urgently at the camera. 'They took us into the sands one day. Drove us there. Miles from anywhere. They said, this time it's not an exercise. There's bad guys out there. We want you to take them.'

'The boy soldiers.'

'That's who they were. But we were told they were the real thing.' He shook his head. 'We were told to bring them home alive.'

She hardly dared ask. 'And did you?'

'Christ, yes.' He was still shaking his head, as if it were all some big story. 'They were kids. Six of them, too. But they didn't know a thing, they were kids. They weren't soldiers.'

Something was stirring in her memory: fragments of bulletins, and loud denials in the press. 'They were Iraqi, weren't they?'

The look he gave her was pure scorn. 'Well, of course they bloody were.'

Six Iraqi conscripts who had perished in a storm on the Syrian border twenty months ago. Who Iraqi ministers claimed had been captured – murdered – by Western troops.

It was Sarah's turn to shake her head. She didn't want to

look at the TV screen and know there was a war happening. She didn't want to know any of this at all.

'Tell me,' she said.

The circles he'd drawn on the maps rendered the towns targets. Ground zero was a railway station. Red dots were hotels. (It was far from foolproof – nobody had to tell Crane that – but rapidly becoming a compulsion.) Blue dots were B & Bs; there were probably unlicensed places in both towns. Which put them off the map. And there were green dots for hostels, homeless shelters; places they'd have had to bluff their way into, but which he couldn't completely ignore. Of course, it would take weeks to check, by which time Downey and his woman could be anywhere. But long shots were always worth playing. Every week, some fool won the lottery. When that happened, they stopped being fools.

Howard drifted back in. 'Are you staying here forever?'

'If that's how long it takes.'

Crane's desk was a junkyard accident. He'd already broken the phone, for ringing when he wasn't ready. Splintered ends of pencils formed a tepee shape on top of his computer casing: you had to do *something* while you were waiting for the bastard to search a database. And a shredded polystyrene cup, little white flakes of it, adding the impression that Crane was having a bad hair day: Howard looked at all this but made no comment. Which provoked Crane more than anything.

'Haven't you got papers to shuffle? Chits to sign? We need more pencils round here. Isn't it you who buys the pencils, Howard?'

'We're a government agency, Amos. We don't operate for your sole benefit.'

'Govern-Ment-A-Gency. I can just *hear* the capitals when you speak, Howard. Did you learn that at university?'

'Your brother fucked up. I'm sorry, Amos, but that's what he did. Now we can draw lessons from that, which would be a *useful* thing to do, or you can sit here steaming, planning your revenge. It's a job, Amos. And it needs to be done. But it needs to be done properly. You go off the deep end and fuck this up too, I'll hang you out to dry. Believe it.'

Amos whistled through his teeth.

'I mean it. You go solo and spill unnecessary blood, your days here are over. You might as well book the plot next to Axel.'

'Unnecessary blood?'

'You know what I mean.'

He laughed. 'You ever wonder what it's like at the sharp end, Howard?'

'Don't start. I had enough of that from Axel. Laugh at the desk-man. Who knows nothing about anything. But you tried driving a desk on this one, Amos, and look what happened. Your brother's dead, there's civilians *this close* to official secrets, and you're looking for a needle in a haystack so you can go do the John Wayne bit. Very bloody impressive.'

'I'll find him.'

'So you said. You also said Axel could handle it.'

'Careful, Howard.'

'Don't threaten me. You've no friends in the Ministry, Amos. Downey may be the target, but there were a few sighs of relief when he bagged Axel.'

Amos jabbed him in the throat with his forefinger.

It was curious, he thought, as he watched Howard drop to his knees and scrape at the air for a breath, how stress brought out the best in some people. Here's Howard, a man born to be office furniture, learning to speak his mind. Probably been having shit poured on him from above. Once a month or so, poor Howard was summoned for a bollocking from a bloke whose *name* he didn't even know: now that was sad. Crane knew the name, of course, but that was because he believed in making the effort.

He leaned forward now and breathed in Howard's ear. 'I will find him, Howard. If not now, later. When he comes for the girl. And when I find him, I'll kill him. And if I have *any complaints* from you on the matter, I'll drop you from your office window. Clear?'

There was little point in waiting for an answer.

He patted Howard on the cheek. 'When you can breathe, get up and leave. Don't talk to me any more.'

And he turned to his screen, already thinking: Big hotels. Chains. The kind of places with a network he could break into. He didn't hear Howard leave. That was because Howard left very quietly.

They had fought all day, Michael said, though 'fought' wasn't the word, not really – the boy soldiers had fired a shot or two, but nothing that came near causing danger, then tried to dig themselves in at the top of a dune. It was easy to see they were scared witless. Screaming at each other, probably about whether to surrender or not; one of them stood up at the end, stretched his arms skyward; babbling in obvious prayer. Tommy Singleton shot his knee off.

'They were kidnapped. Brought there. For you to practise on.'

Michael said, 'I think so. Yes.'

She couldn't believe it, or wished she couldn't. Wished she couldn't see it in her mind, either, helped along by images on the TV screen: the scared boy standing, screaming at the world to leave him alone. The bullet picking him off like a tin duck at a fairground.

After that, Michael said, they all folded. Threw their guns down the hill, and waited to be captured.

'So you didn't kill them.'

'No. We didn't kill them.'

He closed his eyes then, as if deep in the effort of remembering, though in fact, Sarah suspected, trying to forget.

They had a truck and they'd marched the boy soldiers to it, single file, the way they'd been taught. Piled in the back, with Tommy and another up front.

'We thought that would be the hard part. Finding the way home. But Tommy said he knew. He was good at directions, Tommy. He hardly ever got lost.'

'Even in the desert?'

'You trust your mates. That's what it's about. He said he could find the way home, so we believed him.'

But they'd not been driving half an hour before they heard the helicopter.

'We were trying to talk to the boy soldiers,' he said. 'Two of us were. But they didn't speak a word of English. Except "cigarette" and that. The kid Tommy shot, he was lying on the floor of the truck. We bandaged his leg up, but it was a right mess. It didn't make a difference, though.'

When the helicopter came, it opened fire.

'We were expecting it, kind of. The rest of it, it was too easy. They were just kids, they weren't soldiers. Not really.'

'It shot at you?'

'To the side of the truck. Trying to knock us over, I guess. So Tommy hit the brakes, and we all piled out.'

. . . *Sand crunched under his feet as he fell from the truck, and the whine of the chopper above was the loudest noise in the world.* He shuddered. Sarah almost reached out to him: just to let him feel her touch, and know he wasn't back there, however vivid the pictures in his head.

'Have you ever fired on a flying target?'

She didn't even bother: he was talking to himself.

'You see it in films and that and it looks dead easy. It's almost impossible, though. It buzzed us again, and we emptied most of our weapons, then it flew far off, and turned, and came back in.'

The light was creeping from the room now. She had no idea

how long they'd been there: time was an intruder in this place. Reality was happening elsewhere.

'We could see him hanging off the side. Wearing a harness, so he wouldn't fall.'

'Who?'

'Doesn't matter. He was whoever he was. He was like us, just doing his job.'

There was no bitterness in his voice. Probably, Sarah thought, he believed it: that if you were just doing your job, all manner of things were forgiven.

'And then he dropped it. Just a small thing, about the size of a tennis ball . . . There was a 'chute attached, so it drifted down, and we all stood watching like we were hypnotised or something. The boy soldiers with the rest of us. And we knew we were dead. We all knew we were dead. It can't have taken more than a dozen seconds, somewhere round that, but that was plenty of time to work it out. When you know it's your last twelve seconds it seems like forever, but it passes too fast.'

He fell quiet. She didn't push him. She was remembering her own bad moments: hanging on to life in her kitchen while Rufus – who'd called himself Axel – tightened his rope round her throat. It had felt like she'd spent half her life there, waiting for death, but it was over in a blur, too; had all happened between one breath and the next.

'But it wasn't a bomb.'

He stood abruptly. She reached for the water, poured him a glass, and handed it to him without a word; he took it the same way, and drained it in a single flourish. Then tensed his fingers round the glass, as if he were searching for its shattering point.

'Michael.'

He looked at her.

'Tell me.'

He told her. 'It wasn't a bomb. Or else, it *was*, but not a conventional one. They were testing us. Painting us. That's why we were there. We were guinea pigs.'

'What happened?'

'It went off. There was a sound like glass breaking, and the air went muzzy. That sounds stupid. I can't describe it better. And then . . . it was like I was burning. There was this incredible pain. I thought, it shouldn't be like this, it was a *bomb*, I should just die, it shouldn't keep hurting, but the pain went on and on. I think I was screaming. I guess we all were.'

He put the glass down, very gently, on the floor.

'I remember someone grabbed me, it must have been Tommy. He was screaming too. He kept yelling "Don't look! Don't look!" And I'm half dying with this pain, it's like my skin's being scorched off, and there's this tiny part of my mind going *What's he on about? Don't look at what?*'

Sarah felt her own mouth dry up, but didn't reach for the water.

'And then I saw. I looked up.'

He closed his eyes.

'He was talking about the boy soldiers, Tucker. They weren't screaming. They were melting.'

Each time Howard tried to swallow, he could taste his own gristle. It was as if his throat itself were a lump he couldn't get down: making a rattle of his breath; blurring his vision. Six years working for the Department had left him inured to many forms of violence, but a very big exception was any kind involving himself. On paper, he dealt with it. Had always found it regrettable, but he didn't brood. Amos Crane, though, had never left him crawling on the floor before; for several moments, he'd thought he was going to die. Instead of a vision of his past life flooding before him, he'd had a sudden clear picture of the amount of paperwork this would cause somebody else.

He was standing by his window now, on the floor above

Crane's office. He held a jug of water in one hand, a glass in the other.

Twice in the past hour he'd lifted the phone to call Security: Crane's attack hadn't simply been a breach of conditions of service, it had been criminal goddamn assault. But twice, his nerve had failed him. If Crane didn't feel like co-operating – and he wouldn't – it would take more than Security to subdue him. You didn't train a Crane, then expect him to go quietly. That was the whole trouble, of course. Pit of snakes, this job. It had been true what he'd said to Amos, and Howard himself had been among those feeling more than a twinge of relief when Axel was cancelled. It didn't take genius to see that the day had anyway been coming when somebody, probably Howard himself, would have signed the paper authorising an executive accident for Axel Crane: something quick and easy – he'd been a servant of the Crown – but definite. He was glad the decision had been taken out of his hands. Not because he'd have hesitated to sign (he wouldn't), but because if he had, and the accident had gone wrong, he'd have had Axel Crane paying him a visit. And even if it had gone right, he'd have had Amos doing the same.

His hand strayed to his throat once more. There was no telling whether there wasn't permanent damage there: something ruptured, fatally bruised. The rest of his life he might spend taking soothing drinks every half-hour. Show him the paper on *Amos* Crane, he'd sign it without a blink.

. . . There was paper on his desk now, the file on Michael Downey. The one on Thomas Singleton had been black-ribboned, which didn't mean he'd never have to refer to it again but did mean it was pretty conclusively closed. Not the way he'd thought it would happen, six–seven months back, whenever it was. Downey he'd marked as the weak link, Singleton the danger. From right back on Crows' Hill, Singleton had been the leader: that was the way Howard read the files.

Crane had said to him, 'They've tasted blood. The files don't mean shit.'

Howard had demurred. 'Some things are fixed. People don't change, not as quickly as all that. Character's a constant. Like Blackpool through the rock.'

'Look in your files there,' Crane said. 'Tell me where it says he'd take three prisoners, shoot them dead. If the army had known that from the start, they'd never have taken him.'

Howard shuffled paper.

Crane said, 'But that's the army for you. *We'd* have taken him like a shot.'

And maybe Amos had had a point. The records marked Michael Downey as a dog soldier: he'd follow orders, then lie down. But he was on his own now, and he'd already aced Axel Crane. Who might have been borderline psycho, but was hardly what you'd call a soft target.

Amos was better. Always had been. Howard poured another glass of water.

Amos was better than Axel, and the pair of them had been the best field agents the Department had ever had. *A happy worker is a good worker*, Howard's predecessor had told him. *That pair like their work.* Some parts in particular, Axel had liked too well: his specialised tastes had got him into trouble more than once. The Department's function was to clear up other people's messes, Howard had frequently had to remind him. Not make our own. Axel, then, would become petulant, and seek to lay the blame on whoever else had been involved – a useful choice of scapegoat, as they were rarely alive enough to object. Howard, frankly, had been sick and tired of him, though he'd been careful to pretend amused affection.

Amos, the elder, had been more controlled. Not today, of course. And his record was far from spotless. But of late he'd been prepared to adapt: unlike Axel, he'd realised that the days of guns and roses were numbered, and if he'd wanted his career to last, he'd better be prepared to take up a more executive role. Not that he was suited for it, but experience mattered. He had a calm head. Nothing flustered him. He accepted the outrageous at face value. Axel, though, he'd always indulged, which had been fatal to the current op, and alone gave Howard enough of an edge to give him the chop, even without the assault. Howard rubbed his poor throat once more, and painfully sipped his water. Amos was making things personal: well, he wasn't the only one.

He studied Downey's file again. The man had been a good soldier, once. His bad luck, really. If he'd been a worse one, he'd never have made it past Crows' Hill. As it was he had Amos Crane on his case, not something you'd wish on your enemy, and had somehow managed to involve the woman, Sarah Trafford, too. She *definitely* came under the heading of bad accidents. The mess afterwards was going to take weeks to black-ribbon.

But Downey had killed Axel Crane, remember, and while Amos was better than Axel, that didn't make him invulnerable. Michael Downey, after all, had a cause. What Amos had been banking on from the start: that Downey wouldn't stop until he'd found the child. And a soldier with a cause was a different proposition from a lot of the targets Amos Crane had drawn a line through. Perhaps Crane was stepping in something deeper than he'd realised. The state he was in at the moment, you couldn't accuse him of thinking straight.

Downey surviving this was unthinkable, obviously, but if he despatched Amos Crane in the meantime, it wasn't going to spoil Howard's day. He closed the file, locked it in his cabinet, and after a good hard think about it, crept down the stairs to check on Amos Crane. But Crane was gone, his office in darkness; the dead eye of his computer screen reflecting just the debris of his desk. Among it, Crane's spectacles, neatly folded. He wore them only for screen work, and wouldn't need them now.

*

Daylight was bleeding out of the sky. Above the rooftops of the houses opposite a few last red smears were fading to black, as if an old wound were going bad, and it took an effort for Sarah to remember the obvious: that this was the way it always was, and the sky would be healed by morning. With the pictures in her head mingling with the onscreen images, it was easy to imagine instead that this was the end. Some wounds never got better. The boy soldiers had melted.

She did not press Michael for details: there were some things it was better never to know. And anyway, the word 'melted' contained enough bitter knowledge to last a lifetime. They had sat in silence after its utterance, the pair of them on the floor somehow; Sarah leaning against the bed, and Michael cross-legged, back to the window, so he couldn't see the sky as Sarah could. She wondered if he too would have thought it mortally wounded. Or perhaps he'd have expected a helicopter and the sound of breaking glass: same thing.

'Are you all right?' she prompted gently at last.

'I'm fine.'

'What happened next?'

Michael didn't know what happened next.

He had passed out; wished he had passed out seconds earlier, and been spared the nightmares since. When he came to he was a red sore: his skin flaking, peeling; his hair scorched. He was tied to a hospital bed. He didn't know where he was. He thought . . .

'I didn't know what I thought.'

'You thought you were a prisoner.'

'It was our helicopter. One of ours. I know that now. But back then, tied to that bed . . . I wondered. I thought maybe I'd got it upside down.'

'But you hadn't.'

'We were guinea pigs. That bomb, it was some kind of chemical agent. And the stuff we'd been painted with, that was supposed to protect us.' He paused. 'You used to hear stories, back during the war. About the superweapon. They called it a patriot bomb. You ever hear of that?'

Sarah shook her head.

'It's the Holy Grail. Something that kills the enemy but not your own troops. I don't think it exists, not yet. But not everybody's stopped trying.'

'But that's illegal, chemical weapons, they're . . .'

They were against the law. She didn't bother finishing.

He pulled his shirt up and showed her his stomach. Ugly red weals coloured it, strange blotchy stripes, like the camouflage of a new beast. He didn't comment, having no need to. He pulled his shirt down again. Sarah couldn't say sorry: mostly she felt sick, but not for the sake of his appearance. She said nothing.

'I don't know how long I was there. We were all there, the six of us, but I didn't know that until later. There were tests. Blood tests. A machine, like they use for a brain scan, but for the whole body. They never spoke to me. It was as if I'd dropped from outer space, and they wanted to know all about my planet. You know what happened? I became an un-person out there in the desert. I was just a result, the result of an experiment. And they didn't give a fuck I was also human.'

She would have reached to touch him then, but sensed he didn't want that.

'It was only when I saw through a window I knew I was in England. After that, they moved us anyway. All of us.'

'Where to?'

'An island. Off the west coast of Scotland. I was better by then. Better as I'll ever be. I'm not sure why they didn't just kill us.'

'They pretended you were dead.'

'We learned that on the island. One of the guards told Tommy. Funny, we didn't really think they were guards until then. They were just guys, a bunch of guys, there to make sure we were all right. That's what they told us. And every time we asked, which was every day, they'd say we were going home soon, and it was just a few things needed sorting, that was all. Tomorrow. Maybe the next day. I can't remember how many tomorrows I lived through, waiting for the boat. Must have been hundreds. Then one of the guys, one Tommy got really friendly with, told him we were all supposed to be dead anyway. In that helicopter.' He laughed, but didn't sound amused. 'I've never been to Cyprus. Never been dead, either.'

'What did you do?'

'That was the end. The end of pretending. They weren't armed just because the regulations demanded, and we weren't kept in cells for protection. We were already dead, it was just nobody had pulled the trigger yet. I don't know. Maybe there were more tests they wanted to do. Maybe they wondered if we'd all die anyway, through long-term side effects. Or maybe – and this is what I think really happened – they couldn't kill us without heavy back-up. Like a signed letter from the prime minister, for instance. We were members of Her Majesty's forces, for Christ's sake. They weren't going to execute us without covering their backs. But they weren't going to let us go, either. Not now they'd told the world we were dead.'

Sarah said, 'Jesus wept . . .'

'Yeah. Right.'

He stood abruptly, and went to look out of the window after all. It occurred to her, the way she might cotton on to the plot halfway through a TV drama, that the reason people wanted to kill him was because of everything he knew. And now she knew it too.

'What happened?' she asked.

'We left.'

'Just like that.'

'No. Not just like that.' He turned back to look at her. 'Tommy and I left. That was all.'

'What about the others?'

'Dead.'

'And the guards?'

'Dead.'

'Did you . . .'

'We were still at war, don't you get it? It's just that nobody had explained whose side we were on. There were four guards, six of us. Only Tommy and me walked.'

'I don't blame you.'

'I wasn't asking your forgiveness.'

'I wasn't saying that. I meant—'

'Or your understanding. I'm telling you what happened, that's all. Okay?'

'Okay,' she said softly. She could hardly make him out, now. The room so full of shadows, she couldn't tell where they stopped and he started.

He shook his head, then turned and drew the curtains. There was a small lamp on the bedside table he turned on, then offered her water. She wasn't thirsty. He poured a glass to the brim, and drained it in one long swallow.

'What was it called?' she asked. 'The island?'

'I could find it on a map.'

'And where've you been since?'

'When?'

'All the time you've been playing dead. Where did you hide?'

He didn't answer, but picked up the remote control, and buzzed the TV back to life: artillery traces swept across a black sky like screaming angels. And Sarah thought of snipers cloistered high over city streets; of mortar shells wrecking schools and marketplaces. She thought of dark nights and roadblocks, and civilians poured into mass graves. There were only so many livings a soldier might earn.

'Did she know?'

'Who?'

'Maddy. Tommy's wife. Did she know you were—'

'No. She thought we were dead.'

He snapped the TV off again, as if underlining a point.

She felt she needed breathing space, a time to absorb the information he'd given her. In a former life, she'd have headed for open air: walked her limbs ragged and cleaned her lungs out, given her mind a chance to catch up. Tonight, she didn't want to leave this room. The story he'd told her: it was as if the reality of it was waiting outside, and it was only in here she'd be safe. As for what had happened to *her*, her own sad tale, she'd hardly begun to believe it. Though already a full day had passed since Rufus attacked her, making ancient history of everything that had gone before. And she wondered what poor Maddy had thought, finding her husband delivered from the grave. She must have believed her life was starting over; all the time Rufus was waiting to take it away.

It was as if he'd read her thoughts. 'Tell me about him.'

'Rufus?'

'If that was his name.'

'He called himself Axel,' she remembered.

'Tell me anyway.'

So she told him about Wigwam instead; not about the wacky clothes and the sixties mindset, but about the woman who was her friend, who had struggled to bring up four children despite an abusive partner who had popped out one day for the legendary can of lager, and never come back.

'Literally,' Sarah said. 'A can of lager.'

Michael looked away.

And then Rufus showed up. To call it a whirlwind romance underestimated the weather. Sarah had dropped in one morning and found Wigwam had a husband.

'Cover,' Michael said.

'I know that *now*.'

'He was waiting for Tommy. An agent in place.'

'They knew he'd turn up?'

'They knew where Maddy and Dinah lived.'

Some men buggered off in search of the eternal off-licence; others just buggered off, period. Some went into hiding to save their lives, but had to come back for their children.

'So what about you? Why didn't you just disappear again?'

He didn't answer.

'A man's gotta do?' she asked, surprised at her own venom. 'Nobody blows up your best buddy while you're around?'

'Oh, macho, sure.' He looked at her. 'There was something Tommy used to say. "Remember Buddy Holly's last words? Fuck it. We're all going to die."'

'And that's how soldiers talk.'

'He was a soldier, yes. It's how he talked, that's all. What's Dinah to you, anyway?'

'She was a child,' Sarah said after a long pause. 'I just thought somebody should make sure she was all right.'

Michael said, 'That guy. Rufus. Axel? The day after the bomb, he was hanging round the house, or what was left of it. And every day after.'

'But there were loads of people like that. Sightseers.'

'He wasn't watching the fire crews. He was watching the people *watching* the fire crews. He was waiting for me. Besides, I recognised him.'

'You knew him?'

'Knew the type. He was a killer.'

'*Rufus*?'

'Was I wrong?'

He hadn't been wrong.

'I knew he killed Maddy and Tommy. If anyone knew where Dinah went, he did.'

She had Dinah to thank for her life, then. If Michael hadn't been following Rufus, he'd never have heard her alarm.

'I'd have killed him anyway,' he said.

She knew that too. It troubled her that it didn't upset her more.

'Why haven't they found him?' she asked.

'They have.'

'It would have been on the news.'

'Depends.' He'd been thinking about this, she could tell. 'Depends who found him first.'

'Mark must have got home—'

'Within the hour,' he said. 'That was him at the station, right?'

She hadn't told him that. He knew anyway.

'So, he gets home and finds a body. You've done a bunk. Does he go to the cops?'

'He goes to the cops.' She was sure about this.

He showed her his open palms. 'And first thing they do is pass the buck. This guy, Axel, the killer, he'll have had ID. The local cops take one look at it, they're on the phone to the Home Office.' He yawned suddenly. Hugely. 'Next thing you know, there's men in suits all over your house, deciding what did and didn't happen.'

'You're tired.'

'Exhausted.'

'You should sleep.'

'So should you.'

For a quick moment their eyes met, as their situation hit them anew: two of them, and just one bed. But it was only a moment.

'I'll take the chair,' he said.

'Don't be ridiculous. The bed's big enough.'

'I'll—'

'Oh for God's sake, I won't bite you.' She bit her lip instead.

'Look. Suppose they come? Suppose they find us? You're dead on your feet. You need to sleep.'

'I'm okay.'

'You're not.' You never will be, she thought. 'Just lie down, all right?'

He gave her a crooked sort of smile, an out-of-practice one.

She was thinking of the weals on his stomach, wondering if his whole body was like that. As if he'd been flayed with a red-hot whip: and she shuddered, and hoped he didn't notice.

For some reason, looking up at the hotel in the darkness, he was reminded of a ship: one of those ocean-going monsters he'd never been on but imagined readily enough; ploughing through night and weather, impervious to both. Lights here and there showed where crew were still on watch. The canopies and flagpoles were the rigging. Amos Crane shook his head to dispel the fancy. Middle of the night, one long drive done, another yet to go: in between he'd get to kill people, if his guesswork proved solid. It was hardly the time to indulge his imagination.

The hotel was part of an upmarket chain; upmarket enough that the register was on a database, into which Crane had found his way with no trouble. Late last night – the night *before* last – there'd been a couple who had paid cash for a double room, without reservations, and – according to an unticked box on the screen – nothing in the way of luggage, either. Smithson. As if somebody had started saying Smith, and their brain caught up half a beat later.

It was a one-shot deal. If they weren't here – and he'd stopped looking once he'd found this pair – then he'd not find them before they were on the move again. But that was okay. He liked these odds. *Never let them tell you it's not a game*, Axel had said once. It was good remembering that, after too many months pretending to be a suit. And one way or the other, he didn't expect his desk to be waiting for him once he got back home. He got out of the car and carefully buttoned his raincoat. It was the kind of detail that lingered in the memory of others. Once, he'd done a job in full view of four witnesses, wearing a bright red scarf. *Wearing a red scarf*, the descriptions said afterwards. Other than that, he'd been a ghost.

He crossed the car park, his steps echoing hugely in the dark, and entered the hotel.

The lobby was large and dimly lit; the walls wood-panelled, the carpet a deep thick red. Soothing. There were prints on the walls, historical scenes, Crane registered without actually looking: he was focused on the desk where a porter watched him advance, not with suspicion exactly – not visible suspicion – but in the expectation of receiving an explanation any time now. It was late for a guest to be arriving. Crane reached the desk; reached too for an expression befitting a weary traveller. 'Archibald,' he said.

'Mr . . . ?'

'Archibald,' he repeated. 'I rang earlier.'

'Mr Archibald,' the porter said. He ran a riff on his computer keyboard, opening his screen to the evening's page. 'And what time was this, sir?'

'About nine thirty.' It had just gone one. 'I was held up. I've driven from London. I'm very tired.'

'Of course you are, sir.' He'd found the reservation Crane had entered himself: *Archibald*. 'If you'd just sign here . . .'

It didn't take more than five minutes and he was given the key, shown the lift; he ordered an early call he had no intention of being around for, and wished the porter goodnight. If the man were observant, he could deliver a thorough description of Crane to whoever asked: he had, after all, just spent five minutes in a one-to-one. But, thought Crane, it didn't matter. The die was cast. When the opportunity to kill Downey arose, Crane wouldn't be put off by the presence of a night porter.

On the third floor, like an animal, Crane explored the dimensions of his new surroundings. Bed, wardrobe, trouser press. A dressing table at which he sat for a few moments, studying with genuine surprise his reflection in its mirror. Some days, he felt a stranger to himself. A grey face, the skin stretched tightly over bone: it didn't do him justice. He really thought it didn't do him justice. But it was too late to change face: he stood and checked out the bathroom. Reasonable size. The water pressure wasn't brilliant. In a little basket by the sink he found shampoo, shower gel, toothpicks; even a little needlework kit, bound in white cardboard marked *With Compliments*. It awed him, this descent into the ordinary. That there were people who'd *ooh* and *aah* over this stuff; over any stuff. A trouser press, for Christ's sake. It was like wandering into a situation comedy.

The window gave out on the main street. He could see a man walking a dog; a few shop windows, lit against burglars, cast his shadow as he went.

Crane could feel the excitement building. As if he were here for illicit sexual purposes rather than as a matter of professional pride.

While Michael slept he made small noises in the dark; not words exactly, though expressive enough: speaking in tongues you might call it, like a common or garden hysteric. Translation, in general terms, was not difficult. Whatever he was dreaming he had already lived through, just as Sarah sometimes felt that what she lived through now she had dreamed in her other life: that there would be days like this, locked in a room with a stranger, who mumbled at night when his bad dreams tracked him down.

She remembered another night, waking to hear a child crying in the street. When she reached the window, there was nobody there. Probably there never had been. Was this what it was like to be a mother? To be attuned to random distress, even imaginary distress, on the off chance you could offer consolation? Sarah looked at Michael now as she might at a child, but there was no deceiving herself: wherever he was, he was untouchable, and nothing she could do could tone down the pitch of his nightmares. He had seen war. She had seen death. It was a small overlap, not one that amounted to much. Michael would say it counted for nothing. It had never been her finger on the trigger.

She lay very still, very gently, counting breaths. Soon his whimpering quietened, and soon after that he awoke.

'Did you hear anything?' he whispered, already knowing she was not asleep.

'No,' she said. 'Not a thing.'

After a while his breathing steadied again.

But Sarah couldn't rest. She felt hunted; even here, in this prison-cum-haven, she could feel outside events circling like wolves. Her mind buzzed like a TV screen, all of its pictures uninvited: Rufus – *Axel* – being blown out of the picture, his blood a fine mist in the air of her kitchen; Mark kissing a stranger on a railway platform . . . She had not spoken to Wigwam. She had not spoken to *anyone*. And here she was on a bed in a strange town, next to a man who had already slain her a dragon but wasn't what Sarah would have imagined if she'd ever imagined herself a knight. His edges were dull; they had nothing in common. Except for Dinah, of course. That was what they shared: the image of a small girl lay between them like a sword.

Perhaps she dozed after all. When she opened her eyes, she was looking at the outline of the door: lit by the corridor outside, it was edged in light like it led to another world. But even as she blinked the border was broken; a dark shadow stepped on the fine golden thread, as if an outside force were gathering in the corridor, preparing for invasion . . .

She thought she saw the handle turn.

'Michael—' she began, but he was already pushing her over the side and scooping a heavy glass ashtray in his free hand as he vaulted the foot of the bed and launched himself at the door.

Crane slipped from his room into the dull corridor. Sympathetic lighting: while the hotel guests slept, the world around them dimmed to a pleasant murmur. The air hummed too. It was the suppressed energy of a large building, full to bursting with machines and sleeping people. It was electricity dormant; power waiting to spill.

From a distance Amos Crane heard a faint *ting*, which was either the bell on the desk in the lobby or a lift reaching its floor. A place this size wouldn't ever be wholly asleep. He didn't need to take risks like this: so he told himself, but took them anyway. It all depended on how you defined *need.*

. . . Crane patted his pocket where his skeleton card sat. He'd tried it on his own door and it worked without a squeak. One of the benefits of working for a government agency, along with the pension, the technology, and the wide-ranging sanction for violent misdeeds.

The Smithsons – the *Smithsons* – were in room 231. The 2 meant second floor. Crane didn't take the lift, which tended to be where video surveillance was heaviest; instead, he padded along to the stairwell, behind a heavy fire door. *In the event of a fire*, he remembered reading once, *shout Fire! and try to put it out.* All kinds of emergency descended upon the unwary. Downey, of course, wouldn't be unwary, but that was where the thrill came in. Crane himself was wholly unarmed. That wasn't the challenge, though. The challenge was keeping it quiet, and stopping once the job was done.

He let himself into the corridor below. Three doors along he reached 231 and paused for a while on the threshold, allowing the moment to sink in. Then reached for his key.

★

Michael hit the door cleanly and in one fluent moment unsnapped the lock, turned the handle, and pulled the lurking figure into the room, tripping it as it came, and dropping on top as it hit the floor. Outside in the corridor, a woman screamed. Sarah jumped back on the bed. Michael's hand, full of ashtray, rose and started to fall—

'*Don't*!'

The woman screamed again.

'Don't,' Sarah said.

Michael stopped.

'Shit, feller,' said the man on the floor.

'It's just people,' said Sarah. 'Only people . . .'

Michael lowered his arm, and put the ashtray down.

'Wrong room,' said the man on the floor. He was young, American, slightly drunk, or had been. 'Sorry, man, but *Jeezus*, what's your problem?'

There was activity outside now, as the hotel responded to the woman's screams. She had quietened down; came a timid two steps into the room and said, 'Sorry, we thought this was . . .'

'It's okay,' Sarah said. 'You scared us.'

Michael allowed his captive to get to his feet, then dropped back to his hands and knees as if the effort had all but killed him. He started to cough. The American staggered up and backed away –

'*We* scared *you*?'

– just as a man in hotel uniform turned up, carrying for some reason a torch. 'What's the problem here?'

Michael was still coughing. Sarah dropped to the floor, and touched him on the arm. 'Are you okay?' But he couldn't stop.

The hotel man asked what the problem was again, and the two Americans both tried telling him at once. 'We're next door. We got the wrong room, that's all, but—'

And then they all shut up as Michael spat loudly into the

ashtray: a bright red stream of bloody phlegm that, once it started, didn't look as if it was going to stop . . .

'Jesus,' said the American.

Sarah gripped Michael's arm, and held on tight.

And Crane let himself silently out of the room, and padded back to the stairwell.

It was as well to be philosophical about such things. Hadn't Axel once accused him of philosophy? So he would be philosophical this once, and practise one of its rare consolations: just imagine, he told himself as he slipped into the quiet of his own room, what it would be like to be somebody else. A Smithson, for instance. Lying asleep downstairs right now, unaware of Crane's brief joyless visit. They'd never know how close they came, or that the rest of their lives were a gift from him. Perhaps he should have left a card for them. *I think, therefore you are.*

Worcester had been a mistake, though, he told himself as he undressed. He should have gone to Malvern.

21

LIGHT AGAIN. LIGHT PLAYING over furniture in patterns she already recognised: Sarah had lived in houses where she'd not been as familiar with the way light swam across the arrangements in its path. She imagined an old age in which she looked back and reconstructed all of this, including the trouser press; an age in which she mulled not at all over a forgotten home in Oxford. These were tricks her brain played on her to pull her out of the present, which comprised Michael lying on the bed once more, his coughing fit passed but his face pale, his eyes watery – not knowing what else to do, she had placed a wet towel over his forehead and made him drink water. He wasn't asleep. There was a trace of fever, though, or had been: it seemed to have faded with the dawn. Now he had removed his sweatshirt, and she could see the red blotches on his arms that matched the weals on his stomach. It was a piece of corroboration she could have happily done without.

I don't have a normal life any more. I won't ever have one, if we don't finish this.

He would try to get rid of her now, she guessed, because she'd told him all she knew, which was nothing. But she couldn't stay here and she couldn't go home, because when she thought of all she might find there – Wigwam, Mark – her future dissolved in a watery mist.

Michael turned his head to one side; laid his forearm across his eyes. When she was sure he was sleeping, she left the room quietly. All she had brought from Oxford was her purse, and as she waited for the lift she fished in it for what change it held: a small handful of silver, some useless coppers. The lift took her down to the lobby. In a cubbyhole by the entrance to the bar, she found the phone, and piled money on the shelf while she ransacked her memory for her own number: a sure sign of guilt that she couldn't recall it, but knowing that didn't help much. Let your fingers do the walking, she decided, and shut her eyes and punched in the number by touch – it came automatically, and her hand shook as she heard the connection made, and the ringing begin in her own front room, so many miles away. But nothing. But not even the answer machine. As if she were a ghost, thwarted in the act of haunting; unable even to leave her voice floating in an empty room.

She should call Wigwam, she thought, hanging up. Wigwam would be home. But her heart gave way at the prospect, and she knew that she couldn't talk to Wigwam yet.

But her fingers were dialling again, as if they'd adopted a dangerous habit of their own volition. It was almost with surprise she heard the voice in her ear, reciting the partners of The Bank With No Name as if it were a mantra enjoyed by the holy: so much surprise she didn't respond at first, not until the woman on the switchboard repeated the magic words. Then she asked for Mark.

'I'm sorry . . .'

'Mark Trafford. It's his wife.'

There was a long moment of silence which stretched nearly to breaking point. Then: 'Putting you through.'

For a while there was only space noise, as she travelled the loops and whorls of the bank's system. She would hear Mark's voice any second, and just the thought of it was like imagining walking on the moon – being somewhere totally familiar and utterly strange all at once. Would he already know it was her when he heard the phone ring? Once, he'd been able to do that; they both had. Or had told each other they had. But even when it had seemed to happen, it was just another trick the mind played: and this time, if Mark knew who it was, it was because a switchboard operator had told him.

'Can I help you?'

It wasn't Mark's voice anyway.

'Hello? Can I—'

'I'm calling for Mark Trafford. Is he there?'

The woman didn't respond. And Sarah had the sudden crazy notion that all these events, even this one, were part of some raddled, toxic dream: that she wasn't who she thought she was; there was no Mark; she had no life. That the woman down the line would disconnect her any moment, and she would wake into a world completely different.

'Is he—'

'Is that his wife?'

'I—yes. I'm his wife. Yes.'

There was another strangled silence. Jesus Christ, it's not just me, thought Sarah. Everyone is totally round the twist.

'You . . . don't know?'

'Don't know what?'

. . . There was no sense of panic, eerily enough. Instead a deadly calm, and a shift in her perspective, as if the cubbyhole had suddenly become very distant from the rest of the lobby. And the woman had sounded almost close to tears . . .

'Don't know *what*?' she repeated.

'He doesn't work here any more.'

She had been so sure he was dead that she almost laughed.

'Is that *all*?'

'. . . I don't . . .'

'Who'm I speaking to, anyway?'

'My name's Treadwell, Emma Tre—'

Sarah slammed the phone back on its hook.

In the lift again, heading back up to the room, she remembered a moment from ancient history, and a morning spent complaining to Wigwam about her boring life. No job. Housework. 'You know what he said to me the other day? . . . I was handing him a cup of coffee, and he said *Thanks, em, Sarah.*' No he hadn't. He'd said 'Thanks, Em—Sarah.' Bastard. She reached the room in a mood to kill. And then that vanished too, and there was very nearly real panic this time as she pushed the door open on an empty bed in an empty—

'Michael? *Michael*!'

'What?'

He came out of the bathroom, a towel hanging limply over his shoulders.

Sarah pushed the door shut behind her, and leaned on it for support.

'I thought you'd gone,' he said.

Redundantly, she shook her head.

'Anyway, we've been here too long. We should both be going.' He went back into the bathroom, but left the door open. She could hear water running down the sink. She sat on the bed, and waited.

22

THE ROOM WAS STILL on the same floor and had the same old calendar on the wall; the same window provided the same view of, probably, the same traffic snaking through the same lights. C had the same mane of silver grey hair, the same look of repressed fury, and the same tension headache was creeping up on Howard as he stood in the same place he had last time: just in front of the desk. That mark on the wall hadn't been there before, though. Looked like a spider had been squashed about halfway up.

'Let's recap,' said C.

Yes. Let's.

'You let Axel Crane, who was barking mad, go ballistic on an operation that called for finesse. He blew up a nice suburban house, scoring exactly fifty per cent in his attempt to eliminate the targets, Downey and Singleton. He also killed Singleton's wife, and came this close to killing his young daughter, whom *Amos* Crane has since spirited away for use as bait to draw Downey out. Who meanwhile has killed Axel Crane, apparently to prevent him from murdering a local woman who got too nosy about Singleton's daughter's whereabouts. Said nosiness consisting in part of hiring a private detective, whom Axel *successfully* murdered. Did I miss anything important?'

Howard shook his head.

'Good. Now, here's the really interesting question. If only

one part of that was to appear in the papers, which part would you like it to be?'

'The bit about Downey killing Axel,' Howard said.

C closed his eyes briefy. 'Have you any idea how fucking rhetorical that was?'

This time, Howard didn't reply.

From an office somewhere down the corridor a phone rang, which nobody answered. It was late afternoon, which in the Ministry for Urban Development counted as the wee small hours of the morning. Its name is MUD, Howard thought, inconsequentially. That gave them something in common, at any rate.

'You're supposed to be running a secret department, Howard. You don't officially exist.'

Howard thought: sure. Fine. But the problem with running a place that doesn't exist is, you have to staff it with people who do. Which means creatures like the Crane brothers. Not much point in trying to get that across. 'I'm aware of that.'

'So why is Downey still on the loose? He's been out of our hands since almost last Christmas. He's been back in the country three weeks at least. Have you any idea how much damage he could do if he started talking? If anyone listened?'

'Nobody would.'

'You'd like to guarantee that, would you, Howard? You'd like to sign your fucking name to the promise?'

'He's a war criminal. We can prove it.'

'Oh, brilliant. He's also technically dead, Howard. We can prove that too.' He shook his head. 'We are at *war*, Howard. Along with our good allies across the water. Protecting the proud name of democracy, and all the rest of the bollocks. Do we really want the world to know that it's our fault this time? Because some mad bugger with more ribbons on his uniform than brain cells in his head wanted live targets for the latest chemical toy? We won't look quite so fucking noble all of a sudden, will we? You ever wonder what it's like on the receiving end of sanctions, Howard? Or Scud fucking missiles, come to that? Because that'll be the least of our bloody worries if Downey lives long enough to talk.'

'If he was going to talk, he already would have. He's been on the loose long enough.'

'Didn't have a woman with him, though, did he? Just him and Singleton, right? Combat conditions. It's not like that now. And where's Amos Crane, anyway?'

'He's, er—'

'Back at the office? Don't piss me off, Howard. I heard about your contretemps. That's a bit more fucking French for you, you seem to like it. Put you on the floor, did he? He's a fucking animal. Always has been.'

'I don't know where he is. I think he went after Downey.'

'Nobody ever claimed he didn't enjoy his work. But it's gone too far, Howard. Thanks to the piss poor job those bastard brothers have done, there's another civilian on the dead list. And given the hard-on Crane's got now Downey's boxed his brother, it's not likely to be a pretty death, either. I don't want to read about Mrs Trafford being found in six different locations. Alastair Bloody Campbell couldn't make that sound accidental. So Crane's off the job, got it? Yank his leash and bring him home. As far as I'm concerned, you can pension him off. But do it properly. No amateurs. And I don't want *his* body turning up anywhere, ever. Clear?'

'Can I have that in writing, sir?'

'Fuck off. Now, what happened to Mr Trafford? He been secured?'

'I think so.'

'How excellent. If I were interested in what you think, Howard, I'd be saving up for your memoirs. Has he been secured or not?'

'We've got him with his fingers in the till. His job's gone, obviously, but as far as his bank's concerned that's the end of it. Reputation to maintain and all the rest. But we're holding criminal charges open, and one squeak from him and we'll bury him.'

'Who made that clear?'

'Amos Crane.'

'Good enough.'

. . . Amos had told Trafford, apparently, to expect no chance of a holiday in an open prison, improving his squash, followed by an early release with temporary senile dementia. Amos, in fact, had been extremely graphic about just what Trafford *could* expect.

'He's staying with a friend of his, I gather. The story is, his wife's done a bunk. And no noise about finding a body in the kitchen.'

'But he knows the body was in the Service.'

'He couldn't not, really,' Howard admitted.

C sighed slightly, as if picturing another accident happening in the not too distant future. 'How long have you been doing this job, Howard?'

'Six years, sir. Just under.'

'Wonderful. Stick with it another six years and the population explosion could be a nightmare of the past. Perhaps we should send you overseas. Africa, India. One of those very crowded places. Oh, stop looking so fucking resentful. I know it's not entirely your fault.' C scratched his chin malevolently. 'I just don't much bloody care, that's all. Now. Where's Downey headed? Assuming he lives long enough?'

'The child's on the island. Crane expected he'd go there.'

'Does he think Downey's very clever or very stupid?'

'Very stupid, I think, sir.'

'Fair enough. Either way, Crane'll be heading there himself, unless he tracks Downey down en route. I'm serious about this, now, Howard. Crane finds them before they get to the island, he'll leave a mess all over the landscape. On the island, it doesn't much matter. We can hose it down and forget it. But I don't want more of a pig's ear made out of this than you've managed already. So stop Crane. If he reaches the island first, fair enough. Let him do his job. But I don't want him leaving it. I don't mean to be harsh about this, Howard, but he's like a pit bull that's tasted blood. You can never trust him again.'

'I think I know what you mean.'

'And stop pretending it's a painful duty. I'm sure you'll piss on his corpse. Now get out.'

There was a spring in Howard's step as he walked back across the park. It wasn't often a revenge fantasy received official sanction. Almost enough to make up for the amount of shit he'd had to eat to get it: that man was a foul-mouthed bastard all right. Still. One fantasy at a time.

He hoped Crane made it to the island first. He also hoped Downey still had a gun.

SIX

THE GOOD SOLDIER

23

THE HIRE CAR WAS a red VW, one of those compact, city models. Michael put his new rucksack in the back, along with the canvas bag Sarah had inherited from him. Two days ago, she'd left home with nothing. Already she had luggage; was accumulating a new history. It wasn't that easy to leave everything behind. You junked what you could, and new junk came right along and took its place.

At least there was a new Sarah, though. She turned the windscreen flap down, and checked herself out in the vanity: in Boots, she'd bought a dye pack, and transformed herself from an average, mouse-brown woman to a raven. She wasn't sure how many washes it would take. From the state of the towel when she'd finished, not a lot. But it would do. She no longer looked like the other Sarah Tucker. She looked like her own woman.

Michael saw what she was doing. 'I told you,' he said. 'It looks fine.'

'Thanks.'

'You could be anybody.'

'Thanks,' she said again, but he didn't register the difference. They were on the road now, leaving the town behind. She saw a pair of buzzards hovering over a concrete bridge. It was sad, with all the space their wings might afford them, that they chose to live by the hard shoulder.

'How did you hire a car?'

He looked at her briefly.

'Don't you need ID? Aren't you supposed to be dead?'

'I've got ID.'

'Whose?'

No answer. She went back to landscape gazing. Once, on a drive with Mark, they'd passed a buzzard sitting on a post. It had been much larger than they'd have expected. Unafraid, it had stared them down with an angel's contempt for the earth-bound, then returned to surveying its field. As they drove on, Sarah's main feeling had been one of guilt. She did not know why this was so, and never would.

Another time, in Oxfordshire, they'd driven past a field of ostriches. Dozens of them: out of place, and wicked, and down-right delightful.

'His name was Fielding,' Michael said.

'Fielding.'

'James Fielding.'

'Sounds like a stockbroker.'

'He was a wino. Living on the streets.'

'And you bought his identity?'

'He wasn't using it any more.'

Once you had the social security number, everything came easy. Driving licence, credit cards . . . Even junk mail, if you had an address.

Michael kept driving. They didn't pass any ostriches.

After some hours, they were in London. And then, before she felt truly ready for it, Michael was finding a parking space for the VW, and she was alone on a leafy street, walking through dappled shadows among houses that sang of summer, and light and money.

Gerard's Hampstead home had none of the rural insecurities of his Cotswold cottage: he might be faking it with the county set, but he had nothing to prove in the suburbs. His house was large, detached and mostly hidden from view by a high and surgically perfect hedge whose purpose was less to secure privacy than to underline that, in a street like this, conspicuous expenditure was unnecessary. If you'd made it here, you'd made it. Scrunching up the gravelled drive, she admired the potted bays flanking the big front door; the way that, though a car was parked nearby, no tyre tracks betrayed that it had been driven rather than built there. Probably each stone was numbered and allotted a position. Probably Gerard had full-time staff, organising this.

All of which supposed it was Gerard's home. But memories of conversations about Hampstead had steered Sarah to the appropriate phone book; she had little doubt she'd got it right. Especially when the car turned out a Porsche. Her only disappointment being, when she rang the bell, Inchon answered the door himself. She'd been hoping for something in livery, or at the very least a French maid.

'Good lord,' he said.

'Not at work?'

'It's a holiday,' he said automatically. Then, 'Sarah? What on earth are you doing here?'

'It's a long story.'

Michael appeared behind her. He'd moved silently over the gravel; had possibly floated an inch or two above it.

Gerard glanced at him briefly; said, 'I think you have the wrong house.'

'He's with me.'

'Really?'

Confirming it would have put her at a disadvantage. She simply waited until he said, 'You'd better come in.'

So they followed him through a wide, immaculate hall to a room at the back; a broad, sunny room with French windows, a baby grand, and large, comfy chairs. From outside came what

Sarah thought was the chirping of crickets but turned out to be a water sprinkler. Its reach didn't quite make the windows, but the patio sparkled wetly, and rainbows danced off the spray with each pass. Summertime in England. She half expected a string quartet to kick off.

'Drink?'

'No thanks.'

He said, 'Some people have been worried about you.'

'Other people have been trying to kill me.'

'There was some debate as to whether Mark was among their number.' He sat down heavily. 'There were traces of blood, apparently. On the carpet? But it turned out not to be yours.'

'That wasn't in the papers.'

'I didn't say it was. I made it my business to find out, Sarah.'

'Really.'

'*Noblesse oblige*? I did warn you, after all. I was worried you'd had it out with Mark, and he'd reacted badly.'

'You *warned* me?'

'You were rather drunk. Maybe you don't remember.'

She shook her head. 'I wasn't drunk.'

'I told you you'd be wishing you were bored again. That trouble was coming. A bit cryptic, but what could I say? That your husband was a crook? You'd have broken my legs.'

'Batten down the hatches,' Sarah said.

'Do you know,' Gerard mused, 'he even tried rifling my palmtop? He wanted me to think that was you.'

'Imagine. So you thought he'd killed me.'

'I wasn't that worried. I'd have backed you against him. You might as well sit down, you know. Is he always like that?'

Michael was by the door, head cocked for company. But his gaze never left Gerard.

'Yes.'

He didn't pursue it.

'What was he doing?' Sarah asked. Part of her didn't want to know. The other part had to.

'He was laundering money, Sarah. Not criminal money, sanctioned money. Emanating not a million miles from the Persian Gulf. He was channelling it through a series of offshore trusts he'd set up in Jersey, Liechtenstein and the Cayman Islands, and when it came out the other side, a tiny percentage stayed in an account with his number on it, and the rest, which was by now to all intents and purposes stateless money, was funding arms purchases. He's going to claim he was duped, but he left a paper trail a boy scout could follow. And I *always* investigate before I take on investment advisers. Mark should have known that.'

'So you turned him in.'

'To the police? No, I didn't. I don't approve of what he did, but the thought of taking it to the police, do you know, I just couldn't stomach that either? Too many *Boys' Own* stories as a kid. Nobody likes a sneak.'

'You told his boss, though.'

'A weasel called Mayberry. I tipped him the wink, yes. You might call that a duty. If somebody working for me went fast and loose through the regulations, it'd be nice if I got to hear about it.' His mouth twitched. 'Not that I'd need to be told. That man's in charge? He couldn't run a tap.'

So there it was. Mark wouldn't be making a fuss about her disappearance, because he'd have been told not to, in very direct terms.

Now Gerard's voice gentled somewhat. 'I wish it hadn't turned out like this. You must feel dreadful.'

Sympathy from Gerard was a new horror. She preferred him savage, chopping other people's beliefs. 'Not that dreadful. He was having an affair. Woman in the office. Did you know that? Or would that be *sneaking*?'

'Are you sure you won't sit down?'

She was tired suddenly. Tired of fencing, tired of company. Tired of Gerard already. 'I didn't come here for a rest.'

'What for, then?'

She didn't answer. She was registering a change in the area; some subtle difference she couldn't put a finger to. Then realised it was the sprinkler, changing direction.

'I'd be happy to help, but I don't know what you need. Do you have money?'

'She needs a gun.'

'He talks,' Gerard said, but didn't look at Michael. 'Is that right? You came here for a *gun*?' He seemed amused.

'I told you. People have tried to kill me.'

'Which people?'

She couldn't trust this man. Or didn't that matter now? 'You remember Rufus?'

'That rather strange friend of—'

'It was his blood. On the floor.'

Gerard raised an eyebrow.

'You collect guns. You said so.'

'But I *never* lend them to—'

'Don't try to be funny,' Michael said suddenly.

Gerard ignored him. 'Are you seriously telling me Rufus tried to kill you?'

'The guns,' Michael said, 'are in that case over there.'

They both looked at him now.

'Some of them,' he added.

Sarah looked at the case he meant. She'd thought it some kind of dresser; an upright wooden coffin, that when you opened its doors would surprise you with willow pattern plates. But saw now that its doors were padlocked, which was a little uptight even for this neighbourhood. Unless Gerard knew something about crockery futures.

'I can get in there if I have to,' Michael said.

'No you can't.' Gerard rose, and Michael stepped towards him. The heavier man froze.

'Michael,' she said.

He didn't step back, but relaxed somewhat. Gerard brushed past, and found a key in the drawer of his desk. 'Be my guest.' He tossed it to fall short, but Michael's hand snapped it from the air.

The padlock opened easily. Behind the door was a sheet of glass bordered by a metal strip, in the top corner of which a small red light winked facetiously. Behind the glass, an array of, even to Sarah's eyes, ancient-looking guns.

'These should be in a museum,' Michael said.

'Of course they should. I'm a collector, not a psychopath. And working handguns, these days, are very much against the law.' He looked at Sarah. 'Interesting friends you have.'

'This isn't a game.'

'That doesn't mean there aren't rules. Are you seriously planning on shooting people?'

'Somebody tried to *kill* me.'

'And wound up with their blood on your floor.' He nodded at Michael, still studying the rows of weapons. 'I suppose Superman had something to do with that.'

Michael, busy tracing a finger down the metal strip round the window, ignored him. As they watched, he drew his arm back suddenly, as if to slap a fist into the glass.

'I hope he does that,' Gerard said. 'My money's on the glass.'

Michael lowered his fist.

'Wired into the alarm, too.'

'They're antiques,' Sarah said. 'It's a waste of time.' She should have known: why would Gerard – even Gerard – collect lethal weapons? These were simply expensive items of violent history.

'So who was he, then?' Gerard asked. 'This Rufus?'

'If I was you,' Michael told him, 'I'd mind my own business.'

Gerard glanced at him with contempt. 'I may be a physical coward,' he said, 'but I have no intention of grovelling before implied threats in my own home.'

'He wasn't threatening you,' Sarah lied. 'Gerard, I know you don't like me but—'

'If I didn't like you, you'd know about it. I'd have set the dogs on you the moment you arrived.'

'Dogs?' said Michael.

'Figure of speech. Can I bring you a comic or something? A rubber ball?'

'You want to keep those teeth?'

'You should have him on a leash, Sarah.'

Why didn't they just drop pants and compare? 'Are you finished?'

Michael shrugged; Gerard nodded a short apology. Behind his back, Michael mouthed a word. *Kitchen.*

'Do you think,' she asked, 'I could have a cup of tea?'

If the switch fazed him, he didn't show it. 'If you don't mind bags. I've never mastered this leaf business.'

'Gerard, it's the twenty-first century. *Nobody* minds . . .'

He gave her his superior smile. If wrong-footing were an Olympic event, he'd be drowning in sponsorship money.

He led them to the kitchen, filled the kettle, switched it on. Michael picked a mug from the draining board, and filled it with water from the tap.

'Help yourself,' Gerard invited him.

Michael set the mug on the bench by the kettle, and stood there with his arms folded. Looking at him, Sarah remembered boys she'd known, in her teenage years. The ones who turned encounters with her parents into embarrassment-endurance ordeals; not actively offensive, just obstinately sullen, as if their presence were the only favour you'd ever get.

'This isn't just about Mark, is it?' Gerard was saying.

'Well, hardly—'

'You were caught with drugs, weren't you?'

'They were planted.'

'By, er, Rufus?'

'Yes!'

'Who then tried to kill you.'

'Look, I know it sounds—'

'It sounds absolutely bloody ridiculous, Sarah. Which is the only reason I'm prepared to hear you out. Because you're intelligent enough to concoct a better story than that if you needed to.'

This was hearing her out?

The kettle began breathing steam. Gerard opened a cupboard and pulled teabags from a box. 'Wanting a gun, though, that's absurd. I'm hardly going to let you leave with one even if I had one you could use. A cup of tea, that's different. You certainly look like you could use it.' The kettle snapped off even as he spoke and, plucking it free of its lead, he poured hot water into the teapot. In the sudden blush of steam, neither realised what Michael was doing till he'd done it: picked the lead up, still jacked live into the socket, and dropped the end in his mug of water. A blue bang tugged at the hair on Sarah's neck. Then the fridge hiccuped off, along with the overhead light.

Gerard said, '*What*?' But Michael was already leaving the kitchen, Sarah tagging at his heels.

The light on the gun cabinet's metal frame had stopped blinking; was a dead red eye fixed on nothing. Michael was aiming a chair when Gerard arrived. Another two seconds, and he'd have breached security the hard way.

'Don't bother,' Gerard said.

He lowered the chair.

'Lateral thinking,' Gerard said. 'He'll be doing long division next.'

'Give him the key,' said Sarah.

Not a key but a piece of credit card-shaped plastic with a

pattern punched into it: when Michael slid it into a slot on the frame, the window swung open. Michael reached in and pulled out an ancient pistol; probably a musket, Sarah thought. It didn't look any younger than the Civil War, that was for sure.

Gerard said, 'Now, I'd like you to be very very careful with—'

'Where are the others?'

'There aren't any. I'm a collector, not a—'

'Psychopath. We know.' He nodded at a framed certificate on the wall. 'But you shoot. Competition standard.'

'*Used* to shoot. There was a slight change in the law, probably they didn't announce it down at the zoo.'

Michael was holding the gun in both hands, and bracing his leg against the desk now, making sure Gerard could see what he was doing. *He can't possibly*, thought Sarah: but on the other hand, the barrel looked mostly wood.

Gerard thought he might possibly. 'Do you know how much that cost?' he whispered.

'I don't care how much it cost. I'm after something newer.'

'I don't have any—'

Michael, obviously, had had second thoughts about the strength of his knee, and brought the barrel of the gun down on the side of the desk instead. It didn't break, but made a splintering noise; something metal fell to the carpet. Even Sarah closed her eyes. When she opened them, the first thing she registered was the scarred desk; a wound of bright wood gleaming against its rich dark surface. Guns don't hurt people: people hurt guns. Also expensive furniture.

'You fucking *bastard*,' said Gerard.

Michael dropped the once-valuable gun and picked its partner from the cabinet behind him. 'Where are they?'

Gerard, confirming Sarah's opinion of him, didn't fight losing battles. 'In the cellar,' he said.

'Where?'

'The door's through the kitchen.' Michael took the plastic card with him.

'Would it help,' Sarah said, 'if I told you we needed to do this?'

'Not really.' He went round the desk, and picked up the gun Michael had damaged. Sarah thought he was on the verge of crooning to it.

'Was it very old?' she asked.

'Yes.'

'And—'

'And valuable. Yes.' He looked hard at her. 'How long do you think you'll last? Do you think you'll get to the end of the road?'

'Are we talking metaphor?'

'I'm talking Hampstead. Stealing guns? The Met do armed response, Sarah. I don't want to see you hurt.'

'Thanks.'

'Your friend, I'm not bothered. They can turn him into mashed potato as far as I'm concerned.'

'You're not going to call the police, Gerard.'

'What does that mean, I'm not going to call the police?' He placed the bent weapon gently in the cabinet. 'You've already cost me thousands.'

'Because anything Michael finds that he can use, you shouldn't have in the first place. Isn't that right?'

He pursed his lips now. They were still tight. Below them, or somewhere anyway, they could hear Michael rootling around in wooden cupboards. 'What's going on, Sarah? What's going on *really*? Did that . . . *retard* actually kill your absurd friend? You're telling me that really happened?'

'He wasn't my friend. But yes, it happened.'

'Nobody's said anything about that.'

'It was his blood in the floor. You knew about the blood.'

'I already told you. I made it my business.' He shook his head wearily. 'Does this have to do with your drugs trouble?'

'They were planted on me.'

He didn't respond.

'They were planted because I'd been looking for a girl, the child who lived in that house, remember? The house that was bombed. I went looking for her with a friend, and he was killed, and I was framed.' Her voice broke. She took a moment to get it together. 'Then I started looking again, and Rufus tried to kill me.'

'Like having a pet dormouse turn on you.'

'I'm glad it's funny. We aim to please.'

'And who's the soldier?'

'How did—'

'He moves like one. Come on, Sarah, where'd you find *him*? He looks like a non-speaking role in a spaghetti western.'

'He was Singleton's friend.'

'Singleton?'

'Whose house it was. That blew up that night.'

'Another soldier?'

'Yes.'

'Sarah. He died years ago. It said so in the paper. Whoever was in that house—'

'It was him.'

She could tell he didn't believe her. Oddly, this mattered to her. Here he was, the capitalist monster, and he'd been worried about her – she could tell he wasn't faking. And along with this came the knowledge that if she asked, he'd keep quiet about their visit. Not because of whatever Michael might find downstairs. But because she'd asked.

Even with the thought, Michael was back. He held a handgun in one hand; a longer gun she thought was a shotgun in the other.

Gerard said, 'You think I'm just going to let you walk away with those?' But even Sarah knew he was bluffing.

Michael ignored him. He said to Sarah, 'We should go.'

'That's a Purdey. It's a very expens—'

'Gerard. I'm sorry.'

'I hope you know what you're doing, Sarah.'

'Rufus tried to kill me. Remember that.' She put her hand on his shoulder, stretched lightly and kissed him on the cheek. 'We're looking for a little girl. And we really mean to find her.'

Because there was nothing more to say, they left then. Gerard didn't say goodbye. He didn't rub his cheek, either.

In the car, Michael said, 'Did you have to do that?'

He'd put the guns in the boot. The street had been empty; nobody to see him do so. Not as far as they were aware, anyway.

'Do what?'

'You know.'

She knew. She didn't bother replying. 'We should go. Remember?'

'Go where?'

'The only reason they've got Dinah is because they want you to come looking for her. Right?'

'Right.'

'So it stands to reason she's somewhere you can find her. Somewhere you know.'

'I'm not stupid, Tucker.'

'I think she's—'

'On the island. Yes?'

'I think she's on that island. Yes.'

He put the car into gear, and started to drive.

24

HOWARD STILL HAD THE letter on his desk, words like 'fulsome' and 'sincere' dripping from it like honey off toast. When Amos Crane took the piss, he didn't muck about. But there it was anyway: a written apology, with a coded reference to an incident definitely not described as violent assault. Crane might have farted at a departmental meeting for all the detail offered. In a lot of ways, then, an admirable achievement, and for all Howard knew, maybe Crane would have made it behind a desk after all. The letter would go in his file, of course. Just before the black ribbon went round it.

Crane was now, the letter said, taking a few hours off, catching up on some sleep; would be into the office later, to tidy up before leaving for Scotland. Howard already knew the first part of that, because he'd been having Crane's flat watched. A team of three: two in the van with THE FABULOUS BAKIN' BROTHERS daubed on the side, next to a picture of a large rabbit eating a cookie, and one in the launderette further down the road, the same load of washing cycling round in circles while he waited for his portable to beep. All three were freelance; this, Howard lied to himself, out of respect for Amos's feelings: he couldn't send colleagues to see him off. Insult to injury. Though his real reason was, nobody who'd ever worked with Amos would take him as a target: not for feeling, friendship, loyalty, but fear.

That was how matters had stood three hours ago.

Now, Howard was buttoning his jacket, unbuttoning, buttoning, unbuttoning . . . Catching himself at last, he forced his hands to the desktop. Slight tremor. More than slight, actually. *Extreme* a bit nearer the mark. He picked up the letter once more, put it down. Three hours. That was when the boys in the van called to say the product had just come in, and would be despatched as soon as possible. And since then: nothing.

There was always the danger that things would go wrong. One day he'd have a sampler made of that, and hang it on the wall behind his desk. When things go wrong, there is always danger. Amos Crane was no longer a spring chicken, of course, and the three hard tickets he'd sent were young, enjoyed their work, and not overburdened with self-doubt: it was always possible that they'd finished the job and popped off for an early supper, forgetting to phone in first . . . Perhaps he should have flying pigs added to the design on his sampler. Amos Crane had never been a chicken of any description. The three hard tickets were young, enjoying both their work and an exaggerated sense of their own abilities. There was a world of difference between, say, arranging an accident for an overweight minister whose carnal appetites were in danger of becoming a public embarrassment, and preparing an early grave for a pro like Crane. They hadn't forgotten to call, Howard knew that. They were beyond the reach of any mobile, that was all.

Very soon now, he was going to have to go out and see for himself.

In the end, Howard did what he had to do: because it was his job, because it was his duty, and because so long as he was the first to find out what happened, he'd get to choose what spin to put on events. He didn't drive – he rarely did, in central London – but took the Tube instead, just a few stops down the line, and made his way through a still pulsing Soho to the hungry-looking block where Amos Crane had kept a flat these past months, above a dying record shop and an apartment whose occupant offered French lessons. Crane moved several times a year, whether from professional caution or simply an inability to settle down, Howard had never decided. Certainly, he had never asked. He wondered now, somewhat belatedly, if there were anyone who *would* ask Crane such normal questions; anyone who offered him the basic low-grade human contact most people took for granted. Not now Axel was dead, Howard concluded. Possibly not even before that. The Crane brothers, it was hard to doubt, did not put a value on social contact any higher than the one they put on human life.

. . . He wondered sometimes how he would end, and whether it would be anywhere like this: in the ashtray of the city, surrounded by thieves and no-hopers. It wasn't altogether impossible. While the job paid well, and only went to the highest of flyers, there were obvious disadvantages. Officially, you didn't much exist. To those who asked, you were a middle-ranking civil servant. Such anonymity brought its own pressures, especially when it was enforced, undeserved: actually, Howard wanted to tell people (tell women), I'm James fucking Bond. As good as. Actually, I'm *M.* I tell James Bond what to do . . . Had his career path gone a little differently, a little more traditionally, he'd be within striking distance of Attorney General by now, two, three Parliaments down the line. He'd have wielded less power, but been offered much more deference. The evenings he spent brooding on this disparity tended to be those he drank too much. This job had a high burnout rate. You got a quiet knighthood, but your career was comprehensively over. And even *dream* about your memoirs, and you woke up one morning at the foot of your stairs with a broken neck, and stone cold dead.

None of which was what he should be thinking about now.

Crane's flat was up two flights; the street was busy, though anybody watching would assume he had a French lesson coming. Chance would be a fine thing. The Fabulous Bakin' Brothers were nowhere in sight; the launderette, he'd already passed. There were women in there, but no man; and a large pile of very clean, untended laundry in a basket. The more he thought about it, the more the word his mind came up with was 'bugger'.

The stairs were dark, and unpleasantly damp. Cheryl's flat – first floor – had a severely scarred front door, noticeable for the word 'fuck' ornately designed from cigarette burns. People always find something to do in a queue, supposed Howard. His breathing had become more complicated; he told himself it was the stairs, the damp. Ahead of him was the top floor flat, its own door ajar, and he realised he was unbuttoning his jacket again as he approached it, exactly as if he were preparing for physical exertion, for confrontation, which was not what he had in mind, exactly, but what *was* he going to do when he found Amos Crane in there, and Crane asked him why he'd sent three amateurs to do a pro's job? . . . Duty seemed a ridiculous word all of a sudden. Rank stupidity was what this was. Crane was no respecter of seniority; Howard's still sore throat bore witness to that. And here he was, though, pushing open the door, walking into the spider's parlour. And here was Crane, his hands and teeth still bloody, louring at him from an unspeakable corner of his flat, the bodies of his would-be assassins draped messily from the fixtures . . .

No.

Howard had to sit. The flat was empty. From an open window, a draught rushed through the rooms, carrying with it the noises of the street below: the thieves, the no-hopers, the honest stiffs and the working girls, all of them busy about their lives, which were still going on right now, just like Howard's.

★

He went home. First he went back to the office to check on incoming; then he went home, because he felt he deserved an early night in the company of a decent Sauvignon and one of his special videos. Amos Crane had gone to ground, and God Almighty couldn't find him without an effort. Effort, at present, was beyond Howard's reach. He felt uncharged, fried out; felt, in fact, like the proverbial wet rag. What he'd done would have to be paid for, he knew that. Get in first, the manuals said. Do the other guy while he thinks you're a friendly. But if you do all that and *still* don't get the drop, you have to be prepared to get bloody.

. . . That was what was waiting for him when Amos Crane broke cover. Meantime, he'd go home, have a rest, do some thinking.

Another trip by Tube, then, which more and more resembled, these days, a visit to the underworld. Crowds of ill-smelling, nervous passengers, all crushed up too close together; many of them, he suspected, secretly enjoying the fact. On hot days, the blasts of air through the tunnels were pure sulphur. There weren't as many rats on the line as there used to be, though. Howard assumed poison was set for them, and wondered if that too tainted the air; another invisible addition to the perils of capital life.

Disembarked, relieved, back in the world, he stopped at his local deli and treated himself to hummus, ciabatta, olives, then bought an evening paper at the corner. A world-famous rock star had just joined the choir eternal in dubious circumstances: it was impossible for Howard not to take a professional interest, however much he tried to view it as simple entertainment. Amos Crane, inevitably, came back to mind. Amateurs, he'd told Howard once, assumed that if you left targets with their pants down, an orange in their mouth and a pair of tights wrapped round their neck, nobody asked questions. Forensics, in fact, were a real sod in such cases. You were better off tipping them out a window . . .

Thank you, Amos, he'd said. I'll keep that in mind.

He let himself in the front door; checked the mail out of habit. Nothing. His flat was ground floor, and getting in was a major security operation, calling on three keys. Inside, he dumped his shopping on the floor while he shut the alarm down, then put the shopping in the fridge, opened the Sauvignon, poured a borderline-insensible measure into a very large glass and drank most of it standing there, fridge door open, staring unfocused out of his flat's back window, and its view of not very much. Sometimes the view through the window was the same as the view in his head, he decided: just a blank, formless space, as if somebody important forgot to fill in the details. Christ, and this was his first glass of wine. Much more, and he'd be speaking in French. He refilled the glass, shut the fridge door, and took his wine into the drawing room: a large, excellent place which always made him feel calm and comfortable, where, sadly, the first thing he saw was the sheet of writing paper on the glass-topped coffee table, and calm and comfortable left the agenda.

Howard,
I'll take the events of this afternoon as constructive dismissal, shall I? I won't go into how very upset this leaves me. Perhaps it's as well you're not in, or I might have acted in a way you'd regret.

I shall expect emoluments, pay in lieu (notice, holiday, etc.) to be arranged with your customary attention to detail. Meanwhile, I'm off to Scotland. Funny how some jobs you just can't let go, isn't it? Downey is mine. Remember that. I'll attend to you when I get back.

Sorry about the mess in the bathroom. Believe me, Amos

He finished his wine first, because there was no longer any particular hurry. But having done that, the need to use the bathroom overcame him.

The mess wasn't as bad as he'd expected, actually. At least Amos had left all three in the bath.

25

THESE WERE THE MISSING days. Sarah spent them living a road movie: not the American variety, all sand-strewn horizons and miles of cattle wagons trundling over a prairie, but a home-grown version in which damp hedgerows featured largely, and the scenery lacked visible rhyme or reason. Dry-stone walls appeared out of nowhere, ran humbly along lanesides for a mile or two, then vanished into the ground. Who decided that's where they should be? Fairy-tale trees, tough and withered as witches, jutted at dangerous angles from hillsides. She remembered Mark saying once that all the best road books and films – he was an infallible source of opinion – were the product of foreign eyes celebrating things the natives never noticed: Nabokov setting American geography in motion; Wim Wenders discovering Texas to the sound of a steel guitar. Okay then: maybe she should have packed a pen or a camera. She had the refugee's eye all right; she was an alien in this landscape. A visitor from outer space.

They had chosen to drive the back roads – *Michael* had chosen to drive the back roads – because, well, because that's what he'd chosen to do. She did not argue; if anything, they needed space in which to conduct a reality check. It was not a reality she had ever expected to find herself in – a hire-car with guns in the boot: you read about this happening in the States. It was always described as a spree, and there were always bodies left by the roadside. It ended with somebody strapped to a chair, waiting for the punishment to start.

She had to jerk herself out of these reveries. Remind herself whose side they were on.

The first night, they stopped at a farmhouse some miles from anywhere: if it had been possible to drive clear of Britain without noticing, they'd have managed it that day. The B & B sign by the verge also offered eggs, tomatoes, and, peculiarly, reconditioned fridges. The depredations on the farming industry had obviously been farther-reaching than she'd imagined. They took two rooms, the only two rooms, and in response to the landlady's raised eyebrow Sarah managed something about just being friends. They were not just friends. There was no word available to describe their relationship. That night she fell straight into heavy sleep, to be woken in the small hours by a barking dog, followed by the muttered cursing of, presumably, the farmer. The dog fell silent. So did everything else. Sarah got out of bed and went to look from the window; the surrounding countryside was dark as the far side of the moon. But as she gazed out, a car crested a hill in the distance, its sudden headlit appearance throwing everything into relief. She could make out the hillsides then; the occasional raggedy outbreak of hedge. Three trees in the near distance, their configuration an echo of a Station of the Cross. When the car passed she returned to bed and slept once more, though this time there were dreams: savage, confused things over which hovered, somehow, the horror of crucifixion. The next morning, when they passed those trees, they were innocent in the early light; neither young nor ancient; merely trees. She could as easily have had nightmares about the car she'd seen; a black demon chewing the darkness with its twin electric swords.

Michael never referred to his coughing fit. When she asked him directly he shrugged, and changed the subject.

That second day, still early, they parked on the edge of a

wood. While Sarah watched for traffic, Michael fetched the guns from the boot and carried them into the trees. There she followed him, picking carefully over roots and fallen branches; skirting mud puddles and suspicious piles of leaves Michael didn't seem to notice, though he didn't stumble either. He stopped in a clearing and laid the shotgun on the ground. He had not broken it the way you were supposed to: the code of the countryside. Presumably he followed a different set of rules.

Out on the road, a car drove past. Its engine noise tugged at her heart; the ease with which it left the area, disappeared into somebody else's future.

He found a tin can lying under a tree – there wasn't an empty space in the country you couldn't find a rusting can – and lodged it in a branch before pacing the clearing, measuring ten steps. 'Any further than this,' he said, 'you're definitely going to miss.'

'I'm not going to shoot anybody.'

'Are you going to let them shoot you?'

'I don't suppose it'll be a straight choice,' she said.

He loaded the handgun. 'Use both hands. Use your left to steady your right. On the wrist, like this.' He demonstrated. 'It'll kick back. Not a lot, but you need to expect it.'

'I don't want to fire your gun, Michael.'

He ignored her. 'Don't aim dead centre. Take your bearing and fire a little low. That way, when it pulls up, you're already compensating. When you're new to it, it almost always pulls up.'

'Fascinating. But no.'

'You know your problem, Tucker? You haven't sorted out yet which part's real and which part isn't.'

He turned, apparently casual, and shot the tin can from the tree. It made a lot of noise: not just the gun itself, whose low crack sounded like the splintering of last year's wood, but a racket all around as birds and unseen beasts took fright and fled. And then there was just a settling down, with, somewhere in the distance, a bass pulse, as if the gunshot were still out there, heading like hell for the hills.

Michael retrieved the can and showed her its jaggy, bone-dry wound. 'See? It's made of tin. You can shoot it all you like, you'll never hurt it.'

'So what's the point?'

'We're not in Oz. Whoever's got Dinah, it's not the Tin Man.' He held the gun out for her. 'You might never have to use it. But if the time comes you do, you can't say "Stop, I haven't practised."'

It was heavier than she'd have imagined. This was appropriate: machines that were made for taking life should have heft to them. You wouldn't want to take them lightly. This one, he'd already told her, was a German gun. A Luger. Not as old as the gun he'd broken back at Gerard's, but a wartime piece just the same. 'A collector's item.'

'But still illegal.'

When she looked at the can, it was miles away.

'Just imagine it's Rufus.'

This was crude, unnecessary, and did not work. Her first three shots went wide; only with the fourth could they measure how wide, because that time her bullet wound up buried in the tree itself. About a foot from the can.

'You're pulling to the right. Aim to the left.'

He showed her how to load, but didn't make her do it. He did make her try again. This time she emptied the gun, and came within a few inches of the can with her last shot: he said. She wasn't sure how he could tell.

After that, he picked up the shotgun.

(Back at Gerard's, while Michael smuggled the guns out, Gerard told her about the shotgun. 'Don't let him fire it without taking the plugs out,' he'd said.

'Plugs?'

'The barrels are plugged. Keeps dirt out. That's a bloody expensive gun, Sarah.'

'What would happen if he fired with them in?'

'He'd ruin it.' After a moment or two he added, 'Blow his hands off too, mind. Serve the bugger right.'

And she knew it was her he was thinking about. That he didn't want Michael handing her the gun; saying, 'Here. Have a go with *this*', and Sarah blowing her hands off.)

She didn't need to bring it up. He broke the gun open, peered down the barrels, then upended the gun and pulled a cork from each with his little finger. They looked like corks: red ones, each with a loop in the end for easy removal. He dropped them into a pocket of his denim jacket, then scooped a handful of shells from a box liberated from Gerard's cellar, and shovelled them into another.

'Watch.'

He loaded it, his eyes watching her rather than his hands; making sure she was following. Then cracked the gun back into a piece, pulled the hammers back, and with an action so smooth he might have been dancing brought the stock to his shoulder, levelled the barrels and fired.

The can disappeared. A good part of the branch went with it. This time there was no follow-up noise; no local creatures left to go crazy with shock. Anything left in the area was already stone deaf or dead, themselves excepted. And she wasn't sure about her own hearing, once the roar of the gun had died away.

'You okay?'

'You hit it, then.' Her voice sounded funny in her head. As if it were echoing in a large, empty room.

'Missing it would have been a better trick. If it comes to a straight choice, use this.' His voice was level, serious. It always was, but holding a gun lent him gravitas. 'You point a handgun at a soldier, he'll take it off you. But if you're carrying one of these, he'll keep his distance. Here.'

This, too, was heavy. But in those first moments, she had nothing to compare it to: couldn't remember picking other things up. It was a tool for a job outside her scope, and only a sudden heavy scent of woodland carried on a draught through the clearing gave her the bearing: it was like work for an autumn day, work you did with the house behind you, and woodsmoke drifting on a steady wind. Like shouldering a rake once you're sure the job's done; or wielding a yard broom, clearing rubble from the foot of a tumbling wall.

It was not like housework.

'It'll kick,' Michael said. 'The thing is, don't drop it.'

She raised it to her shoulder, the way he had.

'Uh-uh. You'll end up with a bruise the size of Ireland. Fire from the hip. Just let your eyes point the way. We're not going for long-distance marksmanship here. All you need do is prove you're not afraid to fire it. Most situations, that'll get you the benefit of the doubt.'

When he was satisfied she was holding it correctly, she fired.

It kicked, yes: she felt the tug on her arms as if she were about to take off backwards. What she had been aiming at, she wasn't sure, but the shells tore a hole in a bush she could have put her arm clean through. This was something she did not notice until regaining her balance: but she did not fall, did not drop the gun. For a short moment her vision pixelated, but that was all. The dead bush, the trees around her, were a vast confusion of blurred dots, as if she were standing too close to the screen they projected on to. And then it cleared, and the bush had a hole in it, and Michael was taking the gun away, showing her again how to break it open, feed it, lock it.

'One more time,' he said.

'No.'

'Don't think that's it. Shooting at people, it's a lot different.'

'I imagine,' she said, on her way back to the car.

'Bushes don't shoot back,' she thought he said. But by then

she was deep among the green, tracking her way out of this narrow world of leaf and mud, and couldn't be sure of his words, or whether he meant that made it easier or harder.

That second night she had curled up on the car's back seat in a search for comfort calling on resources she didn't know she possessed. When she closed her eyes, her dream landscape rolled by at an unwavering forty miles an hour, with, every so often, the same barn, the same clutch of houses drifting past. Like a pointless ring road, her dream circled nowhere, endlessly, and trying to break free of it, she could only spin into the void. The trick was to keep going. Even a ring road had to lead somewhere.

Michael slept outside, on hard ground. It was a fine night, with a bright moon but cloud cover enough to keep frost at bay. He had bedded down worse, he assured her. And woken operational.

Earlier that day, they had crossed the glass border: that was what it felt like to Sarah. One moment they were driving along the road; the next they were doing exactly the same thing, only in another country. An invisible transference. In Scotland the sky was still blue; the radio, when they could hear it, still squawked war news. Sometimes, clearing gaps in the roadside, sudden winds buffeted the car, and she felt her heart leap sideways, bang against her ribs.

'Where do we go now?'

'North. Still north.'

The island, he told her, was offcoast from a village called Barragan. He had found it on a map, and was sure that was right.

They had other maps, but Sarah wondered if each didn't merely describe the area in which they were lost. Maps were a means to an end, but only took you so far. Wasn't there a fable about a king who demanded a map of his land so accurate, it would show every ditch, every bush, *everything*? And his map-makers had produced one on a scale of 1:1, and laid it over his land like a shroud . . . You might as well be stranded in the dark as blinded by the light. And besides, if they knew where their journey would take them, they'd end it here and now.

That afternoon, they parked in a lay-by where a van sold mugs of filthy sweet tea, and one of the other customers – a man in a green sleeveless pullover: for some reason, that detail stuck with Sarah – was driving a car with a for sale sticker pasted to the rear side window. The car was a Citroën 2CV. A blue one. He was asking four hundred and fifty pounds, and his sign gave an abundance of detail about age, road tax, MOT: Sarah didn't pay attention, being more enthusiastic about the toilets, which were the other main feature of this lay-by. But when she emerged, she found that Michael had bought the car.

'We've already got a car.'

'Now we've got a different one.'

'We just drive it away?'

'He'll take the VW.'

So Michael carried the guns from the old car in a jumble of jackets and a thin blanket; carried them so casually, it was as if they'd lost shape in the process. That must be what it's like, having guns a part of your life. Carry them like kitchen equipment, and nobody looks at them twice. Sarah, though, watched him, even if the man in sleeveless green was too busy double-counting his money; wondering, probably, if he'd not just been ripped off in a manner he hadn't tumbled to yet. Sarah felt like Faye Dunaway without the blonde; Michael, too, was no Warren Beatty. Besides, they were the good guys. But still: here they were, swapping cars, concealing guns. Unhappy feelings kicked inside her.

In the new car, this tinny thing, the wind's buffetings struck a lot more drastically. Sarah was driving now; had to learn to cope with that at the same time as picking up the car's habits.

When she felt the gusts she had to lean into them, making the wheel a part of her own motion. This was the other trick of it. You had to bend to what was happening. You had to accommodate, to keep from being blown away.

All this time, a sense of their shifting status had been growing on Sarah. Quick glimpses of her stranger's face in the rear-view – the sharp dark hair; the face narrower than she was used to – reminded her that they were on the run; that she had adopted this new identity, non-identity, to throw their followers off the scent. But there were no followers. They were not fugitives. The flight from Oxford, the time in the hotel: these might have been the results of a misread script, because nobody was looking for them at all. She was assumed, if Gerard had told the truth, to have fled a crooked husband, and while this put her under the heading of missing, it did not mean she was actively sought. If what she had once read was true, thousands of people went missing every year. She was simply one of a huge population, a vast herd on the run from what had been their defining characteristics: passports, driving licences, credit cards – roaming now at will like invisible buffalo through indifferent landscapes. As for Michael, he was not part of the equation. Nobody but Gerard knew they were together.

And Gerard hadn't reported the theft of his guns.

So there was no need to worry each time a police car hove into view. Whatever crimes she had been involved in, they had an element of perfection about them: there was even a killing so unobtrusive, it left not a body behind. Though still she flinched when the memory caught her unawares, and in her mind's eye trapped Rufus, or Axel, falling backwards, his blood a fine spray in the air.

It was an image that haunted her dreams that night, as she slept curled up on the car's back seat, looking for comfort that never came.

*

Next day she drove again; too wired to doze in the passenger seat. Michael traced their journey with a finger on the map: the roads afforded glimpses of the lochs. Spots of rain threatened, but never made good. The drive took three hours.

Three hours, and by the time Sarah drove the 2CV into Barragan she was beginning to suspect they'd bought a clunker: loose noises were rattling under its bonnet, as if some mechanical emergency were trying to break free. So much for the man in the green sleeveless pullover; you'd have thought, if you could trust anybody, somebody with an anti-culling sticker on his windscreen would be a good bet.

Michael said, 'You want to get something to eat?'

'I'm not hungry,' she said, without thinking about it.

'Well, I am.'

So was she. It was as if her body were admitting, at last, that she couldn't get by without it.

There was what amounted to a village square, though it wasn't square, and this was where she parked, under the low branches of a large tree. This stood in a plot of earth maybe three yards by four, around which, some time ago, concrete paving slabs had been laid. Now they were cracked and jutting at jagged angles, as what had been intended as some sort of framing device had become a testament to the inexorable defiance of trees. A row of shops lined one side of the square; houses two others; a garage and what seemed to be a health centre the fourth. One of the houses was a pub. This was where they went to eat.

The food was okay, nothing special; the service friendly, if distant. Michael ate like he did most things; as if it were an exercise, and you got marks for efficiency. She wondered how long it would take to get to know somebody like this; and if, after all, the effort would be worth it. Perhaps he'd been different once – hell, *everybody* was different once – but perhaps he'd been different before that time in the desert; before the helicopter and the small glass bomb, and the melting boy soldiers. And still she wondered, too, why he had been chosen to be there in the first place. And if there were sins he'd yet to tell her about.

'We'll stay here tonight,' he said suddenly.

'We'll what?'

'Stay here. Tonight.'

So that was another decision taken, she thought bitterly. But knew, too, that the bitterness was token, was reflexive; because she had no other plans, and nothing to do with her life. Other than finding Dinah, of course. Meanwhile, she might as well stay here as anywhere.

So they booked a room in the inn after eating; a double room, because that was all that was on offer. Not that the village was heavily popular, but one double room was all the inn had. They didn't have much luggage: a couple of carrier bags. The changes of clothing Sarah had bought en route. The guns, they left in the boot of the car.

Afterwards Michael slept, while Sarah went for a wander round the village. By her watch, the wander didn't take more than fourteen minutes: on her second circuit she stopped at the newsagent's and bought a Reginald Hill paperback, and retreated to the bar where she read it cover to cover over the space of the next four hours. It was the calmest afternoon she could remember. Joe was much on her mind, though. This thought kept intruding every time she raised her eyes from her page: that she'd killed him, as good as; that if not for her he'd be in his office now, waiting for the phone to ring, or rabbiting on to a new client about old clients he'd had . . . Zoë, too. Just a few days ago, though it seemed as many years, Zoë had pumped her full of salt water and emptied her of drugs: not a soft woman, Zoë. And she'd promised to check up on Sarah, though Sarah hadn't hung around long enough to be checked up on. Perhaps she should call Zoë. At least let her know she was all right.

That was another thought that wouldn't go away, once she'd had it. It felt like she'd run from a lot of responsibilities lately, and letting Zoë Boehm know she was alive would at least give her a small piece of credit: that was what she told herself, dialling Directory Enquiries from the telephone near the bar, and scribbling Oxford Investigations' number on the pad provided. But when she rang it, that was all that happened; it rang. Not even an answerphone. She pictured a vacant office, dust slowly thickening on its shelves; absence accruing minute by minute, as the empty room waited for a Joe who would never return. She had to hang up before her thoughts caused her to cry.

—Oh God, she thought, dear Joe. Missing out on the rest of his life, because of her. Poor Joe, she wished him peace. Out there with the cosmos now. She had a sudden urge to see the stars.

The inn had a back garden where she found a bench and sat, suddenly overwhelmed by the luxury of being alone. For all the relatively early hour, it was dark now as a city girl could wish it, and though it was mild, she shivered under the big night sky. There were countless stars, each already dead perhaps, but the world wouldn't know that until the unborn generations had come and gone: all part of the cosmic joke that ensured that most important truths stayed well and truly out of reach. The time it took to see the light, the world itself had darkened. There was a degree of comfort in this, Sarah decided; that, divinely ordained or accidentally slam-dunked into being, the arrangement of the universe was not without humour. Which in itself you could take as a sign that prayer was not without purpose.

The wind rustled leaves across the way. An unseen dog barked. Something skittered in the darkness and she exhaled slowly.

. . . There was this to say about the inky background of the cosmos, it covered a multitude of sins. And maybe the stars didn't know they were dead yet. Maybe that was why they continued to shine. Looking up at them now, Sarah understood for maybe the first time what a very tiny part of everything the world was, in a universe which was anyway expanding. This world itself would hardly be missed. What mattered were the little components that went up to making human life. If Dinah didn't matter, nobody did. One of the few important truths within Sarah's reach.

'There's always a good night sky here,' Michael said behind her.

She hadn't heard him arriving.

After a while, he added, 'We used to look at the sky a lot, when we were on the island. One of the others, he knew we were in Scotland. He could tell by the stars.'

'Was that Tommy?'

'No. But it's how Tommy and I knew where we were when we landed.'

'Where was that?'

'A little way up the coast.' He gestured. 'We found a church by the side of a wood. Well, a chapel. Deserted, it was. Funny place for it, really. We sheltered there that first night. Sanctuary, you'd call it.'

He said no more but stood, like her, drinking in the vast spaces above them. And Sarah was surprised to find that she had grown comfortable with his company. Liking didn't enter it. Liking was for people you met, then chose to meet again. This was trust, and trust was for those who taught you to use a gun, then stood close while you fired. Years ago, she'd come through a baptism of pain to find a life with Mark, and had thought she could trust him because she'd imagined it was something they'd come through together. But Mark had simply been on the sidelines; picking up the pieces and arranging them how he'd wanted. And when that fell apart, or at least when his hopes did – for the books and the successes; the life of academic achievement he'd come to expect – he rearranged it all again, and settled for the money. In time, even that hadn't been enough. She wondered how long it had taken him to rationalise his crime; to talk himself through to the other side of the scruples he'd once had. And supposed that when you were denied what you really wanted, you didn't see why you shouldn't have everything else. The money. The mistress. The works.

She turned to look at Michael. He had bathed, shaved; wore a clean shirt and a pair of jeans. In the dim light his face was all crags and valleys, and she had to suppress an impulse to reach out and touch the scar on his chin. He'd probably be no less surprised if she made a grab for his crotch.

To shake the thought from her head, she said, 'Tell me about Tommy.'

'Tommy?'

'You're in this for him. He must have been special.'

'He was okay.' For a while it looked like that was all she was going to get: *He was okay.* Then he said, 'What did you want to know?'

'Anything. Just what he was like.'

'What he was like,' said Michael. He had a can of beer with him he popped now, and offered her a swallow. She shook her head.

'We were in this bar once, Tommy and me. On leave. We'd had a bad day. Tommy liked to bet, and he'd lost heavily that afternoon, and he was really pissed off. Looking for a fight.'

He took a long pull from the beer can, then rubbed his lower lip with a thumb.

'There was a man in the bar, Tommy decided he was the one. I don't know why.' He rapped a quick tattoo with his knuckles on the can. Some way off, the dog barked again. 'You ever see one of those arguments where one guy just wants to live quiet, and the other guy wants to break bones? There was nothing he could say Tommy didn't take wrong. He'd be, Let's buy you a drink, and Tommy was, What are you saying, I'm an alcoholic? You calling me a drunk? Guy must've thought he'd wandered into a nuthouse. He'd say, I'm leaving now, Tommy said, No you're not. Everybody knew what was going to happen. Nobody got in the way.'

Sarah felt the breeze shift direction. From inside the inn came the sounds of crockery, as the staff cleared up.

'He wasn't built or anything, this bloke, just average. Tommy was like me to look at, but you could bounce bricks off him all night long. Anyway, it happened. He followed this bloke outside, someone he'd never met, had never done him harm, and beat him half to death. I pulled him off eventually. I could have put an end to it sooner, but only by killing him. The way you have to some kinds of dog.'

He turned and placed the empty can on the arm of the bench. Then looked at Sarah.

'Well, what did you expect? He was nice to animals, kind to children? You want to hear about him carrying Maddy's picture, crying himself to sleep over Dinah? He went with whores, Tucker, and he got in fights, and if the other guy was better than him, he'd hit him from behind. Because that's what he did. He was a soldier, he was a good soldier. But he wasn't a nice man.'

'And he's the reason you're looking for Dinah?'

'No. Maddy is.'

It was as if a picture she had been looking at turned out to be upside down, and no revision of her former opinion was going to make her look less foolish. But Michael didn't hang around to hear about how she'd got things wrong. She looked up at the stars once more, and then looked round for him, but he'd left.

Sarah Tucker, she thought. You complete and utter idiot.

She wasn't sure how much longer she sat there in the dark. When she went inside at last, and up to their room, Michael was already in bed: she slipped into the bathroom as quietly as she could, and had a tepid shower. Exhausted. *I am exhausted*, she thought – her mind still racing from untamed thoughts. Using a fresh T-shirt as a nightie, and pulling a pair of pants on, she went back into the bedroom, which was small, with thin curtains no match for the moonlight, so a bluish cast settled on all it held: the electric fire, the dusty shelf with its scatter of tourist objects, the small bedside table on which sat an unused ashtray. The bed itself. Michael lay still as a corpse beneath its covers, though, Sarah knew he was awake, and knew, too, that he knew she knew. *I know you know I know you know I know.* All those hours in that hotel room: he'd know her by her breathing in the dark. By the smell of her hair when it needed shampoo.

She sat lightly on the side of the bed. He made no movement, nor any noise, but his eyes shone wet in the blue light, a trick of the moon suggesting him capable of tears.

'Michael?'

No reply.

'She's your daughter. Isn't she?'

'She's Tommy's kid.'

'You know that for a fact?'

'Who knows anything? For a fact.'

'Don't run from this.'

Then his hand appeared from darkness and gripped her own by the wrist. 'What do you want me to say?' He held her so tight she could take her own pulse. 'That I loved my friend's wife? That I wanted *his* life?' He let go. She'd have a bruise by morning; a bracelet of used pain, to match the necklace Rufus left her with. 'We both fucked things up, Tommy and me. But I had more excuse. If I'd had Maddy, I'd never have . . .'

'Never what?'

'I wouldn't be here. Maybe none of us would.'

There's something he's not told me, she thought.

He sat up, the sheet falling from his bare chest. It was curiously hairless: a boy's torso. The red weals cast him like a tiger, or its cage. 'I've seen how you look at me when you think I don't notice.'

(She could hardly deny what was coming.)

'I'm a killer, right? I shot that guy in front of you, and it doesn't matter he'd've killed you, it puts me down in your eyes. I shot him, and that chokes you off.'

'I don't care what you've done.'

'You don't know half of it.'

'Michael—'

'I loved her. Okay? And he treated her like shit. I saw the bruises, you think that didn't matter? I've killed people, so what's a knock or two? Fuck it, I'd have ripped his heart out. But she'd have spat in my face while she fitted him together again.'

'Why did you stay with him?'

'She asked me to.'

He brushed a hand across his forehead: wiping the thought away.

'Did you ever . . .'

'Fuck her?'

'Okay. Fuck her.'

'What do you think?'

Of course he had. Else he'd know for a fact he wasn't Dinah's—

He said, 'It doesn't matter. None of it matters.'

'Tommy had to go and see her,' she said softly. 'That's why . . .' It was why they'd been killed; what gave Rufus – Axel – his opportunity.

'It's not that he had to see her. He had to make sure she wasn't seeing anybody else.'

'Did he know—'

'Oh, sure he knew.' He lay back, his eyes reflecting the pale insignificant light. 'Sure he knew,' he said again.

Which was what hurt, she thought, lying down now beside him. That he'd only stuck by Tommy for his love for Tommy's wife. And that Tommy knew it.

Neither spoke for a long while, but when Sarah shivered suddenly – a goose running over her grave – Michael lifted the sheet so she could slide beneath it. And there she put her arms round him, finding this not so very different, after all, from the other night they'd spent in the same bed. Like cold figures on a stone tomb, she recalled. And now, though wrapped together, there was still that sense of epitaph in their embrace, though over whose grave they were joined tonight, she could not imagine.

But in the morning, when she woke, the room was empty: just a blank cool space in the bed next to her; and, over the back of the chair by the window, Michael's denim jacket – almost like a promise that he'd be back: but a promise, she knew, he had no intention of keeping.

26

THERE WERE LIES AND double bluffs and twisted reasons justifying crooked ends, but first of all, and mostly, there were secrets.

Sitting on the train, Amos Crane remembered being recruited to the Department; remembered the double talk and the veiled hints of the unorthodox. Recalled some buffer who'd been involved in the assassination of Reinhard Heydrich lecturing him on the dark heart that beats in the chest of government; on how what made democracy a fair and just system was that this dark heart was kept hidden rather than used to promote terror and obedience. Death squads were for fascists. In a democracy, accidents happened.

Crane's secret was, he didn't need the lecture.

But he sat anyway, and nodded, and tried to look like he was learning hard lessons. Agreed that it was better – for instance – that a very minor royal should fall getting out of the shower than that the entire royal family should tumble into the dust, and that this was not – was *not* – a matter of sweeping paedophilia under the carpet, but simply pragmatic problem solving. The obituaries elevated the minor royal into a glory-that-might-have-been just this side of sainthood, and a nation mourned untroubled by nasty realities, then forgot him. The boat remained unrocked. This was important.

Sure it was, Crane agreed.

And sometimes, guilt and innocence became relative. When people were in unnecessary possession of troublesome facts, it wasn't crucial to ascertain that they meant to *do* anything with the information. Possession, after all, was nine-tenths of the law: which made it mostly legal to ensure discretion was permanent. Many senior civil servants, the old buffer told Crane, anticipate a K at the end of their career; but if, hypothetically, a particular senior civil servant opened the wrong file at the wrong time to learn, say, that the American air bases then in Britain held weaponry of a type not formally disclosed to the people's elected representatives, he might look forward, instead, to an accident on an icy stretch of road. It did not necessarily matter that his loyalty was never in question. What mattered was that the secrecy was preserved intact.

This wasn't a problem, Crane assured him.

And so Amos Crane, at the tender age of twenty-three, entered the twilight world of expedient operations, a world in which the barbarians were not only waiting at the gates but had copies of the keys. Despite the pep talk, it wasn't all wet work. There were milder ways of silencing potential embarrassments, most involving photographs, women, boys, animals, money, surgery or drugs; though once or twice he was allowed to become creative, which was when his talent for the job became wildly obvious. When an East End pimp acquired pictures of the then foreign secretary wearing only a pair of pre-teen girls, Crane, working on the ABC principle, took out not only the pimp himself but eight other hustlers within two days, sparking a lot of editorials about gangland war that muffled serious investigation. The only shadow cast over this achievement was Crane's documented suggestion at the outset that it would be cheaper and simpler to take out the foreign secretary, thus rendering his susceptibility to blackmail moot. Howard's predecessor pretended to believe this was a joke. Amos, once he'd noticed which way the wind blew, pretended likewise.

And two years into the job, he'd put his young brother up for recruitment.

'It's not a bloody club,' he'd been told.

'No need to blackball him, then.'

'Amos, the fact that he's your brother doesn't mean he's our kind of material. My own brother works for ICI, for God's sake.'

Didn't surprise Amos one bit. 'The point is,' he said, 'he's not exactly a novice. That thing with the pimps . . .'

'Don't say it.'

'Nine in two days? I'm good, but I'm not *that* good. Axel did two of them. The one in the car and the one with the scissors.'

'Oh Jesus Christ . . .'

'He's versatile. You have to give him that.'

There'd been an emergency session that afternoon Amos was only supposed to find out about afterwards. He also guessed the outcome correctly: that there'd be strong support for black-ribboning him and his brother both, but sweet reason would prevail. As the original old buffer said, a pair of talents like that, you never knew when they'd come in handy. And he'd quoted LBJ or Edgar Hoover or whoever, on it being better having the bastards inside pissing out.

'We fought a war against people like that,' the buffer was told.

'Damn nearly lost, too.'

'It was their kind ran the concentration camps.'

'Do you really think,' he'd said, 'that over in Moscow they're turning talent down because it's too *nasty*?'

'It's not Moscow I'm worried about. It's Washington.'

'Fuck Washington.'

It was generally agreed afterwards that it was this remark that won the day.

That had been the real beginning, Amos reflected now; the

day Axel was recruited alongside him, at an age when most boys his age were awaiting their O-level results. And for a shade over twenty years, life had gone on the same: successes outweighing failures for the most part, which was a pretty acceptable margin of error for government work. And there had been room for sentiment too. Taking the old buffer out had been an act of pure heart. The old man had taken to wetting the bed, and telling his life story to his nurse: that wasn't the way he'd have wanted to be remembered, even if he'd been allowed. Amos had seen to him quickly and quietly, and was very proud of the resulting death certificate, which cited heart failure. As for the nurse, she'd been sideswiped on the M1 the following week, on her way to a newly offered job: Amos wasn't sure what the death certificate had read in her case, but was pretty sure they could have slipped it into the same envelope her remains fitted in. Room for sentiment, sure, but there was no sense getting carried away.

And now it was over, and Amos Crane couldn't help thinking they'd been victims of their own success: too good at what they did to be allowed to try anything else, they'd been obvious candidates for downsizing once the winds of fortune changed. Axel's downsizing had happened in the field, of course. But Amos had been targeted, no doubt about it, and all because his first desk operation – his *first* – had chalked up a few minor casualties: it was getting so you weren't allowed any mistakes, which hadn't been office policy in the good old days. He blamed political correctness. And what was worse, Howard had sent freelancers, *amateurs*, to do the job, which was cheeky as well as being a fucking liberty. Howard would pay for that too. In his mind's eye, in fact, Amos was starting to make out a queue: a lot of people demanding his attention. Michael Downey was still at the head of it, blood being thicker than water – Amos Crane could vouch for that. These clichés didn't get where they were by not being true.

And that was a lesson Michael Downey knew too, Crane reminded himself: the lesson about blood. Downey had also served an apprenticeship. Not quite the same league, but he'd been to the edge, which in his case was a place called Crows' Hill, a camp for Iraqi prisoners where he'd served three months as a guard towards the end of the Gulf War, along with his friend Tommy Singleton, always the better soldier. Among those at Crows' Hill were a small group captured at an Iraqi military compound, where a torture chamber had been discovered – electric batons, ceiling chains; a bathtub streaked with blood, though no bodies were found. A school of thought held this irrelevant. No bodies were found because the bastards buried them. One dark night Singleton, Downey and a handful of others – probably drunk or high: Crane neither knew nor cared – took the group of three out to the wire and shot them dead.

They could have been shot themselves. (Probably ended up wishing they had been.) But it was a popular war, and nobody wanted to spoil the party, so the fix was put in instead: that couldn't have been particularly difficult, Crane reflected. Removed from Crows' Hill, Singleton's crew was kept in close confinement for the duration; even after the war, the army didn't much know what to do with them. For years, they were a scandal waiting to happen. When they were co-opted en masse for 'special services', you could hear the sigh of relief in An Najaf. And it was only once these special services were over that they were delivered into the hands of the Department: officially dead – a cover story lacking subtlety, but avoiding loose ends – they'd become embarrassments, and the Department Crane worked for dealt with embarrassments. But there was still curiosity about how long it would take them to die from the effects of the nerve bomb: the experiment had been a failure, immunisation having worked at only seventy per cent, but that didn't mean the statistics weren't worth keeping. So they'd been sent to the Farm, itself a hangover from the days of germ warfare, the idea being that they'd remain there until their various cancers took hold. After that, they'd be chucked. Before that, though, they'd escaped.

. . . Crane tutted like a disappointed teacher: they'd *escaped*. Actually, when you thought about it, that was what had put him here, on this train . . .

Because after dealing with Howard's bob-a-job boobies, he'd headed straight for King's Cross: morally certain that Downey would have worked it out by now, he wanted to be near the island when the soldier came looking for Dinah. It wasn't *that* difficult. Dinah was bait, Downey had to know that; and who put bait somewhere their prey would never find it? . . . Besides, he had the woman with him, and Axel had said the woman was smart. Axel was no great fan of women, so if he'd said it, it was probably so. Sarah Trafford, née Tucker. Dumb enough to get involved, but smart enough for Axel.

Perhaps he scowled at the thought, because the short man sitting opposite asked, 'You all right then, mate?' He had a harsh northern accent, so irritating to the civilised ear, and wore a scarf no sane man would admit to.

'I'm fine. Thank you.'

'Only ye look like death warmed up, like.'

'I doubt that.'

'Y'what?'

Crane sighed, and leaned forward. 'Have you ever seen death, warmed up? Have you?' The man pulled back, but Crane continued: 'The skin pops and blisters like an overcooked rice pudding. The eyeballs burst. And the lips peel back so the teeth look big as tombstones. Believe me, if I looked like that, you wouldn't be making polite conversation.'

'Ye're a fockin' lunatic.'

'It's been said.'

He closed his unburst eyes and leaned back in his seat, while his fellow passenger went to find somewhere else to sit. The train rattled away beneath him, carrying him off to Edinburgh. From there he'd pick up another train, or hire a car. Something. It was a damn shame he didn't have all his equipment with him – especially after carting the bear all that way – but hell: into each life, a little rain must fall. Round about wherever Downey was now, it was coming on cloudy, that was true.

The train jerked, and he opened his eyes involuntarily to see a woman walking past carrying packets of sandwiches and a plastic cup of coffee: a woman in her forties, with dark curly hair and a deeply harassed expression. She was none of his business. He hoped she wouldn't sit down. He didn't want company and he didn't want chat. But he needn't have worried because she was on her way down the carriage, and barely glanced at him on her way past.

Turning to look out of the window once more, the first thing he saw was his own reflection. *Death warmed up indeed*, he thought: no, not that, never that. What he in fact was was cold all of a sudden, as if he'd just had a glimpse into his own future. Everybody's future is the same in the long run. What worried Amos Crane for a moment was how very short the long run suddenly seemed.

27

SARAH WALKED DOWN TO the sea that morning, and sat on a bench to watch the waves beat on the noisy shingle. Somewhere out of vision, lost in the grey haze of the day, was the island where they were holding Dinah, whoever *they* were – that was what she told herself, and she'd come too far to accept that she might be wrong. Or to give up just because Michael had abandoned her. She was wearing his denim jacket, in a pocket of which she'd found a bundle of notes: tens and twenties, more than enough to pay the bill, though she felt mostly detached from such mundane obligations. *It is very important*, she remembered thinking at some point during the madness of the last few days, *when your life is falling apart, to focus on one thing and one thing only*. For better or worse, that had become Dinah. The invisible girl. To get this close and no further was more than flesh and blood could stand.

The wind shivered the shingle, shifting specks of sand. For a moment, it looked like ghosts were chasing each other down the beach.

When she looked round, because she thought she was being watched, Sarah saw a woman approaching down the path. Could be any woman. Wearing a red jumper, as if she liked to be noticed.

She looked back to the sea. One of the things about which

was, there was so bloody much of it . . . Like a great grey blanket, covering most of the world. When they drag us down Cemetery Road, she thought, that's what'll be left: the sea.

She was hardly surprised at all when the woman sat on the bench next to her.

Because of the curious lethargy which had overtaken her – as if her body were remembering all those tranks – it was no effort for Sarah not to look around. Not at first. But her silence didn't seem to faze her new companion: for a number of long minutes, the two women sat without talking; both watching the sea, though probably thinking different things. The wash of the waves had a tidying effect, Sarah decided at last. It tended to smooth your thoughts out: no wonder it turned up so often on those meditation trance tracks . . .

'I suppose I was expecting you,' she said at last.

'Hey. Missing persons, a speciality.'

'I tried to call you.'

'I know.'

A cigarette was waved in front of her face. 'You want one of these?'

'I don't smoke.'

'I know you didn't last week,' said Zoë Boehm. 'Just thought you might have upgraded your lifestyle since.'

Sarah turned to face her. Zoë hadn't changed much, but then, it had only been a few days. 'Nice jumper.'

Zoë blew a ring, to show how much she cared. Then eyed Sarah critically. 'You're not in the state you were. Doped to the gills, I mean. But you're a different sort of mess, still.'

'Thanks.'

'But given how many people you've pissed off in the last few days, I'd say you're on course for a full recovery.'

'Lately I've thought it a wasted day if nobody tries to kill me,' Sarah agreed. 'So tell me, what brings you to this neck of the woods?'

Zoë stared at her a moment or two, then tossed her curly hair and gave a laugh. 'You sure land on your feet, don't you? If Joe hadn't—'

'I've seen a man die lately. I nearly joined him. I might yet. Don't tell me how lucky I am, I don't want to know.'

'Okay.'

'How did you get here?'

'You called me, remember?'

'But you didn't – Oh.'

'1471. One of my favourite numbers, that.' Zoë tossed her cigarette, and the wind grabbed it, sent it sparking to the beach. 'One of the few times I've been glad I forgot to turn the damn answering machine on. I'm always doing that. Shit, the number of jobs that must have cost us.'

'I bet Joe never forgot,' Sarah said.

'That's right. He never did.' She fumbled for another cigarette. 'Anyway, when I got into the office and checked the phone, the most recent call was from Scotland. And I don't know anyone in Scotland.'

'So you immediately thought of me.'

'Nope. Took hours for the penny to drop.' She flicked her Bic lighter, and got her latest nicotine hit up and running. 'Once it did, I rang the number and gave the guy who answered your description. Your new hair threw him at first. Apart from that,' she shrugged modestly, 'it was easy.'

'He told you? Just like that?'

'I had to promise him a blow job. I might also have given him the impression I was teenage and blonde, but if he demands payment anyway, you can expect it to have a hell of an impact on my expenses.'

'I don't remember hiring you.'

'It was a joke, kiddo. It was a joke.' From her leather shoulder bag, Zoë produced a small bottle of vodka. 'I read once you should take salt on a long journey. To liven up what you catch and eat.' She unscrewed the cap, passed the bottle to Sarah. 'I always thought that was an interesting point of view.'

Sarah took a good long swallow. It was mildly like being struck over the head: probably more pleasant. As she handed it back, she glanced inside the bag Zoë had put down between them; one of those amazing arrangements whose insides hold more than their outsides promise, and into which you could fit most of the average wardrobe. Clothes it held, too, but something else besides: small and silver, it winked at Sarah, and she couldn't pretend not to have seen it.

Noticing her look, Zoë pulled it out.

'Six shots,' she said. 'A real handbag gun.'

'What do you need that for?'

'Same as the vodka. I didn't know whether I'd *need* it or not, but I felt better bringing it along.'

'You know, don't you? Do you?'

'Know what?'

'Everything that's happened. Someone tried to kill me.' It still felt strange, dropping that into a conversation. Saying it was a way of getting used to it. 'But Michael shot him.' Stupid: Zoë didn't even know who Michael was.

Gun in one hand, cigarette between the fingers of her other, bottle between her knees, Zoë nodded. 'I heard a story. Someone on the local force who was there. But there were a lot of official denials that anything happened at all. So I presume he was a spook, the guy who copped it.'

'A what?'

'A spy.' She took a drag on her cigarette. 'Any way you look at it, I thought it best to bring the gun.'

'It's pretty small.'

'Joe gave it to me.' Maybe, somewhere in Zoë's subconscious, this was a relevant response to make.

Sarah had all but forgotten, in this recent stretch of her life, that the worst losses had been suffered by other people. And that Zoë, for one, needed to know the facts. 'It was Rufus,' she said.

'Rufus?'

'Who killed Joe. Who tried to kill me. Who was a . . . spook.'

'The one you told me about? Married to that friend?'

She nodded.

Zoë said, 'Fuck.' After a while she said it again, but after the second time she was quiet a lot longer, looking out to sea as if there were answers to questions she hadn't even thought of yet floating out there somewhere, out of vision, out of reach. For a few moments, Sarah wondered if Zoë were disappointed; if she'd hoped to kill Joe's murderer herself. And then dismissed the thought. Revenge, bloodshed, killing – that was a job for life's soldiers, which was why so many of them were dead.

Without speaking, Zoë handed the bottle to Sarah. Who took it, drank from it, and then began to speak: bringing Zoë up to speed on why she was there, who Michael was, where Dinah was . . . What happened. Everything.

And Zoë said, 'Jesus . . .'

A flock of gulls had descended on the strip of gravelly beach before them; were swooping and screaming now, disinterring the remnants of an uncomfortable picnic. Maybe thirty or so. Impossible to count. Sarah remembered, as if it were a scene from a film long ago, seeing a similar flock drop on a scattered packet of crisps on a busy main road in Oxford. Ignoring traffic, they'd come screeching down, snatching crisps from under the wheels, while the unlucky hungry ones were left hovering over the junction at head height; their wingspans making them as much of a threat to cars as the cars were to them. She'd been standing at the lights, waiting to cross. It was like walking into a Hitchcock film, but then again, so was this.

'Bloody wept,' Zoë continued.

'Yes.'

That didn't leave much to say, for the moment. They sat watching the birds wheeling in front of them, as if in celebration of the gift of flight. Though actually, Sarah thought, birds didn't do that: birds were just birds, no more capable of taking joy in their gifts than men were. Ha! She must still be tired; she was definitely talked out.

Zoë lit another cigarette.

This time Sarah stretched her hand out, and Zoë dropped a cigarette into it without comment. The lighter flared. She felt the first drag catch the back of her throat, and her cough was pure reflex: a real hacking, throat-killing experience, her first in years.

Zoë said, 'That sounds really bad. Have you thought about giving up?'

'It's crossed my mind,' Sarah said, when she could speak.

'Course, it's not gunna kill you that much faster than anything else.'

That went past Sarah the first time. Then she thought about it, and nodded. 'I know.'

'You given much thought to your options?'

'I thought, the press.'

'Could be. Kind of depends on how much credibility you've been left with, though.'

'How do you mean?'

Zoë ticked them off on her fingers. 'You were caught packing dope. Your husband's a thief. You can't prove Rufus was anywhere near your house because the spooks disappeared him . . .'

'What about your friend in the force?'

'Uh-uh. He's not a friend, he's a contact. And he's got a family to support and bugger all qualifications. That's why he joined the force in the first place.'

'Oh.'

'Plus, your friend Rufus isn't dead. That's the story, anyway. Word is, he's got terrorist connections, was using your friend

Wigwam as cover – I think the word "dupe" was mentioned – and went to ground when he was rumbled. And the press have already been told they can't print a word of this, so obviously they're convinced it's the truth. As for your friend Michael, he died years ago, remember?'

'Singleton's body . . .'

'Wasn't Singleton's. By which I mean, nobody's gunna have an easy job proving it *was*. Particularly given that what's left of him's been cremated.'

'So I need Michael.'

'Looks like. Pretty urgently, too, you ask me.'

Sarah looked at her.

'Sweetie, if I can find you, they can. And in case you've forgotten, we're fighting a war at the moment, rather than 'fess up to revolting toxic warfare experiments. If the spooks catch you now, I doubt a fake drugs bust will be their method of choice. Not now you've been in close contact with Downey. Even if he hadn't told you everything, they're bound to assume he did. There's no pretty way of saying this. They're going to kill you, Sarah.'

She nodded dumbly. She knew they were going to kill her. Hearing somebody else say it still had a raw edge to it somehow . . .

'But finding Michael Downey again, well, that would be a start.'

'He's gone after Dinah.'

'Yeah.'

'On this island. Somewhere out there.'

'I've got a map.'

Of course Zoë had a map; she probably had a car in the depths of that bag of hers. While she rooted it out, Sarah finished her cigarette: the first in a hell of a long time but, such was the familiarity of it, probably not the last. Not the quickest way to kill yourself, after all . . . A sudden vivid flash, and she was looking at Joe again, slumped over his desk, the razor still in his hand. Rufus had done that. Killed him, arranged him, left him there: you didn't do a job like that without practice. And Rufus might be dead, but there'd be others just like him. Brothers under the skin.

Zoë hadn't seen Joe dead, but she'd buried him . . .

'You should go,' she said suddenly.

'You what?'

'It's like you said, they'll be after me. Sure. But they're not after you. They don't even know you're here.'

Zoë nodded. 'Probably not.'

'So go. You think, when they find me, they'll let whoever I'm with disappear? When they find me, they'll find you too.'

'But they haven't done that yet. Sarah. I'm not gunna make a big thing of this. But I can't just walk away. That would make me bad as them.'

'Better than being dead as me.'

'You're not dead yet, you silly bitch. You've done all right so far. Would you walk away and leave Dinah be?'

'If I'd done that, I'd not be in this mess.'

'But you didn't. So shut up. Look.' She spread the map out in front of them: the wind tugged at its corners, making a paper earthquake of the landscape. 'No islands.'

'Maybe we're on the wrong stretch of coast. Michael—'

'Michael might have been wrong, sure. But if he was, and we're somewhere else entirely, then at least nobody will think of looking for us here. And if he was *right*, then the island's out there. It's just not on the map. Okay?'

'Can I have another cigarette?'

'Help yourself. So, first thing we do is, find a boat.'

'A boat?'

'Unless you were thinking of swimming. Or flying. Whatever. But personally, I think a boat. For crossing water, it's traditional.'

'You want to go *find* it?'

'Quickest way of finding Dinah. And you can bet that's where Michael's headed. He's already spilled blood on this one, Sarah. I doubt he's the type to give up.'

'No. He isn't.'

'The harbour's the other side of the bay. There's boats, they're common in harbours. We should be able to hire one.'

'If the island's there, if Dinah's there, it's because she's the bait in a trap.'

'I know. But the trap's been set for an ex-soldier, not a couple of innocent tourists. I don't think shoot to kill's an across the board policy yet. And you don't look like Sarah Trafford any more, you know? You look a lot sharper. Someone else entirely.'

'Thanks.'

'Hey. You're still a mess. You want a light for that?'

'I'm not sure yet.'

'Well, give it back. They're not cheap.' Zoë took it from Sarah's mouth and put it in her own. 'You okay?'

'I think so.'

'Come on then. Harbour's that way.'

She packed the map, the gun and the bottle back in her bag, and stood up. This thrilled the gulls, who wheeled into the air again in a noisy pack: their yammering, Sarah thought, could give a girl a headache. But it wasn't the loudest noise she'd hear in the near future. She stood up too, and followed Zoë back down the path. That red jumper could give you a headache too. You could pick Zoë out of a crowd, no sweat.

28

THE HELICOPTER BUCKED AGAIN on its second pass over the Farm, and Howard nearly lost his lunch. He was certain the pilot was doing this deliberately. At Howard's feet sat a briefcase (mostly full of electric doodads); round his neck his usual tie – he was an obvious suit, and yahoos like helicopter pilots hated suits. All he could manage in return was a piece of fake nonchalance: 'I can't see anybody down there,' he shouted.

The pilot, who didn't give a fuck about suits, yelled, 'They're not supposed to come out and wave, are they? Nobody's supposed to know they're there.'

Which was true, as far as it went, but didn't mean they weren't all, in fact, dead.

'You'd better put me down.' Howard didn't want to be put down. Howard wanted to go home, lock his door and start looking for another job, because while he was pretty sure he'd beaten Amos Crane to the Farm, that didn't alter the reports about a stolen motor boat the local cops had logged that morning . . . He was pretty sure that had to have been Downey. Howard didn't want to meet him either. But going home and locking his door wasn't an option. Amos Crane, after all, walked through locked doors, and Howard didn't want to be on the other side of one after putting Amos to that kind of trouble . . . Fuck. If he hadn't sent those talent-free bozos to whack Amos, he wouldn't be here now.

'There's something over there.'

'What?'

'Something. Can't make it out. Might just be a rock, the place is made of bloody rocks . . . I'll put you down close as I can.'

Take me far away instead, thought Howard. But shouted nothing: just clung for the rest of his life to the strap across his chest, while the bucking chopper – *that's why they call them choppers!* – dipped dangerously close at an extraordinary angle to the very hard surface of the island: it was indeed made of rock . . . But the machine levelled out for the final few seconds, and touched down more or less evenly, for Howard to more or less fall out.

The pilot made some gestures: his thumb, his watch, the sky. Probably, Howard decided, meaning something about how he was flying away now, but would be back in a certain amount of time . . . Right at that moment, Howard was too glad of the ground beneath his feet to sort out whether this meant an hour, a day, a week: he nodded, waved back, and watched the chopper swing round clumsily like a drunken dragonfly, and lift away into the wild grey yonder. As it droned into the distance, became the size of a pea, Howard felt very alone, very much the desk-man, and he reached down and patted his briefcase nervously, as if it were an odd-shaped plastic dog.

It was a while since he'd been on the island. The Department had inherited it years ago; every so often he'd lie awake wondering what would happen if some wide-eyed auditor questioned why the Ministry for Urban Development numbered a deserted Scottish island amongst its acquisitions . . . Some miles away, he had no idea how many, lay another government-owned island, which had been used for testing an anthrax bomb during the war. It still wasn't safe to visit. At least no actual testing had taken place here, so it was still safe to . . .

Safe to what, his mind refused to supply. Howard had reached the 'something' the pilot had seen, and it was a body.

Afterwards, he was quite impressed with his own cool. He had placed his briefcase on the ground, knelt for a closer look.

He wasn't an expert, but this was a pretty muscular specimen. Many of these muscles were largely intact, but the back of the head was smeared with what looked like its recent contents . . . Another thing that impressed Howard afterwards was that this didn't finish the job the helicopter ride had started; all expectations to the contrary, he held on to his lunch.

He straightened up; had hardly realised how low he'd been bending. Violent death. He'd sometimes been tempted to think there was no other kind: that even the gentlest quietus was a wrench. We're all dragged kicking and screaming from the planet in the long run. Peg out immobile in your own bought bed, and there's still a spark in your brain death stamps on to put out. However. Looking at this mess, brain tissue smeared on rock, Howard knew he'd been wrong to think like that. Not all deaths were violent. This one proved it, by being just that.

Hey-ho, he thought.

Leaving the body where it lay, Howard set off for the Farm. Stupid name: doesn't matter. There were no paths to guide him, but he knew it lay nearby; the island, anyway, was too small to get seriously lost on, if not so small you couldn't die here . . . *That doesn't require a lot of space*, a small voice insisted. *Anywhere precisely the size of your own body will do, and no one's been anywhere smaller than that . . .*

Yes, all right, thank you, shut up. He nearly said this aloud. He found the second body just outside the Farm. A man, blond, and still wearing the spectacles he'd needed when he could see. He lay on his back, one arm across his chest, the other outstretched as if he were still reaching for the apple which lay on the ground just beyond his grasp . . . Or not *just* beyond his grasp, amended Howard. Absolutely and beyond all comprehension unattainable for evermore. That was the idea, anyway. He wasn't sure how this one was supposed to have died, and didn't feel like asking. Presumably went quietly, though; if he'd been armed with just the one apple, it couldn't have been that pitched a battle.

Hey-ho, he thought again.

The body twitched.

Enough of this. Briefcase in hand, he left and approached the low stone building of the Farm. It had been built into a depression, or else a hollow had been dynamited out of the rock; he could never lay eyes on it without thinking he'd been thrown back into medieval times . . . One thing, though: he did not belong here, and that was the truth. His job was pulling strings. A step up, it occurred to him now, from bringing about a man's death. Arranging the fix so the man had never lived: that was the ideal. In Howard's world, that was perfection. But even as the thought was forming, he felt a disturbance in the air around him, and for a brief moment – but long enough for his mind to travel whole continents of fear – he thought it was over; that he had failed some fundamental test, and that Downey – or *Crane*: nothing's impossible – was still there, was behind him now, ready to wrap the black ribbon round what was left of his life. Just a brief moment. And then the door in front of him, the door to the Farm, opened, and instead of Downey, or even Crane, there was a woman standing in front of him, an attractive woman with dark curly hair, wearing a big bright jumper, pillar box red.

'Jesus!' she said. 'Who—'

Howard took a step back.

'Can you help? Are you a doctor?'

'I'm not a *doctor*,' he said regretfully.

'Quickly. Down there.' Zoë pointed back through the open door. 'She's hurt. I think she's dying . . . I think she's dead.'

SEVEN

CEMETERY ROAD

29

Zoë AFTERWARDS DECIDED THAT thinking Howard was a doctor wasn't such a wild surmise: he was carrying a briefcase, for Christ's sake; he was wearing a *suit*. Not conclusive, okay, but these were hardly exam conditions . . .

She also decided, afterwards, that everything had happened too damn fast.

At the harbour they'd found three crewed boats, if a single man counted as a crew: Zoë had unhesitatingly chosen the youngest, a twenty-something in a thick pullover and three-day beard, who looked like he might be malleable given a bit of vamping and a fair amount of cash. His name was Jed, and Jed had never heard of any islands hereabouts, a bit of a dead giveaway as far as Zoë was concerned: tantamount to not noticing he lived next to the sea. But the way he dressed, the way he grinned toothily at their landlubber accents, he really looked like he thought he knew everything. She was betting he probably did.

'Only we've been told there's a place worth a visit.'

'I can't imagine who told ye that.'

'So you do know it?'

'It's likely just a lump of rock.' He scratched his bristled chin. 'There's better places.'

'I'm sure there are.'

Sarah pulled Zoë away. 'Is this getting us anywhere? He says he's never heard of it.'

'He's lying.'

'You can tell?'

'Trust me.' She turned back to Jed, who was crouched on the deck of his blue boat, coiling a length of rope into a neat pile. 'Just give me five minutes.'

'You're sure it'll take that long?' Sarah whispered harshly, sarcastically, but left all the same; walked the jetty to the end, and stood staring out to sea, possibly in the direction of an invisible island.

Zoë said to Jed, 'You hire out often?'

'The boat?'

She laughed. 'Yes. The boat.'

He considered. 'Well, there's tourists. Like yourselves. After the fishing.'

'We're not after fish.'

'An' there's some like to see the coast at night. Aye. I'll do tourists.'

'And there's others like to see the islands.'

'Not much in the way of islands, lady. Just lumps of rock.'

'But you still get visitors. And they pay you well. And they pay you extra to keep quiet.'

He eyed her thoughtfully. It was always possible, she admitted to herself, that she'd made a right bollocks of this. That was something worth considering, so she considered it as she reached into her bag for her cigarettes. She offered Jed one, but he shook his head. He had his own. She was amused, though not side-splittingly so, to see they were much lower tar than hers.

'An' if that were true,' he said at last, when they were both puffing away, 'an' I was paid to keep quiet, I mean.'

'Yes?'

'Well, I'd be daft to open my gob. Wouldn't I?'

She'd been here before. They were past dancing. She blew a big happy cloud of smoke. 'Well, that'd depend,' she told him.

'Oh aye?'

'On how much you were offered to change your mind.'

He nodded deeply, as if he'd rarely come across a point so well put. Twenty-something going on fifty, Zoë amended. Whatever game they'd just embarked on, he was an expert. This was going to cost.

By the time Sarah rejoined them they were each on their second cigarette, sealing a deal notable mostly for Jed's refusal to budge from the first sum mentioned: two hundred pounds, significantly more than Zoë carried with her. Possibly more than her bank carried on her behalf. There was going to have to be a serious conversation with Sarah before too long. On the other hand, if she did nothing now, Sarah might not be alive before too long. One of those situations it was difficult to put a price on, so probably two hundred wasn't excessive.

'Did you remember an island, then?' Sarah asked, a shade hostile.

'I'll be forgettin' me own name next,' said Jed.

'He'll be posing for bloody *post*cards next, more like,' Sarah told Zoë, who was writing a cheque and ignored her.

'I'm trusting that won't bounce,' Jed said.

'And we're trusting *that* won't sink,' Zoë said. 'So we're even.'

Jed patted the rail of his boat with affection. 'I've sailed this lady through high waters,' he said. 'It'll get you through a millpond like today.'

Millpond, Zoë was thinking ten minutes later. *The Cruel Sea*, more like. She could feel her stomach shifting location in counterpoint to the rolling of the waters all around. She was a *city* girl, a fact which was patently clear: that's why Jed thought he could get away with pretending this wasn't a typhoon they were in. But he couldn't fool Zoë's stomach. Currently it was hanging on to the railway sandwiches she'd eaten last night, but it was a matter of minutes, that was all, or a matter of moments. *The Sea Shall Not Have Them*. Bugger that. The sea would get what was coming.

Sarah seemed okay, or at least wasn't hanging over the edge heaving her guts up. It was hard to get a handle on her, Zoë thought. Joe had liked her, that was for sure. But then, Joe had liked most everybody. It was the single most irritating thing about him.

A sudden dip in the air all around her as the boat fell into a trough. *Fuck!* But she recovered, at least temporarily. She put her knuckles to her forehead and rubbed, very hard. They came away wet. Sea spray, obviously, but also sweat: she was losing buckets here. She couldn't remember the last time she'd felt this bad without being drunk. The joke said first you were frightened you'd die, then you were frightened you wouldn't. Except it wasn't a joke, feeling this ill. It was very fucking serious indeed.

She tried to dip into her mind for a good memory, something to chase this away. But all her memories were of Joe, for some reason, and though they weren't all bad, they all *ended* badly. Joe had ended badly. Nothing she tried to remember, or failed to forget, could change that fact. Joe had ended, his throat cut by a stranger, and if you skipped all the details, that was the reason she was on this boat now . . .

Forget about the boat, Zoë.

So she remembered instead, years ago, watching a TV programme with him: it was about bloodhounds, for Christ's sake, which was probably the reason they were watching it. 'That's me,' he'd said. It had never mattered how she'd treated Joe, how she'd responded to his dumb enthusiasms or his injured pride, he never failed to open up for her, to give her all the ammunition she could want. 'That's me. The archetypal bloodhound. Once I'm on the trail, I never stop.' *Well, sure, Joe.* She couldn't recall how she'd replied, but she remembered well what she'd been thinking. Sure you are, just like a bloodhound: creased and baggy and slinging drool all over the place . . . He was an emotional dribbler, Joe; he slobbered over people. He'd fall in love with total strangers and tell them his life story; worse, he'd want to hear theirs. It had driven Zoë mad and it had driven her away, but here she was years after the blood-hound show trying to follow this trail to its end, because Joe had started off on it, and never got to finish.

It was a long time since she'd imagined they'd actually grow old together. But remembering him now, remembering he'd never grow old at all, she wanted to cry, or shout, or hurt someone. Larkin, she thought. He'd always been fond of Philip Larkin. *Give me your arm, old toad; Help me down Cemetery Road* . . . He'd been helped down Cemetery Road, all right, but it hadn't been time for him to go, and he hadn't expected such help. Maybe the man who did that was dead, like Sarah said, but that didn't mean there weren't debts outstanding.

Jesus Christ. *Bloody* Joe.

There was a sudden upsurge, and an equally sudden upchuck. Before she knew it, her grief was coming up into view like so much lunch: she was spewing it on the waters, though that wasn't the end of it, everything cast on the waters came back . . . Seasick. And getting so fucking delirious she'd be spouting poetry herself next.

There was a hand on her shoulder, a voice at her ear. 'Are you okay?'

'No. I'm dying.'

'He says we'll be there soon.'

'You can bury me on the beach.'

But in truth she was feeling better; was feeling, at least, that she might live. Probably an improvement.

Probably, but she'd been wrong about the beach. All there was was rock: this great grey chunk sticking out of the sea like it had been dropped from a large height or thrust up from the depths: whichever, it wasn't anywhere worth visiting. She groaned again – as a form of communication, this was increasingly appealing to Zoë: it made clear her feelings on most subjects, and was a lot simpler than forming coherent sentences.

'You sure you're dying?'

'Just fuck off, okay?'

'Okay.'

'And get me a cigarette.'

'Okay.'

Sarah fetched her a cigarette, but didn't fuck off. Instead she stood next to her at the stern – stern? The flat end – smoking too: that was another wonderful moment for Zoë, knowing she'd dragged a convert kicking and screaming down Nicotine Lane. But she was glad of the company. Funny thing about seasickness: it ironed out the minor things in life, like your future, and made you glad for what comforts there were.

'He says it's just a chunk of rock.'

'He what?'

'Jed. He says, for a chunk of rock, it's mighty popular.'

'Since when?'

Sarah shrugged. Then, because Zoë wasn't looking, added, 'He's not sure. He's only been hiring out this past year. But he says before then, there used to be helicopters going over. He swears he saw one land there once.'

'And the locals don't ask questions?'

'Hey. Do you think he's the only one made a bob out of it?' They both turned as Jed shouted something from the wheelhouse. He was pointing towards the island, which had got a lot closer very quickly. 'I think he's taking us in,' Sarah said.

'Dry land,' Zoë said with feeling.

'Wet rock.'

'Just so long as it's stable.'

'The luck I've had lately,' Sarah told her, 'it'll probably turn out an active volcano.'

*

Jed dropped them in what looked like a natural harbour, though a flight of steps had been fashioned out of the rock. Zoë felt them buckle beneath her as she stepped off the damned boat, unless it was her knees doing that; it was too early to tell. It was up to Sarah to extract promises from Jed as to when he'd be back; more importantly, she extracted the cheque Zoë had written him . . . He seemed to accept this as a legitimate business tactic, rather than an indication of mistrust.

'Don't see why he can't just bloody wait,' Zoë said sourly.

'If he's found, it could cause him problems.'

'Heaven forbid he should have problems,' Zoë muttered. But she was starting to feel better; feel the difference between the fresh air you got on land and the kind on sea. She reached for a cigarette to put this hypothesis to the test.

'Should you be doing that?'

'Most doctors smoke.'

'I meant, won't it give us away? The smoke? The smell?'

'I was never a boy scout,' Zoë said. 'I failed the medical.' And just so it wouldn't look like she was surrendering the initiative because she'd had the good sense to feel nauseated on the water, lit up anyway.

At the top of the steps they surveyed what they could of the island. True, it was greener than it looked from the water, but what life clung to what soil there was must have had a hellish, hard-scrabble existence. Zoë pointed out what was pretty clearly a track.

'Follow the yellow brick road?'

'Might as well,' Sarah said. 'I'm pretty sure we're not in Kansas any more.'

It was, anyway, the obvious way to go.

Twelve minutes later they found the first body, face up a matter of yards from what looked like some kind of farmhouse, an old stone bungalow built into a dip in the rock, so their heads were more or less level with its roof. The body was, or had been, holding an apple. Zoë had little doubt his death had been violent – he was too young to have just keeled over, and anyway, she had the distinct impression people who did that did it face first. Still, she wasn't about to roll him over to check. Middle of nowhere, she didn't fancy mucking about with a corpse.

'Another one,' Sarah said.

'A what?'

'Another body.'

She didn't mean another one apart from this, Zoë realised: she just meant this. 'I guess your Michael's been here.'

'I guess.'

She sounded disconnected. Zoë didn't want her coming apart: not here, not now. She reached into her shoulder bag and took out the small silver gun she'd shown Sarah earlier. 'You want to stay out here?'

'Why, where are you going?'

Zoë pointed to the farmhouse. Bungalow. Whatever. It seemed to be crouching: a little bit of atmosphere went a long way. Although she'd already done so once that morning, she checked the gun again now, checked it was loaded . . . Actually, she'd never fired a bullet, though Joe had insisted she practise squeezing the trigger, so she'd know the proper way if things ever came to the crunch. He'd been an expert, of course. Not that he'd done it himself. Always leave the chamber under the hammer empty, he'd told her. Case of accidents. Thanks, Joe.

'I'm coming with you.'

'Okay.'

Okay because Zoë had no way of knowing whether it was more dangerous inside the building than out.

With Zoë leading, they approached the door. Before they'd found the body, everything had been quiet; now, it seemed to Zoë, the island was full of noises – the wind shifting loose pebbles, straining through knotty tussocks of grass; the waves beating at the rocky edges all around them . . . She wondered how far Jed was; whether, if she fired her small pistol in the air, he'd hear and come back to fetch them. Even being seasick might be preferable to staying here, and finding whatever there was to be found. But she was already pushing open the heavy wooden door as she had that thought, so she filed the notion away in that part of her mind labelled instant regrets.

There are those who claim they can tell when a house is empty. Zoë felt the air, colder inside, wrap itself around her as she entered, but it offered no clues about occupation. Empty, maybe. Or there were people here being very quiet. Time would tell.

It told. There was somebody indeed being very quiet in the first room Zoë entered: a room off the hall – just to the side of the staircase, leading down, that she was ignoring for now. The room was a kitchen: obvious for its fittings, the oven, the sink still stacked with dirty dishes . . . The person being very quiet was dead. Obvious for the stain on his chest, like a map of one of the larger continents; deep black fading to red against the blue cotton background of his T-shirt. Shot, Zoë thought. She could feel a numbness creeping through her body, a paralysis mixed of shock and fear, but her mind was still going about its business coldly enough. *This man had been shot. He was now dead. But so far nobody had shot Zoë or Sarah, so things were going pretty well, considering.*

Behind her she heard Sarah's breathing catch, then give; behind that, a deeper noise, like an angry buzzing insect somewhere way overhead. Then it faded.

'You okay?'

'—I thought . . .'

'You thought it was Michael?'

Sarah nodded.

'But it isn't?'

Sarah shook her head.

And are you glad or disappointed? Zoë wondered. But didn't ask.

She looked back to the body, which seemed to be growing smaller. A trick of perspective. Above it, a stainless steel draining board; above that, a window showing the view out back to be the same as it was out front. Nothing those eyes would see again.

'Shall we check for a pulse?'

'You see that grey stuff?'

Sarah nodded.

'It's brain matter.'

'Oh Jesus . . .' Sarah said.

'Come on.'

'. . . Where?'

'Somewhere else,' said Zoë.

But there was nothing more to be found on this level; no bodies, living or dead. Two tidy bedrooms, pretty monastic-looking. A living room, or what passed for one, with an untidy, uncomfortable sofa and an unswept fireplace. No evidence of a child. No evidence of anything much, as if whatever passed here had been strictly temporary, and left clues no deeper than the empty gaze of a dead man in the kitchen . . . But they hadn't been downstairs yet.

'It doesn't sound like there's anyone down there.'

Anyone alive, Zoë amended silently.

'Can you see the lights?'

They couldn't find the lights.

And Zoë didn't want to go down the stairs. Movies and books were well past the stage where the heroine went down the stairs (and it was hard not to think herself the heroine at this point); instead they fluttered around at the top, thinking about all the movies and books where the heroine went down the stairs . . . In the really scary films it was *safer* down the stairs. Here and now, though, she had no choice. Though they were carved into the stone, these stairs, the way they were in the older kind of crypt.

Dark, too, but that was the point; the stairs were *always* dark . . . Gripping the silver gun firmly, her free hand on the wall for guidance, Zoë went down into the gloom, taking each step like an invalid, trying not to think about what had happened here early this morning . . . just one man, this Michael man, with a gun, and bodies dropping everywhere. Like an avenging angel – or devil. For there was no apparent justice in this aftermath; no satisfaction in evil vanquished, just the overwhelming sense that *nobody* deserved to take another person's life, not when it meant leaving that blank stare in the kitchen . . . She wondered whether Joe had been left like that. He'd been sitting at his desk with an open throat, but nobody had told her about his eyes.

. . . And there was the noise again, a distant beating hazing in and out of hearing. Helicopter?

But it was too much to be expected that she should think about helicopters when she was heading down into the dark. Sarah was a step or two behind her, which was a comfort; the staircase turned a corner into total dark, which was not. Her hand traced the angle of the wall. And then, with a lurch, she was on flat ground again, in what seemed to be a corridor, though it was hard to—

Light exploded all around her and Zoë jumped, had to swallow a scream.

'Sorry. There was a switch,' Sarah said.

'Christ, woman, have you no—'

And a sound like a wet hiccup, like a sob, from behind a closed door.

She supposed, afterwards, that Sarah's first thought had been Dinah. Her own was a blank, was reflex; it was amazing how her reflex took her towards the sound and not away. There were heavy wooden doors, much like upstairs, lining this corridor like a dungeon, and without knowing which the noise had come from she chose the nearest, pushed it, watched it swing open without a sound only to thump softly against an obstacle in its path . . . Another body, Zoë thought. Something soft, not offering much resistance. And so small a body, it could only belong to a child.

There was movement to her left and she dropped to a crouch, forgetting the gun in her hand entirely, then almost dropping it in her haste to cover her lapse. And there was another wet hiccup like a bubble bursting, and Zoë was looking at a woman, she realised: not an armed woman, just a woman, frightened and hurting and bundled up against the wall as if it were the only thing stopping her from sliding off the planet. Not dead. But plainly hurting. Zoë stood slowly and dropped the gun back into her bag, which had slipped from her shoulder. Then she approached the woman the way she might a wounded cat, if she'd ever felt the urge to offer one assistance.

The woman was blonde, though her hair looked streaked and muddy in the shallow light. Curled foetally, she looked up as Zoë approached. *Oh Christ*, thought Zoë, *just like everyone else on this damn island . . .*

'Is she alive?' Sarah said, behind her.

Zoë bit her lip. 'I think she's been shot. There's been a bloody *massacre* round here . . .'

'Let me see.'

Zoë crouched instead, put her hand to the woman's forehead. Felt normal. So? And what do you do? she thought miserably, realising that the woman's hands, folded over her stomach, were leaking red; what do you do with someone hurt like this? Do you sit and watch her die?

'Zoë?'

She moved away. Let Sarah deal with this. And as she stood she saw on the wall above another ghastly pattern, like a mortal Rorschach; a spray of blood about level with her own head.

Beside her Sarah knelt, began murmuring to the woman. Just a babble of comfort, like a stream washing over its bed . . . She remembered the beating she'd heard, remembered thinking *helicopter.*

'I'm going back up. I think there's somebody else here.'

'Be careful,' Sarah told her, not looking up.

Yes. She'd be careful. She took the stairs two at a time, ran out, found a man with a briefcase . . .

Before all that, she stopped to see what it was had obstructed the door. And found, with no conscious sense of surprise at all, that it was a teddy bear; a great big blue teddy bear.

30

David Keller was approaching fifty, still on the road, desperate for a cup of coffee – the very next place, he promised himself: Little Chef or roadside spoon, he was stopping. A shot of hot caffeine. He was supposed to bring it down to three a day, and this would be his fourth (and it wasn't yet lunchtime) but listen, he said to himself – if doctors knew everything, they'd live forever. The rest of us, we'd get old, sick and die, but doctors, none of that would happen to them. If they were so clever. But they're not.

It wasn't a spoon he reached next, but one of those squeaky-clean franchised places where they wore uniforms and hoped you had a good day. He didn't mind that. And say what you like, they served good coffee. They could dress up as frogs and sing 'The Sun Has Got His Hat On', provided they served good coffee.

He parked out front. Used the toilet on his way past. Paid for his cup of coffee – okay, his *pot* – and sat, like he always did, where he could watch the road . . .

For almost thirty years he had been driving this stretch of the country, a big stretch – right up the west coast, and as far south as Carlisle, so *two* countries, you wanted to get technical – plying his trade as a rep for a pharmaceutical company . . . Pharmaceuticals. It had got so you couldn't use the word in company without encountering the knowing wink, the finger tapping the nose, the bark of surprised laughter . . . Sad, really. Nobody worked the roads these days not knowing it was no joke, that 'recreational' drugs were no joke. Kids he stopped to give lifts, you could see it in their eyes, in the loose, jangled rhythm of their movements; you could tell by the fragments of conversation they thought were normal that they were strung out so far you couldn't haul them back with rod and line. This was what was happening. Children – he knew they grew up faster now, but they were still *children* – being used up and tipped on the scrapheap before they were legal to buy a drink, and some people still thought they could raise a laugh saying 'Ah, *pharmaceuticals*' when they met a rep in a public bar. More than sad, it was sick. But don't get me on my hobbyhorse, he said now: said it to himself. One of the drawbacks of this line of work. Not just that you talked to yourself, but that you'd said it all before.

Which was one reason he gave lifts, but not the only one. Get to hear somebody else's voice for a change. But also, if you reached fifty without ever needing a lift yourself, well, you must have been born rich or lucky. So David Keller was in the habit of stopping when he saw somebody looked like they needed help, and it was another sad reflection on the state of the world – so many sad reflections this world has, it's like living in a hall of crazy mirrors – that even that was open to misinterpretation. Pick up many hitchers? men asked him in bars, when they heard he worked the roads. Pick up many *girls*? Aye, David Keller had picked up girls: he'd picked them up, taken them where they wanted to go – miles out his way, sometimes – and left them with a wave, some advice if he had it, a couple of quid if they needed it. Other stuff, taking advantage – you'd have to be a monster. He really meant that. Teenage girls, these men wanted to know about. Men old enough to have teenage daughters themselves. When he heard that question, he'd switch off. He'd get up and walk away. It wasn't like he was a saint or anything. He just thought there were standards, or ought to be; that it should be possible to live, even this day and age, doing more good than harm and not end up in your closing days looking back on the damage you'd done.

Which was another thing about getting older: you did far too much philosophising over a single pot of coffee.

After a while he finished his drink, left a tip and went back to his car. The skies were still grey, he had miles to go, but he didn't feel unhappy about it. Say what you like about the state of the world, each day came minted new. That wasn't just the caffeine talking, either. You put your head down, you got on with things, and mostly life took care of itself. It was true.

It was true, but later that morning David Keller would give a lift where he saw it was needed, and that was the last mistake his good heart would ever make.

Sarah knelt beside the dying woman. There seemed little doubt about this fact, that the woman was dying, or no doubt in Sarah's mind . . . For the first time in what felt like hours she was in full control of her own thoughts, her own actions. She'd been sidelined, perhaps, by Zoë's presence. But now she was back, though helpless in the face of this woman's pain.

'Die,' the woman said.

'*Shh*. Rest quiet now.'

'—Nah.'

'. . . Dinah?'

But there was only that wet hiccup in reply, as if the name had been escaping air, bubbling up through damaged channels to burst in the liquid gloom.

Sarah put her hand to the woman's cheek. She didn't dare move her; didn't anyway know *how* to move her, or where . . . It occurred to her now, they hadn't stopped to check the body outside, just taken on trust he was dead. What else would he be, stretched out like that beneath the grey sky? . . . When she looked around, she noticed for the first time the pitiful decorations Blu-tacked to the walls; a child's renderings of other children, animals, the sky, the sun, a house. The earth, in these pictures, was always a strip of green along the foot of the paper; the sky a strip of blue on the upper edge. Dinah.

There was a bear, too, a big blue teddy bear. It lay by the door, exactly as if it had been—

Oh, yes, shot.

This had been Michael, she supposed. He was fading in her memory, she was surprised to find; probably because she was having difficulty putting what he had *done* here next to who he *was*. Who she thought he'd been. But he had come in the night, or early in the morning, and left this mayhem behind him; taken Dinah . . . She felt sick. For a moment it was a worse wound than this woman lying here had suffered: she had *lain* with that man, and what was he: a war criminal? Filled with revulsion, she forced her mind further back: would she have let him save her life if she'd known him capable of this? Somewhere between that point and sharing a bed, she drew the line, and somewhere on that line, he'd been balancing for years. Maybe Maddy Singleton had been the only hope he'd had, and even that hope was a dim reflection of betrayal; she was married to his brother soldier . . . Even now, Sarah had barely an inkling of the bond that had held those two together. But knew at least that it had been sealed with blood, and couldn't be broken by less.

She went to fetch the bear. There was nothing else she could do. It wouldn't have surprised her if the woman had died in the moments it took to collect it, but she was still breathing when Sarah knelt by her once more with the ridiculous blue toy in her hands. The light in her eyes was flickering, or that might have been a trick of Sarah's own eyes; watering now, making candlelight out of the gloom.

There was a noise upstairs. Zoë coming back.

'Die,' the woman said again.

'Dinah. Yes.'

'Dine.'

Dying. There was somebody with Zoë; Sarah could clearly hear two pairs of feet on the steps. How had she known they weren't alone? Was that Michael? Or would he just have killed Zoë like he'd killed everybody else?

But it wasn't Michael. It looked, instead, as if Zoë had brought her bank manager along; a neat, medium man with a balding head and a cheap briefcase, who smiled pleasantly when he saw Sarah, as if he'd long been denied the pleasure of an introduction.

'Can you help?' she asked him.

'Oh, I do hope so.'

'She's been shot. We think she's been shot.'

'What a pity. You must be Sarah Trafford, is that right? Sarah Trafford, née Tucker, late of Oxford?'

'. . . Who are you?'

'And your friend is—?'

'Not important,' said Zoë. 'Look. Can you help her? She's dying.'

'I expect she is. Downey did all this, I presume? He's a better soldier than we thought. Or else the child is just very, *very* important to him.'

He stepped further into the room, and put the briefcase on the floor.

'The funny thing is, she's not his. Did you know that? The blood work was done. She's definitely Singleton's.'

'I don't know who you are,' Zoë said, 'and I don't know what the fuck you're on about, but the question is, can you help her? She's *dying*, for pity's sake.'

'Oh, we're all doing that. Downey's dying too, did you know? Caught something nasty in the desert. Long term, but definitely fatal. Just a little bit,' said Howard, 'like life.'

'Are you mad?' Zoë asked him.

'Mad, no. Maybe a little disoriented.'

But Sarah wondered.

The man came closer, knelt by the dying woman. Something heavy in his pocket dragged at his jacket, ruining the cut. It looked awfully like, Sarah thought—

'Die—'

'Yes,' said the man sadly.

A gun, Sarah thought. It looked very like a gun.

Amos Crane was using *binoculars*, binoculars he had found in the boot of the car. Now he sat on the harbour wall, scanning the sea for traffic; not sure yet what he was looking for, but confident he'd know it when he found it . . . Where the sea met the sky was just a thin grey stripe. Ideally there'd be a boat bobbing on that stripe, a boat with a big white sail with a blue and gold target stitched into it.

My, he felt grand. Oh, he felt really fine.

On the train he had slept at last, a sleep punctuated, bizarrely, by dreams of the woman he had seen, the woman in the red top, with the coffee and the railway sandwiches. But he'd woken refreshed. And the morning since had passed like clockwork, if about as slowly; he'd found himself delighting in the detail, savouring the moment, as if this were less a routine nutting than a swansong . . . Well, of course it was a swansong. He'd been present at a lot of those. He'd just never been the swan yet. He didn't intend to be one now.

. . . 'Nutting' was an Axel word. It was one of many. He'd been a magpie with his euphemisms, filching them from other contexts: sex and drugs and sports. He'd spoken of twatting and spliffing, and he'd always meant one thing. Rarely used the same word twice. Never had to explain himself. Back in the rarefied air of the office, it was all *black-ribbon* this and *expedite* that . . . Like working in a bank. Axel's approach had been more honest, you couldn't deny it. When you did a job on someone, you weren't *expediting* them. You were splatting them, basically. It was a fact of life.

. . . He wondered if Howard were here yet, and concluded: chances were. *Howard* probably came by *helicopter*. No budgetary restraints for *Howard*, thank you very much. Amos closed one eye, and imagined the black circle he was looking through a gunsight. Pretty soon, he supposed, he'd be after a new lifestyle – new identity, new country, all the rest. Howard, though, would be looking for a new plane of existence. Along with Downey, the woman, the child . . .

The child, yes. He'd taken her a teddy bear, but that hadn't been sentiment, it had just been the job.

He shifted a little, to ease the growing cramp in his leg. Doing the child wasn't something he was looking forward to, obviously, but he'd never been one to shirk the painfully inevitable. So as was his habit, he put this detail from his mind. Let the next thing happen in its order. We'll shoot that horse when we come to it.

And way off in the distance a familiar boat hove into view, and Amos Crane thought to himself: *Well* . . .

The woman died two minutes later.

That was what the man had said, bending low over her, his hand to her pulse.

Hard to know, Sarah thought, whether it was relief or defeat. For the woman, that is. Two minutes of struggle, then she stopped – sudden as that; no winding down, just a full stop instead of a comma. Sarah had left the room, walked up the stairs, come out here into the light and air – birds wheeling about now, couple of hundred yards away, as if they'd found something on which to feed. She kept expecting to cry, but didn't. Inside her something welled and gathered, but she wouldn't let it burst.

She heard sounds now familiar behind her: a soft footfall, a cardboard rustle, the hiss of a plastic lighter.

Zoë said, 'There's nothing we could have done.'

'I know.'

'Maybe if we'd got here earlier . . .'

'Or been surgeons.'

'Or been surgeons.'

'What the fuck happened, Zoë?'

'Your friend Michael—'

'He's not my friend.'

'No. What I think happened, what it looks like happened, he got here, probably stole a boat, killed the guards, took Dinah and left.'

'And who's—'

'I don't know. One of *them*. Hush.'

Whoever he was, he came out and joined them now: something of an absurd little man, Sarah couldn't help feeling, with his suit and tie, his briefcase, on this grey lump of seabound rock. But he'd known her name. So yes, obviously, one of *them*.

And something weighing down his pocket which might just be a gun. Who's to say it hadn't been *him* who caused all this?

She said to him, 'Dinah was here, wasn't she?'

'. . . She was.'

Zoë said, 'Sarah—'

'A little child. A four-year-old girl.'

'Four years, yes. Something like that.'

'You bastard.'

'Sarah—'

'She was *bait*. You bastard.'

The man tugged at an ear. Then said, 'Well, yes, technically. But she wasn't meant to get hurt.'

'You thought Michael would just turn up and ask for her nicely?'

'Sarah—'

'*Anything* could have happened!'

'Anything more or less did,' he pointed out.

'Sarah, would you pack it in?'

'Huh?'

Zoë was looking at her strangely; trying to pass messages with her eyes . . .

'The question is,' the man said, 'where is he now?'

'He's left.'

'Yes, very good. He's left. You wouldn't happen to know *where* though, would you? Mrs Trafford?'

'I've got no idea.'

'Perhaps now would be a good time to give it some thought.'

'Thing is,' Zoë said, 'we've got to be off.'

'You've got to be off.'

'Boat to catch. You know how it goes.'

'Leaving the scene of the crime?'

'It's not our crime.'

'So you say. But you *are* the only other people here. There's bound to be an investigation, yes? You're witnesses to a death.'

'Thing is, Mrs Trafford here's already been witness to one of those. And by the time you lot were finished with it, it turned out it never happened.'

'My lot?'

'Spooks. Spies. Men in grey.'

'Yes, well . . .'

'And what's worrying *me* is, you want to disappear this little massacre, you might get ideas about disappearing us. You follow?'

'I think you're being unnecessarily—'

'Fine. Think what you like. But I'll say it again, we've a boat to catch. The same guy who dropped us here. Who knows who we are. Who has a *cheque* with my name on it. Who has friends who know where *he* is. Am I making this clear at all?'

'As crystal.'

'Great. We'll be off then.'

The man's hand, which had dropped to his pocket, dropped away again. And, Sarah noticed, Zoë withdrew her own hand from her shoulder bag: it was holding her lighter, though she already had a cigarette going . . . Sarah herself was holding the blue bear. She felt like a shoplifter, an attention-seeking thief. Hadn't even realised she'd brought it out with her.

'Sarah?'

'. . . Yes.'

Zoë was backing away, not taking her eyes from the balding man. Who watched, politely, saying nothing; he looked like, if he'd had a hat, he'd have tipped it.

'Sarah? Are you coming?'

'I'm coming.'

Bear tucked under her arm, she came. And back along the track they went together, watched a good part of the way by the strange little spook, who frankly looked more accountant than spy . . . 'Fucking amateur,' reckoned Zoë.

Hey-ho, thought Howard.

He walked over to where the corpse lay, the second corpse he'd found, and idly kicked its apple at a nearby rock. There were a lot of nearby rocks on the island. The apple bounced, bruised; a sizeable chunk flew up, and flopped to the ground. Perhaps he'd kicked it harder than he'd intended.

Howard looked at the corpse. 'So what are you supposed to have died from, then? Fright?'

The corpse rolled over. A large and not particularly convincing wound stained his shirt front.

'I was on my back initially. But it wasn't too comfortable. I rolled over.'

'You realise you twitched?'

'Rigor mortis,' said the corpse cheerfully. 'Or something.'

'And what's his name, Paul? Paul's created a work of art in the kitchen.'

'He reckoned the deader he looked, the less chance they'd check too careful. It worked, didn't it?'

'It worked. No thanks to Dodo.'

'Deedee.'

'Whatever. We're not handing out Oscars this week. That's the longest dying scene since *Reservoir Dogs*.'

'She was pissed off. About the kid.' The former corpse, Brian, stood up. 'Paul had to smack her about a bit. Last night. Bring her into line.'

'What about the kid?'

'She didn't want to let her go. Deedee,' he amplified, 'didn't want to let the kid go.'

'But she did.'

'Downey came. About four hours ago? Early morning, anyway. Motor boat. We could have taken him.'

'I didn't want him taken.'

'I thought that was the point.'

'The point's changed.' Amos Crane had changed it, but Howard wasn't getting into that. 'And he took the child.'

'Like I said on the phone. We left her in the kitchen, he must have thought it was a trap.' Brian shrugged. 'He took her anyway. Back to the boat, voom, he was off. We were watching from over there.' He waved vaguely in the direction of the first corpse Howard had found. The indisputably dead one. 'Next thing we know, Jed's on the bell. Two more passengers coming. Christ, nothing happens for weeks on end, then it all comes down at once.'

Paul came out of the house wiping gore from the side of his head. 'Was that fun?' he asked them. 'Was it fuck.'

Howard nodded.

'They came nowhere *near* me,' he added. Aggrieved.

Brian said, 'We could have just hidden.'

'Where?' Howard asked him.

He grew vague. 'There's places.'

'Downey didn't find you because he wasn't looking. Once he got the child he was away. Those two,' he waved in the direction the women had gone, 'they'd have looked.'

'Who were they?'

Howard just stared at him.

And also, he added, if things went wrong from this point in, and they wound up telling their story to anyone, well, it wouldn't help their credibility when they testified to deaths that never happened . . .

Brian said, 'They're bait too. Aren't they?'

Howard nodded vaguely. Sure they were bait. He was assuming they'd lead Amos Crane to Downey . . . His best bet for coming out of this was to have them all wind up in the same place, then get the drop on whoever was left standing. He hoped that wouldn't be Amos. Still, he'd have to be prepared.

The helicopter was over them already. Brian said, 'You following them in that thing? It's a little conspicuous.'

Howard shook his head. He didn't need to. So long as Sarah Trafford kept hold of that bear, he'd know where they were.

He pointed over to where he'd found the first body. 'You planning on burying that thing at all?'

'Had to get the blood from somewhere,' Brian said.

'An' I always hated that bastard cat,' Paul said.

'You've still got some of its brains in your hair.'

Paul was still scrubbing while the helicopter took Howard away.

31

SARAH STOOD AT THE stern, watching the wake scar the sea-surface . . . Only the sea healed without mark; wiped the white scar so cleanly, it had never been there at all. And that didn't count the invisible pollutants . . . Hard to think about Michael, now. Invisible pollutants in his case, too, and not just the toxic explosion in the desert – what kind of worm ate into the soul so deep, it allowed you to kill whoever lay in your way? She thought of the trap that had been laid for him, and shook her head in weary disgust. Last time they'd put Michael on that island, he'd left bodies behind him. Why had they thought this time would be any different?

Zoë asked, 'Are you okay?'

'No . . . How about you?'

She made a face. 'They should put stabilisers on these things. But it's not as bad as it was before.'

Though the boat rocked as she said that, and Sarah saw white ghosts crawl over her.

Looking back to the sea, Sarah said, 'I can't believe he did that.'

'Killed them.'

'Did he have to? Wasn't there another way?'

She wasn't really asking. Zoë tried, anyway. 'He thinks Dinah's his.'

'He doesn't *know*.'

'No. Is that important?'

'That man, he said it wasn't so. He said she isn't *Michael's.*'

'He did say that. And maybe he was telling the truth, and maybe he wasn't. Either way, Michael doesn't know. And even if he did, do you think he'd really care?'

'But—'

'Sarah.' Zoë put a hand on her shoulder. 'You don't even know the child. You've come this far. Do you think *he* should have just walked away?'

'I don't *know.*'

'Maybe he didn't either. But he does now.' Zoë turned and spat over the side of the boat. 'Shit, I wish they'd built a bloody bridge. Sarah? Maybe they shot at him first.'

'He had a gun, didn't he?'

'That creep? Yeah, he had a gun.'

'And so have you.'

'And so have I . . .'

'Would you have done it? Shot him, I mean?'

Zoë gave her a look. 'We'll never know, will we?'

They heard a buzzing overhead, a giant mosquito whine, and looked up to see light glinting off the fishbowl windscreen of the helicopter as it flashed past, heading towards the island. Sarah caught the impression of a man in helmet, goggles, leather gear. Already he was into the distance.

'That'll be his lift,' Zoë said.

'Do you think this boat goes any faster?'

'Now would be a good time to find out.'

He had retreated from the harbour wall, and watched the boat dock from the doorway of a waterfront shop, where, for amusement as much as protective colouring, he'd been writing a postcard: *Enjoying retirement! Will catch up with you later!* This, he'd send to Howard's boss.

The sky was grey; the sea was grey. Only the car, parked thirty yards down the road, was blue.

Amos Crane turned his attention to the scene unfolding by the water's edge; two women disembarking; one of them – Sarah Trafford – handing a piece of paper to Jed. The other wore a red top, and as he focused on her face – not using *binoculars*, not here on the street – he felt the dizzying sensation he'd had before when he noticed disparate events falling together in a tidy heap. It was the woman from the train. The one who'd stolen into his dream.

He didn't know who she was, but then she didn't know him either . . . You could look on that as level ground.

He also noticed something else funny; that Sarah Trafford was carrying the bear. *Bet that'll please Howard*, he thought; quite pleased himself. He had, after all, brought it here. Looked like Howard would be reaping the benefit, though.

Amos pulled his wallet from his pocket; pulled a stamp from his wallet. Dabbed it on his tongue, and attached it to the postcard. It was nearly time to go. Either these women would lead him to Downey, or they would not. Either way, they couldn't remain on the board much longer. This had turned out to be one of those games where you burned your pieces as they fell . . .

Nutted. Scorched. *Splatted*.

He popped the postcard in the waiting box. When he looked up, the women had gone.

'Ladies,' Jed said.

'It's been your pleasure,' Sarah assured him, handing back the cheque Zoë had signed an hour before.

Zoë said, 'And Jed? We were never here.'

'Never where?'

'Good point.'

'I don't trust him,' Sarah said, once they were fifteen yards away.

'Well, that's pretty shrewd, Sarah. Seeing as we already know he takes bribes.'

Sarah hoisted the teddy bear under her arm. She couldn't keep lugging this toy around; on the other hand, she couldn't just dump it in a bin. At least she *could*, but it wouldn't feel right, somehow.

Zoë caught her by the arm. 'What now?'

'I don't know.'

'Try having a think.'

'I just want to put as much space between us and that place as possible.'

'Now you're talking. Any special direction? Are you still checked in anywhere?'

She was, but suddenly that didn't seem important . . . She could leave, *they* could leave; she could settle her bill later. Send them a cheque. She owed Zoë money, too. Better get her life in order.

'We should head for a city. Head for Glasgow if we can. Get a train back south.'

'You need to talk to someone,' Zoë said.

'I know.'

'Press. Someone big.'

'Who'd believe me?'

'Believe us.'

'. . . Thanks, Zoë.'

'Bus stop. We need a bus stop.'

Sarah hadn't said all she wanted to say. Thanks was not enough. But Zoë was already on her way, as if the bus stop wasn't going to hang around if they didn't get a move on. She swapped the bear from one arm to the other, and took off after her friend.

The copter put Howard down right where it had picked him up: the corner of a field just out of sight of the main road: not too far from his car; a bit too close to a herd of cows. Which scattered. All but one, who held her ground, lowered her head;

watched the crazy machine through huge brown eyes as it tilted up and pulled away. With her right front hoof she prodded a lump of grass, which until recently had commanded her full attention.

Howard dropped his briefcase. Picked it up. Looked at the cow. He was certain it was a cow: bulls have horns, cows have tits, and that was a rule of nature. But there was no point hanging round, so tucking the briefcase under one arm, he half marched, half trotted across to the nearest gate, scrambled over it without damaging anything important, then kept on at the same ungainly pace until he reached his car, a hundred yards down the track. The cow had forgotten him by then; was deeply involved in her grass.

Behind the wheel, Howard luxuriated for a moment in motionless comfort. Then, hey-ho, back to work. From his briefcase he took a laptop; this he opened, and tipped a switch. A blue screen flickered into life. He adjusted its radius until it was operating within a two-mile area, which still left both major points in view, *A* being the laptop itself, dead centre, and *B* being the bear. Unfortunately, the area was laid out on a grid Howard couldn't actually drive along; without a map, it was worse than useless – he had a map; he unfolded it, spread it over the passenger seat. All he had to do now was work out where he was, superimpose his position onscreen *mentally* – and, theoretically, he'd be able to follow the bear.

What he really needed now, he decided, as point *B* began to move, was someone who'd operated one of these damn things before.

The bus stop had the air of long-ago abandonment. It was just a metal upright with, chest-height to Sarah, what had once been a timetable hooped round it, but was now a mating diary for the local blades: DAZ LOVES PEANUT. DISH 4 TRAJ. What hellish name abbreviated to Traj? Or Daz, come to that. Shit. Her mind, which had slowed to the point of stopping – the inertia born of emergency – was now all fizz and pop: none of it, though, any use at all.

Zoë said, 'Maybe we'll get lucky.'

'Yup.'

'We're *bound* to get lucky.'

'Yup.'

Think about it: we've had bodies, bombs, drugs, thunderstorms . . . Life was a country song: if it wasn't for bad luck, I'd have no luck at all.

There was a car coming, a blue car, and it slowed as it reached the stop.

'Local rapist,' Zoë muttered.

A man leaned out of his open window. He was alone in his car. He said, 'You weren't waiting for a bus, were you?'

Before Zoë could make any one of a dozen responses, Sarah said, 'We are, yes.'

'Because unless they've changed things recently, that bus doesn't run any more.'

'You local?' Zoë asked.

'No. But I work the roads. I've driven this stretch for years. Trust me.'

Oh, sure . . .

'The name's Keller. David Keller.'

'Uh-huh,' said Zoë.

'And if you're heading this way, I can give you a ride. Far as the next town, anyway. Somewhere you might find a bus.'

Zoë looked at Sarah. Sarah looked right back.

'Thanks,' said Sarah. 'We could use some help right now.'

So could Howard. He'd had to alter the tracker's parameters already: four miles and counting – either they'd got transport, or that bear could really move. On the main road, where he could locate himself on his map, he'd pulled into a lay-by and was fussing over details: a power pylon to his right, or probably east, meant he was either *here* or *here* . . . So they were back on the water or heading down the coast. Something of a toss-up, really. But he had no choice but to act like they were still on the road.

And at the back of his mind, with that part of his brain he used for crosswords, sexual fantasies, and other mental activities demanding attention to detail, he was clocking through the possible identities of a woman in a red jumper and, he was halfway definite, a gun in a leather shoulder bag.

The detective. That was what his subconscious came up with a minute or so before passing it on. She was something to do with that detective Sarah Trafford had hired, and Axel had pacified.

That was the trouble with loose ends, he decided, starting the car up again, heading in what he hoped was the right direction. You didn't pay attention at the time, the whole blasted ball of wool came apart.

He didn't know yet if he was capable of wrapping this up himself. Maybe he'd get lucky, and Amos Crane would do that for him. But one way or the other, he was going to get his hands dirty, because if he didn't put Amos Crane away first, Amos Crane would bury him . . .

Point *B* slowed to a crawl and stopped. Maybe that was his luck changing direction, Howard thought . . . then realised he couldn't swear as to whether his luck so far had been good or bad.

Images of something else buried flashed through Sarah's mind: the sun on heavy leaves, and old stone, and decorated glass. The kind of image that tugs at you and you can't pin down, because it never actually *happened*; it's a detail from a radio show or a page in a book – something described that your mind has coloured in, allowed to become as real as memory. But what was stone and glass and hidden among the trees?

'. . . Pharmaceuticals?'

'You'd be surprised how many people give me the wink when they hear that word.'

'Stop the car,' she said.

'Sarah?' said Zoë.

Zoë was up front, talking to . . . David Keller; that was his name. And she'd turned round now, frowning at Sarah, wondering what the hell was up *now*; you couldn't blame her, Sarah decided; I act like I'm bonkers half the time these days. Maybe I am. And none of this is happening.

'Sarah?'

'I'm sorry. David? Could you stop the car, please. I've just realised something.'

Obediently, he stopped the car, and turned to look at Sarah too. 'Are you in some kind of trouble?' he asked.

Shrewd. Maybe. Though it didn't take a genius.

'Kind of. Do you have a map? A local map?'

'I might have. There's all kinds of stuff in the glove box.' He nodded at Zoë, meaning: sure, go ahead, look in the glove compartment.

There were maps: also packets of extra-strong mints, sunglasses, wet wipes, Opal Fruits, much of which tumbled into Zoë's lap when she released the catch . . . Three maps down she found the one they were after, and handed it to Sarah without a word.

A little way up the coast. We found a church by the side of a wood. Well, a chapel.

'Is it something special you're looking for? I do know the area quite well.'

Deserted, it was . . . We sheltered there that first night. Sanctuary, you'd call it.

'Sarah?'

'I know where they are.'

'What makes you—'

'Zoë, *please*. Trust me. I know where they'll be.'

She fell back to her map reading: never one of her greatest skills. But she knew a little cross when she saw one: bang next to that densely green patch, which must be Michael's wood.

'I know this is none of my business,' their driver began.

'David. I'm sorry about this. We both are. You can let us out here, there's somewhere we need to be.'

He turned in his seat to face her. An old face, or looking older than it actually was, perhaps – funny, Sarah found time to think, how some people can look older than they appear to be. He'd stopped to help them, and here she was telling him they didn't need his help. Didn't seem the type to turn nasty, though. His face crinkled when he spoke.

'I see a lot of people on the roads . . . I don't mean you look desperate. But you get a sense for it, after a while. You need help. That's okay. I can take you where you need to go.'

'She doesn't know what she needs,' Zoë muttered.

He looked at her.

'Sorry.' Zoë turned to Sarah again. 'But listen, I thought we'd decided this? We head for the nearest exit.'

'They're near here,' Sarah said. Sounding stubborn, mulish, even to her own ears. But hell, she'd come this far. 'I know they are. And you said it yourself, we need Michael. Without him, who's going to listen?'

'But—'

'And he's got Dinah.' And he's dangerous, she didn't add. Didn't need to. He's killed people; for all we know, he'll kill her too – kill himself, kill her, who could tell, after everything else he'd done?

'Sarah—'

'I'm sorry, David. This isn't fair on you. And thanks for your offer, you're a kind man, but I can't drag you into this. It's okay, Zoë.'

'No it isn't.'

'I can manage—'

'Shut up.' Zoë opened her door. 'So we're going. Or staying. Whatever. Come on.'

The car rolled forward a couple of feet, and she almost fell out.

'What the fuck?'

'Did I get your attention?'

'David?'

'Sorry,' he said. He turned to Sarah once more. 'Miss? I'll say it again. You want to go somewhere, I can take you. I don't like leaving you here, the side of the road like this.'

'But—'

'It's not for your sake, it's for mine. You know? This way I don't lie awake all night, wondering if you got where you needed to go.'

She was still holding the map, folded over now so the little cross, the dense square of green, looked a hop and a jump away. But why walk when they could ride? He could give them a lift, then drive off: his good deed done.

'Are you sure?'

'I'm sure.'

Zoë shut her door again. 'This is what I like. Firm decisions, swiftly taken.'

He held his hand out; Sarah handed him the map. Showed him with a finger: 'It's that church. Or chapel, or whatever it is. I just remembered . . .'

'It's of consuming historical interest,' Zoë finished.

'So we go there,' he said. 'Five minutes. Okay?'

And proved to be good as his word.

*

Two more things:

Howard, who'd worked out where he was, started after point *B* just as point *B* started to move . . .

. . . and Amos Crane, who'd been following all this, smiled, as he moved too.

32

THERE WAS A SMALL wooden door, very old, with fresh splintering around the handle; with iron nails stamped into it like bullets. There were bushes round this door, clawing their way out of the stony ground like an illustration of a parable.

There was a stained-glass window too; a somewhat Celtic cross. There was no name to the chapel that Sarah could see. Nothing to tell you where you were.

There was a blue 2CV parked lopsided to the back of the building; its rear left wheel an inch or so above the ground, as if its front right had found a ditch.

Sarah stood taking this in while Zoë waved distractedly at the car now heading away from them, reversing up the track through the trees, towards the main road. 'Nice man,' she said.

'Hmm?'

'He didn't have to help us.'

'No.'

She was going to take a few steps forward, push on the door, go right in. Any minute now. That was what she was going to do.

'So what's the story, Sarah? Ten minutes ago, you had no idea where they were.'

'I remembered.'

'You remembered he said he'd meet you here?'

'I remembered he talked about it. Back when he and Tommy Singleton escaped. This is where they hid.'

Zoë took it in. Shook her head. 'Well, if you ask me,' she said, 'it's fucking spooky,' and she reached into her bag for her gun.

Sarah didn't notice. She was taking those few steps forward, pushing on the door. Which swung open.

. . . What it reminded her of, those first few seconds, was the chapel in that awful place where she'd first gone looking for Dinah. Arimathea. Here, now, walking into another chapel, she suffered again that sense of old air, of air locked in stone, and the feeling crashed in on her that this was what had become of her life: it had degenerated into a succession of moments, each of which had to be lived through in turn. Brief flashes of memory ignited for her, like sudden views of a bright room: the distant *thump* of a house collapsing, and sparks flying upwards into a dark sky; a man with blood like a necktie pooling down on to his desk; another with a rope of dental floss he was trying to kill her with . . . And herself, all those years ago, falling from the roof, with lights cartwheeling like a circus attraction. All of that. And all leading to where she was now, in another old, cold chapel, looking for a girl who was a survivor, as she was herself. So far.

There were no benches in the chapel. No altar. No furniture of any kind. Just a bare room with a filthy stone floor, some old cracked windows and naked beams low overhead. And a man sitting against the wall opposite, with a small child in his arms . . . Dinah.

Michael was levelling a gun at her.

That was almost it. Right there. Not a matter of her past life flashing before her eyes – not again – more a case of seeing her future, all of it, folding into a single instant, an instant in which he fired the gun, she fell, the world went black . . . None of it happened. Instead he lowered the gun as she stepped out of shadow, raised it again as he saw Zoë – who was right behind her – then put it down once more. No matter Zoë held a gun. He looked, Sarah thought, so tired – so tired, he was maybe half dead himself.

'You came,' he said.

'You forgot your jacket.'

A stupid thing to say, she knew; one of those flippant comments she'd be embarrassed about afterwards, if there was an afterwards. She came forward, his jacket feeling baggy on her shoulders. 'This is a friend of mine.'

Zoë nodded at Michael. She was still holding her gun. Michael simply stared at her, then looked back at Sarah.

Only a matter of hours, after all, but what had he done with them? Killed how many people? And look at him now, holding a small child, who seemed very like she might be sleeping: what did she say to him? What did she say to Dinah?

I left my life behind to find you, and I can't remember why . . .

'You didn't have to kill them,' she said. The words had a life of their own. Too much life for Michael, perhaps, who put his head on one side, as if getting out of their way. 'Michael? You didn't have to *kill* them.'

Zoë brushed past her. Michael seemed not to notice; he'd put his gun on the ground now, and folded his arm back round Dinah.

Sarah was swimming on dry land; her thoughts as waxy and monstrous as jellyfish. Was this *it*? Was this the end?

'Sarah?' Zoë said. She had her hand to Michael's forehead.

'. . . What?'

'He's sick. Did you know that?'

Buzzing now, loud as a car. She felt sick herself. Had to snap back to reality; pull herself out of whatever pit she was falling into, just as she felt the draught at her back, and the door to the chapel opened.

*

Amos Crane came walking down the track.

This was *it*, this was *the end*; here was where he closed with flesh and bone. And it was odd, but it was happening the way it always did, with a slow gathering of detail, and the heightening of all his senses. He'd thought this would be different. It was his brother's killer, after all. He'd thought there would be a mad rush, and a sudden descent; that for one berserk moment, he'd be free of all thought, all feeling, and come back to himself only once it was over . . . When the flesh and bone were done.

But everything was as it always was, and Amos Crane was walking down the track.

The chapel didn't look much bigger in the world than it had on the map: that was his thought as he stood in the clearing, casting a critical eye. Not that size mattered. All that desk work, all those months of waiting – all those blips on the screen. And here they were, under one roof. With a woman in a red jumper for an extra.

It was a pity about the child. But sometimes things didn't work out quite as cleanly as you'd have liked.

He put a hand on the roof of the 2CV. It felt cool to the touch. This was where Downey had come, then, after taking the child. Crane wondered how easy that had been. He wondered if Howard had made it easier somehow; if Howard had his own ideas about how the end should be played. As well for him if he did. As far as Amos Crane was concerned, Howard was part of the ending.

On the main road, he heard a car slow, then stop . . .

But it was too late for that, too late for anything else. He walked to the door, put a hand to it. All the blood within him, all the *atoms*, singing free.

This was where he closed with flesh and bone.

Or was that somebody else coming down the track behind him?

*

Sarah, dully, said, 'Oh. Hello.'

'Hello.'

'We thought you'd gone.'

'I came back.'

Zoë frowned up at him. 'Well, you shouldn't have.'

He shrugged.

Sarah forgot him then, put David Keller out of mind just like that, and stepped forward to crouch by Michael and look at the child. Dinah was not asleep. She lay quiet – a small blonde girl with large green eyes, who looked unblinkingly back at Sarah for a moment, then turned her head to stare into Michael's chest.

'She looks like Maddy,' Michael said.

'. . . She's beautiful.'

And she was. She was even worth it. *Because if Dinah isn't worth it, nothing is . . . Just a tiny girl, how can they* use *her like this?* Thoughts she'd had way back when, staring at the night sky, adding up the stars . . . Last night. That had been last night. And yes, she was beautiful.

Michael wasn't. He looked ill and drawn, was fading at the edges. Around his T-shirt collar was a spray of blood, and Sarah knew he'd had another coughing attack . . . As if he could start to let go, give up, now that his search was over.

He was talking to her. Saying something like: 'I didn't kill anybody. Not this time.'

Zoë shrugged.

'Just walked in and took her away . . . Didn't I, sweetheart?'

Sarah said, 'Okay. It's okay.' All those bodies on the island, but he hadn't killed anyone. Okay. She stroked the child's shoulder, drawing her attention away from wherever it was it had gone. 'Here, I brought you this.' The blue teddy. The kidnapped bear. Who had come from the island where all the bodies lay, though *Michael* hadn't killed anyone.

Dinah reached a hand out, and touched the bear on the nose.

'Do you want to hold it?'

She shook her head.

Zoë stood, keeping her movement as smooth as possible. Not wanting to disturb anyone, to cause ripples round the scene.

'Are you sure? I brought it for you.'

Dinah shook her head again, then regarded Sarah gravely. Who felt something give in her heart; as if strings were being stretched; as if her heart were an instrument, played by a child.

'. . . Can I hold her?'

Michael nodded. It seemed an effort. Not the dip of the head, but bringing it back upright, to rest against the wall.

Zoë frowned, as if she'd heard something outside.

Sarah held her arms out. 'Do you want to come to me, Dinah? Give Michael a rest?'

It felt like the longest moment, crouched like that, with outstretched arms. Did Dinah want to come to Sarah? Sarah had come far enough for her, but the child didn't know that, the child shouldn't care. All that mattered was the here and now. Her mother dead and gone, and Dinah wouldn't even know that yet . . . And yet she snuggled there in Michael's arms as if she trusted him, and knew he'd hold her safe.

'It's okay, sweetie. You stay where you are.'

But the child wriggled in his arms then, and held her hands out for Sarah.

She placed the bear in the dust by her side, and lifted Dinah to her. There was a lot of weight and warmth in the exchange; a whole new world of smells, of heavy sounds. She could feel Dinah's body working, that was what it was; could feel her lungs filling and emptying, her stomach churning away at nothing . . . Christ, the child would be *hungry*. Needed feeding. Needed sleep. All the things small children needed, though all Sarah could offer was a moment's peace.

'That man again,' Dinah said, pointing at the teddy.

'That's a bear,' said Sarah.

'*Man. That* man again.'

And Dinah pointed at the man she meant, and Sarah and Zoë turned to look at David Keller . . .

. . . Though Keller, in fact, lay dead some miles away, not far from the road stop where he'd drunk that final cup of coffee.

Pharmaceuticals . . . You'd be surprised the way people raise an eyebrow when they hear that. But Amos Crane had not raised an eyebrow, had given the matter no thought at all, and had killed David Keller, whose only sin had been to give Crane a lift, with a similar absence of reflection, or indeed regret – because it was, after all, necessary, or if not necessary desirable, or if not desirable . . . about to happen. That was what it was. You could not argue with what was about to happen. David Keller hadn't. Amos Crane needed a temporary identity, and David Keller had yielded his with no more than a wet murmur. Amos Crane needed a car, and dead David Keller wasn't using his any more. Sarah and Zoë had needed a lift, but dead David Keller hadn't been there to oblige.

They looked at David Keller now, but Amos Crane looked back.

He came forward and crouched down too, all of them almost on their knees now, bar Zoë, in a chilled empty space built for worship. He smiled kindly, and Sarah saw his history in his smile; saw Rufus – Axel? – leering at her in her kitchen, shortly before he began to kill her. And she thought: all this distance, to end the same way it began. Everything stops where it started. It wasn't an answer she was happy to find.

Zoë dipped for her gun, but it was already in Amos Crane's hand.

Michael reached for his – but Zoë's little pistol was nuzzling into Sarah's ear, burrowing there like a maggot in the apple of her head.

And here was another moment she was called on to live through: the one that might be her last. Her exit.

'Pass that gun,' Crane said.

Michael slid his gun across the floor. It made a clattery, bumpy sort of noise – this gun, too, had come a long way; all the way from Gerard's collection . . . Michael, then, slid *Gerard's* gun across the floor, making a bumpy, clattery sort of noise: at least until Zoë stood on it.

The barrel of the little gun pressed harder into Sarah's ear, and she might have screamed, but she didn't drop Dinah, who was starting to twist and wriggle in her arms.

Zoë picked the gun up.

'I will,' said Amos Crane, 'blow a hole in her head.'

'Not with that you won't.'

Oh please please don't tell him please don't bluff him please don't say

'It isn't loaded.'

So Amos Crane pulled the trigger.

Howard heard the shot from outside, where the day was brightening at last after a slow start – he was under the trees now, of course, but their leaves cast mottled shadows on the ground before him as he walked; lent even the air itself a dappled quality, as shadows brushed his face. He had parked the car back on the road. He no longer needed his suitcase. The gun, his hand tightened round now, though he did not draw it from his pocket.

He ought to be very frightened, very nervous. In truth, he was at one remove from any kind of emotion: the nearest he could call to mind was sitting an exam – a very important exam, or at least one that seemed so at the time, and he'd felt, walking into the examination hall, a great weight lifting from his shoulders, or anyway his mind, because it didn't *matter* any more, it was out of his control. Anything he hadn't already done wasn't going to happen. Whatever was put in front of him, he'd just cope with the best he could.

But everything about him was intense: the sunlight through the branches, and the breeze that stirred the stones. The gunshot from the chapel, which sent birds clamouring into flight for as far abroad as he could imagine. Like an exam, he reminded himself. Like an unseen. He took the gun from his pocket slowly, slowly. Watched as the door in front of him started to open. Then faded back into the shadows like a ghost, like an unseen.

From the ceiling now, a shower of dust, of grit and plaster, falling like a benediction; it settled on Zoë to give her an extra few years' grey. Which was about how much she felt she'd just aged. Above them all something creaked ominously, as if the shot she'd fired above her head had weakened the structure, though that was surely too much damage for a single shot to cause, even from a gun as heavy as Gerard's.

Sarah, who had slumped to the floor at that deafening *click*, scooped Dinah into her arms once more. The child was frightened, whimpering, and shook like a leaf on the bough.

'Are you okay?' Zoë asked.

She nodded, unable to speak yet.

Amos Crane, still on his feet, dropped the useless silver pistol and put both hands in his pockets. Sarah, cradling Dinah, looked up at him. Now that he wasn't David Keller, for all he occupied the same body, there was a near palpable change to him; still far too close, she could almost feel his heat. As if whatever drove him ticked quietly in the cool air. The engine of his hatred. Hatred, certainly; it was impossible to kneel by his feet and not sense that. Whatever he was here for, it wasn't just a job. But it was ridiculous to say *whatever*, for she knew full well what he was here for: he was here for their deaths. He was here to guide them to their exits.

'Take your hands from your pockets. Very slowly.'

Michael said, 'Shoot him.'

'Now take two steps back.'

'Give me the gun. *I'll* shoot him.'

'I said out of your pockets. And two steps back.'

'*Give me the gun!*'

Amos Crane rocked on his heels. He might have been silently laughing.

Sarah pulled away from him, scrabbling a little in the dust, still with one arm wrapped round Dinah, though the child was fighting it now; didn't want to be held any longer. Something knocked against her hand. Zoë's little gun. Why didn't you load it, Zoë, she wanted to say. What was the point? But Zoë was busy, and not answering questions.

'Back. *Off.*'

And still Amos Crane rocked on his heels, and showed her wolfish teeth.

'Kill him,' Michael said.

Sarah said, 'It didn't fire.'

'Always leave the chamber empty,' Zoë said. She bit her lip. 'Sarah? Will you just get out of here?'

'But what about—?'

'Sarah. Just go. Take Dinah, and go.'

'I don't know—'

'*Go!*'

She went. She took Dinah and went. Didn't pause at the door to look back: just opened it, and went.

Amos Crane said, 'Always leave the chamber empty?'

Outside, it was impossible to believe there was such a place as inside; the sun had come out, leaves were painting the air green. There were bushes, clawing their way out of stony ground; there was a stained-glass window.

There was a blue 2CV, half parked in a ditch.

She wasn't thinking, she was running on automatic. She opened the back door, still on automatic; put the grizzling child on the seat on automatic. Leaned forward and brushed the child's hair with her lips . . . 'Hush, Dinah. Everything's going to be all right.'

'Gnah!'

'Sit still. It's okay. We're *both* going away.'

But as she shut the back door on Dinah, opened the front door for herself, she knew they weren't going anywhere, because she didn't have the keys.

Back inside. But she didn't want to go back inside. Wasn't taking Dinah back inside, and wasn't leaving her out here alone . . . She could walk, she decided. Up to the main road. It wasn't very far. Flag down a lift . . .

But she couldn't flag down a lift. Look who the last lift turned out to be.

The thoughts rushed through her mind much faster than it would take to say them. Even as they did, she was seeing what she saw: over there, in the trees, a shadow, moving. Not in time with the other moving shadows. A shape, then, rather than a shadow: the shape of a man.

She shut the front door of the car. Moved round to the back.

It was a man; it was the man from the island. Like everybody else these days, he carried a gun.

Back on automatic – it was important to do these things on automatic – she turned as if she hadn't seen him, and opened the car boot. It'll be locked, she thought – but it wasn't locked. It'll be gone, she thought, raising the lid – but it wasn't gone. I won't be able to use it, she thought – but picked it up anyway.

Sarah turned smoothly, and pointed the shotgun at Howard.

He stopped, and pursed his lips . . . a pretty minor reaction, on the whole.

Behind her, Sarah heard a soft thump from the car. Dinah, falling off the seat, maybe . . . and knew, as surely as she'd ever known anything, that whatever was going to happen next, it couldn't happen anywhere near Dinah. Better the child was left in the car on her own than be near what happened next.

So she turned and ran into the trees.

Follow follow follow . . . She didn't know what she'd do if he didn't follow. She didn't know what she was going to do if he did. But that was what happened: he did. Waited the beat of her heart in the clearing, then took off after her into the trees.

He was still carrying a gun, she knew, but he wasn't firing it: that was good. And she was still holding the shotgun, though knew she wouldn't be able to use it herself. She remembered those other woods, that little copse, where Michael had made her point it and shoot, and she'd blasted a hole through leaf and branch, none of it offering any more resistance than the human body would . . . No, she wasn't about to shoot anyone.

But if he killed her, what was to stop him killing Dinah, too?

The thought made her faster. She jumped a fallen log. The denim jacket she wore – Michael's – snagged a branch, but she tugged it free. Behind her, she heard him fall, maybe on that same log, and for a moment his English swearing filled the Scottish air . . . She half stumbled, and nearly dropped the gun. This wouldn't do. Wouldn't work. Any moment now she'd fall, and blow her own brains out . . .

And burst out of the trees with that thought in her head, into a clearing of stubby grass, and rabbit shit, and picnic litter. With the shotgun in her hand, and Michael's jacket, and maybe a minute to spare . . .

A minute was all it took. Then Howard was in the clearing with her.

'Always leave the chamber empty?' said Amos Crane. Slowly, he drew his hands from his pockets.

'Don't even *think* about it.'

'Would that mean what I think it means?'

'Don't even think about it.'

'Shoot him,' said Michael.

'Shut up.'

Amos Crane smiled. It was amazing where you found the edge. Here in a disused chapel miles from anywhere, with the man he'd come to kill and a woman he'd dreamed about. And women always hesitate; leave that whisker of a chance.

'Are you comfortable with that?' he asked.

Zoë tried not to answer . . .

'. . . Comfortable with what?'

'A head shot,' said Crane. Without pointing, with just a nod of his head, he indicated the direction of the gun barrel: levelled straight between his eyes, in hands steady as most rocks. 'Don't get me wrong. Head shot's what I'd go with.'

'. . . So?'

'Just *shoot* him for Christ's sake!'

'So most people aren't as fast as me. You hit me, I'm dead, no question. But it's kind of a small target, don't you see? And if you miss, well . . .'

Zoë didn't twitch a muscle.

'. . . Well, if you miss, you're dead. You and him both.'

'Kill the fucker!'

'On the other hand,' blithely as if Michael had not spoken, 'you go for the chest, say, and it might not kill me straight off. Oh sure, shot to the heart, *pouf*! I'm dead. But otherwise, well, there's lots of complicated body parts in there, as I'm sure we both know, and you'd do me so much damage I'd probably die whatever. But maybe not immediately, you know what I'm getting at? And then we're back to plan B. You're dead. You and him both.'

'Look, you dumb bitch—'

'Shut up,' Zoë said evenly.

The silver gun just lay there in the dust by Amos Crane's

feet. She had no idea on earth how long it would take to reach his hands.

'Gut shot, well, same again. I've seen people live for hours with a bullet in the belly. Well, I'll rephrase that. I've watched people *die* for hours with a bullet in the belly. That's assuming lack of medical intervention, of course. But that won't bother you one way or the other, will it? Because you'll be dead. You and him both.'

'Be my guest.'

'And, well, anywhere else . . . You're not planning on shooting to *wound*, are you?'

She shook her head.

'Fine. If you were, I hardly need tell you . . .'

'I'd be dead,' said Zoë flatly.

'Uh-huh.'

'Me and him both.'

'Uh-huh.'

'Do you want to take those two steps back now? Because I'm not asking again.'

Amos Crane took half a step back, and half a step forward again. 'You don't remember me, do you?'

'Shoot him!'

'I know you don't, or you'd never have got in the car.'

'*Shoot* him!'

'I was on the train. I watched you walk past. You were carrying,' he said dreamily, 'a cup of coffee and two packets of sandwiches.'

'I'm counting to three now,' Zoë told him. 'One.'

'And you know the really funny thing?'

'Two.'

'I dreamed about you,' said Amos Crane – a fact both absurd and utterly true, though he never knew whether it was the patent absurdity or simple truth of it that caused Zoë's eyes to flicker when he spoke, a flicker long enough to allow him to drop . . . And Amos Crane did not drop like other men. There was no stooping, no bending of the back. One moment his feet were on the floor, and the next – the next, he might have had no feet at all, and it was certainly true, he knew, it was certainly true that whatever came of this, his knees would never be the same again, not after allowing his whole weight to come down on them on a dusty stone floor. In a disused chapel. In the middle of nowhere. Reaching for a gun. All of it so unnecessary, when he had his own gun, strapped under his right armpit, but it had been too thrilling, too edgy, to walk in here empty-handed, and see what the gods dealt out . . . a woman in a red top, who would certainly shoot but would probably miss. All of which Amos Crane was not precisely thinking at that moment; he was feeling, rather; just as he felt the floor hit his knees with a crack, felt the gun jump into his hand. He had never had trouble with guns, Amos Crane. Never met a one he didn't like. This one would do just fine. This was the gun he would reach and point, and once he'd shot the woman, he'd take longer over the man, because this was the man who had killed his brother. Michael Downey was going to die slow . . .

But Zoë didn't hesitate.

And Amos Crane ceased to be a problem.

He arrived at the grubby little clearing – limping – to find Sarah waiting for him: a shotgun in her hands like she was Annie Oakley. His own gun more or less dangled from his wrist. He had fallen, doing something pretty unpleasantly painful to his knee in the process, and now had the nagging feeling that nothing was going the way it ought to. That some kind of rewind needed putting into operation, so he'd be back at his desk in London, reading about this through others' reports.

But he was pretty sure he'd heard a shot back there. Whichever way you looked at it, loose ends were being clipped.

Sarah said, 'That's far enough.'

Howard stopped, because he wasn't a fool. He said, 'It's okay, you know. It's all over. More or less.'

'Drop the gun.'

'I'm not going to hurt you. See?' He tossed the gun into the trees. 'You can put that down too, if you like.'

Sarah didn't loosen her grip on the shotgun.

He said, 'You want to see my card? I have ID.'

'Not particularly.'

'You just got involved in—'

'I know what I got involved in. I got involved in bastards like you covering up toxic war games. Chemical weapons? Out in the African desert? Am I ringing bells?'

'None of that had anything to do with me.'

'Oh, sure.'

'I'm serious. Frankly, it pisses me off too. It doesn't matter if you don't believe me.'

'I don't. But you know what really gets me? That you used a *child*, a four-year-old *child* as part of your cover-up. First you poison her father. Then you kidnap her as *bait*!'

'Her father—'

'I don't care.'

'Her father was no better than a war criminal. Did you know that?'

Sarah didn't answer.

'Same as your friend Downey. Shooting unarmed prisoners. Sound like the sort of thing he'd do? Think about the island, Sarah. What happened on the island. He's a bloody maniac. You must see that.'

'You used him as a guinea pig.'

'He volunteered.'

'I don't believe you.'

'I think you do.'

Oh, she could believe him. Howard saw that right enough.

She would believe anything right then. Up to and especially that she was in a coma, and this the fevered dreaming of her damaged mind.

He started to feel better about life. Even his knee stopped throbbing. 'Mrs Trafford,' he said, 'Sarah. Hear me. Nothing that happened to your friend in the past had anything to do with me. With *us*. No matter what he did, what happened to him was a crime. And as far as I'm aware, those responsible were punished. They crossed a line.' He shrugged. 'You can't always prevent such things. You can only clear up afterwards.'

'But nobody ever *knew* about it. Those boy soldiers were killed—'

'That's the point. Nobody ever knew about it. You think people are happier knowing the truth, Sarah? About everything? You think they *want* to know what goes on in the margins of their democracy? They don't. That's my job. That's what clearing up means.'

'But you used a *child*—'

'Who is *all right*, Sarah. She's *all right*. You think we'd have let anything happen to her?'

'Anything almost did!'

'Right. On the island. But that was Downey's fault, Sarah. Not ours. Certainly we wanted to . . . make contact. Bring him back into the fold. We weren't to know he'd go haywire.'

'You blew a house up. Somebody tried to *kill* me!'

'Same agent. You want to hear me say I'm sorry? Well, I am. Believe me, I'm sorry. Especially about what he tried to do to you, but all we can say on that is, he paid the price. He went rogue, he paid the price. I don't honestly think we can be held responsible for his actions, Sarah. We really have to be reasonable about this.'

But she was shaking her head, as if she weren't convinced that they did.

'Look, Sarah, cards on the table. There are two ways we can

go with this.' He spread his hands, palms up. 'The first is, you put the gun down, come with me, and we get your life back for you. Simple as that. Obviously you'll have to sign a few papers, official secrets, stuff like that, but that's pretty much all there is to it. You put this behind you, start off like it never happened. And we can work out your husband's difficulties. Sure, he's been neck deep in some serious sins, but nothing we can't straighten. Not with a little goodwill on all sides. Okay?'

'And what's the other way?'

He shuffled, humbly. 'I think we should stick with way one. You know my speciality, Sarah? What I'm good at? Fixing it so things never happened. We can do that here. Trust me.'

'And the other way?'

Howard showed how unhappy he felt, brooding on the other way. 'You must understand me, it really is very important Downey's story goes no further. And if you show yourself too, ah, *intransigent* on this point, well, everything gets blown out of proportion. That's all.'

'And the other way?'

'The other way, Sarah, is you don't put the gun down. You even use it.' He shook his head and smiled shyly, as if it were a secret they shared, that way two was never really going to be an option. 'You use it. Obviously, lots of things aren't going to matter to me at that point. I'll be spread a little thin to worry *then* about what comes next. But you ought to bear in mind the consequences.'

Sarah didn't say anything. He sighed deeply.

'The consequences. I might not be around any more, but the, ah, department I work for will be. And I'm afraid they'll have to go into overdrive at that point. Which means that you, your friend back there, Downey, the child, your husband, your old friend, er, *Wigwam* . . . Everyone you might have had contact with, really. Will all meet major accidents.'

'I ought to kill you.'

'That's your choice. But you won't just be killing me. You'll be starting something you can't stop. You've been lucky so far, you know. Very lucky. We've been a little stretched. Turn this into a full-scale emergency, and what's happening in the Gulf right now will look like teatime. Now, perhaps I ought to give you a while to think about this, but that's hardly crucial, is it, Sarah? I mean, this isn't a difficult choice you're facing. Happy ever after, or let's fuck everybody. Pardon my French.'

'You're not human.'

'Compared to some of my colleagues, I'm a teddy bear. A teddy bear that's been awarded the Nobel peace prize. Now, I really think you ought to put the gun down, Sarah. Before everyone you know and love gets hurt.'

And to his deep relief, he saw that she was considering doing just that.

He breathed in, breathed out. Somebody's life passed before his eyes . . .

Howard stepped forward, and picked the gun from the ground where she'd dropped it, then took a number of steps back, and raised the barrel so it pointed at Sarah.

'What's the matter?' she asked him.

'Let's not be obtuse.'

'But you said—'

'I said you could sign some papers. I'm sorry. I lied.' He raised the gun and sighted down the barrel.

'But—'

'But no. I'm sorry. You're brave. I'm sorry.' He lowered the gun. At this range, he was hardly going to miss. No need to make a production of it.

'But—'

'I'm sorry.'

He fired.

And Sarah . . .

For one split moment Sarah was standing at the end of a long long corridor, watching a bright light rushing towards her at one hundred miles an hour. With it came a noise, something like an angry wind or a whole gang of lions roaring at once, and it changed colour as it approached: now red, now green, now red, now white, now red. In the end it was all red and it swallowed her up just as the noise vanished, and it was like having a telescope she was looking through shatter, leaving her disoriented but exactly where she should be. Then the noise came back, only this time without lions: just a high-pitched scream which scaled the trees, looking for a way to break the sky.

Sarah took a deep breath, and knew she was alive.

The man lay on his back a few yards away, the appalling stump of his right arm gushing blood, though he gripped it by the elbow with his left as if that might help. Sarah had never heard another human issue sounds like this. It was what people meant when they spoke about banshees. His face growled at her, all his features colliding, as if the bland disguise had dropped away, showing the child of darkness beneath. The darkness, though, was mostly made of pain.

The shotgun was a twisted mess of metal at his feet.

She opened her mouth to say something, but found nothing to be said.

After a while she undid her belt and knelt by the screaming man; slipped it round his arm below the elbow, and drew it tight. His remaining hand clawed at her face but when she pushed him down, he subsided. The scream became a whimper. All around his mouth was a thin white paste. The belt looped his arm four times before she could fasten the buckle, and even then, as far as she could see, had no effect whatsoever. But she was no nurse, and you did what you could, that was all . . . The word haunting her was 'cauterised'. But he'd have to take his chances.

'Listen to me.'

Her own words, transmitted from somewhere outside space.

'Are you listening? You have to lie still. Thrash around, you'll bleed to death.'

Lie still, you'll also bleed to death, she thought. Listen: whose fault was this anyway?

'I'll bring help.'

He spat: a bright gob of phlegm which spattered his own shirt front. In his eyes she could read approaching death. It was like looking down another tunnel, whose distant light was an oncoming train.

'God forgive you,' she said.

When she stood, Michael's denim jacket flapped loosely in the breeze. Dipping into its pocket, she scattered the last of the shotgun shells; gold droppings fell to earth like magic goose shit. Though as they winked at her from their brand new hiding places, Sarah was thinking not of them but of the bright red plugs tidy Michael had tucked in his pocket. One fragment of which she could see now, poking blindly from the wreck of the shotgun stock.

And back she walked through the trees, sunlight dancing in her footsteps. Back she ran, actually, filled with sudden fear: for Zoë, for Michael . . . Most of all for Dinah, whom she'd come a long way to lose in a hurry.

I came all this way to find you, and I do remember why. Because we're survivors, the two of us. We survive.

Alive, she ran through the trees, then; and in an astonishingly short while reached the chapel: old stone, straggly bushes, blue 2CV. Her legs almost gave way at that point. As if she were faced with an unexpected hurdle, Sarah found herself weak in the calves; almost stumbled, almost fell; had to reach out and steady herself with both hands on the roof of the tinny car. Through whose window she looked down to see Dinah, looking up at her.

She opened the door. The child wasn't crying. Something of a miracle. On the other hand, all she'd been through, well: *she's probably tougher than me*, Sarah thought. *Probably is. Not that I ever set out to prove anything.*

For a moment, she felt a jagged memory intrude: of a cat seen through a window, mocking her from the far side of the glass. Then it went.

She reached down and took Dinah in her arms. The child thought about it, but didn't struggle. Opened her mouth to say something, but must have changed her mind.

Sarah reached for words of comfort, while behind her a door opened, and someone stepped lightly into the sun, flicking a cigarette lighter.

'Everything's going to be all right,' Sarah said. Then she turned and smiled at Zoë.